I0736004

PRINCE OF KITARRA

THE SANARII CHRONICLES

BOOK III

ANDREA GIBB

www.andreagibb.com

WIND&ROOT
www.windandroot.ca

*To the Crones
(you know who you are)*

Those who were strong are now weak,
With healing hands, the babes will speak
Light turns to dark and colors shift,
Two rivers join when two lovers rift,
Watch for the child of two thrones,
Born with magic in his bones,
A child lit by the stars,
Watch for him, for he shall be ours.

After he has proved love's true form,
With spear in hand, the child will breach the storm
A king, a prince, a fox and a crow, four a circle make.
To send the dark one to stars for true love's sake.
Snap the tether, set him free,
Restore the river of magic to its rightful tree.

CHAPTER 1
RHYL

RHYL WAS A PRINCE and the child of the prophecy. And it was his nineteenth birthday.

There was no doubt in Rhyl's mind that his parents had overdone the festivities.

The largest courtyard of the Queen's Keep had been transformed into something from an old tale. Colorful lanterns scattered beams of light and dancing shadows around the garden, flowers grown just for the occasion flocked in arbors and vases. The amount of food was ridiculous. Pastries from the finest bakeries of Kilev. Rare cheeses from the mountain town of Withe. Even the sunset cooperated, casting red and gold light as if on cue over the glittering crowd of Kitarra's court.

Perhaps it was a good thing Talo was still traveling because Rhyl was certain his party was bigger, brighter, and more elaborate than Talo's nineteenth birthday had been. Not that Talo would be jealous… but he would use it to goad their parents endlessly.

Rhyl took another full glass of fruit wine, wondering if nineteen was really worth the celebration. Yes, Rhyl was a prince, just like Talo. But he was not Kitarra's prince. Not really. He was a prince stolen from his land and brought to another because of a prophecy spoken to a living queen by a dead Guardian. The child who would one day save the Kitarrans from an invisible threat. No one knew why Kitarran babes died so soon, or why the land was rotting away. Rhyl knew little about it. Because no one would tell him. But then, he hadn't exactly asked.

A niggling suspicion he couldn't dismiss was that his parents created this grand event to celebrate him entering his twentieth year because they worried he would not see a thirtieth. It was a morose thought, and he knew it, but he had thought it often enough that it was old company. He'd seen the sideways glances from his mother, the worry around her eyes. Rhyl was the child of the prophecy, after all.

He tossed back another sip of wine and let the thought slide away. The wide arches of the courtyard looked west. The dying sunlight glinted like fire on the Ilba River below. Rhyl thought it looked like a painting. Or a battle. The guests oohed and aahed, then danced and drank as the colorful lanterns lit up all around the courtyard, swaying in the gentle evening breeze. It was damn near perfection.

Rhyl's attention returned to the crowd as another young woman approached with another ornately wrapped package. This girl was very pretty. Rhyl didn't quite catch her name, and after a moment of polite (and memorized) pleasantries, he placed her gift on the growing pile and the young woman was on her way, blushing hard. It was a performance Rhyl had repeated countless times already that evening. Kitarrans were generous and even though Rhyl had it announced to the realm that he wanted no gifts, the gifts kept coming, usually carried by someone's eligible daughter.

Rhyl sighed. By Attin's nipples, he wished Talo were home and not sailing the ocean halfway between Kitarra and Rodan. Talo would stand beside him and mutter amusing observations in his ear. They were both princes; the shared tedium of the position made it tolerable. Talo was his brother, his confidant, his balance, his friend. They had never been apart for so long since Rhyl was brought to Kitarra as a young child.

Well, as the child of the prophecy, Rhyl might lead a doomed life, but there were some advantages. Like magic. Rhyl was *sanarii*. He could control the elements. Fire. Air. Water and earth were more difficult, but Rhyl wasn't the best student. *Sanarii* magic also infused Rhyl's body, his mind, lending his skill and strength that even he admitted were otherworldly and gave him an advantage. He had tried to deny that he was better and faster with a sword and latha because of practice and athleticism, but no it was magic that made him impossible to beat. Talo, as a Kitarran, his strength and reflexes faster, better than a human, could almost best him. Almost.

But a party was not a battle. Thankfully, with his magic, Rhyl could talk to Talo, mind to mind. His consciousness left the party behind as he reached with his magic, reached for his brother, who was on a boat in the ocean.

Talo.

Rhyl. Bored already?

Yeah. You're not here to make things interesting.

Tsk. Surely it can't be that bad.

It's not. I just wish you were here. What are you doing?

Playing cards.

Oh? Cheating, no doubt.

Of course not!

Rhyl could feel Talo's laughter touch his mind.

"My prince."

And just like that, Rhyl was snagged away from his magical connection to Talo. The jolt was not comfortable, but it was soon forgotten as Rhyl recognized the young man beside him.

"Corri! I thought you were in Withe," Rhyl exclaimed, a smile growing on his face to see his friend. Corri looked thinner, paler than when Rhyl had seen him last fall.

"My father invited me back home." Corri gave him a lopsided smile which restored his handsome features and held out a box wrapped in gold ribbon. Rhyl took the gift, muttering a hasty thanks.

"It's a vase."

"Thanks."

"There are probably a hundred vases in that tower of gifts," Corri remarked, gazing at the growing mountain of boxes.

"It's highly likely. I have no idea what I am supposed to do with all of these." Rhyl waved vaguely at the pile. Mua would tell him it was not about the things so much as letting the people show their love for him. And she had been queen of Kitarra for what Rhyl suspected was a thousand years, so she knew a thing or two about royal duties. The gifts made him cringe inwardly (though he would never tell Mua). As a child, Rhyl had never questioned his place in Kitarra. But now, turning nineteen, meant expectations. It made him feel…out of place. Every gift felt like payment for a deed unfinished.

Rhyl noticed that the music had stopped, and the crowd parted.

Oh no.

Rhyl's parents approached, grinning proudly. His father, First Defender of Kitarra, a man known to be of great worth and heart. And his mother, an Allati princess, a *sanarii*. They looked every bit as royal as their birthright suggested, though neither would ever wear a crown. His mother's silk dress was the color of the dawn sky, the Defender's a slightly darker hue. They walked arm in arm and eyed each other in a way that made Rhyl want to cringe and roll his eyes. His parents loved each other deeply, and that love poured over to those around them and to Kitarra itself.

Behind them walked Stone—Prince Arrain, looking every bit like the legend he was. Kitarra's true prince, its lost and then found prince, Eva's amourii, known to his close friends simply as Stone.

They were going to make a presentation. Speeches. Rhyl had expected it, but still, the reality was much worse. Rhyl's face was on fire already. Corri patted his back, winked, and stepped into the crowd.

Aralis and Bren appeared as if from nowhere, as usual, wearing identical expressions of mirth, eager to bask in Rhyl's embarrassment. The little demons. The rest of Rhyl's family arranged themselves around him: Queen Arrah, her crown of delicate, ornate chains and beads tinkling, a queen's guard at her elbow to support her should she need it; Aisha and Tilley, who had traveled with Turk and Bellah from Pinnae to celebrate;

and Murryn and Tarran with little Tavi, who was not so little anymore, lurking at their elbow.

Aiyan and Mila were absent as they had accompanied Talo to Rodan. Rhyl thought of those gone, and it was a lash to the heart. Old wise Mehmet and his endless stories. Loyal Anfru who had always looked the other way when Rhyl and Talo raided the cook's larder. Gods, sometimes he missed those old men so much he couldn't breathe.

Rhyl turned his attention back to his parents and Stone. Stone's white fur gleamed, and his black markings looked like jewelry. His tailored vest and trousers were green and gold. Rhyl's father wore the sigil of the First Defender in gold upon his shoulder. His dark hair and short beard were flecked with gray, but he was still very much a man in his prime.

Rhyl looked at his mother. Eva's hair was long and silver-gold like his own. Rhyl had the same eyes as his mother–how many times had they been commented on? Now that he was older, Rhyl could see her fragility when he had only ever seen her strength. And yet, he knew she would fight the world for him.

Stone held out his arms to get the crowd's attention. Rhyl noticed the slightest jitter in Stone's hands, but no one else would.

"Tonight, we celebrate." Stone's deep voice echoed easily through the courtyard. "Tonight, our young prince turns nineteen. We brought him here when he was but a wee boy. We took him from his home and gave him ours—a decision not made easily. And he has become our prince, our child of the prophecy, and we couldn't be more proud of how he has grown."

Then Illiah, as First Defender, stepped up, his voice no less regal or commanding. "Rhyl, my son. If I had known that day when we were taken from Jullayah, ripped from our family and friends, that I would see you grow safe, sound, and healthy into the young man before me, I would have urged the Kitarrans faster. Kitarra is our home, our land. And we are proud to see you as one of them."

"To Prince Rhyl!" His mother's voice rang above the crowd.

"Prince Rhyl!" the crowd echoed with cheers and laughter.

"Now, Rhyl, dear heart, the three of us each have a gift for you." Eva spoke loud and clear, not just for him, but for all those gathered.

Stone stepped forward first and bowed low, offering Rhyl a dagger of Kitarran steel, bright and short. The kind of dagger used for many things–cutting, hacking, killing. But it was also beautiful. The blade was layered steel in a pattern that reminded Rhyl of the whorls and curves of a tree. Before Rhyl could thank him, Stone stepped back and Rhyl's father stepped forward.

The Defender handed him a small box. It fit in Rhyl's hand easily and looked suspiciously like a jewelry box. Rhyl lifted the lid to see a ring, but not for a finger. It was larger. It took Rhyl a moment, but then he laughed in delight. "Really?"

"He is yours."

Rhyl bounced. The ring was from a horse's bridle–Honey's bridle. A horse that his father had been training for years. A horse that Rhyl had fallen in love with, as much as one could love a horse. Rhyl hugged his father tight and received a thump on his back for his effort.

Rhyl looked at his mother. She grinned at him. "Here." In her outstretched hand was a sword. Small, lightweight, but well crafted. The handle leather was oiled but aged. The little etched Cendari leaves glinted in the steel like a secret. His mother's sword. Rhyl could handle a bigger sword, and well. But he had always loved his mother's sword and often pirated it away for practice, much to his mother's amusement and dismay. The little sword was his preferred weapon, even over a latha.

"Thank you," Rhyl said, feeling the words bone deep. He embraced them each. His family. "I wish Talo were here," he murmured into his mother's hair. She squeezed him harder.

"I know. Me too."

Then, in Kitarran tradition, a great cake was brought out. As tradition dictated, it fell to Rhyl to cut it and serve his guests. Well, not to everyone–that would take all night–but he served it to those closest to him, and the servants did the rest.

"So, how long are you obligated to stay at your own party?" Corri asked, sidling up to Rhyl, licking the frosting off the spiced cake.

"A little while longer, I imagine," Rhyl said reluctantly.

"Want to come by my place after?"

"Sure," Rhyl answered with a grin, knowing it was a terrible idea. Talo was always warning Rhyl that Corri was a bad influence. (There *was* the time Corri bribed Rhyl to drink an entire bottle of fire wine, and they had to drag his sick, nearly unconscious body to Aiyan). But Talo was in the middle of the ocean on a grand adventure while Rhyl was stuck in Kilev. Rhyl was itching to get away from the confines of the palace to do something stupid. "I can be there in an hour."

Corri smiled, his eyes flashing.

"Was that Scytt's son?" the Defender asked, coming up behind Rhyl.

"Yes. Corri," Rhyl told him. The Defender said no more. Corri's father had been First Defender before Illiah. There was no love lost between the two older men. Rhyl didn't particularly like Scytt either, but Corri stayed out of his father's way, so Rhyl had hardly any dealings with the previous Defender.

The hour wore on. The night covered Kilev like a silken blanket. Rhyl danced with more young women—they seemed to multiply. He danced with the queen, then his mother. Then little Tavi, Murryn's eleven-year-old daughter, insisted he dance with her before she was forced to go to bed. He obliged, even though she was half his size, and it was more than a little awkward, and the whole dance she muttered about noblewomen and their fine clothes and perfect hair and how did they keep their dresses so clean and their shoes from fraying?

"But Tavi," Rhyl leaned down to whisper in her ear, "none of them can turn into a wolf."

Tavi beamed, because, of course, as a descendant of the *heera* people, she could turn into a wolf just like her Uncle Aiyan and Aunt Mila.

After Tavi, Rhyl decided it was time to sneak away from his own party. He made his way to the edge of the garden but caught sight of a young man who looked vaguely familiar. One of Irri's spies, he was sure. He would be followed. He did not want to be followed. Even if Rhyl was the deadliest person in Kitarra, possessing the ability to control the elements with magic and unbeaten with sword and latha, he was still followed like a little child toddling too close to a cliff. He swallowed his annoyance and came up with a plan.

He wove through the dancers and plucked out a young woman who had previously whispered a very generous birthday offer in his ear. She smiled like a vixen to see him approach and leaned against him as he looped her arm in his, leading her away from the party. She was a bit tipsy from too much fine wine, so Rhyl decided he was likely doing her a favor. He kissed her in the hallway and felt her arch against him. She tasted like wine. He pulled her up stairways and halls toward his chambers.

Just outside his door, once he was sure Irri's spiders had not followed him out of decency, he found a servant.

"Jean, Lady Yola is not feeling well. Can you see her home?" Rhyl asked.

Yola pouted, then glared at him. "Maybe the rumors are true," she muttered. Jean bristled, but Rhyl signaled for him to stand down.

"Come, my lady," Jean said, taking Yola's arm in his. Rhyl patted him on the shoulder in thanks.

Once Yola and Jean were gone, Rhyl tossed a dark cloak about his shoulders, pulled the hood over his bright hair, and slunk through the palace into the city streets.

The night was tame. The lingering snow adorning Kitarra Peak glinted against a sky pricked by a thousand stars. The air was crisp and promised warm summer nights and bright summer days to come. A soft breeze came down the mountain. The smell of the forest filled Rhyl's nose.

Corri's family estate was not far from the public bathhouse. It was a lovely house, but a bit too far from the forest for Rhyl's liking. The garden was just beginning to bloom and old trees lined the gravel lane leading from the main road up to the big house.

Rhyl ducked around the trees, abandoning the crunchy gravel to wend through the kitchen gardens to the servants' entrance. It was late, and the servants would be sleeping. It would be easy to sneak in unseen. He paused for a moment. Why did he feel the need for secrecy? What difference did it make if people knew he was visiting Corri in the middle of the night? He shrugged.

He put his hand on the latch, but the door opened before he could twist it.

Corri's grinning face emerged, cast in lantern light. The front of his shirt was unfastened, and Rhyl caught a glimpse of smooth skin and muscle. Corri's eyes flashed with a fiery light that made Rhyl's vision teeter. The *varing* pulsed around Corri like heat from a fire. Rhyl could see the dark magic because he was not just a *sanarii*, he was also a *candarii*. A sorcerer. He was one of a kind, destined to fulfill a prophecy and bring balance to magic and life.

The dark magic smelled of burning metal and ash, yet it was sharp and enticing. The *varing* dancing in Corri's smile called to him, welcoming him, pulling him.

This was a terrible idea, but he stepped inside, anyway.

CHAPTER 2

ILLIAH

ILLIAH GRIMACED AS HE SAT DOWN at the table laden with fresh baked goods and early summer berries. He took a slice of bread, spread it with honey, but couldn't bring it to his mouth. His head ached.

Who did he think he was, some young pup? He had overindulged at Rhyl's party the night before.

The duties of the First Defender did not give way to celebrations. Illiah had been up at dawn to meet with Irri. Irri, his master of spies, preferred early conferences so he could slip away afterward like a wisp of morning fog.

Approaching footsteps pounded in time with his headache.

"Tell me what Irri said," Stone said as a way of greeting. The big Kitarran took a seat opposite Illiah. He grabbed a bun from the breakfast platter and slathered it with jam, taking a giant bite. Clearly, Stone was not feeling the aftereffects of Lord Susor's ale.

"Irri returned during the night. He said Drenev was—"

"There you are!" Eva burst in, her presence both demanding and welcome. She took one look at Illiah and frowned. "I told you that Withe winter ale was strong stuff and that Susor is a deviant old tooth."

Illiah took a spiteful bite of his breakfast. He swallowed it with effort.

Eva put her hands on her hips. "You met with Irri? What did his spiders say?"

Illiah gave his wife a level look and his mouth twitched into a smile, which she echoed. Even when she was peeved, Illiah could make her smile. She hated it. Illiah loved it. "As I was saying to Stone before you interrupted with your grand entrance," he continued, "Irri reported that the village was the same as Firdale. No sign of struggle. The people were gone, but not their belongings."

"How many?" Eva asked, her smile vanishing.

"Fifty, perhaps."

Eva bit her lip. Stone fidgeted with his cup. His fingers trembled slightly.

"And there was no trace?" Eva asked, eyeing Illiah. She didn't say it, but he knew she meant any trace of *magic*.

Illiah shook his head. He was not in the habit of lying to Eva, and it wasn't quite a lie. Irri had said nothing about magic. But Illiah could not tell Eva about the dreams or the whispers that made him believe that the missing persons were somehow linked to the *varing*.

"So we add them to the list," Eva concluded.

"The list of the missing grows long," Stone muttered.

The list of Kitarrans who had mysteriously vanished was in a book kept between the three of them. But people were asking questions. Over the past two years, there had been some disappearances. A herder here. A farmer there. Then a well-known swordsmith went missing, and his son. Then a merchant from the coast. Then the foreman of the public bathhouse in Kilev. Then the tiny dwelling of Firdale by the coast. Now Drenev, a village proper. A whole village was impossible to dismiss. The people of Kitarra would demand answers. And it was Illiah's job as First Defender to find them. So far, he had none.

"How many is that since the spring thaw?" Illiah asked.

"Over one hundred," Stone answered.

Too many names for one short season. Illiah rubbed his forehead with the heel of his hand, silently cursing Susor and his ale.

"We need to make the list public. Send it out to every inn and cross-road," Eva said. "We need to find them. Someone must know something. Irri must have clues."

Illiah closed his eyes. Thinking. But all he could see were snatches of dreams filled with violence and terror where men killed and maimed with eyes glazed by blood lust. The *daeum*. Illiah had fought them twenty years ago. He had come face-to-face with them in Rodan thirteen—how could it have been so long?—years ago. But the dreams that haunted him at night were not memories. The missing people were not taken by *daeum* because the *daeum* and their tyrant emperor were dead and gone. No, his dreams were driven by something else. Illiah was terrified the missing people had been turned into *revenant*s. But Irri had not found any proof that Illiah's worst fears were reality. Maybe Illiah was just seeing ghosts where there was nothing more than shadow.

"Irri and his spiders, as you affectionately call them, are looking for clues. Discreetly. I think we should avoid causing a panic," Stone said so Illiah didn't have to.

"I know, I know." Eva sat down and leaned on her elbows. "The uncanny thing is, all the missing are human."

"There are far more humans in Kitarra than Kitarrans," Stone reminded her. "It could be a matter of ratios."

"What if this has something to do with the prophecy, with dark magic?" Eva asked.

"Eva, you think everything has to do with dark magic," Stone said, petitioning Illiah for backup. Eva smacked Stone's shoulder.

"I agree with Stone. It's a big conclusion to leap to," Illiah told his wife without meeting her gaze. He wasn't lying to her. He didn't think every disappearance was caused by magic. Though he was certain that what happened in Drenev was caused by magic. "But there is a way we could find out."

It was as if a winter wind whipped through the room. Stone's tail twitched.

"Illiah, you know I can't use magic," Eva said.

"Can't or won't?"

"Illiah." Eva's warning was quiet.

A familiar anger rose, simmering inside Illiah. He blinked, trying to displace the clawing at the sides of his eyes. He blinked again and the shadows of the room grew thicker, deeper, more alive. "You could use your *sanarii* magic to find answers. Don't the people of Kitarra deserve to know what happened to their loved ones?"

Eva's eyes glinted like a battle-ax. "Illiah, I can't do it. I can't." Then her voice softened, a telltale sign that she was hurt as well as angry. "How could you ask this of me?"

"It was thirteen years ago, Eva!"

"Don't. Just don't." Eva's chair scraped against the floor as she stood abruptly, her eyes flashing. Then she left with a breeze that smelled like lavender and mint, and Illiah felt it settle over him along with raging guilt.

"I think you may have pushed her a bit far that time," Stone said quietly.

Illiah groaned, his face in his hands. It had been cruel to ask her to use the magic that had destroyed the cendari tree and killed Tayeh. What was he thinking?

"She will forgive you," Stone cooed, patting Illiah's shoulder.

"She will. But should she? I don't deserve it."

Stone sighed. Then cursed. Then laughed. "You two. I should be tired of babysitting your relationship after all these years. And yet, running a realm is not nearly as entertaining as watching you two. It's like watching a dog chasing its tail."

"Thanks," Illiah grumbled.

"Your relationship aside, what are we going to do?"

"First, we need to make sure the families of the missing people are taken care of."

"Of course. I have already talked to Larren about compensation. If only we had Aiyan and Mila to see what they can sniff out."

Illiah regretted Aiyan's absence. It had not been easy to see the wolf leave Kitarra with Mila and Talo, if only for a short trip to Rodan. Without Aiyan close, Illiah could easily imagine the monster that lived inside him breaking free. Thirteen years had passed since the man made of *varing*, of dark magic, had taken over his body. Thirteen years since he had almost died and been reborn. Thirteen years he had lived with the fear that someday he would not be strong enough to keep the monster chained. He still felt it, clawing at the back of his mind. Whispering in his nightmares. And after Drenev…Illiah's unease gnawed at him like a beast.

Stone chewed his lip. "We could ask Rhyl to look."

Illiah grimaced. "If Eva doesn't hate me now, she will have my head if she finds out I encouraged Rhyl to use his magic."

Stone gave a bark of unamused laughter. "Do you think she is right?"

"I don't know. Which is why I haven't forced the issue. And what if she is right and it is dangerous? How can I put my son in that position?"

Stone nodded in agreement. Over the years, Illiah had always been thankful Stone could be trusted to offer logic and a cool head. Or just a listening ear for his musings.

"Rhyl says Talo won't be home for another week." Speaking of fathers putting their children in harm's way. Not that Stone put Talo in real danger by sending him off to Rodan. But still, it was a long journey for a young man.

"Rhyl and Talo's bond is a blessing." Stone looked thoughtful. If Eva weren't terrified of using her *sanarii* magic, Illiah knew Stone could have had the same bond with Eva. A bond shared between a Kitarran and *sanarii*. Magic allowed them to speak mind to mind, like Aiyan and Mila. Illiah wondered if Stone resented Eva for not nurturing the magical link between them. He didn't seem to.

And Illiah knew Stone loved Eva in a way Illiah could only imagine. Like a sister, but more than a sister. A friend of the heart. Stone had tried to describe it to Illiah once, back when Illiah had been adjusting to Stone being a permanent fixture in their family. That jealousy had been short-lived, thank the Guardians.

"It's unfortunate Talo missed Rhyl's celebration," Illiah remarked.

"I'm sure Talo is most aggrieved," Stone said with a snort.

"Maybe that was his plan." Illiah laughed. "I know Talo hates Arrah's parties."

Stone grinned. "I remember when I came of age and all of Kitarra showed up. I thought I would die of embarrassment. I was sure all of Kitarra would think me a great disappointment."

"Oh, a little embarrassment is not the worst thing a nineteen-year-old could experience."

"Agreed. If only Bren and Aralis had succeeded in commissioning that statue," Stone said wistfully. "They told me it was going to be a nude likeness of Rhyl with only a sword about the waist." Stone's eyes crinkled with mirth.

"If only it wasn't going to cost a small fortune, it might have been worth it to see Rhyl's expression," Illiah managed between fits of laughter. "We need to give the twins more to do."

"Good luck. They are too headstrong. Wonder where they acquired that trait." Stone's grin was wicked.

Illiah sighed and stretched his arms. "I need to go find Eva and apologize."

"Be careful. I'm her amourii. If she orders me to cut off your head, I will have no choice but to do it," Stone teased.

Illiah gave him a mock bow. "It would be my honor to die under your blade." Illiah winked at Stone. Illiah had almost died under Stone's blade once, long ago. He could tease Stone all he wanted about it now, but that night in the dark crypts of Cotoch's house still haunted his nightmares.

Illiah found Eva beside the dead cendari tree in the palace courtyard, gazing up at the forest, her arms wrapped around herself. A memory of the first time Illiah saw Eva as a young woman came to mind. She had been sixteen, her light gold hair damp, her blue-green eyes full of the forest. Her clothing clung to the curves of her body. That first time they met, they fought. Over a horse. Illiah couldn't help but smile. Yes, over the years they still fought and argued, but they loved and laughed and held each other through grief and fear and lost themselves in love and tenderness countless times. He would not trade his life with her for anything.

Now, years and three children later, to him, she did not look like she had aged or changed at all. Which was an illusion, and yet not. Illiah knew Eva had changed. She had grown more beautiful, sharper and softer, stronger and braver, yet more fragile.

But at that moment, she stood as still as the dead tree beside her. Like a wild thing sensing danger.

"Eva?"

She didn't turn. The stiffening of her shoulders was the only indication that she heard him.

"Eva, I'm sorry." He came over and stood beside her. "I shouldn't have said those things."

"You don't see it, Illiah."

Illiah pressed his lips together. Eva turned to him and laid the palm of her hand against his chest, over his heart.

"There is…still a darkness in you, Illiah. I lost you to it once. Sometimes I wake at night from a dream full of emptiness, of that pain knowing you were unreachable and hurting." A few tears trickled down her cheek. Illiah reached and wiped them away with his thumb. Eva leaned into his hand. "I saved you once, but it cost so much. What price would you have me pay next time? Our sons? Stone? Kitarra?"

"I am only trying to save our people."

"I know. But magic is not what we thought. It's dangerous."

Illiah knew Eva believed it. But he couldn't agree. Was it dangerous? An ax could kill or maim, but it was also an essential tool for survival. Fire could ravage and destroy, but without it, the chill of winter would be unbearable. Just because something was dangerous didn't mean it was untouchable.

"You came to apologize, but you are still angry with me," Eva said, stepping away from him.

If he reassured her that was not so, it would be a lie.

"Leave me alone, Illiah."

Illiah debated not listening to her. Part of him wanted to solve this problem, to reunite their hearts, but her coldness made his anger surge. He turned and left, knowing if he pressed her, it would make things worse.

Stone stood in the doorway, his face as dark as night.

"What is it?" Illiah asked.

"It's Rhyl. He is missing."

CHAPTER 3

RHYL

RHYL'S HEAD FELT LIKE SLUDGE. Rhyl's sight, his mind, felt blurred, rough around the edges. His hand brushed the skin of his naked chest. He didn't remember taking off his shirt. As his eyes adjusted to the faint light, his head cleared a little. A shape came into focus beside him. Corri. He lay on the floor, eyes closed. Rhyl decided not to think too hard about why Corri was wearing even less clothing than him.

Rhyl sat up slowly. Gray light painted the room in muted colors as the daylight failed to penetrate the curtains. Something dark and wet coated the floor around Corri. Why was Corri so still? Rhyl swayed, blinking hard, falling onto his hands and knees. The black ooze was the *varing*. He knew that. He could smell it. He could feel it pulsing around the room in waves, brushing up against his bare skin like a caress.

No. That was not right. Rhyl crawled over to Corri and felt a wet stickiness on his knees and recoiled. The ground was stained with something more tangible than magic. It was blood. Corri's blood. Rhyl's hands began to shake. Was Corri breathing? Rhyl couldn't tell. He pressed his finger against the artery in Corri's neck, desperate to find a heartbeat. Corri's skin was white in the pale room. Rhyl reached for his healing *sanarii* magic, but it was dull and unresponsive. He reached harder, frantically pulling the *simul rami* to him, pushing it into Corri, trying to heal him. But all he could feel inside Corri's veins was the *varing*, a black, thick wall of magic that he could not cast aside, he could not heal.

What was happening? Everything was tipped. Rhyl was a *candarii*. He was a *sanarii*. Magic was his to control. Despite his mother's wishes, he had spent years working with Attin, a Guardian, for fuck's sake. Why could he not help Corri?

There. A faint heartbeat, then another pulsed against his fingers. Rhyl bent over his friend, held his breath so in the absolute silence he could listen for Corri's breath and watch for the rise and fall of his chest. Rhyl saw it, but Corri's breathing was slow, so so slow. Rhyl tried to find a wound, anything, but for his efforts, all he got was blood all over his hands. There was no visible wound.

Desperation cinched around his heart. From his lessons with Aiyan at the Healer's Hall, Rhyl knew a person could only lose so much blood before death was inevitable.

"Help," he said, his voice wobbly and rough. "Help!" he shouted, running to the door, leaving a smear of blood behind him. He threw open the door and hoped Corri's servants weren't far away. "HELP! Help me!"

They came running. A particularly round woman Rhyl recognized as Corri's maid wailed when she saw her ward sprawled in his blood on the floor.

"Get him to the healers," the woman said in a stern voice, gesturing for the others to pick up Corri.

Rhyl just stood by, watching, feeling like he had sunken into a frozen lake. He couldn't breathe enough air into his lungs. His chest felt like he was being crushed. Someone put a hand on his shoulder, and he jumped. It was one of Corri's guards, a big man and he glared at Rhyl like he was the worst kind of vermin. He felt something shrink inside under that look. Rhyl noticed too late that he had rubbed his bloody hands on his naked chest, not remembering he had no shirt.

"Best run home, little prince. Looks like you've done enough here," he said, his voice full of venom.

Rhyl shivered, fighting to stay upright as another wave of dizziness overcame him. The sour, ashy smell of the *varing* made it worse. He hoped he wouldn't faint. Corri's servants and guards eyed him with malice. Rhyl felt a strong urge to run, run, run.

He tripped over his feet as he made for the door. The guards were lifting Corri's hurt body. There was nothing Rhyl could do to help. He found his discarded shirt and pulled it over his blood-smeared chest before he turned and fled from the bustle of the servants as they tried to save their young lord's life.

He stepped outside, and the daylight was blinding.

Rhyl staggered through the gardens to the side path that led back to the main road and therefore back to the Queen's Keep.

"Rhyl!"

Rhyl swallowed. If he stopped moving, he might fall over. It was Irri, the spider himself. Irri gripped his arm. Rhyl winced.

"Gods, what happened? Where were you? You foolish boy," Irri hissed.

A weight lowered on Rhyl's shoulders. Irri had taken his cloak and tossed it around Rhyl.

"Are you ill? Hurt? I'm taking you to the healers."

"I'm not hurt or ill. Take me home. Please," Rhyl added in a quiet voice.

"Fine, come along."

"The pools, Irri. The back way. I need to clean up." Rhyl's voice shook. Irri nodded sharply. There were hidden paths, discreet ways only Irri and the inner royals knew of. At least Rhyl would not need to walk through the entire palace in his state. The rumors would not be kind. Ha. Rumors were kinder than the truth. Rhyl almost sobbed at the thought.

The private courtyard was empty. Rhyl peeled off his remaining clothes and slipped into the hot mineral water with a clumsy splash and began scrubbing his hands and body. Irri left him. Rhyl wondered absently what kind of panic his absence had caused. Nothing compared to the panic once his parents found out about Corri.

Wet and clean, he turned to his pile of bloodied clothes and lifted his hands. He called fire and with great relief watched the blood-soiled clothing ignite, turning to ash under his magic.

He didn't understand his impulse to hide the evidence of…of what? He couldn't remember anything after stepping through Corri's door. He didn't think he'd drunk enough wine and ale to be inebriated enough to forget the entire night.

He closed his eyes, the smell of ash still in his nose. The *varing* tingled against his skin like a layer of silk. He searched his mind, trying to remember. He opened his eyes and looked for a vision within the *simul rami*. The mineral water made connecting to the source of magic easy.

The *varing* slammed into the *simul rami*, causing a cascade of visions and sensations to burst into Rhyl's mind. He opened his eyes, gasping. *Candarii* magic wrapped around his chest, making his body feel alive. He slowed his breathing and disentangled the visions. Corri's eyes, bright and fiery. Corri's smile twisting his handsome mouth. Corri laughing, or had he been crying? Corri slipping a gray powder onto his lips.

Rhyl rubbed his tongue along the inside of his mouth. Had he taken culla alongside Corri? Could he have been that utterly stupid?

Rhyl leaned his head onto the stone edge of the pool, watching the mist disappear into the morning light. Above him, the black branches of the cendari tree stretched and rose. He could hear them creak against the slight breeze. The night had begun with gold and splendor, but now everything felt gray and muddled. His gut churned.

He barely made it out of the pool before he vomited. He lay on his back, relishing the cold wet stones against his hot skin. He had never felt so wretched. If Corri died…he didn't even know if it was his fault.

"Rhyl," a voice called. Rhyl managed to sit, staring into the forest. "You look awful."

Rhyl had never been more grateful to see the Guardian of Allati. The spirit man often appeared when Rhyl least expected.

"Attin, I feel awful."

"I can sense the *varing* all over you. What have you been doing?" The Guardian's voice brimmed with concern.

"I—I blacked out, Attin. I can't remember. I think my friend…my friend is hurt. Dying, even. I don't know what happened."

Attin came over to him and placed his hand on Rhyl's brow. The Guardian's touch was soothing, and not quite real. Like a waking dream. Maybe Rhyl was still sleeping and he would wake on Corri's bed with Corri there beside him, alive and laughing instead of passed out in a pool of blood. But no, the Guardian was as real as the cold stones pressed into his bare knees.

"The *varing* is getting stronger," Attin mused.

Rhyl shivered but still felt too ill to move. "Corri—my friend—was full of the *varing*. And he took culla."

"You should not have gone to his house," Attin clucked.

"I know. It was stupid."

Attin sighed. "I think the time has come, Rhyl."

Then Rhyl felt the Guardian's magic, the magic of the *sanarii*, wash over him. He was propelled into the *simul rami*, into a vision. Since his eighth birthday, Rhyl had spent one day out of every five in the forest with Attin learning the ways of the *sanarii*. He had learned to seek visions in the *simul rami*. To ride the air to find visions of the present, to look into the water or fire to find visions of the past. To use the elements. To make fire burn from his fingertips and move the wind at his command (not as satisfying as fire; Rhyl liked to watch things burn). It was not the first time Attin used his powers to force a vision onto Rhyl.

The *simul rami* took Rhyl to a forest. Tall trees stood around him. *Tall* was too simple a word for them. They were immense. Ancient, their roots anchored by moss and ferns. Filtered sunlight crept through the branches, making the air dance as if rejoicing in the return of the morning sun. A quiet came over him, letting him breathe, dulling the memories of panic the other visions induced.

A young man sat on the moss. His hair was a mop of lazy black curls, his eyes as blue as a mountain lake. The corner of his mouth quirked as if he could see Rhyl and found him amusing. Beside him sat a white fox. In the vision, Rhyl felt the fox's searching eyes calling to him.

"We need you to come here, Rhyl," the young man told him. His voice was lilting and mellow. "Soon. Now. Time is short."

Rhyl felt himself nod. Yes, he knew that. He had been dreaming about the Great Forest and the white fox for months. The handsome young man with the laughing mouth and serious eyes was new…and Rhyl remembered that this was a vision, not a dream.

"I'm sorry about your friend." The young man's bright smile faded along with his voice and the Forest. The *simul rami* and its vision slipped from Rhyl's mind.

Rhyl was still in the courtyard lying on the cold stones. Attin was gone. Rhyl groaned. His head felt like it had been split by a latha, his skin clammy and covered in goose-prickles.

"Rhyl," a soft voice called, and he felt warm hands on his face.

"Mummy," Rhyl said. He decided his mother was infinitely wise as she said not another word, didn't ask a single question. All she did was wrap him in his towel and lead him to his room and kissed his forehead as he crawled under his feather blankets. Once he heard the click of his door closing, he pulled his blankets around his head to block out the vision circling in his mind. He clenched his hands into fists and bit his knuckles, trying not to think of Corri's sticky blood. His blankets smelled like lavender and he inhaled, hoping to cast out the memory of the sour *varing*.

When he slept, finally, he dreamed of a black-haired man with blue eyes and long fingers that turned into claws which he plunged into Rhyl's naked chest. And in his dream, he licked the blood from those claws and relished in his pain.

CHAPTER 4

CALYPSO

THE STONE SANK to the bottom of the forest lake after ten skips. One skip for each year of Calypso's childhood he'd lived as a raven in the Keep, outside the Great Forest.

"A coincidence," he muttered.

Calypso threw his second stone with force instead of finesse, and it sloshed instead of skipped.

He sat down on the shore and watched a kingfisher dive into the water, emerging empty-handed—or rather empty-beaked. Calypso pitied the hungry little fellow, forced to dedicate its life to mere survival. Find food. Find a mate. Rear a clutch. Calypso was a *velidar* and he lived in the Great Forest. He never felt the pang of hunger or the cold of winter. Magic gave him everything his body needed. But he still felt hollow. His insides were gnawed by a different kind of hunger.

Life had been simple when Calypso was just a raven. He had lived alongside Eva. The people of the Keep had fed him. Called him their friend. Well, as much as a bird could be a friend to a human. And then magic had pulled him into the Great Forest and the Allmakers had summoned him, forcing his human form from his raven body. Then everything changed. Now, he was *more*. And sometimes, it irked him.

Or perhaps it was just that he was no longer a child.

Perhaps it was that he was stuck in the Great Forest.

Perhaps it was because he was lonely.

In his frustration, he'd wasted his last good skipping stone. He could create more, call on the magic of the Forest, but it took effort to manipulate magic into something real and solid, even for him with his amplified magic—a gift from the Old Spirits, the mysterious Allmakers. Calypso didn't want to put in the effort. He flopped onto the moss, watching the trees sway above, the blue sky bright.

Fuck, he was bored.

He wondered if Rhyl would come. Surely, he would. Rhyl had seen the evils of the *varing*. Felt its coercive nature. Especially after what happened to Rhyl's friend. Rhyl knew what was at stake…didn't he?

"What must I do?"

Thirteen years had passed since Calypso had asked the Allmakers that simple question. Thirteen years since the Allmakers had shown him a vision of death and evil and pain. Not a vision of the past or present but a possible future where the *varing* broke free to destroy the *simul rami*.

The Allmakers' answer, it turned out, was far more complicated than he could have imagined. Mostly because the Old Spirits were ancient beings and the ways of the world and the shifting seasons had made their methods of communication frustrating and obtuse. They spoke to Calypso in whispers and odd visions. He would wake in the middle of the night from a dream that was a vision, a gift, a curse–he could never decide.

Rhyl…time is short. Bring him to usss, the Allmakers had begged in voices weak as grass in the wind.

What choice did he have? So Calypso used his magic and sent a vision to Rhyl. And now he had to wait. And wait. And wait. Kitarra was a long way from the Great Forest.

"Rhyl, get your princely ass here or I shall die of boredom," Calypso told the sky. A terribly empty threat. Rhyl couldn't care less about Calypso dying of boredom because Rhyl didn't know who Calypso was. (Calypso had been a raven, Rhyl wee boy.)(It didn't count.)

Now the child of the prophecy was all grown up. Calypso couldn't even imagine what it was like, being the Child of the Fucking Prophecy. It was a huge thing to put on a child, even if that child was now a man. Worse than letting a *velidar* believe he was a raven. Fuuuck.

But Rhyl was a prince, lived in a palace, and wanted for nothing, as far as Calypso could tell. Maybe Calypso shouldn't feel bad for him. Rhyl had brothers, parents, a grandmother–people who loved him.

Calypso drove his fingers into the moss. Calypso had the Great Forest. A place of magic and trees and beauty and quiet and more magic. But it wasn't enough. And yet it had to be, because as a *velidar*, if he ventured outside the Forest he would be once more stuck as a raven. He would be forced to live half a life.

And long ago in the Allmakers glade, he had agreed to be their voice, their tool. He had let their magic infuse his. He had felt worthy, and now he just felt afraid. Because time was short and soon Rhyl would come.

CHAPTER 5

ILLIAH

ILLIAH DIDN'T CARE for the pitying look Irri cast his way as he left once he finished his report. Irri had found Rhyl and deposited the prince, uninjured and safe, in the royal courtyard, the heart of his home. Upon hearing this, Eva had gone to tend to their oldest son while Illiah stayed to hear the rest.

The relief that Rhyl had not been kidnapped or assassinated was heady. The initial panic fled, leaving behind a dull ache, a memory of that fear. But the panic had all been for nothing. Rhyl had merely sneaked away to spend the night with a friend.

But something had gone wrong. And Rhyl's friend …

Irri didn't know the details, but he would find out. It was what Irri did best, after all—ferret out whispers and truths where there were only silence and shadows.

The door to Illiah's study creaked, and he looked up to see Eva slip inside. She came around his table and settled onto his lap, wrapping her arms around his neck.

"Did Rhyl say what happened?" Illiah asked, folding his wife into his arms, cradling her against him.

She shook her head against his chest. "I didn't press him. He is shaken. Sick. But not from injury. He is resting now."

"A messenger arrived from the Healer's Hall. Corri is dead."

Eva clutched him harder, burrowing her face into his shoulder. He held her tighter. "Rhyl was with him?"

"Irri thinks so. Rhyl managed to leave the Queen's Keep last night without Irri's people knowing."

"Oh, Rhyl. What was he thinking?"

Illiah didn't comment. Rhyl was a handsome young man, a prince, charming in his way, and it came with advantages any young man would snatch up. But there was no point discussing Rhyl's nightlife with Eva.

A knock came at the door.

"Come," Illiah said.

"Defender, Lord Scytt is begging an audience," Diea announced.

"Does he know about his son?" The question was difficult to voice.

"He does."

Illiah looked at Eva. They could not deny him. His son was dead. "Bring him to the Petal," Illiah told his captain.

"Do you need me to come?" Eva asked once Diea was on her way.

"No, I don't think so."

Eva sighed. She kissed Illiah's neck before extricating herself from his lap. "I will go see about arrangements for Corri's body. It's the least we can do." Her voice cracked.

Part of Illiah desperately wanted to call Eva back to him, to have her at his side. But it was likely better to see Scytt alone. Eva never had kind words for the former First Defender, especially when it came to his son. Scytt seemed a less capable father than he had been a First Defender. Illiah had been under the impression Scytt had banished Corri to Withe. What had brought the boy back to Kilev? Rhyl had said Corri had been glad to get out of his father's control. He must've come back for Rhyl's party.

Scytt stood with his back to the door, gazing at the map of Kitarra that hung on the wall of the large council room Eva had termed the Petal. The map had been a gift from Eva years ago, commissioned by an artist. It was as tall as a man and twice as wide.

Scytt had softened over the years, but he still begrudged Illiah for taking his position. And for being a foreigner. But now Scytt was a father grieving a son, and that took Illiah's breath away.

"My lord, my heart aches for your loss," Illiah said.

Scytt turned, his blond hair now fully silver. His eyes were rimmed with red and his jaw worked and clenched.

"My son,"–Scytt's voice caught–"he is dead. Because of your son. Because of the child of the prophecy."

Illiah sucked in his breath and bit back his anger. The man was grieving. "Why do you say that?"

"Your son corrupted Corri with his…debased ways. They were together when Corri died. The healers say there was no wound, no injury. What could have caused his death but for magic? Your son is unnatural. A disease infecting Kitarra's roots. He should go back to Jullayah."

Illiah held up his hand. He had expected grief from Scytt, and questions, but this? "I am more sorry than you know that your son is dead. But I won't listen to you call Rhyl an abomination."

Scytt took a threatening step toward Illiah. The tightly coiled knot that burned inside Illiah cinched but did not back down. "Eva is arranging for your son's wake. And I assure you we will investigate the cause of his death."

"Ha! It was Rhyl. He killed Corri. I know it." Scytt's outrage made Illiah's blood simmer. His nails bit into his palms.

Illiah took another leveled breath before speaking. "You are dismissed. A guard will escort you."

Scytt growled and looked like he might draw a knife. Then he noticed Diea at his elbow and wilted, but his anger still radiated as Diea escorted him out.

Alone, Illiah let his hands rest on the table. He hung his head and waited for the grief and anger to dispel, for the dark magic rising like bile in his throat to settle.

"Da?"

Illiah snapped his head up to see Rhyl standing at the door. Rhyl's face was as pale as his starlit hair. Illiah didn't have to ask if Rhyl overheard Scytt's harsh words, it was clear he had.

"Rhyl."

"Mum just told me. Corri is dead. What if what Scytt says is true? What if I killed him?" Rhyl sounded so young, so afraid.

"No. You would never hurt your friend."

"Wouldn't I? I don't remember what happened last night! All I remember is the *varing*." Tears streamed down Rhyl's face. "I woke… and Corri was…he was …"

"Shhh." Illiah moved across the room and pulled Rhyl into an embrace. "Rhyl, you are *sanarii* and *candarii*. You are strong. Your heart is *good*. You did not kill that boy."

"But I have killed before."

"As a frightened child. In self-defense." Illiah cupped Rhyl's face in his hand and tethered his son's gaze to his. "If not knowing is what torments you, look with your magic. At least then you will know."

Rhyl's eyes widened. Clearly, that wasn't what he'd expected his father to say.

"I'm afraid to try," Rhyl whispered.

"Afraid to try or afraid to know? You are strong enough to carry the truth, Rhyl." Illiah knew how dangerous the truth could be.

"What about Mum?"

"She won't like it. But she is also strong enough to watch you use your magic, Rhyl. Don't worry about her. She is strong as Kitarran steel, your mother," Illiah said with a small smile.

"Will you help me?" Rhyl asked.

Illiah's heart faltered. He gave his head a slight shake. "I can't."

Rhyl nodded. Rhyl had been taught that *candarii* magic was…difficult. Unreliable. Coercive. But he didn't know the whole truth of it. Illiah almost opened his mouth to tell him why he couldn't help Rhyl search for a vision. But he didn't. How could he put that darkness on his son? If Illiah had his way he would die without telling Rhyl the terrible things *candarii* magic could do. About the darkness, the void living inside Illiah's head, inside his soul. How Illiah kept that darkness, that void, on a tight leash. If he helped Rhyl, he would risk releasing the *varing* and the chaos it so desperately wanted to create.

CHAPTER 6

STONE

STONE GAZED UP at the manor house that belonged to the previous First Defender of Kitarra. Illiah had taken Scytt's title, and even though it had been Queen Arrah's command, Scytt never forgave Illiah the slight. Long ago, Stone had known Scytt when he worked under Emri, but Stone was surprised his mother, his dear queen, had appointed the man as First. But that was in the past.

It was a good house. Old. The gardens were grand, and beautiful, if a bit bland. Scytt had inherited the estate from his father not long after his demotion. He had already fathered a son by then. Stone could not remember what happened to Corri's mother…But it wasn't the history of the house or the gardens that drew Stone's attention now. It was the sense of fear and dread that held him there, on the front path. It wasn't just the sudden tragic death of the heir, or remnants of the grieving house staff. There was more to it. Stone could sense magic. But it wasn't the *simul rami* that he could sense behind the dark windows.

As a Kitarran, he was connected to the *simul rami* differently than humans. Aiyan could see that connection with his *heera* wolf magic. Aiyan could see anyone's connection to the *simul rami*. He called that connection a dicidium. Aiyan had told Stone that a Kitarran's dicidium, that slice of magic inside every living being, looked different, brighter than a human's.

But Stone was different yet. His magic was more. He knew it was because he was broken. He had died and been reborn, his shattered pieces put back together differently, out of order. And that broken thing inside him sensed magic. He had never talked to Aiyan about it. He didn't want to mention it, give it recognition, as if in doing so, he would give the dark dwelling inside him wings and claws to break free.

He could sense the vercuri.

He had not told Eva.

He could see things that were almost visions, but of the dead. Always the dead. Well, they weren't just dreams, they were real. Visions. Like Stone was a damn *sanarii*. He saw *revenant*s, the dead walking. He could see the man beneath Illiah's skin that was not Illiah.

He had not told Eva.

This had been happening since Eva destroyed the cendari tree.

He had not told Eva.

He dreamed of stars so bright, so numerous, they hurt his eyes. He dreamed of water crushing his chest with ever-lasting pain until the pain burst like wings, setting him free. He dreamed of Emri. Gods, he dreamed of Emri.

Stone hadn't told anyone about the dead who visited his dreams.

He had not told Eva.

He should tell Eva.

And now, Stone wanted more than anything to convince himself it was not the truth, that what he saw in his nightmares was just that—nightmares. But he had seen Rhyl's young friend Corri in a pool of blood. And it had come true. If he had known, could he have prevented the young man's death? Could he have spared Rhyl the grief of losing a friend?

As Stone gazed up at the house, he recognized the poison made of magic. A dark spot, right in the heart of Kilev. How far would it spread? Would it infect the houses around? Would it reach the Queen's Keep? He wished Aiyan were home. The wolf had insights like no other.

Dark spots, as Stone had labeled them years ago, had infected parts of Kitarra, growing in number slowly, but never so close to a large population like the city of Kilev. Dark spots could bend the mind and make it difficult to see nightmare from real life. The thought of Kilev's winding streets, its many markets and artisan studios being infected, tainted, made his stomach turn.

And the fear he felt for Rhyl liquefied his bones. He could not bring himself to voice his worry, but he was almost certain that Rhyl had caused this. And that would mean he had failed Rhyl, failed Eva and Illiah, because they should have seen it coming. Rhyl was the child of the prophecy. He was *candarii* and *sanarii*. He had a power they did not understand, had not tried to understand. And now... was it too late? Had they ignored what was before them and left too much to the Guardians, to hope?

Hope. Stone despised the notion that was hope. Hope was a puff of cloud. A ray of sunlight easily covered in shadow. They needed action, not hope. But their enemy was invisible, unknowable. Stone wanted to scream in frustration. Instead, he took a deep breath and moved toward the house, ready to speak words of kindness and condolences, as was expected from the Prince of Kitarra.

CHAPTER 7
RHYL

RHYL'S HANDS SHOOK as he poured the water into the copper basin. Water sloshed onto his feet. He knew if he waited, he would lose his nerve to find a vision as his father had suggested. He needed the hurt and anger writhing in his gut to fuel his resolve. Scytt's words had ripped through the torn strands of Rhyl's heart. He could hardly breathe. What if Scytt was right, and Corri's death was Rhyl's fault? He needed to know. He was terrified to know.

The basin shimmered. The basin had been a gift from Aiyan and Mila. He could not look at the bowl of water without remembering the day he received it. His mother had been furious. Aiyan, in his calm, scary voice, had stated it was necessary–the boy (Rhyl) needed to learn to use his magic, and the basin was a tool for finding visions. Rhyl had been twelve.

His mother had given up magic because she believed it dangerous. Rhyl didn't feel like he had that option.

Ripples chased his fingers across the water. He welcomed the magic into his mind and with it came the image of a young man with ruffled black hair and those blue, blue eyes, the same man from before. Behind the man, the Great Forest was a tumble of mossy rocks and masses of ferns. His face was drawn in lines of sorrow, and Rhyl wished he could push the lines away from the man's mouth with his thumb.

But this was a vision and Rhyl had no power here.

"I'm sorry, Rhyl," the young man said.

And then Rhyl saw the truth.

Corri was talking to his father, his face stained with tears. Scytt's expression was lethal as he took a swig from a small flask. Corri fell to his knees pleading, for what, Rhyl could not tell.

Scytt took a long piece of leather, and Corri's pleading made awful sense. Two guards pulled Corri's shirt from his shoulders. Corri tried to fight them, but he had always been a thin man, not weak precisely, but certainly not a fighter like Rhyl. The guards didn't stop until Corri hunched, naked, in front of his father.

Scytt took the band of leather and slapped it against Corri's skin with enough force that the red welts grew wet with blood. He didn't stop until Corri collapsed, gasping and crying on the floor. Rhyl could not imagine what Corri could have done to deserve his father's wrath. No one deserved such punishment. No, it was not wrath, Rhyl decided. It was disgust. Scytt was disgusted, disappointed by his son.

Varing slunk from the shadows, a force only Rhyl could see, and settled around Corri, feeding on his misery, his pain, the shadows around his heart.

Then the vision shifted to another time and place, and Rhyl saw himself. Watching himself in the vision was a strange sensation. Stranger still was the way Rhyl looked at Corri, with eyes black as pitch. Corri stood in front of him, his eyes burning, his mouth twisted in a smile that was far from friendly or sane. Hungry. Corri looked starving.

Sometimes Rhyl could see magic. From conversations with the wolf shifters, the way Rhyl saw magic was not quite the same as the way Aiyan and Mila could. For Rhyl it was more of a haze, a mist that kissed his skin and his senses rather than the colorful dicidiums Aiyan saw. But sometimes what Rhyl saw was dark and viscous. Alive.

In the vision, the faint tendril of magic moved like a snake between Rhyl's vision-self and Corri. Corri leaped up and lunged at Rhyl, grabbing his arm, laughing, laughing, pulling Rhyl toward him. The *varing* pulsed under Corri's skin electric and volatile. Rhyl could see a tendril of dark, sticky stuff trickle down Corri's chin from his laughing mouth.

The *varing*. Corri became less sane and less animated, and his eyes grew somber, then fearful, then desperate. Then Corri grabbed a knife and held it to his wrists.

"What are you doing?" vision-Rhyl asked.

Corri answered, "Isn't this what you want?"

Vision-Rhyl hesitated. "Yes." His voice was a wraith. A shadow. A monster.

Rhyl watched Corri slit his wrists and his blood pool onto the floor like some nightmare waterfall. Rhyl saw, horrified, as vision-Rhyl did nothing. Then, once Corri was slumped onto the floor, vision-Rhyl crouched beside Corri, his hands on Corri's pale skin.

Corri's wounds healed and disappeared. Rhyl had healed him. He had no memory of it. But it hadn't been enough. Corri still died.

Scytt was right. It had been Rhyl's fault.

CHAPTER 8

ASHA

ASHA LEANED INTO THE BOW of the Kitarran ship and watched the sun rise over the wide horizon like a parting kiss. The waves rose and fell as the bow of the ship cut through the salty water, bringing her closer and closer to the land of her people. Kitarra. She had never seen it. Or more accurately, she could not remember seeing it. She'd been a babe when her parents were captured, shipped to Rodan, and forced into slavery. All she knew about them was that they were dead. All she knew about Kitarra was that it was supposed to be her home.

Talo would tell her (and had) that Kitarra was tall trees and crisp mornings. Birdsong at daybreak, frog song at night. Waves. Gray sand. Jagged lines of mountains. Hidden valleys. Creeks that ran with water hot enough to scald.

She could not imagine it.

But each morning brought her closer to that land. And each morning she would watch the sunrise, and each morning Talo would greet her with, "And how are you this morning, Asha?"

And each morning, she would reply, "I am well, My Prince."

The first time she called Talo "My Prince' out of politeness. Talo *was* royalty. One spoke to princes with manners and titles. Even Asha, who had grown up isolated and confined, knew that.

But it wasn't just that Talo was heir to the throne of Kitarra. He exuded all the things Asha would have thought a prince should be. His voice was soft yet stern. He laughed and jested, but sometimes his eyes were full of mystery and a seriousness that made her want to know his every thought. He was not *just* a prince, a figurehead—he was always charming and wise. Or would be someday when he was grown up. Not that he was a boy. He was older than her by a few years. But he was young. Untested. Even though he was lean with hard muscles and moved with a warrior's skill, he reminded Asha of a new leaf unfurling in the sun. She watched him with the same fascination she would watch a butterfly emerge from its cocoon. And like a butterfly, he was also quite beautiful.

The second time she'd addressed him as "My Prince" he'd laughed and told her to call him Talo. Titles were for court; names were for friends. The third time, she called him "My Prince" just to see if he would smile. He did.

It felt dangerous to know she could make Talo smile. She told herself not to encourage him. But despite her better judgment, every day of their voyage, that was how their day began, him asking her how she was, her answering with a title to annoy and amuse him.

Talo was a restless presence on the ship. The captain, a fierce woman named Astera, must have recognized it on the journey to Rodan, because Talo spent most of the day as part of the crew. Asha had been surprised when Talo told her he'd worked alongside the ship's crew, but now that she knew him a little, she could see why. He needed a task or a challenge. Asha was thankful for it. To be cast under his glow all day, every day was more than she was prepared to handle, even if she wanted it.

On the calmer days when the crew had fewer demands on their time, Talo would wander over to her to make conversation or simply stare at the waves with her.

Asha would never tire of watching the sea. The colors of the water shifting under the sun or the clouds. The hiss of rain—rain!—across the water was like music. Feeling the rain on her fur was music brought to life.

Watching Talo weave around the ship's crew was almost as mesmerizing as watching the waves. He leaped and climbed, his long tail balancing him along the ropes and cross braces of the sails, his long, tawny ears pressed back against the wind. There were other Kitarrans along with the human crew, but Talo was the only one who drew her attention.

Her fingers itched to chase after him, to dance along the rails, the mizzens, up the ropes, to feel the surge of wave and swell from the height of the sails. But that would be foolish. Not that she feared for her safety. She was strong and agile, and the sails were not that tall. But she needed to be Asha, a forlorn Kitarran woman rescued from a life of slavery. That role did not involve aerobatics or competitions. So instead, she watched the horizon that one day very soon would bring her to the land that had once been hers. Kitarra. Talo's land.

Besides herself, the crew, and Talo, the ship carried only three other passengers. Bright sunny Cassandra, princess of Rodan, who befriended *everyone*. Dark, beautiful Mila who was something between Talo's maid, healer, and counselor. (Cassandra had confided to Asha she would give her right hand to have Mila's curvy figure. Asha scolded Cassandra for being ridiculous.) The third was Mila's husband—mate?—Aiyan. Aiyan was from Rodan but had left for Kitarra years ago. His story was still told in hushed tones around the city of Kara. The story of the wolf was meant to scare children into behaving.

Asha had been warned to avoid him as much as possible. She assumed keeping her distance from the wolf would be difficult on such a small ship, but Aiyan preferred to keep to himself. He was often below deck with his transport of Rodan plants, carefully potted up for the journey. Sometimes Asha saw him conversing with Mila or Talo, but some days he didn't even shift out of his wolf form. He was as fearsome as the stories suggested, but Asha had not seen the violence she'd been warned about.

Asha was thankful for Cassandra's company. The emperor of Rodan's pretty daughter was just as happy to watch the crew work, and happier to play cards or dice with Asha. Sometimes Mila or Talo joined them, but neither was any good at Rodan card games. Asha had been pleased to find Cassandra an excellent adversary. They had nothing to bet, but their games helped pass the more dreary days.

At first, Asha had despaired to learn the journey to Kitarra would be weeks, not days. And then she saw the ocean and smelled the salty water and felt the sea spray on her fur. When she stepped onto the boat and felt it move beneath her feet, her stomach dipped and a thrill ran through her. She had expected the feeling to diminish with time, but it didn't. Even the smell of fresh-caught fish being gutted on deck reminded her of something she couldn't put her finger on.

One day, she confided this to Talo as he sat gutting fish. (Very un-princely.)(Not that she had much experience with princes.)

Talo paused and squinted up at her. His fur was splattered with fish scales glinting in the sun. "You are from the Long Isles. It makes sense that the smell of fish would trigger something in you. My mother was from the Isles as well. She loved the sea."

The knowledge sank under Asha's skin like a warm drink.

"My mother left the Isles to become the First Defender of Kitarra—a great honor. And to marry my father." Talo grinned like that was a lesser honor.

"I will be pleased to meet her."

"Not possible. My mother died giving birth to me."

"Oh, I'm so sorry, Talo." Asha touched his shoulder before she could stop herself. She cursed inwardly. Then cursed herself for being stupid. Earning Talo's trust was what she was supposed to do. "I often wonder what happened to my parents, my family. But I'm afraid to think of it." It was not a lie. Once Asha learned the truth that her people had been stolen from their homes and sold as slaves, it filled her with deep, unsettling anger. But fear was stronger than anger.

"My mua can tell you who your family was. With your distinctive fur, they must have been well known. The marks on a Kitarran's fur are passed down through family lines. My fur is the same as my father's when he was my age." Talo's face twitched. "But I have my mother's eyes."

"You have very nice eyes," Asha admitted, then bit her tongue because that was *not* what she meant to say.

Talo turned back to his fish, but he was smiling.

"I don't know about you, but I'm getting tired of eating fish," Talo muttered.

"Yeah, maybe a little."

Talo grinned to see Cassandra come over to them, holding her silk skirt above her ankles to avoid the fish mess. Cassandra ignored the looks from the ship's crew as she passed them at their chores.

"Don't worry. There is plenty of variety in Kilev. Oh, here's Cassandra to batter me with more questions about Rhyl. What fun."

Cassandra was journeying to Kitarra as an envoy for her father, but also with hopes (high hopes) to form an alliance with Prince Rhyl. And she was not subtle about her intent to woo him. Quite the opposite. Talo was tired of Cassandra's interrogating, that was plain. But there were only so many ways on a ship to keep boredom at bay, so Talo gave in every time. Asha suspected some of the things Talo shared about his human brother who was not a brother (Talo's description) were pure fabrication, just to annoy Cassandra. Cassandra's cleverness extended beyond cards and dice. She became suspicious. Her questions turned into a guessing game of true or false. She learned that Rhyl was afraid of slugs but not spiders. That he couldn't see someone vomit without vomiting himself. He despised meat pie. Cassandra assured Talo sarcastically such facts would surely help her woo the young prince.

"Don't worry. Just befriend Eva, Rhyl's mother. She is determined to find him a wife."

"Really?" Cassandra's eyes brightened hopefully. "She would force Rhyl into a match?"

"Hardly. But she would try."

"Why is she so keen to see her son wed?" Asha asked.

"She wants him to be happy. To find true love and all that."

Asha huffed silently. As if true love was the only way to find happiness. But what did she know of finding happiness?

Cassandra, however, melted against Asha as if the possibility of true love made her lose physical strength. Asha couldn't help but roll her eyes. Cassandra was the same age as Asha, but she seemed younger. Cassandra had grown up cosseted and loved, wanting for nothing. But Asha couldn't hold it against her. Cassandra was kind and thoughtful and fun. Maybe Rhyl *would* fall in love with her. Though, for Cassandra's sake, Asha hoped not. Love seemed…cruel. Like a dagger that could twist deep and true.

Talo tried to meet her eye, but Asha refused to look at him.

Cassandra grew thoughtful and sighed audibly. "Tomorrow we arrive in Kilev. I am *so* ready to get off this ship."

"We all are. Except maybe Asha." Talo flashed her one of his alarmingly charming smiles.

"I am looking forward to being…home," Asha admitted.

Home. Kitarra. A land Asha did not remember. A home that was ready to welcome and embrace her like the long-lost kin she was. Her heart turned over. She looked away from Talo in case he saw the fear and pain in her eyes. Kitarra would never be her home. Kitarra was just another cage.

CHAPTER 9

STONE

Stone stared at the small pinch of gray culla powder in the center of his palm.

He had been addicted to the drug for nearly two decades. Nearly half his life. His addiction was not as bad as it once was, thanks to Aiyan. But still, the longing at the back of his mouth barely outweighed his self-disgust.

He licked the powder from his skin. The taste was mild, but it hit his nerves instantly. The effects trickled through his veins like fire. He gasped, caught between despair and rapture.

His thoughts raced. He was the lucky one. Aiyan had helped him bring his dose down over the years so the culla wouldn't kill him. Aiyan and his extensive knowledge of poisons and healing draughts had found another herb, belios, to cut with the culla to make it less potent. But the belios made Stone's hands tremble.

Stone took a deep breath, opening his eyes. Now the culla moved through his body, making him feel impossibly strong. Stone took out his latha and began his exercises. Exertion helped take the edge off the dose.

His hands still shook. He grasped the latha tighter. The room moved around him. He was air. He was water. He was light.

The latha shot from his hand and landed with a clatter on the floor. Stone stared at it, trying to understand how it had slipped from his grasp. The rogue blade cut into the plaster, making a nasty gouge. At least it wasn't someone's head. Luckily, he was alone.

Or almost alone. At the edge of his vision, he saw them. Shadows.

Wraiths. The dead. The living. A waking dream. A portent. Fuck if he knew.

Stone braced his hands on his knees and breathed in and out, waiting for his heart rate to settle. For the ghosts to leave. The belios kicked in and the culla eased. His muscles slackened and his mind stepped back from the chasm.

He had not spoken to Rhyl about Corri. The poor boy was grieving. Eva was worried about him. They all were. Rhyl's friend was dead, and Rhyl thought it was his fault. They hadn't spoken of it, but they were all anxious for Aiyan and Mila to return from Rodan. The wolves were wise, and Stone had never realized until that moment how much he relied on them.

A loud knock broke his concentration, allowing him to cast his indecision aside. Jean poked his head through the door. "Prince Arrain, a ship is coming up the river. It's the *Serpent's Daughter*," the steward said.

"You're sure?"

"Absolutely. The flag flying is Captain Astera's."

Stone relished the wave of relief that washed over him. It wasn't that he'd been worried about Talo. The voyage to Rodan was long, but because of the long-standing peace and trade between the two realms and it being late spring, theirs was a safe passage. But still, Talo was his son.

Stone was thankful Rhyl didn't share his mother's fear of magic. Without Rhyl's assurances that Talo was on his way home, healthy and safe, Stone might have given in to the fears and nightmares of Talo's ship being sunk to the bottom of the vast sea. Stone had questioned his decision to let Talo leave the safety of Kitarra to act as an ambassador to Rodan alongside Aiyan and Mila. But the boy—his boy—was a man, a prince. Talo needed to stretch his wings.

"Stone!" Rhyl ran down the hall toward him, his hair escaping its ribbon and falling around his face. Such a pretty boy, Stone thought with a smile. Though there were shadows under his eyes. But it had only been a week since Corri's mysterious death. Maybe Talo's return would bring some life back to Rhyl's expression.

The twins, two lanky boys in their thirteenth year, were at Rhyl's heel, their almost-black hair wild and their identical grins nothing but mischief. Gods, where Rhyl looked like his mother, the twins looked like Illiah, but more careless and good-humored. Stone doubted Illiah had ever been as carefree as Bren and Aralis.

"Talo is back!" Bren announced.

"I just heard–"

"Well, what are we waiting for?" Aralis asked, thumping Stone on the back. At least this time Aralis didn't pull his tail.

"To the river!" Bren exclaimed.

The twins ran ahead before Stone could comment. Rhyl matched Stone's stride at a less exuberant pace.

"Those two have been so well behaved lately, I fear they are conniving something," Rhyl remarked.

"Yes. You and Talo were model children compared to those two ruffians," Stone huffed, thankful for Rhyl's light banter, the slight smile tugging at his lips.

It was a fine spring day. Stone and Rhyl walked out of the palace and into the sun. The trees were lush and full now, and the air smelled like earth and the river. Stone admired the River Ilba as the sun glinted on the waves, and how the silty water was tinged with green in the sun. He spotted the *Serpent's Daughter* without difficulty. Its green sails had faded since she had disembarked from Kitarra three months before.

Stone lost sight of the river as the winding road took them through the trees, easing them down to the water's edge. When they arrived at the royal dock, the ship was just preparing to berth.

"Where are your parents?" Stone asked Rhyl, noticing that Eva and Illiah were not among those gathered on the dock to welcome Kitarra's young prince.

"I couldn't find them," Rhyl replied, his eyes on the approaching ship.

"There he is!" Bren pointed.

Talo's distinct, lanky form was impossible to miss at the prow of the ship with his tawny fur bright as flames. The sun cut Stone's culla-sensitive nerves, but he could see Talo leaning over the rail, hollering at them. Stone grinned.

The ship slowed and ropes were thrown and caught by the waiting dock hands. The *Serpent* was tied to the dock and a wide walkway secured. Stone expected Talo to leap over the side of the ship to greet them, as his personality dictated, but instead, Talo walked slowly. Clinging to his arm was a young Kitarran woman barely more than a girl. Her fur was light gold and black, with striking, distinctive white patches. Her jewel-green eyes were like a wild creature's. Talo had a hand over her arm as if to steady her or keep her from running away. She was clearly the Kitarran Beric had told them about.

When Beric became emperor, he allowed all the slaves from Kitarra to return to their homeland. But somehow, this girl had been overlooked and stolen away from Kara. When she was found, Beric sent word immediately, and Queen Arrah declared a delegation be sent to fetch her home, and here she was. The girl looked younger than Stone expected. She must have been barely more than a babe when she was taken from the Isles. Stone couldn't help the anger that rose, that this girl had been robbed of her people, her family, her heritage.

Talo grinned like a kitten in the cream.

Stone shared a look with Rhyl. Talo had mentioned this girl to Rhyl, but Rhyl had failed to mention the lost girl was a beautiful young woman who Talo was obviously half in love with. Rhyl returned Stone's curious gaze, frowning. There was something amiss about this.

"Talo," Stone said, stepping toward his son, arms out. He would ask questions later. For now, it was a gift to see Talo home and safe. And happy. Talo glowed like a bonfire.

"Da," Talo grinned, falling into Stone's arms for a quick embrace. "This is Asha. Asha, this is my father, Arrain. But most of us call him

Stone. And this is Rhyl. These are Rhyl's brothers, Aralis and Bren, but we generally just ignore them. Feel free to do the same."

"Hey!" the twins protested. Then, "What did you bring us?"

"Spoiled brats!" Talo laughed. Aralis and Bren avoided his swat and went to interrogate Captain Astera and paw at Talo's chests for exotic trinkets.

"Welcome, Asha," Rhyl said with an incline of his head. Stone watched Rhyl's soft eyes, and dear gods, they were full of pity and a wisdom Stone would not have granted the young man just starting his twentieth year.

Captain Astera managed to disentangle herself from the twins and bowed to him, offering him a smile. "I shall have my report to you and the First Defender in the morning."

Stone waved her aside. "Thank you. But don't rush, unless there is something pressing?"

She shook her head, then turned and delivered stern commands to her crew.

A lovely young human woman stepped up beside Talo and Asha. Her eyes landed on Rhyl instantly, and her face grew more dazzling as she smiled at him. Stone saw Rhyl smile back, as if by reflex. Huh. Stone recalled that it had been arranged for Beric's daughter to accompany Talo back to Kitarra. Stone couldn't recall if it had been Eva's idea or Beric's.

"Rhyl, this is Princess Cassandra," Talo said. "Emperor Beric's daughter."

"Prince Rhyl, I am so pleased to meet you," Princess Cassandra said in a sweet voice with a deep curtsy. Stone noticed Rhyl's faint blush.

"As I am you," Rhyl said, holding out his hand to help her down the floating walkway to the dock. Stone's brows arched at Rhyl's transformation into a gentleman. Pity Eva wasn't there to see it.

Stone craned his neck to catch a glimpse of the wolves. Where were they? Ah, Bren and Aralis had accosted them. Aiyan was not the most approachable person, but the twins had never been afraid of him. Aiyan enjoyed their boisterous nature but had been known to nip at the twins' heels, and Stone wasn't sure it was all in play.

Aiyan and Mila, after extricating themselves from Bren and Aralis, made it down to the dock. Aiyan clasped Stone on the shoulder.

"Where is Illiah?" he asked.

"I'm not sure," Stone replied.

"Yes, where are Illiah and Eva?" Talo asked, disappointed not to see his foster parents.

"I don't know," Rhyl replied. "I am sure they will turn up." Talo looped his arm over Rhyl's shoulders and Rhyl leaned against him. Stone reached out and ruffled both their heads with his big hands. Talo was taller than Rhyl now, as tall as Stone. His son was a man grown, with a lovely woman at his side. Why then did Stone not feel more elated?

CHAPTER 10

ASHA

CASSANDRA LEANED against Asha to whisper loudly in her ear. "Talo vastly underestimated Rhyl's good looks. He is so handsome." Cassandra had actually blushed when Rhyl was introduced. Gods, Asha felt instantly sorry for the young prince.

Talo's father, Prince Arrain, assessed Asha somewhat coolly but told her she could call him Stone. Asha wanted to ask why he had two names, but she bit her tongue. Other than in height, Stone didn't resemble Talo at all. His fur was white with black markings. His eyes were an unreal shade of yellow.

A carriage took them along the winding road up the hill from the river dock to the palace.

They were led into the Queen's Keep where Talo left Asha and Cassandra with a kind-faced servant, with reassurances that Asha would see him soon. Asha couldn't help but give Talo a plaintive look as the servant gestured for her and Cassandra to follow her into the palatial keep. Talo smiled at her, but surrounded by his family, Asha knew it was too much to ask him to come with her.

As they followed the servant, Cassandra switched back to the tongue of Rodan so she could comment to Asha on the palace architecture without the servant hearing. Asha tsked her and told her to speak in their new tongue. Asha did not know if she had been taught her native language or if she had always known it. She had no memory of a time when she could not speak both the languages of Rodan and Kitarra.

Cassandra was shown to her room and promised to speak to Asha soon.

"This way, Lady Asha," the servant said, gesturing gently yet firmly for Asha to follow her farther into the Queen's Keep. Asha left behind the last person she was familiar with. They went through a tall door, held open by a guard. Another stood close by.

"This is the royal wing of the Queen's Keep," the servant told her. With a pang of guilt, Asha realized she'd forgotten the servant's name. It had gone in one ear and out the other. Asha had been too distracted by the fuss of their arrival. She felt awkward asking, so she kept her mouth shut. "The queen insisted you be given a place among the royal family."

Asha wanted to ask if that meant Talo's room was close by, but again, she held her questions.

The open-air hallway they emerged into had wide windows overlooking the city and the river. Asha could see a small flickering line on the horizon that was the sea.

"This way," the servant said with a nudge in her voice.

They passed more guards. Asha eyed their folded lathas and long, sheathed daggers with awe. The latha was a uniquely Kitarran weapon. It was mechanized to open with a particular movement, two folded blades becoming one. At first, Asha had been dubious about its merits, but watching Talo practice had changed her mind.

Asha felt the guards' eyes follow her every step, every movement. She was almost afraid they could read her thoughts, but she had been told that mind-reading was not a Kitarran skill.

"This is your room." The servant opened the door, revealing a tall ceiling and wide windows with ruby drapes. The glass panes were clear, and the garden and the forest cast a green light about the room.

The linens were hemmed with fine embroidery. The furniture was simple but well made. There was a fireplace for cool nights. Asha remembered that it snowed during Kitarran winters. Snow. She couldn't imagine it.

"There are clothes, and I see your chest of things has been brought up from the Serpent already." The servant sounded pleased by the efficiency.

"There is a wash basin here, a privy out this door here. And the pools in the garden are for everyone in the royal wing."

Talo had told Asha about the pools of ever-flowing hot water. She peered out the window and could see the corner of one pool set among a beautiful garden. Bright blue water sent flashes of light to dance in the trees.

"I will leave you to rest. The queen will summon you soon. Welcome to Kitarra, Lady Asha."

"Thank you."

Lady Asha.

And just like that, Asha was alone. The silence thundered in her ears. She looked around the room. Her feet felt too firm; as soon as she'd stepped on dry land, she instantly missed the movement of the sea. And as soon as Talo had been embraced by his family, she began to miss him too. His brother Rhyl had been the first to pull Talo into an embrace. Their closeness, their affection, made an old loneliness ache inside Asha's heart.

She changed her clothes. She would sort out her belongings later. She washed. She used the privy, and after, she peered around the corner. The full grandeur of the courtyard garden revealed itself. The steaming pools beckoned, but it was the dead tree that caught her breath. Its tall, arching branches were black and leafless. It made her want to cry. She didn't know why. She returned to her room, thankful she could not see the tree from her window.

She lay on the bed and even though she felt tired, she couldn't sleep. She wondered if she was allowed to leave her room. Where would she go? Could she roam the halls? Explore the Queen's Keep? There were guards around every corner. Could she run into the forest? Could she escape? Would they chase after her? Of course they would. They had gone all the way to Rodan to fetch her.

She was to be summoned by the queen. Talo's grandmother. Maybe Talo would come himself to bring her to meet the queen.

Much later, a Queen's Guard knocked on Asha's door to announce that Queen Arrah was ready to receive her. As they walked, Asha was instructed to curtsy. To be polite. To address the queen as "Your Grace" or "My Queen." And answer her questions honestly—the queen appreciated honesty above all else. It felt like a warning. Asha's gut fluttered as the guard led her through a door into a wide, arching room.

The queen of Kitarra, Talo's mua, was old. She was thin, and her skin was loose, making her fur melt slightly around her fading but proud features. Her eyes were sharp, and very different from Talo's. But Talo had his mother's eyes. Two big dogs lay at the queen's side. They raised their heads and stared at Asha with clever expressions. Talo had told her about the Kitarran dogs, the uandians. Asha had little experience with dogs, but something about them made her want to reach out and run her hand over their fur.

The queen gestured for Asha to come very close, so close Asha had to stop herself from leaning away. The two dogs reached their long noses to sniff Asha's ankles. The intensity of the queen's gaze was like being pricked by needles. And Asha thought Talo's father had been intimidating.

Asha swallowed and controlled her expression as the queen inspected her. The queen put two fingers on Asha's face and turned it this way and that. The scrutiny sent a riot of memories through Asha's mind. They made her body recoil and her heart race. But this woman was not Her. This woman was the queen of Kitarra, and Talo's grandmother. Talo spoke of her with love and admiration. Asha forced her fear down, down, but it was a struggle. It was always a struggle.

Then the queen gave a little smile and a nod. The chains adorning her head tinkled like music. The dogs licked Asha's hands.

"You have no memory of your parents at all?" the queen asked.

"None, My Queen."

"Poor child." The queen looked sad, and tired. "You are undoubtedly a descendant of Lirren. The House of Lirren was well known on the northern Long Isles. The pattern of your fur is distinct and would only be found in a direct descendant of that family."

Asha didn't know how to feel about having a name…it made her numb. Liam would never know his family name.

"Though not much of a child anymore, are you? Do you know how old you are?" The questions were direct, but the queen's voice was kind.

"I'm seventeen, Your Grace. I think."

"Ah. Were you mistreated in Rodan?" The queen's voice had become as gentle as thistle down.

"I don't have any memory of my parents or being taken to Rodan. I was raised in a villa north of the city of Kara. It was secluded, but no, I was not mistreated." But she thought of Liam and the blood on her fur and that day when her childhood came to an end. She could almost smell the magic in her nose.

"Were there other Kitarrans?"

"No. Just me." Surely the queen would sense her lie.

"We are so glad you are home. Kitarra welcomes you. I told Kila to give you a room here in the royal wing, is it to your liking?"

"Yes, Your Grace. Thank you, Your Grace."

"You may stay here in the palace, in Kilev, as long as you like. Or you may return to the Long Isles if you wish. I will have an accountant look into the condition of your family's estate. And I will send a message to Turk in Pinnae. He is Keeper of the Long Isles. You may be the last surviving Lirren. You will want for nothing. And anything you need, just ask." The queen patted Asha's cheek. The queen smiled, and it transformed her into the beloved grandmother Talo spoke of.

"Thank you. You are very generous." Asha curtsied.

"One of the privileges of being queen, my dear. You may pet them if you wish." The queen nodded to the two dogs.

Asha bent down, knowing the dogs would prefer if she was at their level. Their rear ends wobbled as they wagged their tails, licking her hands as she scratched under their chins. Asha felt her face stretch in a smile.

"I'm sure we will see each other soon. Good day, Asha."

The queen rang a small bell. A guard approached Asha, signaling the end of their audience.

Asha sighed as she was shown out. She had lied to the queen of Kitarra. She had been given access to the royal family. She knew it was a victory, but it felt like a death sentence.

CHAPTER 11

RHYL

RHYL WAS UNSURPRISED that Talo's return was met with fanfare. Dinner had been a busy affair. Talo berated Eva and Illiah for not greeting him at the dock, demanding to know what was more important than greeting their foster son who they must've missed very, very much? Stone laughed, winked at Talo, and begged Illiah and Eva not to answer. Illiah offered to take Talo aside and give him the rundown of what he called an adult relationship. Talo rolled his eyes and muttered something that sounded like "Spare me."

Everyone wanted to meet Asha and Cassandra and hear tales of Rodan and the voyage. Rhyl wanted to hear, too, so he was content to listen as Talo rambled on.

Asha added a few comments, but it was clear she was a reserved sort. Cassandra sat beside Rhyl and added her own commentary, her breath tickling Rhyl's ear. She was a pretty girl, and clever, her Rodan accent crisper and more charming than Aiyan's. But Kitarra was full of pretty, clever girls.

When not distracted by the Rodan princess, Rhyl watched Asha watch Talo. Asha had a hard time taking her eyes from Talo. Rhyl couldn't blame her. Talo was considered a well-made, handsome Kitarran. He was kind and thoughtful and funny. Gods, Rhyl had missed him. His heart hurt a little as he noticed how Talo watched Asha. Like they revolved around each other. Once, Rhyl had known that Talo would do anything for him. Now, he knew that Talo would do anything for Asha. But that was good. That was how it was supposed to be.

And yet, there was something about Asha that made Rhyl's skin prickle with unease. Which was ridiculous because she had just spent weeks on a confined boat with Aiyan and Mila. If there was anything amiss or malicious about the Kitarran girl, the wolves would have sniffed it out instantly with their literal wolf's ability to sense lies and deceit.

Rhyl considered his feelings concerning Asha might just be jealousy. Asha and Talo's closeness was like watching someone eat a honey pastry; he wanted it for himself. He wanted that closeness with someone—not with Talo or Asha or anyone in the room—but someone. But then he thought of Corri and the *varing* and the blood and his heart clenched and his stomach roiled.

He excused himself, ignoring his mother's concerned gaze and Talo's confused look. Part of him was disappointed when no one called out to stop him or ask him if he was all right. He was not all right.

Now that they were grown adults, Rhyl and Talo had separate apartments. As children, Rhyl had never felt chafed sharing a room with Talo, but now he was thankful for space to be alone. For both their sakes.

A knock came at his door. "Rhyl?" He recognized Talo's voice.

"Come in."

Talo did. He flopped into the chair by the window, long legs and tail stretched out, examining Rhyl with a look that was difficult to decipher. Rhyl wanted to tell Talo everything. But his tongue wouldn't form the words.

"I missed you," Talo said.

Rhyl smiled a little. "I missed you too. I wish I could have come."

"Me too. Maybe we should go to Pinnae together."

"Maybe."

Talo bit his lip. Rhyl knew he was about to add "We could take Asha."

"So…you and Asha?"

Talo looked at his hands. "No. It's nothing like that."

Rhyl knew it *was* something like that.

"What happened while I was gone, Rhyl? I know something is going on. The parents look at you with more reverence than usual. Like you are made of glass and full of cracks."

Rhyl felt a lump rise in his throat. He didn't want to tell Talo. He wanted to tell Talo. He didn't know if he could speak the words; he didn't know if he could keep them back. Talo was so happy, he didn't want to pull him under his shadow. In the end, it was Rhyl's burden to carry. He was the child of the prophecy. His birthright.

"Rhyl …," Talo chided.

"I—I can't, Talo." Rhyl's voice caught.

"Do you want me to stay and keep away the dark?" Talo asked without a trace of ridicule. Rhyl was utterly grateful Talo didn't push him. It was enough to lift Rhyl's spirits and for his breath to come evenly.

"I'm pretty sure that as kids, you were the one constantly asking for a night-light," Rhyl reminded him.

"So, that's a no, then?" A smile turned Talo's lips.

"I'll be fine."

"I could send Cassandra. I am sure she would be happy to comfort you." Talo's grin turned malicious.

Rhyl threw a pillow at him. Talo dodged it.

"Tomorrow," Talo said.

And Rhyl knew what he meant. Talo would give him a night, and then he would poke and prod until he gave in and told Talo everything. Somehow, the knowledge that Talo cared, that Talo would not leave to carry the burden alone, eased the wild thing inside Rhyl's chest.

Talo let himself out, blowing Rhyl a kiss as he closed the door. Rhyl felt his lips curve in a smile as he closed his eyes. His breathing came easier.

CHAPTER 12
ASHA

THE NIGHT CAME into terrifying clarity. Asha had fallen asleep almost instantly, nestled on the soft bed encased in luxurious blankets.

Asha had opened her eyes to a nightmare.

She was in a different room altogether. Her body was rife with panic, her muscles burning. Iron fingers lunged for her throat, crushing her. She scrambled to understand what was happening. But her lungs screamed in agony, making it impossible for her mind to grasp anything but the instinct for survival.

She recognized the man with his hands around her neck, squeezing the life from her. Rhyl. No. Not possible. It was Rhyl, and yet not Rhyl. His face was contorted—the whites of his eyes were inky black.

"Please." Asha managed to push the plea from her constricted throat just as she had begged Liam all those years ago. Her voice was a garbled whisper. Stars burst in her vision. The fire burned from her heart outward. Everything felt cold.

Then Rhyl released her with enough force that she stumbled and hit the ground, landing on her tail. Her eyes watered from the pain as her lungs gasped and sucked in air.

Her sight blurred and then cleared. The room was swathed in darkness. It was still night, but she was Kitarran and she could see Rhyl standing, his hand raised. Then as if his strings had been cut, he slumped onto his bed in a faint.

Asha sat and took one deep breath after another. Her chest ached.

The pain was already passing. Kitarrans healed quickly. Then Asha noticed the smell. Ashy. Sour. Horribly familiar. It was the smell of dark magic. Her master's magic. That was why she was in Rhyl's room, why she could not remember rising from her bed and walking down the hall in the dead of night. Asha had come to Rhyl under thrall, her body willed by her master's magic, her mind in a cage.

But no longer. The connection was broken and Asha was awake. She looked at Rhyl where he lay. She could see the faint rise of his chest. Was he asleep? Taken into a deep trance by his magic? He was a force, strong enough to break Asha's master's spell, strong enough to squeeze the life from Asha and snap her like a twig. Asha swallowed. Talo had told her nothing about this. Nothing about the dark magic that wreathed his human brother.

The cold from the stone floor seeped through Asha's fur. She almost missed the hot Rodan sun. With the pain and magic-induced fog receded from Asha's mind, it left her with tremors and weakness. Even the tip of her tail shook. With effort, she pushed herself to her feet. She needed to disappear before anyone found her. She willed herself to remain calm. Rhyl was still unconscious on his bed. Would he remember her when he woke?

There was *something* in the dark, in the air around her. Asha spun, trying to see it, but it was only a sense. A presence. Another strong tremor struck her. She tucked her arms and tail as close to her body as possible lest the shadows reach out for her.

The air dipped once more in temperature. *Rhyl. Rhyl. Rhyl.* The shadows sang in voices like knives, slicing Asha's nerves, filling her with intangible dread and a desperate need to flee. Keeping her movements silent, she crept out through Rhyl's door and down the hall bathed in midnight.

There were no guards, but Asha didn't let herself breathe until she pulled the door to her room shut behind her. The painted walls and lavish pillows in her chambers welcomed her. She curled up on her bed. Her hands shook as she pulled her blankets around her shivering body.

Fear gave way to rage. Her anger flooded heat through her but didn't warm her. Her rage was driven by helplessness, an old friend, as familiar as her shadow. Somehow, she'd hoped her master's magic wouldn't reach her in Kitarra, that her master wouldn't be able to enthrall her anymore. Asha had been wrong.

A sob escaped her throat like a roar. Asha shushed herself. She couldn't risk anyone being witness to her shame, to her fear. Yes, she was angry, but she knew it didn't matter. Anger would not save her. Fear would not save her. Nothing could.

She began to remember how she came to be in Rhyl's room. Her mind remembered, even if her body had been controlled by her master. She remembered the silent hall of the palace. How she had walked past the guards and dogs, but Asha was known to them now, and there were no rules about walking around the palace at night. To them, it would look like she was merely restless. And who wouldn't want to stop at the hallway window and admire the river and Kilev at night, bathed in summer moonlight?

She had waited for the guards to move on, and in the shadow between their turn, she'd slipped into Rhyl's room soundlessly.

Rhyl had been sleeping in a messy pile of blankets, his white-gold hair splayed around his face covering his eyes. His face twitched, frowned, a deep crease between his brows, like he was in the throes of a nightmare. Tears fell from his eyes. Tears black as tar.

Rhyl must have sensed her presence, or perhaps he had sensed the magic that enthralled Asha had made her a slave. He had jerked, sitting upright in his bed, his hair falling from his face. Rhyl didn't utter a word. His hand reached out like a viper and caught her, his fingers pressing into the tendons of her neck. Then the thrall had ended.

Had Rhyl's magic freed her? Or had Asha's master fled her body and her mind during Rhyl's attack? She didn't know. What did her master want with Rhyl? Would Rhyl remember everything in the morning?

Asha rubbed her bruised neck. Her tears fell into her fur, hot and furious. Her body convulsed with sobs. She could not stop the memories.

Her memories were of Liam's hands on her neck. Liam's twisted promise in her ear. Liam's eyes that held death but not peace. It was Liam's eyes that haunted her until the morning sun slipped above the horizon, filling her room with pale light.

CHAPTER 13
RHYL

RHYL. *Rhyl. Rhyl.*

The voice was a hiss, a whip, a lash of cold rain.

Rhyl woke. His nose burned from the sharp awful smell of the *varing*. His eyes burned from his tears. In his dream—no, not a dream, not a nightmare—it had been a vision. Of Corri. His wrists slit. The blood. The *varing*. He thought he saw a person slink out of his door, but he blinked, and nothing.

Rhyl leaned over his bed and retched into his chamber pot.

He couldn't tell if it was night or day or somewhere in between. His room swam with shadows and stunk like ash. Then the *varing* touched his skin, tingling down his arm, reminding him of *sanarii* magic, but more potent, more mysterious. Rhyl called fire. The flame rose, green and alive, licking the air around his fingers. The shadows surged.

Rhyl. Rhyl. Rhyl.

A scream resonated in Rhyl's mind. He knew someone was in excruciating pain. Someone close.

He bolted from his room, the shadows following him, the *varing* clinging to his skin. Dawn lit the hallway with a watery light, but still the shadows persisted, calling to him, warning him. His parents' chamber was a short distance away. The door was never locked, so there was no resistance when Rhyl pushed his way in.

"Rhyl!" his mother yelled as he burst through the doors.

"Where is Da?"

"I don't know. I don't know!" Eva wailed. Tears stained her cheeks.

Her eyes were wide, childlike. Rhyl had never seen the expression on her face before and prayed he never would again.

Rhyl's heart pounded in his chest. *Find him*, he commanded the shadows. The *varing* led Rhyl into the courtyard. Pale dawn light streamed through the steam rising off the pools. The forest that edged the courtyard remained dark as night, but against the dark, Rhyl could see his father standing at the base of the cendari tree.

Eva was right behind Rhyl. When Rhyl told her to stay back, to his great surprise, she listened. He stopped a few feet from his father.

"Da."

Illiah turned to look at him. His eyes were black, black, black.

"Da," Rhyl whispered. Rhyl felt like a child again, helpless, afraid. Gods, he was so afraid. The *varing* held Illiah in thrall. Some instinct told Rhyl to reach out and grasp his father's hands, holding them tight. He almost expected Illiah to resist, to pull away from his grasp, but he didn't. Rhyl's skin crawled as his father looked at him with eyes made of *varing* filling his familiar face with a horrible wrongness. Rhyl concentrated on his father's calloused hands in his. He used the touch to tether himself to his father and pull the *varing* from his father's skin, his veins, just as he would use his *sanarii* gifts to heal. It…worked. Illiah's eyes cleared and became green. His face relaxed. The creases softened.

Rhyl's relief came out as a hiccup.

"Rhyl," Illiah said softly as if waking from a dream. Illiah stumbled, but Eva was there to catch his arm, to steady him.

The *varing* still hovered in the surrounding air. Rhyl reached to the dark magic, calling to it. As he did, he felt the *varing* surge, and grow stronger, as if he was feeding it. *What is this? What am I doing?* The questions consumed him. The magic called to him…it wanted… it wanted.

"Oh no," Rhyl choked out. A dark shape solidified from the *varing*, slipping to the ground like a shadow made of ditch water. Rhyl froze, unable to look away from this monster he had called—no, created. It rose and grew, forming legs and hands. It did not have eyes, not in the sense a living thing did, but it had awareness, and Rhyl felt it focus on him. A *vivus*. Aiyan had spoken of the malicious beings made of *varing*. Its featureless form shifted, morphing into another shape, and its eyeless face became human. Rhyl stood paralyzed watching, knowing whose likeness it was taking.

Then it fell, crumbling into dust. Eva stood behind it. In her shaking hand was a wooden weapon.

"Mum!"

Illiah staggered against Eva. "Eva, are you all right?"

Eva nodded shakily.

"I fought it. I did." Illiah's breath was ragged.

Illiah thought this was his fault.

"I know, love. I know," Eva cooed. Rhyl's parents sagged against each other. She dropped the knife to hold her husband against her. The strange weapon thumped on the moss.

Rhyl swallowed his emotions so he could tell his father it was not his fault, that it was Rhyl's, his eyes focused on the knife. Rhyl felt like kicking it away, but instead, he picked it up. It was warm, alive. He could feel the wood singing, the grains were almost glowing. Eva looked up at him.

"What *is* this?" he asked. "How did you know—how did you—is this a vercuri?" He had never seen one before, but what else could it be?

Eva snatched the wooden knife from his hand and tucked it away.

"Rhyl, it is all right," Eva said, which was not an answer to his question. When did his parents willingly answer his questions? He bit his lip. It was not the time for anger. But his mother was wrong. It was not all right. He was both *candarii* and *sanarii*, which meant his magic was something other, something worse, something unpredictable. He was the child of the prophecy, but he was also a monster. He was a weapon unsharpened. An arrow loosed with no target. Rhyl was a danger to them all. He could hardly stand the soft look passed between his parents, so full of *understanding*. It infuriated him.

Rhyl wanted to know everything. He *needed* to know everything. But he knew if he stayed beside them a moment longer, he would lash out in anger. He could hardly tear his glance from where the vercuri was half-hidden in his mother's pocket. He turned and left so he would not speak or do something he would regret.

"Rhyl, wait!" his mother called after him. But Rhyl didn't listen. He kept moving. His legs were the only thing keeping his tears from consuming him. If he stopped, he would drown.

Rhyl stumbled down the palace halls to Talo's room, his throat thick with sobs as he knocked gently on the door.

Talo, face puffy from sleep, opened the door. Rhyl fell in almost toppling him.

"I can't wait any longer. I need to go to the Great Forest. I need to leave before I endanger everyone." Rhyl wiped his eyes with the back of his hand. His sight was blurry with unshed tears. He had black stains on his hands. He rubbed them against his crumpled clothes.

"Rhyl," Talo began, but didn't continue. Rhyl knew it was because there was nothing left to say. He was right. He had to leave. Talo couldn't deny it.

Rhyl tried to pull his thoughts together. He would need supplies. Food. Weapons for fighting. Tools for hunting and foraging. His bedroll. Furs. Summer was coming fast, so the weather shouldn't get cold. He wasn't going to the mountains, after all.

"What happened?" Talo asked.

"I—I—" Rhyl choked on the words. Hot tears dripped down his nose.

"Rhyl." Talo put his hands on Rhyl's shoulders.

"What happened with Corri…I did it. I killed him. Then just now… Da…Gods, I don't even know."

"Tell me," Talo commanded gently.

"I—the *varing*—it was too strong. So strong. Like Corri was a living cloud of *varing*. It was so good, I felt so alive. I could control it. The *varing* feeds on pain and despair, and it— I—it was like using fire, fanning it, letting it grow. Then Corri slit his wrists."

Talo was silent.

"Then I healed him. That was why there were no wounds. I healed them while still in a trance. But when I came to, Corri had already lost too much blood. There was nothing to be done. And Da …"

Talo waited.

"Just now, I woke sensing something was wrong. I found him by the cendari tree, but he was consumed by *varing*. I touched him and the *varing* left him and became a *vivus*. Because of *me*. ME! Then Mum killed the *vivus* with a—a wooden knife."

Talo pulled Rhyl against him and Rhyl dug his hands into his brother's fur. "Is Illiah all right?"

Rhyl nodded against Talo's soft shoulder. He felt Talo's long exhale.

Rhyl pulled away, wiping his cheek with his hand, then wiped his wet hand on his pants. "You can't come with me to the Great Forest," he stated.

Talo tensed. "Rhyl–"

"You need to stay here."

Talo's light blue eyes were troubled and torn. "I should go with you. I *want* to go with you. That is what we planned …"

"Things have changed. You need to stay here with Asha," Rhyl said. Asha…Asha. Why did his stomach churn when thinking of her? "And with our parents."

Talo's ears drooped.

"I can get to the Great Forest alone," Rhyl assured him. He took a breath. Yes. He felt better already knowing that he would leave Kilev. He would find answers. The man in the Great Forest basically promised him as much. He let his exhale out long and slow.

"I know you can, Rhyl…but…it's such a long way."

Rhyl nudged Talo's shoulder. "I'll be fine." He held out his hand and let his fire coil around his wrist like a snake, flaring high enough to make Talo scoot back.

"Show off," Talo muttered. "That is your plan? To burn everyone who might be a danger?"

"I don't have to light them on fire, just scare the piss out of them." Rhyl had never actually used his *sanarii* fire on another person. The thought made him squeamish. But Rhyl had yet to meet anyone who didn't cower witnessing his ability to call the potent element.

Talo sobered. "Did you speak to them while I was away?"

Rhyl shook his head. "Now *that*, I can't do without you."

"You plan to ride across three realms alone but you can't summon the courage to speak to our parents about it?"

"Don't judge me."

Talo grinned. "Leave the parents to me."

Rhyl was so glad to have his brother who was not a brother back. With Talo beside him, he felt stronger.

Talo sighed. "I had hoped for more time with you before you had to leave."

"I know."

"Cassandra is going to weep."

Rhyl rolled his eyes and sniffed loudly. Talo thumped him on the back.

"I will rally the parents, and you can leave by nightfall, if you must," Talo told him.

"Thank you, Talo." Rhyl didn't say it, but for all his talk, he really wished Talo was coming with him. But he felt certain Talo needed to stay in Kitarra. Talo's place was in Kitarra. Rhyl's place was wherever the prophecy led him.

CHAPTER 14
RHYL

"RHYL? They are ready for you."

Rhyl gripped Talo's shoulder, squeezing it, letting his weight shift against Talo's briefly. The corner of Talo's mouth quirked. Rhyl's bones felt unresponsive as he marched into his father's council room.

Morning light poured from the high windows, casting a golden glow on all the faces waiting for him there. Aiyan. Mila. Tarran. Murryn. Aisha. Turk. Stone. Illiah. Eva. Mua, the queen. Talo. The people who had shaped him into the man he was. Their eyes followed him expectantly. Talo had brought them here, but Rhyl had called this meeting. Rhyl was in command. He reminded himself that he was a prince and their chosen one, and he could not collapse into a pile of nerves.

They all stood when he entered and sat as he sat. Rhyl had attended enough of his father's councils to mimic his father's commanding presence, his calm but stern voice, but Rhyl couldn't shake the feeling that he was only pretending to be grown up and the grown-ups were just amusing him by playing along.

He cast the thought aside. As Rhyl had seen the Defender do countless times, Rhyl looked at each of them in turn, holding their eyes. It gave him a blessed moment to gather his thoughts. Was that why his father did it? Was the Defender nervous like a sheep among wolves during council? Rhyl could not believe it.

"Thank you for coming." He cleared his throat. "The time for secrets has passed. The time for treating me like a child is done. I need to know what I must do to fulfill the prophecy. I need answers." He caught Aiyan's golden eyes and saw approval. Coming from the old wolf, it gave Rhyl courage. His mother cut a meaningful glance at Stone, and Rhyl's newfound courage tripped.

"Where shall we begin?" his father asked.

"The prophecy," Rhyl stated.

"It was given to us by Tayeh," Mua said.

Stone shifted in his seat, and Rhyl almost didn't hear him when he said, "That is not entirely true."

But the queen heard him. "Arrain, my son, what have you kept from me?"

Stone looked aged. He leaned forward, elbows on the table, knuckles clenched. "When I was young, I received the prophecy from a seer named Magda."

The queen groaned, covering her eyes with her hand. "Magda was nothing but–"

"Don't start," Stone – Arrain–warned.

"Tayeh came to me and instructed that I bring Rhyl and Illiah to Kitarra," Arrah argued. "He told me Eva was to stay behind in Jullayah and that I was to bring Illiah and Rhyl here. He spoke of the prophecy."

"But you got the prophecy from me first, years earlier," Stone corrected. "Not from Tayeh." Stone glanced at Eva across the table.

"And now you are telling me it was from the lips of—of a seer? Not the Guardian himself?" the queen stated. Gods, Rhyl was thankful the queen had never used that terse voice on him. Another benefit of being her grandson.

"It doesn't matter," Eva said. "It *was* Tayeh's prophecy, regardless of how Arrain obtained it. Tayeh told me of it before Illiah and I fell in love." Eva halted, turning her blue-green eyes on Rhyl. "That summer, long ago, when your father was captive in Rodan, Stone and I went in search of Magda." She rubbed her temple. "We didn't find her, but she left us a note, knowing we would come looking. The note mentioned another part of the prophecy…but we don't know what it is. Or maybe Magda's note lied. Or maybe Tayeh lied. Or maybe Tayeh didn't give us all of it—maybe he planned to someday."

"Where is Magda now?" Rhyl asked.

"We don't know. Stone has been searching for her for years."

"It seems she doesn't want to be found."

"Or she is dead," Tarran pointed out.

"Not helpful," Murryn muttered to her husband.

"So…there may be another part of the prophecy, but we don't know what it says," Rhyl concluded.

"Right."

Rhyl felt a mixture of frustration and rising excitement. He must be on the right track, but the track was a dark, long tunnel. "Tell me about the *vivus*."

Just as Rhyl expected and dreaded at the mention of the *vivus*, the fear in the room felt palpable.

"A *vivus* is an entity made from the *varing*. A poisonous shadow that invades your mind and makes you relive the worst things your heart can imagine," Aiyan said. "Sometimes the *vivus* becomes so strong it takes over a host and becomes a *revenant*."

"There have been no more *vivus*," Murryn noted hopefully. "Not for years."

Rhyl looked at his father. He hadn't told them, then.

Aiyan looked at Murryn. "The dark magic is not gone. It is waiting. I can feel it sometimes. Mila has felt it too." He turned expectantly to Illiah.

It was Eva who spoke. "Rhyl, when your father was taken to Rodan, the *vivus* overtook him."

"No. It wasn't a *vivus*," the Defender said quietly. "It was not just mindless terror and fear. It was an entity. A person made of *varing* took over my mind."

"Illiah almost died," Mila told Rhyl, her deep blue eyes calming like the river at night.

"But he is still here." Illiah tapped his head gently. "I feel him, sometimes."

Rhyl swallowed. "What happened when you…when you were taken to Rodan? No one ever speaks of it." It was a question that had burned in Rhyl since he was old enough to recognize the scars that crisscrossed Illiah's body were not from combat, but from something worse. And when Rhyl was older, he heard the rumors, the stories about how the Defender was captured, sent to Rodan, and tortured by the now-dead emperor, Imal. Rhyl had never had enough courage to ask his parents about that time.

"I made a mistake and crawled right into Cotoch's trap. Cotoch took me to Rodan, as some sort of prize," the Defender said. "I was Emperor Imal's prisoner. He tortured me to harvest the *varing*. He was *candarii*. *Candarii* can harvest the *varing* from the pain and suffering of others."

Rhyl could hardly hear for the pounding of his heart hot in his ears. He swallowed to keep his bile down. "A *candarii* harvests the *varing* from pain? Why didn't anyone tell me?" he managed to ask.

"Rhyl, you are not *candarii*," his father said softly.

"But I am. I'm both *sanarii* and *candarii*." Rhyl tried his best to keep his voice even.

"You are more than *candarii*. That is why we didn't tell you. Because we didn't think it was relevant."

Rhyl didn't point out the obvious fact that *he* found it very relevant. "What happened in Rodan?" Rhyl asked, looking at the almost invisible scars along his father's exposed skin.

"When I was at my weakest, when I wanted most to die, the man made of *varing* came to me. And when I woke and was myself again, the emperor was dead. I killed Imal and tried to kill Aiyan and Mila, but I have no memory of it. Mila stabbed me with a vercuri, and I woke up."

It was uncomfortably close to what had happened that very morning. But why now? Why had his father lost control after so many years? Rhyl could not remember Corri's death; had there been a strange entity that night? Rhyl's only memory was from what he saw in the vision.

"Eva saved your father," Mila said.

"I saved him by destroying the cendari tree and killing Tayeh." Eva's voice was anguished.

"Eva was tricked by Crea. Crea told her the *sanarii* could use the vercuri. What has Attin told you about the vercuri?" Stone asked, placing a knife made of wood on the table. The knife Eva had used that morning to kill the *varing* monster, the *vivus*. He slid it over to Rhyl. All eyes were on the seemingly harmless carved wood. Rhyl wrapped his fingers around the little wooden weapon. Just like before, the knife felt alive with magic. He could feel it *calling* to him. The *varing*. Aiyan tensed beside him.

"Put it down, Rhyl," Aiyan said softly.

Rhyl saw tears trickling down his mother's cheeks, her eyes wild. He put the vercuri down. What *was* he? Was this the *candarii* part of him yearning for the pain of others? He clenched his fists to keep his fingers from trembling.

"Attin told me the vercuri can be dangerous. He told me there are nine of them," Rhyl answered Stone's question.

Stone took out a small wooden bird and another wooden dagger—or perhaps a short sword—and placed them on the table. They were made from the same wood. Rhyl did not reach out to touch them.

"This dagger is two vercuri combined. Do you remember your mother's leaf pendant?"

Rhyl nodded. It was one of his only memories from when he was brought to Kitarra. He had worn it around his neck, but a Kitarran warrior wanted it. He remembered how miserable he felt handing it over.

"The second piece of this vercuri is a dagger your father got from his old mentor–what was his name?" Stone turned to Illiah.

"Eelan."

"Right," Rhyl huffed. His father liked to tell stories of Eelan, how fierce he was as a teacher, making Illiah's rigorous discipline look like child's play. And here Rhyl had half believed Illiah had made him up to bolster the novices at the Forge.

"This dagger I found in Tayeh's Vale. This bird once belonged to Magda. And Aiyan found this dagger in Rodan, but we believe it was stolen from Jullayah, from one of Crea's temples," Stone explained. "Five of nine." Stone looked at Aiyan, who gave a slight nod. "Watch." Stone placed the three vercuri next to each other.

Rhyl blinked, trying to make sense of what he saw. The four objects were gone, melding together to form a new thing, a longer, almost sword-like weapon.

"Tayeh told me once long ago that the nine vercuri were carved from a fallen cendari branch. They can give the bearer abilities." Eva looked at Illiah. "Make you stronger."

"Or let you influence others," Illiah said, his voice heavy.

"But a *sanarii* cannot use them?"

Eva shook her head. "I used the vercuri to save your father, and it destroyed the cendari tree."

Rhyl knew his mother felt responsible for killing the tree, which led her to believe magic was dangerous to wield. But he had not known she had used a vercuri.

"Attin told me the vercuri were created to bring balance to the *simul rami*. To magic," Rhyl told them. His mother nodded. "Attin said there are two in Allati. With Cotoch. When I touch the vercuri, I can feel the *varing*," Rhyl whispered, looking at Aiyan.

"Tayeh once told me that to speak of dark and evil things is to invite them," Eva said. "I think he was talking about the *varing*. How it feeds and grows stronger when surrounded by pain and cruel intentions."

That made sense. Corri's life with his abusive father was shrouded in pain.

"That certainly is what happened in Kara under Imal's rule," Aiyan remarked bitterly.

"But how does this connect to the prophecy?" Rhyl wanted to know.

"*Those who are strong are now weak,*" Eva recited.

"The Kitarran people," Stone noted.

"With healing hands, the babes will speak."

"That could be Aiyan and Mila. How many babes have lived because of their Healer's Hall?" Rhyl stated.

"Yes, it could be the wolves," Stone agreed.

"Light turns to dark when colors shift," Rhyl continued the prophecy. "The *simul rami* clouded by the *varing*. I have seen it."

"I have too. A person infected with the *varing* turns their aura dark and muddy," Aiyan said. Rhyl couldn't imagine seeing magic the way the wolf could.

"Two rivers join when two lovers rift," Illiah said.

"Again. The *varing* and the *simul rami*," Rhyl said. "But who are the lovers?"

No one missed the look his parents shared. But no one had an answer for him.

"Born with magic in his bones,

"A child lit by the stars,

"Watch for him for he shall be ours," Rhyl finished. "But that's not all of it." Stone shook his head.

Rhyl felt like he was falling into a deep pit. Nothing to grab onto. He needed more information.

"You don't know what to do," Rhyl concluded, looking around the table.

"We know the *varing*, the dark magic, is spreading. And if we can't stop it, the realms will fall into turmoil and chaos," Illiah said. "We know that we need the vercuri. And you." The latter was said with regret.

"So, in summation," Rhyl began, "Da has a man made of *varing* living inside his head, and if he takes control, he will cause murder and mayhem. And I have to stop the *varing* from poisoning the *simul rami*. We have five vercuri. We need nine. No one knows where the other four are, but some may be with your greatest enemy." The Defender narrowed his eyes. "Yes, I know things," Rhyl snapped. "But once we have all the vercuri, we still don't know what to do with them."

"There may be a clue," Eva said. "There is a strange spirit woman who is trapped in the crypts below Cotoch's house in Mahlas. She came to me. And Stone. And Illiah, though what he recalls of that time is muddled."

"She came to me and told me I needed to kill Illiah. And I almost did," Stone said, sounding lost.

A chill slid down Rhyl's spine, right to his toes. He met Talo's surprised gaze. When they were children, they had been kidnapped by Cotoch and taken to Mahlas. Rhyl didn't remember much of that time; Talo neither. And what they did remember was fear. Stone and Irri had rescued them. But this was part of that story they had never guessed at.

"Why did she want you to die, Da?" Rhyl asked.

"Likely it has to do with Illiah's connection to the *varing*. She must have foreseen that it would consume him. She was trying to save us," Eva said.

Aiyan fidgeted in his seat, running his thumb over his lip. "The Muro, the *heera* goddess, died to warn me of the same thing. Something about Illiah makes it possible for the *varing* to manifest a consciousness inside him," he said.

Rhyl thought his life had been ruled by the prophecy, but it was nothing compared to the curse his father bore.

"But you know how to control it," Talo stated to Illiah. It was almost a question.

Illiah looked at Eva. She reached to take his hand. "I thought so, but this morning I very nearly lost control to him again."

A few people actually gasped.

"Why?" Tarran asked. "Why now after all these years?"

Rhyl couldn't move. Couldn't speak for the dread that seized his muscles. He knew why. It was him. The *varing* flowed in him, called to him. What if he had caused it to break through Illiah's bonds? What if next time he couldn't stop it?

"Maybe we can ask her, this spirit woman," Murryn suggested. "Eva, she came to you. Maybe you can talk to her with magic."

Everyone looked at Eva. She bit her lip. Rhyl knew his mother was terrified to use her magic.

"Can we go to Mahlas?" Tarran asked. "Send one of Irri's spiders?"

"Our spies tell us Cotoch still visits the city sometimes. And Regent Geral is extremely loyal to Cotoch. It would be too dangerous."

Stone must have noticed the hopelessness creep over Rhyl because he put his big hand on Rhyl's shoulder. "It's all right. We are here to help you."

"There is time, Rhyl," his mother said at her most reassuring.

"We will be your shield, your sword. Anything you need us to be," Aiyan said.

Rhyl wanted to believe them, but something pressed against the backs of his eyes, a feeling of restlessness, like sand running between his fingers. Corri's face hovered in his mind. The *varing* was a monster living inside Rhyl, waiting, lurking. They were wrong. There was no time. He could feel it. They couldn't help him. He knew the journey would take him far from home and the people who had vowed to help him.

This path he would walk alone.

CHAPTER 15

EVA

WHEN EVA NOTICED Rhyl's eyes glaze over, a sign that he was truly overwhelmed, she stood and begged them to end the council for the day. No one argued. Rhyl retreated to his room.

Oh, how she wanted to relieve him of his burden, to shoulder this for him. She wanted to follow him and make sure he was all right. But he was a grown man and she didn't think a mother was what he needed at that moment.

Eva still felt unsettled. Afraid. She was still shaken from waking up at dawn, feeling the choking poison of the *varing* around her, reaching out and finding Illiah gone. She had known instantly that the *varing* had taken him. What she hadn't expected was Rhyl rushing in, as if some premonition had brought him to her. And Rhyl had known exactly where to find Illiah. It wasn't until the *vivus* appeared that she realized Rhyl's intuition was not a blessing, but a curse. The *varing* had called him.

Eva hated dredging up memories of that awful time when Illiah was captured. His torture. How she saved him at the cost of Tayeh's life and the cendari tree, though she didn't know the cost at the time. Laying bare all their dark history to Rhyl was unpalatable. Eva raged at the necessity of it. Her son should be able to enjoy being a young man, full of passion and freedom. Perhaps fall in love. Marry. Make a life for himself, one of his choosing. Instead he was dissecting the horrors of their past to move forward into an uncertain future.

The others left just as Rhyl had, leaving the three of them alone: her, Illiah, and Stone.

Illiah leaned over and rubbed her thigh with his hand. His touch soothed some of her concern. Illiah's eyes crinkled as he smiled at her.

Thirteen years had brought them close. Thirteen years had aged them. Illiah had more than a handful of gray in his dark beard, and Stone's dark spots and stripes had faded more to white. But they were far from old.

"What now?" Eva asked, leaning her forehead on Illiah's shoulder.

"Perhaps it is time to let Rhyl take the lead," Stone suggested.

Illiah sighed. "He is a strong young man, and clever. But I feel like he is keeping something from us."

Eva laughed. "I am sure that is how all parents feel about their children. Don't even get me started on Aralis and Bren."

"At least they are too young to get into any serious trouble."

Eva didn't dare contradict her husband in case it came true. The twins were their own entity. Like a thunderstorm. Or a flood. She just prayed they didn't realize it until they were old enough to form a few more threads of common sense.

"Rhyl will be all right. He is his parents' child," Stone said. "Stubborn and willful."

"Thanks," Eva muttered.

"And there are still things we can do to help him," Stone went on.

"Like find Magda."

"And the vercuri."

"All of which are as elusive as a flea on an alra."

Eva glared at Stone for his ridiculous analogy. "I'm going for a walk in the forest to clear my head," she announced.

"Where to?"

"Raven's Ridge."

"You and your ravens," Illiah muttered.

"Their chicks should be fledging soon," Eva reminded them, not caring that neither Stone nor Illiah had any interest in the pair of wild ravens that lived in the forest around Kitarra Peak. The ravens reminded her of Calypso, the raven she had raised from a poor orphaned hatchling. Even after all the years since she had left Jullayah, she still missed that bird. "I'll be back for dinner. Hopefully, Talo can convince his lovely Asha to join us all tonight. I would like to get to know her."

"Give her time," Stone suggested.

"I know. I know."

"Speaking of young, budding love, did you know that Princess Cassandra was caught sneaking around the palace last night?" Illiah mentioned.

"Oh? Do you think she was looking for Rhyl?" Eva wasn't sure how she felt about girls sneaking into her son's chambers. She guessed it was inevitable; he was nineteen, for goodness' sake.

Illiah shrugged, enjoying her discomfort. Stone merely looked thoughtful but offered no comments. "Don't meddle. Rhyl will not thank you for it," Illiah chided with an amused smile.

Eva rolled her eyes and threw up her hands. "Fine! I won't." She leaned down and brushed a kiss across her husband's lips before heading to the door.

"Stone, will you accompany me to the Forge?" She heard the Defender ask.

Eva left them to their other business and went to find the forest to clear her head.

CHAPTER 16

RHYL

AFTER THE COUNCIL, Rhyl's sense of urgency to get to the Great Forest intensified into dread boiling in his bones. He had to leave. He *had* to go to the Great Forest. It would be a long, lonely road. He had enough skills and magic to get there safely, and he wasn't afraid. Not exactly. His thoughts kept turning back to the man in the Forest with the dark curling hair and the eyes…eyes that made all sorts of thoughts leap around Rhyl's head. But Kitarra was his home…and he had never been alone. Not truly.

He'd always assumed his parents—and Stone—would have the answers he needed. That they were keeping secrets to protect him. And while that was somewhat true, realizing that they knew so little was… unsettling. That they hadn't told him about the true nature of *candarii* magic. Betrayal and disappointment urged him forward. He felt like he couldn't sit still, like his world was tilting and he had to keep moving or he would fall over.

He found himself staring into the clear water of his basin, calling out to the *simul rami*, to whom he didn't know until he found himself in a vision, staring into the face of the Forest man with dark hair and blue eyes. He didn't even know his name, yet he had called him, and there he was.

"Rhyl, what's wrong?" The concern in the Forest man's voice made the beast inside Rhyl's chest settle slightly.

"I'm *candarii*. I—I didn't know—I didn't know what a *candarii* was. Not really. Although the *varing* has always been close…but—my father's scars are from being tortured, from having the *varing* ripped from his pain. I could do that. I feel its pull. It calls to me and…fuck, it feels …" He couldn't finish. He couldn't admit the strength, the lure of the dark magic.

"You are worried because of what happened with your friend?"

Rhyl bit his lip to stop the strong emotion from escaping the back of his throat. He nodded.

The man's brows furrowed, his blue eyes troubled. "You need to learn to control it, to be more than a *candarii*, more than a *sanarii*."

"How?"

"Come to the Forest."

"I will try."

The man swallowed, nodding. The vision faded. Rhyl's hands still shook, but he felt better than he had since the night Corri died.

Rhyl packed his things and discreetly said goodbye to Talo—only Talo. A pang of sadness followed this. He regretted leaving in secret, but if he told his parents, they would never let him go. Or worse, they would insist on coming with him. This was something he had to do on his own—wanted to do on his own. Bren and Aralis would not forgive him for leaving without saying goodbye. No doubt they would repay him in some way, with some prank, when he returned. He didn't know how long he would be gone, but he hoped it was only a few turnings of the moon.

Rhyl thought he'd been extremely stealthy about the whole thing. He waited until nightfall and sneaked to the storeroom for supplies without being caught. He pilfered the palace larder without raising suspicion. But in the stables while saddling Honey, Stone appeared out of the deteriorating twilight.

"I'm not here to stop you."

Rhyl let himself relax, just a little. "How did you know I was leaving?"

Stone shrugged, his ears pointy.

"I'm going to the Great Forest," Rhyl told him.

"That's a long way to go alone."

"Talo was going to come with me, but now …"

Stone's lips softened, but it wasn't quite a smile. "You told him not to."

"He needs to be here." Before Talo's voyage to Rodan, Rhyl and Talo had been inseparable. Now they were living different lives. Rhyl was the child of the prophecy and Talo was the prince of Kitarra. Rhyl had never expected the change to come so suddenly and unforeseen, but it was what it was.

"Here." Stone handed Rhyl a sword. It was not overly long, its curving blade wider at the tip than the cross guard. It was made of wood. The vercuri.

"Mum's pendant. Da's dagger. Tayeh's dagger. The bird. And Aiyan's dagger," Rhyl said. "Five of the nine."

Stone nodded.

Rhyl reached out his hand, then pulled back. "Are you sure this is a good idea?"

"Rhyl, you are the child of the prophecy. Good idea or not, you are meant to hold the vercuri. And if you are going to travel the Midlands alone, I would rather you have it with you. It will protect you. It will give you strength."

Rhyl took the wooden blade, holding it like it was a wild thing. He could feel the magic in it. He could feel it whisper to him. He felt bolder holding it, like he could take on the world. Strength indeed.

"But what if there is need for it while I am gone?"

"Your need is greater."

Rhyl's heart sank.

"Take this as well." Stone unrolled a map. "It's of the Midlands. Here is Tayeh's Vale, where you will find shelter. Here is Stonyhill, where we have friends." He pointed. "How are you planning to go through the Tarm?"

Rhyl met Stone's yellow eyes. "With *candarii* cleverness, *sanarii* magic, and my blade, if necessary."

Stone grinned. "Sounds like something your father would say."

Rhyl grinned right back

"Be safe, Rhyl."

"I will."

Stone rolled up the map and tucked it into Rhyl's saddlebag. He put one big hand on Rhyl's shoulder, the other over his heart.

"May your path be clear but ever winding," he said. The traditional Kitarran farewell.

"Thank you, Stone."

"I love you, Rhyl. We all do."

CHAPTER 17

STONE

STONE WENT BACK to his room to pour himself a strong drink. And hide. Oh, Eva was going to be livid when she found out that he let Rhyl leave without contention or insisting he take a guard. Honestly, Rhyl was the most dangerous thing in all the realms. He needed a guard as much as he needed a nursemaid. But Eva was the boy's mother.

Fuck. She was going to eviscerate him.

Stone was tempted to lie about the whole thing, pretend he had no idea where Rhyl was. "Rhyl did what?" he would say at his most aggrieved. It wouldn't be the first time he had lied to her. Gods, what a terrible thing to think. Eva was not just his *friend,* she was part of his heart.

He downed the last of his strong fire wine—a gift from Illiah's foster brother in Jullayah—as his door burst open. Illiah. Always adept at making an entrance.

"Stone? Have you seen Eva?"

Illuminated by the torchlight, the Defender looked aged. Stone thought of Rhyl and their last conversation and decided not to tell Illiah about his son leaving. At least, not just yet.

"No. Why?"

"I haven't seen her in hours. It's nearly midnight. She's never out late. I can't find her anywhere in the palace or the forest. None of the servants have seen her."

Eva was not in the habit of informing the men in her life of her every move, so there was no reason for the flash of panic in his gut. "She would have mentioned if she was going into the city. There was no note?"

"Nothing. Her horse is in the stable."

The flutter of panic grew into a wave threatening to rob Stone of air. If Eva hadn't told Illiah or Stone about leaving the palace, then… Stone had no words. He didn't even know where to start looking. "Where could she have gone?"

"I have no idea. I have a bad feeling about this." Illiah took a rattled breath.

Together, they stirred the Queen's Guard into action, sending scouts into the city, searching the palace, the forest. They met with Irri and asked his spiders to search for Eva. They sent for the wolves.

"Eva's horse is in the stable as you said, but Rhyl's horse is missing, Defender," Diea reported.

"Where's Rhyl?"

"We can't find him."

"Eva is not with Rhyl," Stone told Illiah.

Illiah dismissed Diea with an unusually curt gesture. "How do you know? Arrain, where is my son?" Illiah only called Stone by his birth name when he was angry.

"Rhyl left. He is on his way to the Great Forest."

Illiah sank into a chair. "Alone?"

Stone nodded.

"You let my son leave on a dangerous journey *without telling me?*" Illiah hissed. The torch flickered in the reflection of Illiah's black eyes. It occurred to Stone that the timing of this particular information could've been better. Eva was missing. Rhyl was gone. Dark things had been buried alive inside the Defender. Dark things trying to claw their way out.

Aiyan, I need you. Right now, Stone called out with his mind. *Heera* magic was a handy thing, especially when one's friend was in danger of transforming into an evil sadist made of dark magic. "Rhyl is a clever boy," Stone assured Illiah. "He'll be fine. Even without magic, he is one of the best warriors. And I gave him the vercuri. All the vercuri."

"Eva would not approve," Illiah growled.

"Which is why I didn't tell her."

Aiyan must have been close because two wolves came trouncing into the chamber. Then, in a blink, the wolves disappeared, replaced by Aiyan and Mila. Both naked. Both beautiful. Like a god and goddess from the dawn of time. Illiah saw them and put his head in his hands, knowing why they were there. Mila put her hand on Illiah's shoulder, her long, dark hair curling around her naked curves. Aiyan cupped Illiah's face in his hands and hummed a *heera* chant. Illiah breathed easier.

"Thank you," he whispered.

Mila took a blanket and tossed it around her bare shoulders. "What happened, Illiah? You haven't lost control for a long time. And now twice in as many days."

"Rhyl has gone to the Great Forest," Stone told them.

The two shapeshifters looked unsurprised.

"He'll be all right. He's a smart boy," Aiyan said. Why did the wolf always manage to sound so reassuring? Stone saw Illiah's shoulders soften. Aiyan's presence was a blessing.

"Also Eva is missing," Stone said.

"No one knows where she is," Illiah spat.

"She went into the forest after the council," Stone said.

Aiyan looked at Mila, who frowned. "We can start there."

"Are you all right now, Illiah?" Mila asked.

"I will be better knowing you are looking for Eva."

"Thank you," Stone said.

"We will do our best to find her," Aiyan stated. They shifted back into wolves and trotted through the door to the courtyard.

"How could you let Eva disappear?" Illiah growled. He stood up and began pacing. Stone could hear the old jealousy, irrational as it was, tear through Illiah's words. "You are her *amourii*."

"And you are her husband!" Stone replied with equal venom. Then he took a deep breath, flexing his fists, trying to subside the trembling. Stone gripped Illiah's shoulders in his large, furred hands, his claws digging through Illiah's tunic. Illiah cringed. "Fighting each other is not going to find her."

"What if she is gone, like the other missing people?" Illiah whispered. He closed his eyes and took a deep breath, but it was a struggle. "Stone…" It was a plea.

"Illiah?" Stone held him harder. "Fight it. Fight this evil, not me. I am your friend. Always. Don't make me call back Aiyan and Mila. We need them searching for Eva."

Illiah opened his eyes. It made Stone's skin crawl to see the dark ribbons of *varing* slide away from the whites of Illiah's eyes, reminding Stone of the shadows, the dead that slunk inside his mind. Something inside his heart sank, knowing he could see the magic. Not everyone could. Aiyan and Mila. Eva. Rhyl. Illiah. *Candarii. Sanarii. Heera.* Whatever Mila was. But no other Kitarran could see magic like Stone could. Which is why he hadn't told anyone. Not even Eva.

"We *will* find her." Stone released Illiah's shoulders. Illiah slid down the wall until he sat, his legs stretched in front of him.

"What do I do?" Illiah sounded bereft. "Go after Rhyl? Stay here and hope for a message about Eva?"

Stone sighed, sitting beside Illiah on the stone floor. "Rhyl doesn't want our help. He will be all right." If he repeated it enough times, would it make it true?

Illiah huffed. "Rhyl has many skills. He is a warrior. He is *sanarii* and *candarii*. But he is soft from living in this palace. He is not used to a rough existence."

"He will learn."

"How is Talo?"

"Distracted."

"Asha."

"Yeah."

"How did we get here, Stone? Our children grown. And us, old, unable to fix their woes."

Stone did not know how to reply. He did feel old. Ancient. His fingers shook more often than not. His body felt dry and thirsty most mornings. Aiyan's herbal remedies didn't erase the growing weariness Stone felt day in and day out.

"If Eva is in trouble, she would use her magic to tell me," Stone said softly. Eva despised her magic, but she was not a fool. "Which means, wherever she is, she is there by her own volition and has decided not to involve either of us." Stone heard the bitterness in his voice. Illiah was not the only one angry with Eva. Illiah was right, Stone was her amourii. If she was hurt, it was his fault. If something had happened to her, it was his fault. If she had left him behind intentionally…was that any less of a failure?

The night deepened, an endless well of a dark. An hour had passed, or more, it was hard to tell. Stone and Illiah were still sitting, slouched by the wall when two wolves trotted down the hallway. One black as night, and one gray like a storm.

They shifted back, looking dead on their feet. "We traced Eva into the forest. We caught another scent, a man. We followed the scent north into the hills as far as we could, but it grew stale and faint." Aiyan looked defeated. Mila put her hand on her lover's shoulder. "There were no scents that spoke of harm or injury, but there were traces of fear and anger. There is no doubt she was headed to Allati."

"Cotoch?" Illiah asked looking at Stone.

Aiyan shook his head. "I never forget a scent. It was not him. Neither Mila nor I recognized it."

"Can you contact her, Stone?" Mila asked.

"I tried. She won't hear me."

"If she is in trouble, she would call you," Illiah stated.

"One would hope," Mila remarked.

"She would," Illiah insisted, sounding resolved—and jealous.

"Da?"

Bren and Aralis appeared in the doorway.

"Yes, boys?"

"Where's Mum? Is she in trouble?"

Illiah took a deep breath and opened his arms, inviting the boys to sit with them. "We don't know."

"How can we help?" they asked.

Illiah smiled at them. Bren sat down beside Illiah while Aralis took up the small space between Stone and Illiah. They were big boys; in a year or two, they would be nearly men, but that didn't stop them from needing the comfort of an embrace. Stone put his arm around Aralis.

"You could find, her, Da," Bren said. "You are a *candarii*. You can see visions."

"Like Rhyl." Aralis.

"Find her." Bren.

"Da. Do it." Both.

Illiah looked at Aiyan. Aiyan frowned.

"I don't think that's a good idea," Aiyan said.

"Why not?" the boys asked.

"The *varing* is unstable. Your father is not strong enough to control it." Aiyan was not one to mince words.

The twins were quiet. Contemplative. Stone had never been more thankful that the twins had not inherited either of their parents' magic.

"Come, let's find our beds," Illiah said, ushering his children ahead of him.

Within moments, Stone was alone, sitting with his back to the cold wall and waiting for the night to dissolve to dawn.

When Stone—Arrain—had been a child, he'd wake from a nightmare and feel like the night, the dark, had taken over everything, that dawn had been murdered by a merciless night. It was the same feeling that had propelled him over the cliff the day Emri died. Stone felt it now. He should know better, he should have been able to cast the sense aside, but he couldn't. All he could do was close his eyes and pray dawn would come.

CHAPTER 18

ILLIAH

FIND *her.*

Illiah shut out the whisper in his mind. He wasn't sure if it was his voice or Mute's that spoke. He'd spent thirteen years suppressing the dark thoughts and the thing living in his mind; he thought he'd mastered it. Then a tendril had broken free. And now, with Eva missing, the darkness came more and more, stronger and stronger.

You are not in Imal's prison, he told himself. *You are not trapped waiting for Imal to come for you with his knife. You are home. Eva is all right. Eva will come home.*

He commanded himself to believe it.

What little evidence they had pointed to the conclusion that Eva had left Kitarra without explanation.

Eva had left him.

He had to trust her. And he did. But he couldn't trust the dark hole her absence created in his mind. It whispered untruths in his ear.

Days passed.

Each day Illiah hoped.

If Eva was in trouble, she would call Stone. He had to trust his wife had sense for that. And she was not dead. Somehow, Illiah would know if she was. Each day he dreaded his intuition was wrong, that he would find out something terrible had befallen her.

Illiah kept himself distracted. He had the Forge, his duties as First Defender. Queen Arrah was aging, so Illiah and Stone took up what responsibilities they could to help the realm. Rhyl was gone, and it was impossible to hide that secret from Kitarra. Gossip had already spread from the palace servants. Rumors gained speed like an arrow racing toward a target. Irri's spiders had reported that whispers claimed Rhyl had been killed, others that he'd gone back to Jullayah, and still others that he had been captured by Cotoch. And some said that he was on a grand quest to save them all and his return would herald the end of the dark time Kitarra had known for a generation. Illiah could only hope there was a shred of truth to the last one.

"Maybe we should let the rumors spread, let them all believe what they want. The truth is of no use to anyone at this point," Stone suggested in one of his more dour moments. Illiah wasn't the only one on edge.

"Spoken like a responsible prince," Illiah quipped.

Stone groaned. "What would you say, then?"

"We could say Rhyl is at an undisclosed location learning about magic."

"Lie?"

"No matter how honest we are, some will still call us liars."

"And what of Eva?" Stone asked. They hardly spoke of Eva. She was a subject too tender to poke with their sharp words.

"We could tell them she is with Rhyl."

Stone cursed.

"Irri told me that Asha has been restless, wandering the halls at night," Illiah said, changing the subject.

"Oh?"

"Irri is suspicious of her," Illiah said.

"Irri would feel suspicious of a butterfly wandering the hallways," Stone quipped.

"Still, we should keep tabs on her."

Stone gave a long growl of a sigh. "You are right."

"I will put Hersha on it," Illiah said.

"Hersha? Talo will not like that."

"You think he will be jealous? Are Asha and Talo …?"

"I don't know, exactly."

"Talo's chosen would become queen."

"Do you think I don't know that? Mua reminds me as often as she can." Stone showed a pointed tooth. "She wants me to 'have a discussion' with Talo about it."

Illiah laughed softly. "Eva would talk to Talo about it," Illiah said, then the pain came. A sharp ache in his chest. Gods, he missed her. "We have to say something official about Rhyl and Eva. It's been days. If we don't, the people will lose trust in us," Illiah reminded Stone.

"I know."

"You want to go after her," Illiah concluded.

Stone didn't answer, but he wouldn't meet Illiah's eye either.

"Do you think I don't? My heart is in shreds not knowing with absolute certainty if she is all right," Illiah told Stone. "You would tell me if she contacted you, right?" Illiah could not keep his voice from cutting.

"I would tell you," Stone said quietly.

Find her. FIND HER.

The voice was like a thousand needles in Illiah's mind.

Illiah dug his nails into his scalp. "I need you here, Stone." It was a plea.

"I know, Illiah."

CHAPTER 19
ASHA

EVEN THOUGH weeks had passed, every night, Asha dreaded the feeling of her master's magic wrapping around her mind. But Asha had not felt her master's magic at all, not since that night. For that, she was grateful.

Rhyl was gone. Eva was missing. Rumors hatched like sand fleas. Asha ignored them all.

The queen gave her money, and Asha could do almost whatever she wished. But the places in Kilev she was most curious about, she was not allowed to visit. Not just anyone was allowed to prowl around the Forge where the Peace Guards trained and lived alongside the Queen's Guard. The large building was walled, as secure as the palace. It was a great honor to train at the Forge, she was told, even if not all who trained there would become guards. Would she have been able to train with a latha if she had never been taken from Kitarra? Would her parents have wanted her to be a warrior? Or would they have wanted something else entirely for her?

Thoughts of what could have been were the result of boredom. Asha despised her wandering mind. Especially when it wandered to Talo. Then her thoughts would be accompanied by a pang of loneliness. She hardly saw him, mostly just in glimpses in the hallway. And he always looked despondent, worried, not the carefree prince dancing along the ship's masts and sails, looking at the horizon like everything was an adventure. His brother and foster mother were missing. For Talo, who had never known his mother, Eva was the closest thing he had. Asha yearned to make Talo smile.

Talo was often busy because he was the *prince*.

Asha found herself busy as well, only because Cassandra insisted she accompany her to visit the markets, the public bathhouses, the docks. Kilev was an inviting city with its many artisans and lively neighborhoods. Concerts by amazing musicians. Asha loved those. Music was so distracting. Cassandra took Asha with her when she was invited to dine with well-known families who hoped to earn Cassandra's favor and therefore the favor of Emperor Beric.

Cassandra still harbored wistful thoughts that she would not go home to Rodan. She made it no secret that she intended to wed someone in Kitarra. She was still set on Prince Rhyl, which made things difficult because Rhyl was gone and no one knew (or would say) when he would be back. Cassandra, an abominably cheerful girl, didn't let this deter her. Regardless of the rumors, she was certain Rhyl would return to Kilev within a month. Her determination was inspiring.

"Talk to Talo, get us invited to more family dinners. I need to make a good impression," Cassandra begged Asha.

"Cass, the royal family is uneasy with Rhyl and his mother gone. I don't think now is a good time."

"Don't you want to see more of Talo?"

"You are the worst!" Asha smacked her friend on the shoulder. Cassandra grinned like a weasel.

"Lord Teriv is taking me sailing tomorrow. Want to come?"

"You are only inviting me because you don't want to be alone with that snake."

"He is fairly harmless, just annoying," Cassandra corrected, wiggling her fingers at Asha.

"Actually, I have an invitation from a young man named Hersha to take a stroll in the city tomorrow."

"A stroll with a young man? How charming," Cassandra teased. "Does Talo know?"

Asha had received many invitations from young Kitarran men

wishing to meet her. Asha wished Talo *did* know. Part of her wanted to go to Talo and tell him. She wanted Talo to be jealous. Maybe then he would come see her…But it was all so foolish. Asha berated herself. And Hersha *was* a nice young Kitarran. He was from the mountain city of Withe, but he was training at the Forge.

"I guess I will have to manage Teriv without you." Cassandra sighed. "What shall I wear?"

Asha rolled her eyes.

As it happened, Asha's wish came true. She was just leaving her room when Talo appeared in the hallway. He stopped and smiled at her. Asha felt the smile down to her toes.

"Asha, what are you up to today?"

"I'm going into the city with a young man named Hersha. Do you know him?"

"I do know him. A fine fellow," he answered somewhat stiffly.

Asha cursed herself silently. She had no business being satisfied by Talo's sudden frown.

"Have a good time." He nodded a bow and left her. Asha wilted. What had she expected? Talo to abandon his princely duties and beg that she spend the day with him instead? She was more foolish than Cassandra.

Hersha was waiting in the public courtyard of the Queen's Keep. The Queen's Guard would not let him, or anyone without royal permission, into the royal wing of the palace. Asha smiled at him but inside, she felt wretched. She missed Talo.

Hersha chatted as they walked past the Forge, then past the public baths and the Healer's Hall—the latter was a simple square building, its only adornments flowers, so many flowers. More flowers than Asha knew existed. Passing the Healer's Hall made Asha think of Mila and Aiyan. She shivered. After spending weeks on the small ship with the two wolf shifters, she still knew so little about them.

"Have you met Aiyan?" Hersha's question pulled her from her thoughts. Asha noted the reverence in his tone. Did the people of Kitarra know Aiyan had been an assassin to an evil emperor? Did they know the terrible things he had done?

"Yes, he traveled with us back from Rodan."

Hersha's face lit up. "Did you see him shift?"

An odd question. "Not directly, no."

Hersha continued, undeterred, "Wouldn't it be amazing to turn into a wolf? A different creature?" The awe in his voice was unrestrained.

We can all turn into different creatures if we must, she thought.

"What is it like, training at the Forge?" Asha asked. She didn't want to talk about Aiyan or Mila. And the Forge was not something she could ask Talo about. She minced her words around the palace for fear they would think she was a spy. But Hersha was open and cheerful, and the question would appear harmless.

Hersha grinned. "Hard. Exceptionally hard. The Defender expects a lot from us."

"He seems like a tough leader, but also good."

"He is. We all respect him very much."

"I have heard that he is…afflicted. What happened to him?"

Hersha was quiet, and Asha worried she had asked something too personal and taboo.

"Lord Illiah was a prisoner in Rodan many years ago. No one speaks of it, but such an experience must make one…afflicted."

"I'm sorry. I didn't know."

"That's all right. That was about the same time the cendari tree died. Some say Illiah's capture and the tree dying are connected. But the queen has never officially said so."

"The cendari tree?" Asha thought of the massive dead tree that sent a shaft of sadness through her every time she laid eyes on it.

"Cendari trees are magic. They are life. Kitarra is built around the cendari trees. In Withe, the tree is at the center of the town."

"Magic…in trees?"

"Well, magic is in all of us. Which is why so many Kitarran babes are born dead. The *simul rami*—the magic of life and light—is being poisoned by dark magic. But someday, Rhyl will set it right." Hersha stopped and turned back toward the Queen's Keep. Asha followed his line of sight to the tip of the blackened branches of the cendari tree poking up beyond the palace walls. "We can't control magic like a *sanarii*, but it gives us Kitarrans fast healing and makes us strong. And without it, the light inside our souls would burn out. My mua taught me that."

It sounded like a silly old maid's tale. She had grown up far from Kitarra; there was no way the tree's magic could have reached her in Rodan. And if Hersha was correct, she couldn't survive without it. But she didn't want to contradict Hersha. Then she thought of Liam.

"Have you ever heard of a Kitarran who was not dead…but had that light extinguished?" she asked.

Hersha huffed an uncomfortable laugh. "I have not and hope I never do. That is why the prophecy is so important."

Talo had explained the prophecy to her and Cassandra. Since it pertained to Rhyl, Cassandra had demanded to know every little detail. Cassandra's eyes had positively glowed thinking of her prince (Cassandra's words) as a hero who would save the world from dark magic. Asha thought it sounded like a horrible burden. Was that where Rhyl was? Fulfilling the prophecy?

"You should see the cendari tree in Withe. It is glorious," Hersha told Asha, his bright smile dancing, an invitation.

Cassandra would've smiled, transforming into her most charming self, and declared boldly that Hersha should invite her to Withe. Asha could change into a bold and charming version of herself, but she didn't want to. She didn't want to encourage Hersha. He was…very sweet. But Asha had no business falling in love with him. She had no business falling in love with anyone. A snake could not fall in love with a mouse.

CHAPTER 20

ILLIAH

ILLIAH FIDDLED WITH the papers on his desk. Recruit contracts to sign. Lists of inventory. Trivial things. He could only make out half of what they said, but his challenges with the written word hadn't hindered him for many years. Not when he had innumerable scribes and underlings at his beck and call. And Stone usually saw to the tasks that required reading and writing.

Stone sat opposite him, gazing at the ceiling, his fingers entwined. The tension blanketing Illiah's study was a palpable, unpleasant thing, woven from guilt. It was not the first time Illiah had chosen a spy based on his young, handsome appeal, but Asha was a friend.

Hersha entered through a hidden door that led to the Defender's study. Only an elite few knew of its existence.

Hersha was a spy, trained to notice minute details and expressions. But if he noticed Illiah's and Stone's guilt, he said nothing. He told them briefly of his day courting young Asha.

"She was curious about the Forge," Hersha reported. "But she didn't ask me to take her there. She didn't ask anything about Rhyl or Talo. She is rather quiet. She did ask about you, my lord."

"Me?" Illiah echoed.

"She said you seemed afflicted…and wanted to know why," Hersha said awkwardly. "And she was fascinated by the cendari trees, but who isn't? She did ask something peculiar."

"What was that?"

"She asked if I had ever met a Kitarran who was alive but their soul was not."

Illiah and Stone looked at each other. It *was* a strange question.

After Hersha had left, Illiah looked at Stone. "What do you make of that?"

"I don't know." Stone looked thoughtful.

"I don't like spying on Asha like this," Illiah stated. "What if she grows fond of Hersha?"

"Asha only has eyes for Talo," Stone murmured.

Illiah huffed.

"Even more reason for us to know as much about her as possible," Stone reminded him.

"You're right. It just feels wrong."

"I thought you knew how this Defender thing worked? Doing unpleasant tasks for noble reasons and all that."

"I'll get them to engrave that on your second headstone when you die for real," Illiah remarked.

"Not if you die first. Then I will have it put next to your statue."

"I get a statue?"

"Of course. Bren and Aralis will design it."

Illiah burst out laughing. "You wouldn't dare."

"Oh, I would." Stone laughed too.

"I wish Aiyan would just do his *heera* thing and we would have everything we need to know about the girl," Illiah said.

"You know why we can't ask that of him."

"I do. I wouldn't." Aiyan had the unusual ability to read someone's thoughts and experiences through touch. But Aiyan felt strongly that using his *heera* gift without permission was a violation. And Aiyan knew firsthand the trauma of being violated. No. Illiah would not ask Aiyan to use his *heera* magic on Asha. Likely Asha was exactly as she appeared, a young woman kidnapped from her home and hidden away. She had suffered enough.

Eva would agree.

"She will come back to us," Stone said.

Illiah hadn't realized he had reverted to silence, that his thoughts had turned to Eva.

CHAPTER 21

CALYPSO

CALYPSO WANTED TO SCREAM. Like the other *velidar*, Calypso heard Timur's unspoken call. It permeated Calypso's mind like a vision from the *simul rami*. It called him by name. A summons. A command. He hated Timur's voice in his mind.

The leader of the *velidar* only used the method of communicating when something was wrong. Like a death of one of their own. Or danger. There weren't many things that could threaten a shapeshifter surrounded by the magic of the Great Forest. But the dire situation didn't soften the feeling of violation.

High Hill was deep within the Great Forest. The hillock was covered in rocks and trees, and at its peak, the forest opened to a mossy glade. Legend told that a giant tree, bigger than any other, once grew upon the hill, feeding its roots with the *simul rami*. But the tree was gone, and if it had ever been more than a tale, there was no sign of it. It was a place where the magic of the *simul rami* was focused and potent. The safest place in the Great Forest for a *velidar*. It was where Timur commanded them to gather.

Calypso perched on a large branch in a big hemlock just on the edge of the glade. The other *velidar* assembled on the moss below. Timur had already shifted from mountain cat into his human form, his white hair braided and pulled away from his face, revealing a foreboding expression. The other *velidar* kept their distance, especially the *velidar* whose favored forms were squirrels and rabbits. They avoided Timur's predatory gaze.

Soon, everyone except Calypso had taken their human forms and stood in a loose circle around Timur. Reluctantly, Calypso spread his wings and dropped to the moss. He shifted to join them. Midna saw him and waved him over, her round eyes wide.

"What's happening?" he asked her.

Midna looped her arm in his, pulling him close so she could whisper to him. "Wanderers."

No wonder Timur's eyes looked like hoarfrost in spring. As their leader, it would be Timur's duty to find and kill the wanderers before they spread death and chaos through the Forest. Calypso shivered. But, if he was being honest with himself, he had felt the presence of wanderers—at least he had felt *something* in the Forest—a cold presence that made his magic sour and foggy.

"How many?" Calypso asked her.

Midna shushed him. Timur was speaking.

"There are wanderers in the Forest," Timur said. His silken voice filled the glade. Gasps and hisses and growls echoed through the *velidar*.

"Who's missing?" someone asked loudly, their voice wavering. The others quieted to hear Timur's answer.

Timur clenched his jaw. "Lera and Torli."

Calypso swallowed the foul taste in the back of his throat. The idea of seeing a familiar *velidar* morphed and changed into a grotesque mindless monster was a *velidar*'s worst fear. A wanderer was a *velidar* poisoned by the *varing*. Knowing it had happened inside the Forest where the magic was pure, was frightening. No wonder the *velidar* looked like wraiths.

"I am preparing a hunt." Timur focused his green eyes on his people, one at a time.

"We will hunt with you." A few *velidar* stood forward, close friends of Lera and Torli. They were big—wolves, other forest cats, an eagle.

"Predators," Midna muttered in Calypso's ear.

"Raven-boy." Timur startled Calypso by addressing him. The crowd parted and Calypso was subjected to the full force of Timur's green eyes.

It reminded Calypso how frail a grounded raven was compared to a stealthy mountain cat. "You can use magic better than any of us. I need your help."

Another day, Calypso would bask in the glow of Timur's rare compliment. But hunting wanderers was the last thing Calypso wanted to do. What he wanted to do was crawl into a dark hole.

"Well, raven-boy?"

They were all big predators like Timur. Ulli was a fucking wolverine, for Guardian's sake. Even now, after Timur's acknowledgment, they still looked at him like he was the maggot on their feast. After all the years Calypso had lived in the Forest, all the *velidar*, except for Midna, still disliked him. Calypso liked to think they were jealous of his close connection to the trees and magic of the Forest, but he knew in his heart that was only a fraction of the reason.

Half of Calypso's life had been spent in the Great Forest. And for that half of his life, he'd always been alone, magic and trees his stalwart companions. Midna was his friend, but she was friends with *everyone*, so he wasn't sure if she counted. The Allmakers had taken an interest in Calypso's life, but he couldn't call magical beings older than the trees companions and certainly not friends. But because of the Allmakers, he had learned to use the *simul rami* better than the other *velidar*.

And now Timur needed Calypso's close connection to the *simul rami* to find the wanderers before the wanderers reached the border of the Forest. If they managed to make it to the human realms, the wanderers would cause carnage and death and the *varing* would spread.

Timur was waiting. Midna let go of Calypso's arm as he walked over to join the small group. Calypso closed his eyes to connect to the *simul rami*, the magic of the Forest. It wasn't necessary, but he was tired of the predators watching him.

Where are they? Calypso asked the Forest. He felt a shiver, a pulse in answer to his question. A wanderer went against everything the Forest was, it was corrupted, diseased. It shouldn't be a surprise that the Forest magic was hesitant and timid.

Calypso blew air between his teeth. "I cannot find them," he told Timur.

Timur bristled. Several pairs of eyes glared at him as if blaming *him*. The indignation of it made him bite his tongue.

"*Look* again," Timur ordered. "Quickly."

Calypso wanted to tell Timur it wouldn't work, but he didn't want to look like he was giving up. The other *velidar* may not like him, but that didn't mean Calypso didn't want to help. To become a wanderer was a terrible thing. Maybe if he could get a better connection to the *simul rami*.

He went and sat at the base of the biggest tree that ringed the glade. The hanging branches of the cedar almost reached the ground, encompassing Calypso, shielding him from the view of the others. He pressed his back into the bark and closed his eyes. His fingers dug into the loamy dirt. With the old tree at his back, and his fingers close to its roots, he closed his eyes and used the *simul rami* to stretch out into the Forest, searching, calling. In his mind, he saw bright coils and patterns of roots and branches. He felt the magic stumble to his call.

But it was not a wanderer he found in the *simul rami*. The Great Forest slipped from his mind, the twisting roots made of light gone, and before him was a row of standing stones and beyond, the Tarm. He had seen the grassy expanse of the Tarm in visions before. The stones marked Kitarra's border. With the end of spring, the valley plain was alive with birds and green grass. A young man rode on a horse, his star-white hair tousled in the wind, his blue-green eyes taking in the lonely landscape, searching, watching with just as much consternation as Calypso was himself.

Rhyl was on his way to the Great Forest.

No, not Rhyl. I need to find the wanderers. Please, Calypso begged the *simul rami.*

The *simul rami* reluctantly brought him to a different part of the Forest.

Calypso could smell the blood even in the vision. Blood and death and rotting. His heart beat faster seeing it, hearing it snarl, its breath labored because it was not designed to be stuck between two shapes, neither human nor wild creature, but a terrible combination of the two. Wrong, wrong, wrong.

Calypso came out of the *simul rami* to find his cheeks wet with tears. He rubbed them away with the heel of his hand.

"One is not far from here, North," Calypso told Timur and the others. "There will be…a blood trail to follow. Torli is already dead."

Timur's green eyes dulled. He nodded. They all shifted and went north. Calypso stayed where he was, thankful Timur did not demand that he follow. The image of that terrible, poor beast stuck in his mind. Calypso knew, *he knew* there was no coming back from it, that once the *varing* took hold of a *velidar* and turned it into a wanderer, the *velidar* could never regain its mind or its proper form. It was lost forever.

CHAPTER 22

RHYL

RHYL BROUGHT HIS HORSE, Little Honey, to a halt. Only half of his name was apt, his fur was honey-colored, his mane a slighter darker hue. But he was not little. Honey was tall in the shoulder with the long limbs and fast pace that made Illiah's horses coveted by most of Kitarra.

The long line of standing stones that marked the border of Kitarra stretched from north to south. The last time he had seen the stones was when he was a child. Rhyl thought the stones would look smaller with his adult eyes, but they still looked immense. Dozens of legends spoke about how the stones came to be, but Rhyl didn't believe any of the stories. They were too fantastical. But still…the stones were as tall as three men and as wide as a wagon. How could they have been moved? Unless they had been moved by *sanarii* magic…Rhyl flexed his fingers but shook his head. No, he was not going to waste his time trying.

The wind teased at Rhyl's short hair. He had finally cut it. He wasn't keen on spending his evenings untangling and rebraiding his long hair. The wind also whispered of magic and visions. He silenced it and kept riding.

Even without the map from Stone, Rhyl knew the quickest way to travel to the Great Forest from Kitarra was through the Tarm.

Beyond the standing stones, to the east, the Tarm lay before him. The long valley plain was coated with thick green grass and scrubby patches of short trees dotted by hidden marsh. Rhyl could see birds. Ducks and pheasants. Little red-winged flickers landed on the arching blades of grass. To the north, snow-capped mountains hemmed the valley. Somewhere to the southwest was the sea. Rhyl could almost smell it, but mostly the air smelled like marsh.

The road stretched on ahead of him, a thin track that looked a hundred years old. People rarely traveled to Mahlas from Kitarra.

Rhyl sighed. The Tarm felt empty and barren compared to the bustling city of Kilev or the sleepy valleys of the mountains around Withe. The Tarm looked…lonely.

By dusk, the weather turned, reminding Rhyl how uncomfortable spring rains could be. Thankfully, the road was more gravel than mud. Rhyl huddled under his cloak. Honey didn't seem to mind the rain. The horse pressed into the wind, his mane tangling with the wet. When it was too dark to ride, Rhyl sheltered under his canvas, listening to the drips and drops punctuated by gusts of wind. He hated it.

Three days of spring rain later, Rhyl was thoroughly wet. At night, he used his *sanarii* magic to make a fire. The flame danced, fed on his magic, the warmth caressing his face. How did a traveler survive without magic? As a child, Rhyl thought it would be amusing to learn to light a fire with tinder. It had been beyond tedious.

The rain stopped and Rhyl spoiled himself by letting the flames burn hot and tall. He changed into his spare clothes (thankfully only damp instead of soaked) and hung his dripping trousers in front of the fire to dry. He held his hand in front of the wet fabric, wondering if he could dry them with his magic. Or would his trousers catch fire? Was it worth a pair of trousers to find out? Why hadn't he experimented with this before the stakes were so high? Where could he find another pair of trousers if he burned them? But if it worked …

"And who might you be?" a gruff voice startled him. A cloaked figure dissolved from the night. There were more, but Rhyl couldn't make out the others beyond the bright light of his fire. His sword lay beside him, sheathed. He had several knives, but they were not the best for fighting more than one adversary. The vercuri was secured in its sheath between his shoulder blades. But he knew nothing about the *candarii* enchantments to use the vercuri.

"Just a traveler," Rhyl replied.

"From Kitarra?" the man asked gruffly.

"Does it matter?"

"We've orders to detain anyone from Kitarra."

"I'm from Allati," Rhyl said and realized he'd blundered beyond repair. Of course they wouldn't believe him *now*.

"That's a load of stinking shit, if you ask me." The man pushed his cloak back to expose a sword at his hip. A sicara. Its long, curving blade looked thirsty. The man wore a leather breastplate. The crest of Mahlas glinted. Mahlas guards. Shit.

Someone yanked Rhyl's hood back, exposing his face and pale hair. Rhyl hadn't heard the man approach. He swiveled, dagger drawn. The men gathered closer to his fire, laughing.

"Look at this pretty boy!" the leader exclaimed. "His face is pretty enough to fuck."

"And such hair."

"Hey, boys, do you reckon this is who I think it is?"

"Nah. There is no reason for the *prince* to be so far from home."

"You're right. Can't be 'im. Impossible. Probably just an Allati runaway. That means we can have our fun with the wee lordling," the leader said. The man cocked his head at Rhyl. Something in the man's expression made Rhyl ill. His muscles coiled like a snake ready to strike.

"You need to leave me alone," Rhyl warned, shifting his dagger in his hands. He could feel the vercuri at his back, warming in response to the *varing* that oozed from the men's vile thoughts like smoke from a fire.

"There are five of us, boy, and only one of you. You'll do as we say like a good little wench."

Rhyl had watched his father take down ten men in practice. Even in this fourth decade, the Defender's skill with the sword was legendary. And Rhyl was his father's son. Rhyl had trained under his father and Stone and Aiyan. His skill with a sword was just as deadly, and his *candarii* magic gave him speed. But unlike the Defender, Rhyl didn't need a sword. He had *sanarii* magic. Magic was his weapon.

Rhyl unleashed fire and air, sending a boiling blast toward the men. The scorching air knocked them into the dark with shouts and gasps. Rhyl pursued, watching with grim satisfaction as their shouts of anger turned to cries of pain and pleas for mercy. The night air grew thick with the *varing*. Rhyl felt the vercuri at his back gather the dark magic like a cup filling with water. *Sanarii* magic was seeing and healing; *candarii* was taking and changing. Rhyl had never pushed his limits or experimented. Attin had told him to be cautious, but it was his parents—his mother—who had forbidden it. Now there was no one to curb him, a*nd* he had the vercuri. Rhyl gasped as the *varing* flowed from the vercuri into his body. *More.*

Rhyl flexed his magic and used it to choke the men, watching as they fell as one to the ground, gasping for breath. The leader was the last to die. Blood dripped from his nose, black in the firelight.

"Please, please don't kill me." One was still alive. He knelt on the ground, his arms above his head. Rhyl conjured a fire to look into his face. The beggar was hardly more than a boy, about the same age as Rhyl. An old bruise on his cheek was barely visible through the grime on his skin. Rhyl pitied him.

"And what will you say when you return and the others don't?" Rhyl asked him.

The young man stammered, trying to form a response. Something about his flummoxed state made Rhyl grin.

"Tell them what you saw here," Rhyl told the poor boy. "Tell them that a sorcerer walks this land and he is not to be trifled with."

The boy nodded, his eyes wide as if Rhyl had just given him gold. He stumbled to his feet and ran off into the dark.

Rhyl put a hand on Honey's neck. The gelding was shaking. "It's all right, my boy. Shh. It's all right," he told himself as much as Honey. Their deaths had been necessary. The vile men deserved no less. Stone and Illiah would have killed them without thought. But Rhyl still felt the *varing* calling to him, whispering *more, more, more.*

Rhyl didn't want to share his camp with the dead men. A night breeze tugged at his damp hair. It was time to move on.

The next day he passed the city of Mahlas from a discreet distance, keeping to the trees along the forest edge so he would be more difficult to spot. Honey's fur blended into the wild behind them, and with Rhyl's *sanarii* sight, he could see the guards and patrols. He wouldn't be ambushed again.

On the hill above Mahlas stood a dead tree. Its charred branches reached to the sky, stark and ruined in the world of green that was the Tarm. Rhyl would bet his magic it had once been a cendari tree.

When his mother destroyed the cendari tree in Kilev, it had killed Tayeh. Who had died when this tree was killed? Was the spirit his mother spoke of still trapped beneath Cotoch's house? Could it sense him?

Rhyl shook his head. It didn't matter. Not now. He had to get to the Great Forest, to the man with waves of black hair and blue eyes. And he still had weeks to go.

CHAPTER 23

ASHA

ASHA SAT AT THE FOUNTAIN, enjoying the morning sun on her fur and the hot drink in her hands, wishing every morning could start with both when a shadow moved between her and the sun. She looked up and her eyes adjusted to see Talo.

"And how are you this morning, Asha?"

Nothing in the world could have stopped Asha from smiling up at him and answering, "I am well, My Prince."

Talo sat down next to her, swinging his legs over the edge. "Good to hear. How was your day with Hersha? I've heard Hersha is not the only young Kitarran plaguing you with invitations. And gifts." He picked up one of the packages from the pile on the ground beside her. She couldn't bring herself to open them.

Asha shrugged. "There are several young Kitarrans set to win my heart." Gods, with Talo the words just fell out of her mouth.

Talo leaned toward her. "I don't like it."

"Why not? They are all admirable young men."

"I have asked myself the same question and come to the conclusion that it is because they are not me," he said in a soft voice, as if someone might overhear.

Asha couldn't speak for a moment. "No, they are not. But you have been…absent lately."

Talo's eyes were such a vivid blue, it made her breath catch. His lashes were dark and tinged with the same tawny color as his fur. Golden. He had a black spot beside his lip. Asha could not help but think it would be the simplest thing to lean forward and kiss it. She wanted to. The wanting was strong and terrifying. She looked away and sipped her tea so her mouth had something to do.

"What's wrong?"

"Nothing. I just—I…have missed seeing you, Talo." And it was so much the truth that Asha felt awful.

Talo reached and took her hand in his, rubbing his thumb along her palm. Part of her knew she had to pull away, but instead she twisted her fingers into his.

"Asha?"

"Yes?"

"What happened to you?"

"I told you."

"I think there is more to you. To your story."

"There really isn't," Asha lied.

"Talo!"

They both turned to see Prince Arrain, his face stern, waving Talo over, obviously in need of a word. Asha's common sense returned. She pulled her hand from Talo's. Talo stood reluctantly. Asha didn't dare watch him go.

She closed her eyes. The summer sunlight kissed her fur, bringing back memories of Rodan. She remembered the hot air heavy with the smell of spices. Every so often a cool breeze would stir the leaves of the citrus trees above her, tickling her fur, where she used to lie in the dust of the courtyard. The big yellow fruit would wobble up in the branches. Liam would tease that the fruit would fall on her nose if she lay among the roots too long.

When Asha thought of Rodan, those were the moments she returned to. The moments of stillness, of warmth. With Liam lying beside her on the dusty ground, the cool shadows of the citrus trees protecting them from the hot Rodan sun. Time ceased to exist beneath those trees. Their master ceased to exist. The rigorous training that made Asha's arms and legs ache and made her insides writhe with fear, almost forgotten in those perfect moments.

"You look bored, Asha."

Asha opened her eyes. The memory of Rodan died. The dry, cobbled walls of the villa were gone, replaced by green forest and mountains. And the twins. Bren and Aralis sauntered over to her patch of sunshine in the courtyard. They were carrying swords the same way a child carries a stick: careless, looking for something to swat.

"Do I?"

"Yeah," Aralis said. At least Asha was *fairly* certain it was Aralis. She was getting better at telling the twins apart, but still…they were identical and strived to maintain the state by dressing the same and wearing their hair the same. They were rascals. But Asha liked them.

"We could teach you how to use a sword," Bren said with a grin, swinging his sword in an elaborate arc ending with a flourish. Asha could not fathom how any two young persons could contain so much confidence. Asha likened the twins to conjoining rivers. No one could stop them.

"I don't think so," she replied. Gods, she wanted to spar with them. But what would be the point if she had to pretend to be a novice? What would be the point if she could not wipe the smug confidence off their charming faces?

The twins shrugged. "What do you have there?" They looked at the scattering of unopened packages beside Asha.

"Gifts," she told them.

Their eyes lit up.

"Want to help me open them?" Asha asked.

"Can we keep one?"

Asha laughed. They were princes. But one would think they wanted for everything. They were like greedy, hoarding crows.

Despite what Talo believed, the gifts were not all from suitors. The queen told Asha the people of Kitarra wanted to show her their support, that her story of being lost for so many years in Rodan, with no family, no connection to Kitarra, had warmed their hearts. Many Kitarrans had lost loved ones when Rodan attacked Kitarra all those years ago. They sent her gifts of jewelry and clothes. A fine belt. A silk scarf to wear over her shoulders. A finely wrought dagger. And letters of encouragement.

If they only knew.

Asha wanted to burn every last gift. To her, they only exemplified her betrayal of their trust.

If they only knew.

"Yes, you can keep one each." She laughed as the twins dug into the pile. Paper and ribbon flew.

Two moons had passed since Asha had come to Kitarra. She felt like she might have gained the trust of the queen's inner circle. Prince Arrain was quick to smile, and yet something in his eyes spread a chill through her. The Defender liked to tease her, or had, before his wife had disappeared. Now, Lord Illiah seemed quiet, and when he spoke, it was with sharp edges. Certainly, Talo trusted her. Asha avoided the others unless Talo or Cassandra was with her.

You will not be one of them, Asha, her master had reminded her over and over.

And it was true. Asha knew that with all her heart. The people of Kitarra treated her with kindness, like a favored pet—a dog perhaps. But if they knew…if they knew how poisoned she was, they would cast her out without question.

And Talo made the worst mockery of Asha's most desperate longings. Not deliberately–Talo was incapable of malice. But with him, her heart beat more steadily. She thought of her fingers entwined with his. But Talo was the prince of Kitarra. His wife would be the mother of queens.

No, if Talo knew the truth, he wouldn't want anything to do with her.

At night, Asha would wake shaking and sick. Mostly it was her nightmares that woke her, but sometimes it was her master's voice in her mind.

You must go farther. Find the other trees.

"Boys, where are the other cendari trees?" she asked now.

"There is one in Withe," Bren explained.

"And one to the north, in the mountains," Aralis added. "The ribbon on this box is too tight." Aralis maneuvered his sword to cut the ribbon. Allowing the boys to carry large *sharp* weapons around unsheathed seemed like a vast indecency.

"That can't be a good idea," she chided.

Aralis grinned. "Nonsense." The blade cut through the ribbon with ease. Asha breathed a sigh of relief to see the boy's fingers were all intact. Although, if he lost a finger, perhaps it would've been a good lesson.

"There is another cendari tree in the east in the small mining city of Endel," Bren mentioned, making a face as he pulled out a wispy scarf.

"We've seen the one in Withe, but not the others."

"It's sad the one here is dead," Asha mentioned.

"Mum killed it."

"When we were just newborn babes."

"It's why she doesn't use magic. But it's a secret. Don't tell anyone."

Asha shivered. She glanced at the giant tree reaching over the pools. Even bathed in sunlight, its bare branches seemed lost and forlorn.

"How did magic kill a tree?" she asked, more to herself than to the twins.

"Dark magic killed the tree," Bren said. Aralis nudged him, and they said no more.

"Do you have magic?" Asha asked them.

"No."

"And thankful for it."

"These gifts are a bit dull," Bren said, running a silk scarf through his hands. Aralis nodded. "Who are they from?"

Asha sighed. "People who knew my parents and grandparents. And perhaps a few young gentlemen."

"Bor-ring."

Asha laughed.

"Does Talo give you gifts?" Bren asked with a sneaky smile.

"No."

"He would probably give you a rubbish gift, anyway."

"Talo has no sense when it comes to these things," Aralis added as if he was somehow more worldly wise than his big foster brother.

Asha raised a brow at them. "And what would you give a young lady?"

"Knives."

"*And* teach her how to use them," Bren added.

"All girls should know how to use a knife. How to defend themselves," Aralis said matter-of-factly.

Asha couldn't agree more. But it hadn't helped her. She knew how to fight with a knife and sword. But she had never been more than her master's knife, a tool, a thing to be picked up and used at will.

CHAPTER 24

STONE

STONE KNEW HOLDING a girl's hand was hardly the worst development. But seeing Talo sitting next to Asha in the sunny courtyard had made something draw tight and uncomfortable in his chest. Once he had Talo away from Asha's hearing, he turned to his son.

"Talo …" And the words just didn't come. Stone didn't know what to say.

"Do you think I don't know the challenges that might come from falling in love with Asha?" Talo stated, proving that he was both clever and observant.

By Attin's saggy nipples, Stone hated this. A pox on pretty girls.

"I know she is more or less a stranger," Talo continued "What if she is part of some plot against us? I know this. I do. But I still…I can't see it."

Stone's heart broke for Talo's ripped affections. He realized sending Hersha to befriend the strange girl had yet another disadvantage. Now Talo was jealous.

"I know that my wife will be queen, someday," Talo continued, "but Kitarra will trust that the woman I love will be the best queen for Kitarra. That is how it has always been when the line falls to a prince. Mehmet taught me well enough."

"Well, Mua will probably live forever, so there is that."

Talo's laugh was shaky. "And besides, Asha doesn't love me."

Stone thought it best not to comment.

"Gods, I wish Rhyl were here," Talo muttered. "Are you worried about Eva?"

"Yes. But also no. I trust that she isn't in danger. I feel it in my gut."

"Yes. I feel that with Rhyl too."

"I only wish Illiah had the same connection to Eva. Their relationship is closer, them being lovers—"

"Eww."

"Child," Stone teased. "But Eva and I share a bond. I feel her in the *simul rami* sometimes. It's eerie." Stone hadn't even told Eva how he could almost see her thread in his mind. It had grown brighter over the years, that thread that linked him to his amourii. Stone didn't know if it was because of his oath, or Eva's magic, or just the fact that Eva was… she was his tether, his roots. For a long time, he thought it was Talo, his son, who kept him sane, a reason to cope with his addiction, and he was. Talo was his breath, his life, his love, but Eva was different.

She keeps you whole.

The voice was Emri's. Was her voice a sign Stone's mind was starting to crumble from his culla addiction? How long did he have before he devolved into madness? He had no idea. Maybe he should tell Aiyan he could hear Emri's voice.

"And so we wait for the *sanarii* to come back to us," Talo said in a poetic voice.

"We are the ones in the tale that no one speaks of whilst the heroes do their work."

"And without us, the quest would fail." Talo grinned. Then sobered. "I hope Rhyl is all right. I hope he doesn't starve to death. He has never been good at hunting. Or sleeping out of doors. Or riding in the rain."

Stone laughed softly. "He'll be fine."

Talo sighed, leaning against Stone's shoulder. Stone wrapped his arm around his son, marveling at how big Talo had grown, remembering the small slip of a thing he had been. How had the years flown by when the last few months since Eva's disappearance had crawled by in slow agony?

CHAPTER 25

RHYL

RHYL WAS EXHAUSTED. And lonely. And hungry.

His supply of nuts and dried meat had dwindled, then vanished. There was plenty of game, but Rhyl was not the best hunter. He managed to take down a goose with his bow (it had been grounded, and Rhyl didn't ask why) but that had been five days ago and he hadn't had fresh meat since. He was better at foraging. He gave a silent thanks for the many lessons from Stone and Aiyan about which plants to eat. And early summer was an excellent time for wild berries. Still, foraging was time-consuming. And a handful of berries did little to slake his hunger. Fortunately, there was no shortage of fresh summer grass for Honey to graze on, the lucky beast.

He rode through the Tarm in five days. Then he entered the Midlands, ruled by no king or queen or law. The Midlands felt endless. He cut twenty more tiny notches into the leather strap on his saddle, one for each day that passed. He'd left Kitarra in spring; now the sun was hot and summer was everywhere he looked.

He made for Stonyhill with all speed. He wondered what he would find there and hoped it would be an abundance of hearty meals. He had no doubt he would be welcomed as a friend of Tarek and Elish. The Iron Wolves spent a fair time at Stonyhill in the winter months. But it was summer. Were the Iron Wolves traversing the Midlands, protecting travelers? Fighting bands of rogues? Eating fresh-caught fish in Fishtown? Rhyl's mouth watered at the thought.

He'd passed a few cautious travelers on the rough road, but they kept to themselves and didn't antagonize him. He asked politely if they knew how far it was to Stonyhill, and they answered in meek voices that the small village was only a few days ahead. He couldn't bring himself to beg a meal from them. They eyed his sword and his latha, so their fear made him hesitate to ask. Or maybe it was his pride.

There were other settlements in the Midlands, but Rhyl had no interest in them. Stonyhill was close to the Great Forest. He really hoped Tarek and Elish would be there. He hadn't seen them in over two years since their last visit to Kilev. He had fond memories of the men who were like family.

The rocky road crested a hill and below lay a shallow valley. Rhyl wanted to shout in victory as he beheld the group of buildings and smoke rising from a few chimneys. He could see folk going about their daily business.

Stonyhill. It was as perfect as he had imagined it.

As Rhyl neared the village, a few men dropped their tasks to approach him. Rhyl could see the cautious set of their shoulders and the tools in their belts that could be used as weapons if need be, but they weren't outright hostile.

"And who might you be?" they asked him. He could not fault them for being suspicious.

"A friend of the Iron Wolves," Rhyl replied. "From Kitarra. My mother, Eva, is a friend of Master Felis." Rhyl kept his hands visible. He tried to smile, but mostly, Rhyl was just hungry. The fields were green and lush and dotted with cows and sheep. A rooster crowed from one of the barns. It was all too easy for Rhyl to imagine a dinner of roast meat and summer squash and berries with fresh cream.

They eyed him up and down. Finally, one of the men said, "Come with us. We will take you to the house."

"Thank you." Rhyl dismounted, taking Honey's reins. The men eyed Rhyl's bright hair but didn't ask any questions. Rhyl was thankful.

"Felis?" one of the men roared as he opened the door to what appeared to be the largest house in the village. The House, Rhyl supposed.

"Coming." The man who appeared was roughly the same age as Rhyl's parents, though he had less gray in his beard than the Defender. The man grinned. "Well, if this isn't a surprise," he said, leaning against the doorframe. "Felis, at your service. And you must be Prince Rhyl."

"Just Rhyl," Rhyl corrected, seeing the wide eyes of the men who had escorted him.

"Ah. You are a handsome lad. Not surprising, your mother is a beautiful woman."

Rhyl didn't know what to say.

"Come in, come in. Lark, take the boy's horse. The boy looks like he could use a good meal. Darla! We have a waif in need of feeding up!"

Rhyl didn't mind being called a waif because he very much liked the idea of "feeding up." He followed Felis into the House and was instantly enamored by the cozy, welcoming feel of the place. The common room was large with a low ceiling black from the large fireplace. From wide beams hung smoked meats and dried herbs.

"Sit. Tell me how you came all the way out here. Alone. And whatever for? Stonyhill is a long way from Kitarra's court. And far less grand, from what I hear."

"I'm on my way to the Great Forest," Rhyl told him. The chair creaked under him, making him flinch. He felt his cheeks heat. "But I…I ran out of food."

Felis grinned, shaking his head, his eyes crinkling. "Poor lad."

"I appreciate your hospitality, Felis. To repay it, I would be happy to work before I move on. I am strong and able."

Felis eyed him dubiously. "I bet you are. I'm sure we can make use of you. And fatten you up a wee bit."

"Thank you."

"Tell me, how is your mother?"

Darla brought several plates of steaming food and two large mugs of ale. Rhyl had never tasted anything better. Rhyl ate between answering Felis's questions. He told Felis about Kitarra. His brothers. His father. Everyone. In return, Felis told him the tale about how Eva appeared at his village all those years ago with the Iron Wolves. Rhyl had heard the story before, but it was different from another's perspective. It was evident that Felis cared for Eva quite a bit, even after many years.

"I offered for her to stay here, with me," Felis told Rhyl with a good deal of remorse. "But she had to find you."

Rhyl smiled. "My mother loves me and my father and brothers very much." Rhyl wondered if Felis had a wife but didn't have the courage to ask.

Felis laughed. "Yes, much to my dismay. How long will you stay?"

"A week to work off my debt to you? Is that fair?"

"Sure."

Felis told him that Tarek and Elish were gone to Fishtown, not due to return until fall. Rhyl was disappointed not to see the men who were like uncles to him, but the people of Stonyhill were friendly, and soon Rhyl felt like part of the community. Old Ferad, the head farmer, even commented on Rhyl's ability to apply himself to any task. Rhyl was told Ferad rarely gave out compliments. And in the evenings, a barrage of children would find him and cling to his ankles or jump on his shoulders, begging for stories and games. Rascals, the lot of them. But Rhyl could not deny them.

Rhyl stayed for two weeks in Stonyhill, and even then, it was hard to leave Darla's cooking and Felis's company. Lark taught him how to track and take down wild geese and the fastest way to pluck and cook them. They teased him for being a pretty prince, but Rhyl didn't mind because they also praised him for his hard work. It was hard to leave their comfort for the unknown of the Great Forest.

"Good luck in the Dark Wood, my boy," Felis said with a hug and thump on the back.

"Thank you for everything, Felis."

"If it were anyone else, I would be begging them not to venture into the Dark Wood. But any fool can tell you almost belong in an uncanny place like that. Something about the eyes…your mother had that look too."

Rhyl smiled and said goodbye. Several of the children had wobbling lips as Rhyl ruffled their hair. Darla had packed him plenty of fresh baking, urging him to eat it before it went stale and hard in his pack, and said not to worry, there were travel cakes in there, too, which would last a few weeks.

It was like leaving home all over again. Rhyl could hardly stand it. But he had no choice. The Dark Wood was waiting.

CHAPTER 26
RHYL

THE CLIFF STRETCHED UP AND UP. Before Rhyl stood the chink, the entrance—the only entrance—into the Great Forest. It was just how he imagined it from his mother's description. The chink looked like a jagged, gaping mouth. It was dark and not at all welcoming. A cold breeze wafted down from the narrow gap between the cliffs, making him shiver.

"I don't want to do this, Honey."

Honey's ears perked as he regarded Rhyl with the corner of his brown eye and seemed to say "Why did we come all this way, then?"

"Too right you are, old tooth." Rhyl took Honey's reins in his hand and led him forward.

The light dimmed as the narrow chasm swallowed them. There were a few loose rocks on the path; he tried his best to guide Honey around them and hope no more decided to fall just then. The ground gradually became steeper as they ascended into the Forest.

At the top, the Great Forest felt like another world. The air smelled spiced. If wisdom had a scent, Rhyl knew it would smell like the Great Forest. The trees were huge, immense beings. The undergrowth was ferns and moss and roots surrounded by a hush that spoke of ancient beings. Rhyl could see what might be a path.

Now what? Should he take the path? Call out to the Allmakers? He stood and listened, hoping for some direction or inspiration.

He could feel a soft, quiet presence at the edge of his mind. Magic. He took a breath and closed his eyes.

I'm here, he told it.

Nothing. Silence.

He started to feel like a fool.

What had he expected? Petals and maidens? Greetings from magical creatures? The white fox and the dark-haired man? Yes. Yes, he had expected—hoped—the fox at least would come find him. The man… sometimes he wondered if the man was a figment of his dreams.

Rhyl sighed. There was nothing else to do but make his way deeper into the Great Forest. Following the path seemed safe. Well, at least safe-ish.

After a while, Honey snorted, tossing his head uneasily. Rhyl brought him to a halt, looking around, listening, feeling with his magic. The Forest was eerily still, but at the same time, it felt alive, alive, alive. He turned in the saddle to see a black shadow briefly in the tree behind him before it disappeared from his peripherals. His heart jumped in his chest. Probably just a bird. He frowned. But was it just a bird? The Forest Folk, the *velidar,* *were* shape-shifters. The Great Forest was a place where anything could be anything.

"Hello?" he called, his voice loud and out of place amid the still and silent trees. "Is someone there?"

No one answered. Honey chewed his bit, unperturbed. Rhyl shrugged and nudged Honey into a walk.

Not long after, he heard wings. He spun. A raven landed in the low branches of a tree to his left. He *was* being followed.

Rhyl dismounted and stood with his hands on his hips. "Who are you? Show yourself." He felt foolish. He might be giving orders to a wild animal with no more smarts than Honey. Honey *was* smart for a horse, but still, he was just a horse.

Rhyl was about to get back in the saddle when the raven flew out of its tree and landed not far from Rhyl's feet and cocked one blue eye at him. Rhyl regarded the bird. Its eyes looked awfully clever. A waft of strange magic ruffled Rhyl's senses, and the raven was no longer a raven. Honey snorted and took an uneasy side step.

A young man stood where the raven had been. He was thin, yet not scrawny. His hair was the same inky-black as his raven feathers and his eyes were round and startlingly blue. There was something boyish about him, even though the lines of his face were sharp. It was the man from Rhyl's dream-vision. The man who had told him to come to the Great Forest.

The man was naked.

In Kitarra, nudity was not aberrant. How many times had Rhyl been subjected to Aiyan's nakedness after Aiyan shifted from his wolf form? And yet, Rhyl's cheeks flushed. He looked away.

"Uhm …," he muttered uncomfortably.

The raven-man cursed loudly. Another pulse of magic filled the airspace between them, and when Rhyl dared to look, the man was fully clothed. Even during a Kitarran court ball, Rhyl had rarely seen an ensemble more dashing, or colorful. Every inch of the man's long coat (indigo) was covered in embroidery (purple and pink). With his fair skin, dark hair, and chiseled features, the young man looked like a prince from a fairy tale. Or an actor wearing a costume.

Rhyl cleared his throat and resisted the urge to offer a sarcastic comment.

"Rhyl," the raven-man said, adjusting his sleeves. "I'm Calypso."

Rhyl almost choked on his tongue. "Calypso? My mother's raven?"

Calypso bobbed his head in what Rhyl interpreted as an affirmation, but it was birdlike.

"She never told me her raven was a *velidar!* She kept you as a pet," Rhyl exclaimed.

"She didn't know what I was."

"I—I *remember* you!" As a child, his mother's raven had seemed huge. Rhyl remembered his cold, pointy beak picking treats out of his hand. "How *old* are you?"

"A few years older than you," Calypso said with some scorn. "Does it matter?"

"I guess not."

One of Calypso's eyebrows rose. He swallowed and gestured to the trees. "Welcome to the Great Forest, Rhyl." He sounded like he was reciting a speech. "The Allmakers have prepared me for your grand arrival."

"Grand arrival?"

"Yeah. I am supposed to help you."

"Help me how?"

"Help you save us all." And he winked. His coat glittered. Magic pulsed through the Forest, and Rhyl wondered what kind of fairy tale he had fallen into.

CHAPTER 27

EVA

THE TALL WALL SURROUNDING the city of Attingard grew in Eva's line of sight. With each step, the anxiety in her chest cinched tighter and tighter. She thought she would only return to the Allati city in her nightmares, yet here she was. But this wasn't some dark dream she could abruptly wake from. It was real. And it was her choice.

When Vagar had approached her in the forest behind the Queen's Keep, she had thought, just for a moment, that he was Attin, the Guardian of Allati. But his eyes were blue-green, not golden like the Guardian's. Not to mention the lack of snow-white wings. But honestly, Eva would have been less surprised by a visit from the Guardian than her half brother. The last time she had heard from Vagar, it had been clear he was Cotoch's puppet. Over the years, Kitarran spies in Allati brought news that Vagar was still King Cotoch's right-hand man.

Eva had almost called for help, but her curiosity outweighed her fear. Vagar had been alone, far away from help and home.

"What are you doing here?" she had demanded.

"I have a message for you. Please, just listen to what I have to say." And she had.

Eva listened, wanting to believe Vagar was lying. That it was a trick. But Vagar did not speak like a man under a spell. And Vagar gave her Cotoch's vercuri. A show of good faith.

"You can just take the vercuri, go home. This short sword is two of the nine vercuri. Cotoch offers them to you as a gift, a sign of his sincerity.

But if you come to Allati, he has information for you. He wants to help Kitarra. He wants to help the child of the prophecy."

Eva had scoffed. "What kind of fool does he think I am? How could I do such a thing? Last time I trusted him, he enslaved me—he raped me, Vagar! Next, he took Illiah, bargaining him off to be tortured to death. And Rhyl and Talo, his niece stole them, took them from their home! How could he ask this of me?"

Vagar's eyes were tired. "I know. I will not pretend that Cotoch feels remorse for his past actions, but I do think he is a changed man…He swears he will not hold you against your will nor harm you in any way. All he can offer are words–"

"Words are wind," Eva said, quoting Stone.

"He wants to help you find the other vercuri. I swear on the blood of my children that Cotoch means you no harm."

"Why send you? Why not come to court in the name of diplomacy?"

Vagar raised a brow. "Diplomacy? He is convinced your husband will imprison any of his messengers."

Eva ran her thumb along the vercuri and sighed. "He is not wrong."

With Cotoch, Illiah would not listen to reason. And Stone would not be any better. Eva bit her lip. If Stone and Illiah were with her, they would tell her there were other and better ways to help Rhyl. But Eva knew the truth. They had been searching for years to find the rest of the vercuri or any clues to help Rhyl. They were slowly drowning in their lack of knowledge. And Rhyl was growing restless.

Eva knew her son–he would not sit around idly waiting for answers. He would go out and find them. And if he didn't have the right knowledge, the right tools to help him, he would fail. He would die. She could not let that happen. And she could not throw away this chance. To help Rhyl, Eva was ready to risk her freedom.

"They will track me," she told Vagar. Was she really agreeing to this?

"Then we need to move swiftly. I have two horses on the other side of the ridge."

Eva looked down the hill, to the palace, her home, her family. Could she do this, leave without warning? Without a goodbye? If she didn't, they would stop her. Illiah and Stone would chain her to the floor before letting her run off to Allati. To be fair, if their places were reversed, she might do the same.

So Eva had tucked the vercuri into her belt and followed Vagar.

Two weeks passed as they traveled through the mountains to Allati. Now, with Attingard before her, a battle waged inside her heart. She didn't regret not calling for help that day when Vagar came to her in the forest. She missed having Stone, her amourii—her protector and friend—at her side. But Stone was not just her amourii; he was a father, a prince. Yes, the amourii oath had made him hers to command, but she would never knowingly put him at risk.

This was her choice, and if it meant her death or enslavement, she would make that sacrifice. But she did not want Stone or Illiah to share her fate.

Part of her felt ill and weak at the thought of meeting with Cotoch. Cotoch had wronged her in every way. But part of her riled at the challenge. She was strong. She was a daughter of Kitarra.

As Vagar led Eva through the streets of Attingard, Eva noticed that the city felt more colorful, more alive, than she remembered. But, the last time Eva had been in the city, she had been recovering from a wound that should have killed her. Years had passed. A different king ruled Allati. Illiah's spies reported that Allati had changed under Cotoch's reign—for the better. Eva had a hard time believing it, but seeing the city now, it seemed vibrant and healthy. Prosperous.

Vagar told her how the nobility were more sensible about the Blood. The Shadow Guard were gone–dead. Men no longer hoarded wives, trying to breed pure-blooded sons and daughters to be passed around or discarded at their whim. He also told her Cotoch's only wife, the queen, had died a few years earlier, and he had only one daughter. Very un-Allati-like from what Eva remembered. She remembered noblemen with twenty wives and buckets of children. Still, she planned to reserve judgment.

Vagar led her to the king's palace at the city center. A young boy in a sharp uniform took her horse. At the grand entrance, tall doors were thrown open to welcome them. A line of servants and guards stood ready to beckon them inside.

The doorway gaped at Eva. Cotoch was in there. Waiting. She mustered her courage. She was a daughter of Kitarra. But she felt alone. Mistrust gnawed at her fortitude. Vagar's words might just be a lie built to deceive her into becoming not Cotoch's prisoner, but his plaything.

"Eva?" Vagar noticed her hesitation.

It was too late. Eva had chosen to trust her brother.

"Come, the king is this way," a servant said, bowing from the neck, gesturing for them to follow.

Eva forced her unsteady legs to move. Vagar put his hand on her shoulder, and she was surprised that the touch felt comforting. The servant led them through another door into a wide room with tall arched ceilings painted light gold. Cotoch stood, his hands folded behind him, his back straight. His dark eyes were the same as in her nightmares. She could almost feel his breath against her neck and his magic choking her will.

She had made a terrible mistake. This was a trap. She had been blinded by a mother's need to protect her son, lured by lies fed to her by Vagar. And she would pay the price.

CHAPTER 28

ILLIAH

EVA, *where are you?*

Illiah felt like a river had swallowed him whole. The crushing weight of worry was drowning him. Uncertainty pummeled his fragile human body against the rocky bottom.

It had been weeks without any trace of Eva. No news had reached him of her whereabouts. He didn't think she was dead. That was inconceivable. Stone assured him over and over that he would know if she was in danger or hurt. But Illiah did not know how much he could trust Stone's intuition.

Illiah fingered the list of missing people. Was Eva with them? How could so many go missing without a trace?

In his bones, Illiah knew the answer. The *varing.*

Illiah sat before Rhyl's copper basin. Eva had been furious when Aiyan had gifted it to Rhyl. It had taken weeks and perhaps a visit from the Guardian of Allati (Eva never did admit to it) for Eva to forgive Aiyan.

Illiah didn't know how to seek a vision. He had never exercised his *candarii* magic (why would he?). *At least not knowingly,* he admitted bitterly. But long ago, before she had abandoned her *sanarii* magic, Eva had talked about the process of vision-finding in a basin of water amplified by an element.

He filled the basin. A little voice in his head warned him he was being reckless, but he dismissed it.

This was his only option. Use his *candarii* magic to find Eva or go mad. Perhaps he was already mad. Why else would he try this?

The water rippled under his breath. He looked into the bright depths of light reflected on the copper. He reached for the *varing* inside him, a constant presence in his heart. An old ache. An old grief. He let it rise to greet him.

Eva.

And there she was, a vision in the water of the basin. Her blue-green eyes were clear. She looked unharmed. She smiled at the man beside her. Illiah did not know him, but by the color of her hair and the set of his chin, he knew it was Vagar, Eva's half brother. Impossible. In the distance was a city. Attingard.

Vagar was Cotoch's man. Attingard was Cotoch's city.

The vision darkened with his fear. Illiah felt the *varing* burn along his veins, his eyes, and his mouth tasted like ash. He felt strong. Powerful. Rage warmed his heart and washed away the uncomfortable fear.

His surroundings came back to him with chaotic clarity. The chamber. The basin. A large brown wolf, growling at him, teeth bared, hackles tall.

Illiah growled back, his arms raised. He would fight this wolf. He would not let it stop him. He would not back down. Not now, not with the *varing* surging in his blood and his beloved in danger.

The wolf landed on his chest. Its teeth sunk into Illiah's arm, and pain traveled into his spine. He roared in frustration.

What was he doing? He went limp, shame eclipsing his anger.

The wolf shifted into a man. Aiyan glared at Illiah, his amber eyes laced with displeasure.

"What were you *thinking*, Illiah?" Aiyan shouted. It was the first time Illiah had heard Aiyan raise his voice. "You would force me to fulfill my promise? You would have me become a murderer once more? How *dare* you."

"I'm sorry, Aiyan."

"You cannot give that thing inside you a reason to get out. You cannot let your fear for Eva weaken you." Aiyan's eyes softened. He knew what it was to love with every fiber of his being. "I know you worry for Eva. But you must *trust* her."

"She is traveling to Attingard."

"To see Cotoch," Aiyan surmised.

"Why would she do this?"

"Illiah, Eva would do anything for Rhyl."

"You think she is going to Cotoch because of Rhyl?"

"I don't know. What does your heart tell you?"

Illiah swallowed and rubbed his bleeding arm with his torn sleeve. "That she is brave and strong. And that I need to trust her."

Aiyan nodded. "Good."

It felt like swallowing coals.

CHAPTER 29

EVA

"LADY EVANGELINE, welcome to Attingard," Cotoch said, bowing to her.

Eva held his eyes. Her fear shifted to anger. The trapped feeling in her chest dissolved as thirteen years of hatred coalesced inside her. She wanted to tell him *exactly* what kind of monster he was, but beside Cotoch stood a young child. Eva swallowed all the vile things on the tip of her tongue.

"This is my daughter, Pena," Cotoch said. He placed his arm around the girl's small shoulders. Even without the introduction, it was clear from her dark hair and dark eyes she was Cotoch's daughter. Her little face lit with a smile. She leaned against her father, tucking her hand into his. The lack of fear in the little girl dulled the sharp edge of Eva's rage. Eva wondered if Cotoch had brought his daughter to soften this meeting. If so, it worked.

Eva nodded curtly but had no pleasantries to offer. Cotoch looked flustered. What had happened to his hubris?

"Come, eat. You must be tired," he offered, gesturing for her to follow him.

"I'm eager to hear what you have to tell me, Cotoch," Eva said, finding her voice. But she *was* hungry. And a bath would not go amiss. Or a soft bed.

"Follow me. Food and explanations will be given freely," Cotoch assured her.

Cotoch led her and Vagar to a small dining room and offered her a seat at a surprisingly modest table. The girl, Pena, walked beside her father with small, bouncing steps. Vagar sat opposite Eva, Cotoch in the chair beside her. The girl crawled onto Cotoch's lap, even though she was almost too old for it. She smiled shyly at Eva. Eva found herself smiling back.

"How old are you, Pena?" Eva asked.

"Ten."

"A good age," Eva said. "My youngest boys, twins, are twelve, and they are quite the terrors." Then Eva clamped down her mouth. It felt too personal to be conversing about her children. Was Cotoch influencing her? She searched her mind for the presence of *candarii* magic but found nothing. Someday, she would have to thank Illiah for giving her so much practice sensing the *varing*.

"Papa says I can be a terror sometimes too," the girl said with a giggle and a glance up at her father. Cotoch smiled down at his daughter with such open affection, Eva want to roar. Cotoch, who had caused Eva so much pain and heartache and filled her dreams with nightmares, had the love of a beautiful little girl, a daughter. He didn't deserve a love so pure and innocent.

"Would you mind if we spoke without your daughter present?" Eva asked Cotoch directly.

"Pena, go find Hella and make sure the rose room is ready for our guest."

"I will, Papa." The girl bounded off her father's lap and ran down the hall.

Once Pena had closed the door behind her, Eva turned to the king of Allati.

"Cotoch." Eva addressed her rapist and the man who almost killed Illiah. "You have outmatched me. All these years I have wished for your slow and painful death, but now, I find myself unwilling to wish grief upon that girl's innocent heart. Well played."

Cotoch frowned. "I do not blame you for your sentiments. Not after what I did to you."

"Tell me why I am here."

"I want to help you."

"Help me, how?"

"I want to help fulfill the prophecy."

"You are *candarii*. You take the *varing* and use its power for your personal gain. Why would I ever believe you want to abolish it?"

"Because I have seen the evil residing inside the *varing*. I know how it feels to hold that power in my hand. And I know it costs everything."

Eva's reply was snatched away from her in her surprise. Cotoch was the villain responsible for her nightmares, for Illiah's sick heart. But she saw truth in his eyes. Longing. Shame. Grief. It was unsettling because it was the same expression, the same truth, she often saw in the eyes of her husband.

"What do you want in return for helping us?" She couldn't believe Cotoch's motives were purely altruistic.

"I want Aiyan to teach my daughter the ways of the *heera*. She is a shifter. My parents were both from Rodan. My mother was *heera*."

Cotoch was *heera* like Aiyan and Tarran? Not all *heera* were shifters, Eva knew that. Tarran, Aiyan's brother, was not. But Tarran's daughter was. Still, it was a shock. "I cannot speak for Aiyan. But knowing his character, I think he would be honored. He runs a school in Kilev, after all."

"A school for healers. Yes, I have heard rumors of it. And I have heard that there is another wolf-child, Aiyan's niece."

"You are well informed. Tavi is eleven. Send your daughter to Kilev, and she will be well looked after."

"I want to accompany her."

Eva narrowed her eyes at Cotoch. Was this part of some other plot? Was he using his daughter to worm his way into Kitarra? Or was he merely a father who could not bear to be parted from his child? Eva knew how that felt. Being parted from her boys was an ache that never left. Eva turned to Vagar. "You will be regent in Cotoch's stead?" she surmised.

"I will," Vagar confirmed.

"You would give up your crown for your daughter to come to Kitarra?" she asked Cotoch.

"Well, I wouldn't say 'give up.' It's not meant to be a permanent move." A ghost of a smile played on Cotoch's lips.

"I certainly have no wish to take the crown from Cotoch," Vagar said with so much affectation that Eva believed him. Long ago Vagar had told her he did not wish to be king.

She looked at Cotoch. He must have understood her unspoken question.

"My reign in Allati began using *candarii* magic, but when I realized Vagar and I wanted the same things for this realm, we came to trust each other. And I don't like to use magic, not when it puts Pena at risk."

"What do you mean?"

The grief in Cotoch's eyes was horrible to see. A monster should not feel such anguish. "A story for another time."

Eva set her curiosity aside. "If you come to Kilev, your daughter will be mentored by Aiyan. You will be given accommodations that reflect your status as a visiting monarch. But I cannot promise Illiah and Stone will not slit your throat while you sleep."

Cotoch made a strangled noise.

"I can attempt to speak with them," Eva offered. "They do listen to me, on occasion. But what will you give me in return? We still have not discussed what you have to offer."

"Knowledge. I have already given you the vercuri."

"Tell me." Eva's throat felt tight with desperation. She'd sought answers for so long.

"The prophecy points to Rhyl. But it does not say much of anything useful," Cotoch began.

Eva decided not to mention the mysterious second part of the prophecy.

"You need the nine pieces of the Stormspear. Once combined, the Stormspear will link directly to the *varing*. Then someone—your Rhyl, I assume—can kill the man in the *varing*. Once he is dead, the *varing* and *simul rami* will be in balance once more."

"Are you sure? He has been killed already."

Cotoch raised an eyebrow. "Is that so?"

"What do you know of Illiah's time in Rodan?"

Cotoch leaned forward on his elbows, his dark eyes glinting. His mouth twitched. "Some."

"Imal tortured Illiah until his mind and body were broken." Even though many years had passed, Eva's voice shook, but it was her anger she forced down. "The *varing* overflowed through the pain and despair of Illiah's soul until it took over, giving him strength, but blocking out his mind. Illiah became someone else. And as someone else, he killed your cousin, Imal, and nearly the city of Kara."

Cotoch didn't speak, so Eva continued.

"The man, wearing Illiah's skin, fought Aiyan. But Aiyan lost and almost died. When Aiyan's mate, Mila, stabbed Illiah with a vercuri, it stopped the man made of dark magic and Illiah came back to himself, but he would have died…if I hadn't healed him." Eva would never forget that terrible day when she used magic to reach out and take something that was not hers to take. She would never forget the feel of the *varing* in her veins, choking out the *simul rami*. And the fire she lit a realm away, a fire that spread down her magic and tore through the cendari tree, killing it. Tayeh's voice as he tried to stop her…But the worst part of her memories was the desire, the longing to burn everything.

The candles on the table flared, their little flames stretching beyond a natural height. Both Cotoch and Vagar watched the strange dance. Cotoch cleared his throat nervously.

"But the man in the *varing* didn't die. He lives still," Cotoch said.

"Illiah can feel him sometimes, on the edge of his mind." Eva hadn't meant to tell Cotoch that. It was a secret only a few knew.

"So, it is not enough just to kill the dark man while he wears another's skin."

Eva shook her head.

"In Mahlas, there is a spirit who lives in the crypts below my house," Cotoch told her. "She is the one who crafted the Stormspear. She is the one who failed to kill the man in the *varing* the first time. Tsuga and the dark man were lovers. Have you heard the tale of the Stormspear?"

Eva shook her head.

"It's a *heera* tale, so I thought Aiyan might know it." Cotoch cleared his throat. Then he *sang*.

The turning of leaf and moon were Tsuga's kin,
Earth and rain nourished Tsuga's skin.
She loved the forest and critters tall and small,
But could not speak their tongue at all.

A great stone fell from the sky,
A rift from forest edge to mountain high,
Trembling thunder shook her throne,
And tore her heart down to the bone.
From the dark chasm came,
Someone who could speak her name.

She saw his eyes of glowing dark,
And knew they had hit their mark.
She took his hand and two became one,
And together they walked with the sun.

But the night does not fast,
And the day does not last.
The magic of her world crept into his heart,
And tore his soul right apart.

"Kill me now, my love," he cried,
Knowing magic took him as its prize.
He told her how, and she agreed,
Tearing a limb from her heart tree.

She watched her tree turn black and dead,
She watched the varing share her lover's bed.
She carved a spear with a tip like ice,
And plunged it through his heart but thrice.
Her love for him was strong as wrath,
And she could not destroy his path.
Trapped in a cage of dark,

The spear she took and spliced apart.
And time passed and slumbers on,
The pieces lost 'till magic's dawn.

But some say her lover lives,
Trapped like her, where no light gives.
And in time, he will break and burn,
Through her betrayal of his turn.

For she was Old and Other.
Nam hei tull a dor,
Nam hei tull a dor.

Cotoch's voice was not as clear and crisp as the singers of Kitarra, but Eva felt the melody flow through her, a lingering feeling of awe in the back of her throat. It reminded her of Aiyan and the power of his *heera* voice. More surprising was the tale Cotoch's song told.

"But the *heera* are from across the sea, how can you be sure they would be speaking of the same spirit?" Eva asked. Though it was too uncanny to be coincidence. A tale of lovers and spirits, doomed and desperate. A fantastical impossible tale, except Eva had met the spirit woman. Illiah had as well; he said her name was Tsuga. And she had seen the dark man.

If the song was true, then Tsuga had trapped him in the *varing*, but now, he was breaking free once more.

"I have spent considerable effort over the years to be sure," Cotoch replied.

Eva narrowed her eyes at him. "Tsuga was your prisoner. Illiah told me you tortured her. Did you kill her?"

"She can't die." Cotoch's voice was as tenuous as spider silk.

"I have met her," Eva told him.

"When?" Cotoch's eyes narrowed.

"The first time was when you imprisoned me. She whispered in my ear to spare your life."

Cotoch sat up straight, clearly uncomfortable.

"And the second time she came to me in Kilev to show me ..." Eva swallowed. "To let me say goodbye to Illiah. I saw you tell Stone to slit Illiah's throat." The years had not blurred that memory. She still dreamed of it sometimes. Speaking brought the memories to life and turned the shadows to ice.

"I see," Cotoch said.

Vagar leaned into the space. "I will not say put that behind you, but Cotoch wants to help, Eva. He understands that the *varing* threatens us all."

Cotoch's jaw tightened. "There are dark creatures living in Allati. People consumed by the *varing*. For some reason, they are attracted to Pena."

Eva swallowed, imagining how frightening that would be. So that was why there were so many guards in the King's Keep.

"*Revenants*. People consumed by *varing*," Eva said.

"Yes. They lose their minds, become violent. Like the *daeum*. Unhinged. Manic."

"Aiyan says the *varing* is attracted to *heera* magic," Eva offered. "But the *revenants* are also attracted to *sanarii* magic." Eva looked at Vagar. "Attin told me that was why the Shadow Guard was created."

"That would explain some things," Vagar muttered but didn't elaborate.

"Have there been many *revenant*s in Allati?" Eva asked.

"A few over the years, but this last season there have been more," Cotoch answered.

"In Kitarra too. And people are missing. We don't know why, or where they have gone. It's as if they have vanished, leaving behind a trail of violence or nothing at all."

Cotoch nodded, his eyes dark with emotion. Vagar looked at Cotoch expectantly. "I can take you to Mahlas," Cotoch said quickly. "I think Tsuga knows how to get the other vercuri. Will you come with me?"

Eva considered. She knew Mahlas and the spirit woman were a good place to start. Her bile rose at the thought of traveling with Cotoch, but what choice did she have? He was right–she needed his help. "All right. I will come with you." Immediately, she felt an old fear and squashed it. "Tell me, Cotoch, how is your niece?" Eva asked, a bite in her voice.

Cotoch's eyes flitted to Vagar with a flash of something—anger, resentment?

"Selene is dead." Vagar grinned like a mountain cat—all teeth and no amusement. "I killed her."

Eva nearly choked on her shock. Their spies had not reported Selene's death.

Vagar continued. "She seduced me. Well, not as much seduced as coerced me with her *candarii* magic. One night, her control slipped. I slit her throat."

"Ella?"

"Fine. I was able to convince her that Selene was *candarii*. Ella believed me, thank the gods. Fortunately, Selene was not brave enough to hurt her or my children. It's an understatement to say I was very angry with Cotoch for not having a tighter leash on the woman."

Eva knew Vagar had only one love–Ella, his first wife and only lover.

"I didn't slit your throat when I had the chance," she told Cotoch. She smiled when Cotoch paled.

"You spared my life, and I saved your man from an army of monsters across the sea," Cotoch countered.

"What are you talking about?"

"When Illiah lay dying on the sand in Rodan, it was I who stopped Imal's ravaging *daeum*. I killed them. If I hadn't, they would've burned the city, along with Illiah and your other friends."

"What? How?" Aiyan had never been able to explain what happened to the *daeum* that day, how they had been freed. Aiyan claimed it had not been his magic. "*Heera* magic?"

"*Heera* and *candarii* both. Let us leave our pasts behind us, Eva. Let us move forward in a truce. Let us find a way to rid the world of dark magic—for our children."

"How?"

"It starts with fulfilling that damn prophecy. Tell me, do you know where your eldest son is?" His cadence suggested he knew the answer and Eva did not, proving that Cotoch had not lost all his arrogance in his guilt. How much of Cotoch's old self, the man Eva had fallen prey to years ago, still lurked beneath his respectable exterior? Eva had a feeling she was about to find out.

CHAPTER 30

RHYL

"YOU ARE so *slow.*" Calypso shifted from his raven form to gripe.

Rhyl glared at him. Every time Calypso transformed, it was with a ready complaint. But at least Calypso was no longer naked every time. Though the clothes he created out of magic were ridiculous. Every time. And the ensembles were never the same. Rhyl was tempted to tease him, but bit his tongue. Ravens, it turned out, have very long sharp beaks.

"If only my magical abilities allowed me to take another form just to make your life easier," Rhyl quipped.

"If only …"

"Although, even if I could turn into a damned weasel, it wouldn't help Honey get through this." Rhyl gestured to the twisting roots and rocks camouflaged by moss. He'd dismounted hours ago to lead Honey through the challenging terrain. He didn't want the poor horse to go lame tripping on one of the many hidden obstacles.

"A weasel? That's the fastest animal you can think of?"

"Hey, weasels are *fast*. And small. And sneaky. Who chose this path, anyway?"

Calypso did something with his shoulders, another one of his gestures that was more birdlike than human.

"I know a man and a woman who can turn into wolves," Rhyl said. "When I was younger and more wistful, I would have done anything to have that kind of magic…instead of whatever mongrel mix I have."

"Aiyan and Mila *are* amazing creatures."

"You know them?"

Calypso made an odd dismissive sound that sounded like "visions."

Rhyl paused mid-stride. Honey butted him with his soft muzzle. "You have been watching me?"

"You are the child of the prophecy. I have been tasked by the Allmakers to help you understand Forest magic—your magic—so you can fulfill your destiny. I have been *studying* you."

"Sounds like a polite way of saying *watching*," Rhyl grumbled.

Calypso's face darkened. "You are from another realm. A prince. The Forest is nothing like Kitarra. I had to know what to expect. How to prepare. And you have magic that doesn't fall into any category. What else was I supposed to do? The Allmakers are old—ancient—their methods of communication are vague. At best."

Prepare for *him*? It seemed absurd. "How long have you been waiting for me to come here?"

"Thirteen years."

Rhyl did the sums in his head. "You have been watching me for thirteen years? Since we were both boys?"

Calypso looked…ruffled. No, that wasn't right. Gods, he wasn't ruffled, he was lonely. Something Rhyl had never experienced until recently.

"I'm sorry. I'm rubbish with people." This Calypso muttered to himself.

"People aren't one of my strengths either," Rhyl said with an attempt at a smile.

They moved forward in silence. Calypso stayed human and walked. Well, he didn't really walk, he hopped from rock to root, often getting distracted by something in the ferns that Rhyl couldn't see, then would run to keep up. Calypso was a lousy guide.

"Ah, here we are," Calypso announced.

Rhyl couldn't tell if they had arrived anywhere. The Forest looked the same. Felt the same. Magic still buzzed just below his senses.

"Can you feel the *simul rami* here?" Calypso asked. "There are some places in the Forest where the magic is stronger. In these places, we *velidar* make our homes. And it is a good place to start."

"Start what?"

Calypso cocked his head. "Learning how to control raw magic."

"Right."

"See to your horse. Then we will begin."

Rhyl unsaddled Honey and tethered him to a nearby tree. Sparse clumps of grass grew here and there among the ferns. Honey set off to find them. A small stream trickled nearby among the moss, but it gathered in a small pool big enough for a horse and a man to drink from.

"Now, I am going to do something, and you need to pay attention to the magic," Calypso said once Rhyl was finished eating and wiping crumbs from his tunic.

"I'm watching."

Calypso shifted his shoulders, glancing up at Rhyl as he placed his palm on the mossy ground. His cheeks looked flushed. Was he self-conscious? Rhyl watched as Calypso instructed. He watched Calypso's face soften. He measured the length of Calypso's impossibly black eyelashes as he closed his eyes in concentration. A small divot appeared between his eyebrows. Rhyl looked down at Calypso's hands which were no less distracting. From between Calypso's fingers, a sapling grew and twined, moving like a snake, up and up and up. Rhyl took a deep breath and tried to sense the raw magic giving life to the sapling Calypso *grew*.

"There." Calypso opened his eyes. The tree was the same height as him, with several thin arching branches adorned with soft spring leaves. An oak, perhaps. Rhyl wasn't the best at identifying trees. Calypso patted the topmost branch of the little sapling like it was a child and not a plant.

"What did you see?" he asked.

Rhyl wasn't about to admit that he'd gotten distracted. "I could feel the magic."

"I should think so. Now come here. The real trick of raw magic is to use it to separate life from death—separate what *is* and what *could be*."

Rhyl felt his limbs go rigid. "What do you mean?"

"I want you to kill the tree. Use the *simul rami* and the *varing* to change life to death, and death to life."

An electric emotion ran through Rhyl, part horror, part thrill. "Why do I need to know this?"

"I'm assuming the Allmakers will show you when we get to the Glen."

"The Glen? The field around the round pool of stars?"

"Yes."

"I've seen it in my dreams."

"I know."

Calypso gestured to the sapling. He closed his eyes. A thick lock of his coal-black hair fell across his face. Calypso's hair was like a living thing. Rhyl forced his attention back to the sapling. It was wilting. Crumbling. Falling. Dying. Shrinking.

"You killed it," Rhyl stated.

"Touch it."

Rhyl did. It felt like death. Like nothing.

"Reach further."

Rhyl scrunched up his lips, but closed his eyes and reached with his magic. Ah, yes. The *varing*. A hint. A tiny trace. The poor tree.

"Now, take the *varing*." Calypso's face looked pained.

Rhyl didn't like the feeling of the *varing* slipping into his veins; it was too intoxicating. But the dead sapling held a tiny fraction of dark magic, not enough to do any real damage. Or so he hoped. He took it. It brushed against his bones and muscles, making him feel stronger. In control. Peaceful. It warmed under his skin like sunshine. It tasted like sweet wine in the back of his mouth.

"Now, you must release it and destroy it."

"How do I do that?" Rhyl wasn't sure he wanted to. To lose the feeling the *varing* gave him? To lose that strength? That surety?

"You are the only one who can do this, Rhyl. Use your *sanarii* gifts and get *rid* of it." Calypso's voice was sharp.

Rhyl locked eyes with Calypso's and saw terror.

Rhyl opened his palm. He knew how to create a flame in his hand. Attin had shown him. So he imagined the *varing* in the palm of his hand, and there it was. It was instinctual. He felt the heat move from his veins, his heart, into his skin and his palm, a dark, but obsequious thing. Like black flames made of oil, thick and glistening. Rhyl could smell sour ash and hot metal.

"Now what?" Rhyl rasped.

"Contain it. If you let it go, it will find another place to take hold."

Like a *vivus*.

"Where do I put it?" Rhyl felt a slight stir of panic. What kind of lesson was this? He was completely unprepared.

"Back into the dark river."

"How do I do *that*?"

"I can't tell you exactly. As a *velidar*, if I touch the *varing*, it will hurt me. But the *varing* is the counterpart of the *simul rami*. I know a *sanarii* takes from the *simul rami*. A *candarii* takes from the *varing*. If you can take it, you can put it back."

Rhyl bit his lip against a colorful litany of curses he wanted to let out and closed his eyes. He searched for the dark river. It felt far, far away, farther than the *simul rami*. Beneath, somehow. He reached past the *simul rami*; he hovered above the dark river of *varing*. He felt it call him, welcome him. He wanted to touch it, but he stopped himself. Instead, he took the *varing* from his hand and pushed it into the river of magic.

He opened his eyes and took a gasping breath like he'd been drowning. But his veins felt clear, and the dark flame was gone from his hand. He'd done it.

"What are you doing?" Calypso asked.

"Fixing the tree." Rhyl put his hand against the withered tree and used the *simul rami* to heal the dying sapling. Its leaves were less vibrant than before, but it was alive. Rhyl sighed. Then he swayed on his feet. He almost fell over. Fatigue pressed against his chest like an anvil.

"You didn't have to do that. Now it is going to take us even longer," Calypso complained, but there might have been a hint of a smile in his voice.

"I'm fine." Well, Rhyl was *mostly* fine. He would just walk slowly until the feeling passed. Calypso's face hovered close to his. Rhyl realized that Calypso was holding him up by the elbow. Calypso chewed the inside of his lip.

"We'll stay here for tonight and continue on in the morning, if you are up for it. Come on." He pulled Rhyl after him.

"Come where?"

"My house."

And out of thin air—or Rhyl supposed, magic—there was a door leading into a tree. Calypso opened it. A warm glow shone out into the Forest, which Rhyl realized was dimming with the oncoming night.

"Your horse will have to stay outside."

"Is it safe?"

"Sure."

The strange house was small but bigger than the tree was round, which made Rhyl's head throb with the illogical nature of it. Rhyl brushed his fingers against the simple furnishings. Everything felt real. *Was* real, he supposed. The stone floor felt sturdy under his boots. The fire in the grate was warm on his face.

"You made this with magic? Just now?"

"No. I made it over years. Improving here and there."

"And you just call to it and it comes?"

"Only in places of the Forest where magic is strong enough."

"Amazing," Rhyl exclaimed.

"There is only magic like this in the Great Forest. And only if you are a *velidar*. Outside the Forest, I have no magic."

"None at all?"

"No."

Rhyl looked around. In one corner sat a small bed, the linens embellished with gold-threaded designs that reminded him of Kitarra. A long mirror stood in another corner. He couldn't help but smile, wondering how much time Calypso spent admiring himself. Rhyl sank into the cushioned chair. Magic extracted its price, and Rhyl didn't think he could stand a second longer. Or ask Calypso if he tried on his magical ensembles in front of the mirror.

"Here." Calypso handed him a plate of steaming food.

Rhyl grinned. "Is it made from magic? Of course it is. Is it safe for me?" Rhyl realized too late that was a dumb question. Calypso was not going to feed him something poisonous.

"Don't be ridiculous. Just eat it."

It tasted delicious. And real. And it filled his stomach as any nonmagical food would. "Reminds me of the tales about mortals eating the food of the fairies and being stuck in their world forever."

"I thought you already knew you were living in an old tale." Calypso smiled with half his mouth. He looked more impish than Bren and Aralis.

"If I were living in an old tale, I would have come across a damsel in distress by now," Rhyl said through a mouthful of food.

"Don't count your eggs before they've hatched." Another plate of food appeared in Calypso's hands. He ate—well, like a raven, in rather big bites, swallowing like a beast. He noticed Rhyl watching him and paused, then grinned with most of his teeth showing. Like a challenge. His manners were as bad as the twins. At least Calypso had the excuse of growing up as a raven; Rhyl's brothers were princes, for goodness' sake. A pang of homesickness made Rhyl's food taste off, but just briefly.

"I learned to do this just for you, you know." Calypso gestured to Rhyl's plate of steaming food. "I don't really need to eat. The magic of the Forest nourishes the *velidar*."

"Well, I very much appreciate it."

Calypso's smile faded, but Rhyl could tell he was pleased.

"But if you had learned to make honey cake, *that* would be a real accomplishment," Rhyl said. Calypso glared but quickly realized Rhyl was only teasing. Rhyl grinned in victory. "So you don't have to eat at all?"

"No. But we *velidar* do, during our Full Moon Revel, mostly just wine and ale. Because, why not?" His impish grin returned.

"Full Moon Revel?"

"Many of the *velidar* gather and dance and drink and…copulate."

Rhyl ignored the last word. "The full moon is in a few days."

"Yes, it is. Want to go?"

"Is it safe?"

Calypso made a noise. "Sure. Don't worry, I wouldn't let anyone copulate with you without your consent."

"That was not my first concern," Rhyl muttered. Suddenly, his arms weighed more than steel ingots. The fire was warm on his face and he wanted to sleep. But…he had questions for Calypso. "What are the Allmakers like?" he asked.

"Uhm. Generally speaking? Rather terrifying."

"What do they look like?"

"I don't know. I have never actually seen them. Time to sleep."

"Unfair. You sleep?"

"Yes. I sleep," Calypso said settling into the small bed, pulling the fanciful blanket around him. "You can sleep on the floor. Here." He waved his hand and a stack of blankets appeared. And a pillow. Magic. Rhyl really did get the short end of the magic stick. Damn the prophecy.

"Thanks," Rhyl said. The blanket was blue and green and reminded him of his room back in Kitarra. There was a basin in the corner and Rhyl figured he had just enough strength left to wash away some of his travels. He pulled off his shirt and dipped his hands into the warm water. It felt like heaven to clean the grime from his face. He felt eyes on him, but when he turned, Calypso was tucked into his bed, curled into a ball. Rhyl couldn't tell if he was asleep.

Rhyl lay down on the floor, a thick blanket below him and a second one tucked around his shoulders to keep away any chill. Though he doubted he would feel cold in a small, enchanted house built by a man who was also a raven.

CHAPTER 31

RHYL

IN THE MORNING, Calypso led him farther, deeper into the Forest. As they went, Calypso told him to practice with magic. It took two days, but Rhyl managed to grow a tree in the same way as Calypso, then kill it, sending the *varing* back to its source. Growing the tree (only to destroy it) was harder than Calypso made it look. Every night, Rhyl flopped onto his bed in front of the fire (it took Calypso a full day, but he made Rhyl a proper bed) and fell asleep.

Now it was the full moon and Rhyl was tired, but he still wanted to go to the revel. Ever since Calypso had mentioned it, it had tugged at Rhyl's curiosity. Who wouldn't want to go to a gathering of magical creatures in a magical forest on the full moon and drink wine made from magic?

Rhyl had no idea what to expect, but he knew it would be unlike anything he had ever experienced.

Calypso explained how night revels were held all over the Forest on the full moon. The closest one, Calypso informed him, was in a glade ringed by three giant cedar trees. The place was aptly named the Cedar Glade. And all the *velidar* from this part of the Forest would gather there.

"How many *velidar* will be there?" Rhyl asked as they traversed the dusky woods.

Calypso shrugged. "I'm not sure. Those who live in this part of the Forest. And those close to Timur."

"Who's Timur?"

"Our leader."

Rhyl heard the music before he saw the glade. Lanterns hung from the swooping cedar branches, illuminating the mossy opening in the trees. The last bit of sunlight turned the Forest pink and golden. The lanterns swayed, bobbing like petals on a lake. Or like stars in the night sky.

Beneath the eerie, fantastical lights, dancers wove and dipped and bounced. The music came from a group of *velidar* playing instruments, drums mostly, their voices shifting in harmony with sounds any Kitarran singer would be envious of. The music was heartrendingly beautiful. As Rhyl moved closer, he could see some of the dancers were animals, others human shaped. They wore gauzy clothes that Rhyl realized on closer inspection were not really clothes at all, but merely decorations. There was no humility, no modesty.

At the edge of the circle lit by the curious lanterns, the not-quite shadows didn't entirely hide *velidar* engaged in other pursuits. Rhyl couldn't see them clearly, but his imagination didn't have to work hard to figure it out.

He stepped into the circle just behind Calypso, and everyone paused to look at them.

Several *velidar* came over to greet them. A few shifted into their human forms, their expression varied between awed and bored, friendly and suspicious. Rhyl couldn't blame them. He was a stranger. And a human.

"Calypso! You brought him! Finally."

"Is he everything you hoped?" a man asked.

"Look how beautiful he is," a young woman said, making Rhyl's face redden.

"Are all humans so beautiful?" another pondered.

"My name is Midna." The young woman with short, tangled hair and sunset eyes hopped in front of Rhyl, holding out her hand in greeting. Her nose was small and pointed, reminding Rhyl of a sparrow.

"Nice to meet you," Rhyl said, taking her hand and kissing the back of it. Girls loved that. She was no different. She grinned, blushing.

"Calypso was so impatient for you to come to the Forest," she told him. "But we weren't sure if he would bring you to the revel."

"Why wouldn't I?" Calypso asked with an edge to his voice.

The girl, Midna, shrugged and blew Calypso a kiss, a very human gesture. She hugged Rhyl's arm against her bare skin.

"Here, take this." Someone put a drink in Rhyl's hand that looked like liquid gold and tasted like sunlight and honey and spices. Its warmth reached his toes. The music was earthy and wild and the drumbeat was getting under his skin, making his feet itch. He wanted to move. He threw a glance to Calypso as Midna pulled him, drink and all, into the center of the ring where dancers leaped and wove. The dance was new to him, but if a rabbit could do it—and one was—so could Rhyl.

The night air was sweet and chill and perfect. Midna's laugh was like bird song. Everything felt intoxicating. *This* was a celebration, Rhyl decided. The moon rose above trees and looked down onto the glade and for the first time in weeks, he felt all his homesickness, his loneliness melt away.

"Why doesn't Calypso dance?" Rhyl asked Midna, breathless, after countless rounds around the dance circle. Rhyl hadn't seen Calypso join the dance. Perhaps the rogue had chosen companionship over dancing. Night had descended, and the Forest surrounding the revel was black and deliciously mysterious. Gods, Rhyl was happier than he had felt in…a long time. He searched the branches bending toward the dancing glade. He saw a watchful owl and two chattering squirrels, but no raven. "Maybe he is jealous that you are with me instead of him," Rhyl said, twirling Midna around.

Midna laughed. "If only…No, dear Rhyl. Calypso doesn't want my companionship. Nor the warmth of any woman here."

"He has a sweetheart?"

"No. Gah, are all humans so thick? Calypso would rather find companionship with another *man*."

Rhyl felt his cheeks redden. He *was* thick. "Ah. So he has a man."

Midna's laughing mouth went small. "No, Rhyl. Calypso isn't *allowed* to join the revel."

Rhyl tripped on a root. He must have had too much *velidar* wine. "Why ever not?"

"Because of what he is."

"A raven?"

"Of course not! Because he is not *natural*."

"Not natural? What does that even *mean*?" But despite his confusion, something in her words stung.

Midna sighed. "I know humans sometimes act…perverse. But *velidar* do not. Calypso's attraction to his own gender is considered an abomination. *Velidar* have children so seldom. For him to only want a *man's* affection is seen as a betrayal," Midna whispered. "Timur punished him, but it didn't change anything."

Any remaining warmth from the drink and the dance froze in Rhyl's blood. "Punished him? How?"

"It's not worth repeating. And besides, Forest magic heals any *velidar* wound. Calypso was never in any real danger—Rhyl? Rhyl! Where are you going?"

Rhyl did not answer her as he stalked away. An abomination? It was maddening. Utterly ridiculous. And worse, punishing Calypso for it was cruel. Cruel. Cruel. Cruel. Away from the circle of lanterns and dancing *velidar*, the dark of night enveloped him. His footsteps were unsteady. The moss beneath his feet was trying to trip him. He could hardly see. How the fuck was he supposed to find a raven in the dark? He heard the shuffle of feathers and a quiet squawk.

"Calypso, is that you? I can't see shit."

A wing tip grazed his cheek. Rhyl sighed and followed the raven away from the revelry of the Forest Folk.

CHAPTER 32

CALYPSO

CALYPSO LEFT RHYL to the revel. A convenient distraction, though watching Rhyl and Midna was as comfortable as sticking his beak into a pile of hot coals.

After a while, Timur came to him, his green eyes bright in the lantern light.

"I'm not sure this is a good idea," Timur said by way of greeting, gesturing to the revel, and Rhyl, behind them. "I can feel his magic from here."

"The *varing* follows Rhyl," Calypso agreed.

"I'm surprised they can't feel it." Timur gazed at the dancers.

"The others are less attuned to the Forest than you and me," Calypso said to appease Timur's pride, but the cat-man only sneered.

"How much longer will he be here?"

"Not long. I will take him to the Glen tomorrow."

"Have you told him?"

"No. Not yet."

"Long ago, when his mother traveled through the Forest, we gave her some of our magic to help her survive her journey to Kitarra. Remember, Rhyl is not just *sanarii*, he is *candarii* as well. His magic will poison this Forest if he stays here too long."

"I have not forgotten," Calypso snapped. Timur believed Calypso was a fool. Timur had never curbed his opinions about Calypso being chosen by the Allmakers to be Rhyl's guide through the Forest. Timur would have seen it as an honor; Calypso saw it as a curse.

But the Allmakers *had* chosen him.

"You must be ready," they told him all those years ago.

"What must I do?" Calypso asked.

"Do you know how your parents died, raven-boy?"

"No." *Of course not,* he wanted to add. Who would have told him? Eva, who had been like a mother to him, believed he was a raven, and the other velidar disliked him and barely spoke two words to him. Midna was an exception, but she was a silly thing and younger than him. She didn't know.

"Your father was turned by the varing. *Once the* varing *consumed him, he killed your mother. And he would have killed you, but Lula managed to hide you with her magic."*

"What happened to my father?"

"He went missing. Years later, he was found outside the Forest."

It was a horrible tale. And even now, Calypso's nerves could not handle the truth about his parents.

"There is another part of this, that Rhyl must never know," the Allmakers whispered. *"To rid the world of the dark man, Rhyl must be strong. Tempered. Rhyl must be broken before he can rise."*

"Why?"

They didn't answer. *"You must be there to make sure someone he loves is consumed by the* varing. *That is the best way to break him. Only then can Rhyl learn the true strength of the vercuri and his magic."*

"Why me?"

"There is no one else. You must learn his secrets, his weaknesses."

"You are making me into a monster," Calypso told them.

A heavy silence filled the Forest. *"We are sorry, Calypso. But this is the only way."*

"Calypso!" Timur barked at him now. "Did you hear me?"

"Yes," Calypso hissed back, though he wasn't sure he had.

Timur nodded, eyes flashing, and vanished into the darkness. The music pulsed behind Calypso; the heady beat of the drums made his bones twitch. Calypso shifted into a raven and flew up onto a branch, fighting the urge to fly away into the night.

From below, Rhyl spoke his name. He dropped off the branch, gliding across Rhyl's path. He brushed a feather against Rhyl's face but was not quite brave enough to land on Rhyl's shoulder.

He shifted.

"Done already?" Calypso asked.

Rhyl huffed, clearly unhappy. Then he smiled, cocking his head at Calypso, running his eyes down Calypso's body. "Your coat is lacking its usual fantastical glamour."

Calypso looked at his magically created attire. It was black. How had his magic even created something so boring? He pulled his magic around him and started at the collar, adding silver embroidery shaped in moons and stars, followed by curling vines of green that went down his arms, twisting around his wrists and waist. Satisfied, he cut his glance away from his coat back to Rhyl to find him staring. Calypso hoped the dark hid the sudden flush of heat rioting across his skin.

Rhyl swallowed. "Now the world makes sense again," he quipped.

Calypso was curious why Rhyl left the revel. He wanted to ask Rhyl why he left Midna's embrace so abruptly. Midna was a nice girl, and pretty, at least by the standard of typical males.

Then Rhyl took a step toward Calypso, making the distance between them very small. They were the same height, their eyes and lips matching. Rhyl lifted a finger and placed it against Calypso's jaw. The touch was light, tentative, making Calypso's blood surge with want. Rhyl's eyes trailed to his mouth. "Can I kiss you?"

Calypso made a noise and nodded slightly. Rhyl leaned forward, closing the distance between them, pressing his lips against Calypso's. Calypso parted his lips to greet him, and every thought disappeared, only the warmth of Rhyl's tongue remained. He tasted like moonlight and *velidar* wine. Calypso felt Rhyl tilt toward him, pressing the weight of his body against his, the hard length of his…Calypso caught Rhyl as he stumbled. Shit. Rhyl was very very drunk. Calypso felt every ready, hard corner of his body replaced with ice.

Rhyl did not even protest when Calypso dragged him back home. Rhyl smiled at him like a simpleton as Calypso tucked him into bed, but Rhyl's eyes were closed by the time Calypso chucked Rhyl's boots onto the floor.

Calypso slept as a raven.

CHAPTER 33

COTOCH

COTOCH HAD NOT really believed Eva would come, that she would follow Vagar to Allati. But here she was, surrounded by her enemies—him. She was braver than he'd thought. Or more desperate. But Cotoch understood her reasons.

Seeing her again was like the passing of time had been nothing, like opening a door into his past life filled with actions he regretted. But, if he had taken another path, he wouldn't have had the ambition that would take him to Allati. He wouldn't have met Ana, and he wouldn't have Pena, his daughter, a gift he still did not deserve. He would move mountains for his daughter.

Yes, Cotoch could understand Eva's motives. She was here for her son.

Cotoch had learned long ago that the *varing* was not just unpredictable, it was dangerous. It was a tool, but at what cost? Cotoch had already lost so much, he was terrified he would lose Pena too. And Cotoch could not let that happen. If Rhyl fulfilled the prophecy, the magic of the world would be in balance. The *varing* would no longer be the violent, evil menace that had taken his beloved from him. And Pena would be safe. Eva's son was the answer.

Cotoch arranged for his most trusted servants and guards to escort them. Wagons were loaded with food and clothing and provisions for any encounter. The road to Mahlas was not long, and it was well-used, but Cotoch never traveled without luxury. He was a king; he had earned nights under lavish tents and a soft wagon to ride in.

Eva refused the wagon he offered. Instead, she picked a mare from his stable and told him she would ride. She insisted that all she needed was her own tent and a dagger under her pillow.

She was a brave woman. Cotoch could not help but feel the old ache of want when he saw her, riding with her straight back, her hair tightly plaited, her eyes keen and sharp. When Pena begged him to ditch the wagon and ride so she could run alongside them as a wolf, Cotoch agreed. It was as much for his own sake as Pena's; he could ride beside Eva and watch over Pena at the same time.

Eva, though older and a mother to three children, was still beautiful. But Cotoch had loved a different woman and lost her. He would never love another. Still, that old part of him remembered taking the *varing* and twisting it around Eva, feeling her bend to his whims, and it stirred an old lust. But he wouldn't. Couldn't. And he could find companionship where and when he wanted, for a night, a week. He did not need more than that.

"Pena seems tireless," Eva remarked, watching the little wolf dart off the road and back again.

"Her energy is boundless," Cotoch agreed. "But she is forced to keep it bottled in Attingard. I cannot risk everyone knowing what she can do. These men and women are loyal to me. They keep her secret safe."

Eva narrowed her eyes at him, no doubt imagining his villainous threats to secure his people's loyalty. He wasn't going to waste his breath to convince her otherwise. And yet he found himself saying, "These people follow me willingly, and I trust them to keep Pena's secret. I am a good king, Eva."

Eva looked away. "We have heard reports to confirm that."

He decided to take that as a compliment. Cotoch wanted to say more, but he did not want to speak of his past where Pena might overhear him. Cotoch hoped Pena would never know the kind of man he had once been and the things he had done for power and lust and magic.

As the day waned, Cotoch told Redi to make camp. Pena looked exhausted, and Cotoch knew it would be a hopeless task to get her to ride in the wagon.

The camp took shape quickly. Fires were lit, even though the evenings were long with summer light. The smell of roasted meat wafted through evening air. Men talked and laughed.

Cotoch found Eva sitting in front of the fire, her face cast in shadow. Her eyes looked round and luminous. Worried. She looked up and her expression became masked, but not before he recognized her fear. She had not been pleased when Cotoch told her of his vision, that Rhyl had left Kitarra and was traveling across the Midlands.

"Here." He handed her a steaming plate of roasted meat and vegetables.

"Thank you," she said quietly.

"I will beg for your forgiveness, Eva. But I hope you know I am sincere in my offer to help," he added softly. "I gave you my word that I would not touch you. I will not break it."

"A man like you, what is your word worth?"

He shrugged. "I can't blame you for thinking that. I have lived in a dark place for many years. I treated you and yours…well, with much jealousy and selfishness and cruelty. And no, I am not completely changed. I enjoy being powerful, Eva. I enjoy ordering people around. I enjoy punishing them for their offenses. I enjoy being a king."

"But you are not a bad king," Eva conceded.

Cotoch's lips twitched, almost smiling. "And I try to be a good father to Pena. She is my life. And if someone did to her what I did to you …"

"For her sake, I hope you will never have to complete that threat," Eva said quietly.

"You have a good heart, Eva."

"I could still slit your throat as you sleep," she reminded him.

"You could."

"Do you know how often I have regretted not killing you?"

Cotoch raised a brow. "I will show my worth to you. I will help you find the rest of the vercuri."

"As part of a bargain."

"Yes," he said.

"I will not argue that you seem…changed. But that does not erase what you have done. And for me, you will always be the villain."

It hurt. But Cotoch could not deny it. It was no less than he deserved. "What experience do you have with the Guardians, Eva?"

Eva bit her lip. Her face was ashen.

"Have you met Crea?" Cotoch asked.

"Yes." Her voice was like ice.

"Crea was the one who set me on the path to you and Illiah, and Rhyl. She wanted me to find the Stormspear. She warned me that if I did not help her, she would find someone who would."

"When was this?"

"Years ago. Just before I came to Allati."

"Crea lied and told me I could use the vercuri to save Illiah. I tried. I destroyed the cendari tree and killed Tayeh."

Well, fuck. That was not what Cotoch had expected.

"Since then, she has not made an appearance," Eva told him.

"I am worried she will try to influence Pena. But Crea said she could not come to Allati."

"She came to me in Kitarra while Tayeh was still alive. She is a liar, Cotoch."

"So it seems."

"Have you told Pena about her?"

"No. Did you warn Rhyl?"

"Attin has mentored Rhyl since he was a small boy. He is safe from Crea's machinations." Eva didn't sound convinced.

"Why, then, is Rhyl on his way to the Great Forest?" Cotoch asked. Eva had been shocked to hear of his vision of Rhyl leaving Kitarra. Alone. He knew the prince was headed to the Great Forest, because in his vision, Rhyl himself had mentioned it.

"It doesn't make sense that Crea would send Rhyl to the Great Forest, if that is what you are thinking," Eva mused, sounding less certain.

"You killed Tayeh?" Cotoch asked. He couldn't help himself.

Eva bowed her head. "I made a mistake. I will never forgive myself."

"I didn't know the Guardians could die," Cotoch muttered.

Eva didn't comment. Her eyes followed the dancing flames of the fire. Cotoch stood without another word and went to his tent. Pena was still awake. She sat on his bed, waiting for him.

"Papa, I don't like her." Pena was talking about Eva. "She is mean to you. I don't want to go to Kitarra."

Cotoch sighed, pulling his daughter close, wrapping his arm around her. She leaned against him. "Eva doesn't like me. And that is all right, love. She and I …" *I raped her. I took her son. I wanted to murder her husband. I killed people, but first I cut them up, bit by bit. For magic. For power.* Cotoch shivered and held Pena tighter. "I took something from her. She got it back…but still."

"Well. I don't like her."

"In Kitarra you will be safe. And there are others like you. Other people who can turn into wolves. Think of the fun you would have."

Pena smiled. "So long as you are there with me."

Cotoch sighed. *They may just slit my throat as soon as they see me.*

CHAPTER 34

EVA

"WHAT IS IT?" Eva asked Cotoch.

The city gates of Mahlas blotted out the sun as they rode beneath. Something about Cotoch's expression made Eva uneasy. Cotoch moved as if to rein in his horse, but the gatekeepers were already ushering them into Mahlas.

"I didn't recognize those men," Cotoch muttered. "But I haven't visited Mahlas for a year. Pena, come ride next to me."

Pena sidled her pony close to her father's, looking around the city with her wide, trusting eyes. Eva was relieved Cotoch did not allow his daughter to enter Mahlas as a wolf. She approved of his choice to keep the girl's abilities a secret from anyone not a trusted guard or house servant.

Mahlas was nearly unrecognizable. It seemed busy. Numerous shops lined the street. Market stalls dotted the main roads. The people looked well-fed and clean. Eva reminded herself it was many years since she'd entered the city with Stone. Her memories were unreliable.

A group of soldiers passed them, heading for the city gate. On their shoulders was not the bear of Mahlas nor the rose of Allati but an eagle. Eva recognized the sigil but could hardly comprehend it.

"What are Jullayan guards doing here?" Eva hissed, moving closer to Cotoch.

"I have no idea," Cotoch answered with such fervor that Eva believed him.

Cotoch continued, leading Eva and their company down the main street. After a while, the street opened into a large courtyard and the grand entrance to Cotoch's house. Eva stopped alongside Cotoch. The tall doorway was blocked by yet another contingent of Jullayan guards. She shared a glance with Cotoch. He looked grim. His expression told her they were of the same mind: it was too late to turn back. Cotoch dismounted and strode to stand before them.

"Where is Geral?" he demanded. "Where is my regent?"

"King Cotoch, you have been expected. Please follow us." The guards stepped aside, and the doors opened wide. Eva followed Cotoch and Pena inside, wondering what in the four realms was going on. Clearly, the Jullayans were not Cotoch's guests, but neither did they seem hostile.

"Come, this way," the guard encouraged, leading them into the great hall.

Eva shared a perplexed glance with Cotoch. Before them, a man and woman sat like royalty. The man …

"Caeris?" Eva could not believe her eyes. Caeris's likeness to Illiah, his twin brother had not faded with age. At Caeris's side sat a woman with long, black hair and beautiful eyes that glinted like ice on a winter night. The woman who was Caeris's queen looked plucked straight from Crea's temple. Eva felt nothing but alarm under her gaze.

Eva lifted her chin and stepped forward to greet her husband's twin, but she only took one step. She could feel the *varing* like a shroud around Caeris and the woman beside him. She cut a glance to Cotoch. His answering look was cool, but Eva could read his alarm.

"Lady Evangeline, how unexpected," Caeris said, greeting her as if nothing was amiss or strange about any of this. It sounded rehearsed. "And King Cotoch, welcome."

Cotoch stepped up beside Eva, and she could almost feel his rage. But he stayed silent.

"What are you doing here?" Eva asked.

"We are on our way to Kitarra," Caeris told her. "Regent Geral has been so kind as to let us stay." Caeris and his queen shared an amused glance.

Eva smiled despite the misgivings writhing in her gut at his statement. "Illiah will be thrilled to welcome you. It's been so long, Caeris." She tried to remember the last message they had received from Caeris or Kaile. It had been over a year. Once Illiah had recovered from Rodan, he'd sent word to Jullayah. When Caeris learned that they were alive, and in Kitarra, he had been angry, calling them defectors, naming Queen Arrah an enemy. But the years had worn down Caeris's anger and disappointment. Messengers had traveled from Jullayah to Kitarra a few times a year, but Caeris had never mentioned making the long journey to Kitarra, even with the invitation from Arrah and Illiah. Eva had heard nothing about Caeris finally taking a wife. She would've remembered. Caeris marrying would mean he could finally father an heir. Rhyl was still the closest legitimate heir to the throne of Jullayah.

Caeris's smile was not reassuring. Eva found herself looking to Cotoch—again—for consolation. "Allow me to introduce my wife—"

"Allia," Cotoch interrupted.

Allia. Why did the name sound familiar?

"Cotoch," the queen purred. "Are you surprised to see me?" Her voice had a familiar accent.

"I thought you were dead."

"Nonsense."

"Should we dine, my dear?" Caeris asked his wife, ignoring Cotoch.

"Yes. Do you prefer wine or ale, Cotoch?" Allia asked sweetly.

Cotoch didn't answer. Eva desperately wanted to ask him who this woman was and why Cotoch's voice was filled with loathing. But she didn't dare. For all Caeris's and Allia's congeniality, something lurked in their gazes that sent a warning up Eva's spine.

"Cotoch, is this your daughter?" the dark woman asked, walking toward Pena. Pena pressed against Cotoch's side, clutching his hand.

"Perhaps over dinner, Caeris, you could tell me why you decided now to travel to Kitarra? The invitation has been long-standing," Eva asked, deflecting the attention from little Pena. Eva did not like the way Caeris's queen looked at the little girl. Like she wanted to devour her.

"You will address him as Your Majesty," Allia tore her eyes from Pena to snap at Eva.

Cotoch raised his brow at Eva in warning.

Caeris stepped toward Eva, holding out his arm as if they were back in the court of Caer Andri. "Of course." His smile caught Eva off guard. For a moment, he looked so much like Illiah. "Magic. We are coming to Kitarra to seek magic," Caeris said with a strange smile. "Allia has the ear of the Goddess. She has opened my eyes, Eva. She tells me that I am descended from the Old Ones. I'm a *candarii*, Eva."

Caeris's arm came around hers, guiding her. Eva wanted to push him away. She could sense the *varing*, and it filled her with revulsion. But she didn't want Caeris, or his strange queen, to notice her fear.

"I thought the Goddess did not allow magic." Eva had kept her magic secret throughout her entire childhood for fear of Crea, the self-proclaimed Black Goddess. Caeris had always been a hypocrite.

"In the wrong hands, yes, of course, magic is forbidden. But the Black Goddess brought Allia to me. The Black Goddess bids me to go to Kitarra."

Eva swallowed. The longing in Caeris's voice was impossible to miss.

Caeris didn't notice her reluctance as he led her down the hall. "Isn't that why you and Illiah have stayed in Kitarra all these years?" Caeris continued. "I have always wondered how Illiah grew so powerful, how he had such *influence*, first in Jullayah, now in Kitarra. I finally understand why he never came back to Jullayah. With the Goddess's blessing, Allia has shown me the truth. Kitarra's magic has made Illiah strong. And I want that power for myself. For Jullayah. For the Black Goddess."

Crea, the errant Guardian of Jullayah could go fuck herself. Crea had always wanted Illiah dead. It was Crea who had tricked Eva into using the vercuri to save Illiah, knowing it would kill Tayeh. Crea was as much to blame for Tayeh's death as she was. Eva risked a glance at Cotoch. His gaze had a certain *I told you so* expression, though it lacked arrogance.

"But why are you here, Eva? Why are you not at Illiah's side?" He narrowed his eyes and glanced at Cotoch.

Eva did not trust Caeris; she never had. And this woman, Allia, was poison. Even without Cotoch's cryptic looks, Eva could feel the malice radiating from her like a stench. If they wanted Kitarra for their own, they would not hesitate to dangle Eva in front of Illiah to force Illiah to do what they wanted. For all Illiah's sound reasoning, Eva was his weakness.

"Time does strange things to men. Illiah is not the man I once loved. I left Illiah and Kitarra to be with Cotoch." Eva could only hope Caeris believed her lie and that Caeris knew nothing of her past or Kitarra's relationship with Cotoch. She gave Cotoch a look that was full of love and desire. Cotoch was clever. His gaze mirrored her own. He even winked, the rogue.

Caeris huffed. "I did warn Illiah, all those years ago, that you were… untameable."

Cotoch bristled beside her. Was he actually taking offense on her behalf? She almost laughed.

Allia took Eva's other arm in hers. Her touch sent shivers down Eva's skin. Something clutched around Eva's will. The *varing*.

"Give me the vercuri, Eva," Allia's voice drifted past the fog in Eva's mind.

Eva didn't know if she took the vercuri from its sheath. Tendrils of dark magic wrapped around her control. The choking, crushing weight of the magic she would never forget. Her chest tightened as her heart accelerated in panic. Cotoch. Had he planned this? Eva pushed against the *varing*, using her *sanarii* magic, but her skills were rusty. She had given up magic all those years ago when she had used it and killed a Guardian.

"Eva," came a faint whisper in her ear. "Keep fighting. It is not me, it is her. Allia is very strong, but I can help you…"

Cotoch.

Eva's mind cleared. She sat at the table with no memory of sitting, her wine halfway to her mouth. Cotoch's hand was on Eva's elbow under the table. As soon as he realized she was herself, he snatched his hand back. "I am sorry, Eva. I was just trying to help you," he whispered.

Caeris was watching her from across the table with a slight frown. The expression was very Illiah-like. It wormed past her fear and made her ache with longing for the safety of her husband's arms and his heart. Of home. "You did help. Thank you, Cotoch," Eva whispered back.

Allia sat, eating meat the same color as her wine. Before her on the table sat the vercuri. Eva's vercuri. Beside Allia, Pena sat with her food untouched.

Eva fought down the wave of panic. This was a trap. She crushed a fleeting desire to use her *sanarii* magic to call Stone. Stone, her rescuer, her friend, her *amourii*. But no. Even a brave man was still one man, and against the Jullayan guards, he had no hope. And Stone would tell Illiah. And Illiah would come…and Eva would not risk that. She needed a different plan.

She was not alone. She had Cotoch as her ally. The man she had once vowed to kill. And now she was pretending to be his lover. She sipped her wine and tried not to choke on the manic laughter that threatened to consume her.

CHAPTER 35

EVA

AFTER DINNER, Caeris snapped his fingers, and ten guards appeared.

At that instant, Eva's fear was confirmed. They were prisoners. Cotoch had known it longer, perhaps, because he stood, his shoulders squared and declared, "Touch my daughter and I will kill you."

Allia smiled. "She is a darling. Liam?"

Eva swallowed her hiss of surprise as a young Kitarran approached Allia. His fur was gray striped with black. Younger than Talo, but still a man. Tall, strong. It was clear he moved with the grace that was both Kitarran and warrior. What was he doing here, in Mahlas?

"Yes, master?" the young man asked.

"Take the girl to the room prepared for her."

"Of course."

"If she runs, kill her. If she shifts into a wolf, kill her."

"Yes, My Queen." Liam's eyes were cold and unquestioning. What was going on here? How did this woman have a Kitarran as her guard?

Eva watched Pena tense as the Kitarran put his hand on her shoulder. She didn't make a sound, but her eyes begged her father for help. Cotoch's jaw flexed with contained rage as he watched his daughter taken away, unable to reassure her, his authority stolen.

"Where did you find the Kitarran, Allia?" Eva asked.

Allia's smile curved into a blade. "Why do you care? You gave up Kitarra for your lover." She gestured to Cotoch.

Eva shut her mouth lest she destroy her lie.

Next, the guards herded Cotoch and Eva down the hall.

Their prison was a well-furnished room with all the amenities for prestigious guests. As far as prisons went, it could be much worse. Eva would rather share a room with Cotoch than be confined to a cold, wet, stinking dungeon.

Cotoch paced the room like a caged beast. A minuscule part of Eva felt gratified by his anger. She knew the cold cutting burn of that emotion. She'd endured it when Selene had stolen Rhyl and Talo from her. The feeling of terror and helplessness was engraved in her mind. But with her gratification was also shame. Pena was innocent. Eva could not rejoice in Cotoch's suffering when it came at Pena's expense.

"Who is Allia, Cotoch?"

Cotoch didn't answer. "They took her," he repeated for the twentieth time.

Eva wanted to reassure him that Caeris would not hurt a child…but she had no way to know what kind of man Caeris was now, and how much of his mind was subject to the whims of his wife. And Allia…something made Eva believe Allia *would* hurt a child like Pena.

"Cotoch, tell me who Allia is," Eva demanded.

The muscles in Cotoch's jaw worked. He pressed his fist against the door. "She is Imal's sister. My cousin. A *candarii-heera*. A monster of her brother's making. Her brother, and his wolf."

Eva swallowed her disgust. She knew only a handful of things Imal had forced Aiyan to do as his assassin. Aiyan's past was a masterpiece of terrible things he had done to survive. But if Aiyan had mentioned Allia, it was without substance. Mila was the only one who knew Aiyan's secrets.

"Why does she have a Kitarran?"

Cotoch barked. "He is *daeum*, I am sure of it. Only, I thought it was impossible to create a *daeum* Kitarran. Imal tried, but he couldn't do it. Allia, it seems, has more skill than her brother."

Eva closed her eyes. *Daeum* warriors had their minds ravaged by the *varing* and existed under the thumb of their creator, a *candarii* sorcerer.

The *daeum* armies and their ruthless lust for violence had annihilated the Kitarran Isles, and Jullayah before that. Did Caeris know that?

The young Kitarran was a travesty. Eva's heart ached for him. His cold eyes had reminded her of Stone on the days when the thirst for culla was all-consuming and Eva had to talk him down from cliffs and edges. Sometimes she could see the turbid water swirling in his eyes.

Cotoch had given Stone culla. Cotoch was cut from the same cloth as Allia. He was *candarii*.

"If Allia touches Pena, I will gut her." A cry of anger and grief burst from Cotoch. He banged on the door until his fists were bloody. Eva let him.

He deserved this.

Didn't he?

Chapter 36

COTOCH

COTOCH SAT WITH HIS BACK AGAINST the locked door, his eyes closed. His hands ached. His knuckles burned, covered with a crust of blood, a small distraction as he forced himself to block the images his mind concocted from his terror. He needed to stay sane. He needed to get out of this room. He needed… he needed …

Eva was lying on the bed. If she was sleeping, he would eat his boot. He wouldn't sleep locked in a room with a madman.

She had surprised him, lying about their relationship to Caeris and Allia. Her choice to lie indicated that the king of Jullayah was not the trustworthy type, even without a serpent for a wife. He hadn't asked, but he guessed Eva lied to protect her family. Being the First Defender's wife and Prince Arrain's amourii meant Eva was an excellent hostage. As Cotoch's lover and a defector from Kitarra, Eva was less valuable.

Another time, he would have been amused by the whole predicament. Another time he would have yearned to rub it in Illiah's smug face. But now all he could think of was Pena in the hands a *daeum* Kitarran and that evil bitch of a queen.

Kitarrans were strong and capable and ruthless. How many years had he had Stone in his employ? How many interrogations had gone faster with the Kitarran's teeth and claws and yellow eyes driving fear into Cotoch's enemies? Cotoch did not know Allia well. He had spent a short time in Rodan, all those years ago. But Imal had told him enough about his sister to make Cotoch's skin crawl. Cotoch could only imagine the ways she used her Kitarran.

"Eva? How did you survive when Selene kidnapped Rhyl and Talo?" he asked, his voice rough. When she didn't respond, he wondered if she had managed to fall asleep after all. But then she spoke, her voice barely a whisper.

"I didn't, Cotoch. I felt like death. Only somehow, my body kept moving."

A soft scratch at the door made Cotoch instantly on guard. Then he heard the smallest whine like a dog. Cotoch knew the sound. He shook the door handle, but like the hundreds of previous attempts, it did not open. He would give his right hand for an iron sledge.

He pressed his face to the crack. "Pena?"

"Papa?" Her voice was as fragile as a newly hatched bird.

"Pena, my love, my love. Are you all right? Are you hurt?"

"I'm all right. I managed to sneak out of my room. I followed your scent here."

"Pena, listen to me very carefully. You must leave. You need to become a wolf, and I will tell you how to get out of this house. Go to Kitarra. They will help you there."

Pena started crying. "I can't. It's too far! I can't leave you!"

"Shhh. You must, Pena. You must."

Eva crouched beside him, pressing her face against the door. "Pena. Go to Kitarra. Where the mountains end, there is a line of stones. And a road. The road will lead you to the village of Faevallen. Find a Kitarran and tell them Lady Eva sent you. Ask to see Aiyan. They will keep you safe, I promise, Pena. I promise," she repeated.

"All right," Pena said. Cotoch could hear her voice waver, and it sent daggers through his heart.

Cotoch explained slowly what Pena needed to do to find the door to the garden at the back of the house and the hidden trail up the hill. As a wolf, she would be silent as the dead, and fast. "Pena, do you understand?"

A whimper.

"Pena, you can do this. You are a *heera* wolf," Cotoch said. "You are as swift as the wind and oh so clever."

"I don't want to."

Eva repeated her instructions. "Use your nose, little wolf. We will come find you in Kitarra, Pena." Eva locked eyes with Cotoch's.

"I–"

"I love you, Pena. Always," Cotoch assured her.

A pause. "I love you too."

Then nothing.

Cotoch sat with his back against the door. Tears streamed down his cheeks. He felt Eva's hand brush his shoulder. Cotoch had experienced enough in his life to know pain and anguish, but this was another beast entirely.

CHAPTER 37

CALYPSO

RHYL DIDN'T MENTION the revel and Calypso wondered if Rhyl even remembered the wine-induced (at least on Rhyl's part) kiss. Calypso didn't know how to ask. And asking Rhyl meant Calypso would have to shift out of his raven form. And asking Rhyl meant *asking* Rhyl. Calypso was willing to admit he was being a coward. As they traveled, Rhyl kept glancing at him with this *look,* but he didn't say anything. It was like the kiss had never happened. Calypso could hardly stand it.

But Calypso couldn't stay a raven, ergo not speaking to Rhyl, forever.

"We are here." Calypso shifted to human to announce.

"Where?" Rhyl scrutinized their destination like he had just come out of a trance.

"This is where the Allmakers are."

Rhyl raised a brow, clearly confused.

"You have to walk between those." Calypso gestured to the wall of trees that formed a protective circle around the Allmakers' domain. Their trunks were so massive, they had nearly grown together. The only space between them was just wide enough for a man to slip through. A raven would have to fold its wings.

Rhyl looked nervous. Calypso didn't blame him.

"Are you coming with me?" Rhyl asked half-heartedly as he dismounted.

"I wish I could." And Calypso meant it. Watching Rhyl, wide-eyed and worried, made Calypso want to take his hand, lead him away— away from the Allmakers and the damn prophecy. He reached out and took Honey's reins instead.

"Go on," Calypso said when Rhyl didn't move.

Rhyl took one step, then another. He put his hand on the tree's bark like it was made of ice. He had to climb up onto the root to slide between the two trees. Before he slipped through, he gave Calypso a look that made Calypso's breath hitch. Then Rhyl turned and was lost from sight.

Calypso felt the magic of the Forest sigh. He crumpled onto the moss to wait. Honey huffed in his ear before turning his disinterested equine gaze into the Forest to look for grass.

After a while, Calypso noticed the white fox beside him.

"Is he ready?" The Guardian of the Great Forest shifted into her human form. Her face was drawn and lined in a way no spirit's should be.

"Rhyl is strong," Calypso replied, knowing it was not the answer she was looking for. "The Allmakers believe time is running out."

Lulanan nodded. "I feel it too."

"The Allmakers want me to go with Rhyl," Calypso told her.

"You're afraid."

"Not afraid, exactly. I just don't know how I can help Rhyl outside the Great Forest."

"You are more capable than you think, raven-boy," the Guardian told him.

Calypso didn't comment.

With foxlike precision, Lula jerked her amber eyes to the glade. A percussion of noiseless waves pushed out from the trees. A rush of pressure and pain and magic. Lulanan whimpered. Honey stamped his hoof, his ears pressed back. Calypso reached for Honey's reins so he couldn't bolt. "It's all right, Honey. Good boy. Don't worry. It's all right," he murmured.

A strange stillness descended on the Forest. Like a breath withheld. A heartbeat stopped.

"No." Lulanan's voice was frost.

Even as the question of *what* formed in Calypso's mind, he knew the answer. The Forest was reeling as a large piece of magic ceased to be. Like it had dropped into a void that no one could see. Calypso had felt it all those years ago when Tayeh died, but this was different, larger, emptier, and it could only mean one thing. The Allmakers were gone.

"No. It was not supposed to happen this way," Lula wailed in fear.

Fear. That was the feeling trickling down Calypso's neck along his spine. Calypso could feel the magic teetering. He could *see* it. The trees surrounding the glade were *oozing*. With snaps and creaks, their bark cracked, fissured then tore, as if raked by an invisible beast. Black *varing* dripped from the lacerations like blood, soaking into the moss, shriveling the ferns. The Allmakers' death had left a void, a hole, and holes could be filled. The *varing* was filling the space the Allmakers left behind. His heart galloped.

The *varing* overflowed through the rift of magic. The Forest would be poisoned. What had Rhyl *done*? Or was this what the Allmakers had planned? Calypso couldn't believe they would knowingly poison the Forest.

Calypso scanned the hurting trees, desperate for Rhyl to emerge. "Where are you?" he muttered through clenched teeth. He stepped back, away from the *varing* creeping across the roots and moss toward him.

Then, the *varing* receded like it was pulled back, away. The trees remained torn and broken and gray but they no longer *bled*. Calypso felt *sanarii* magic. Rhyl must have contained the *varing*, just as Calypso taught him. But where was Rhyl? He would be weak from using so much magic. And pulling that amount of *varing* . . .

"Rhyl," Calypso hissed. He plunged forward, moving between the giant trees, which suddenly seemed less tight.

Thirteen years ago, the Allmakers had called Calypso. He had flown through the narrow gap between the sentinel trees to find himself surrounded by sunlight and golden grass. A different place, a place of magic. At the center of the glade, he came upon a circular pool of dark water. There the Allmakers had talked to him and shown him the path he must take.

Now, as he stepped through, the golden grass was gone. The glade was empty, loud, and hurting. The pool of stars was gone. Nothing but rock, blackened from the fire, remained. At the center, Rhyl lay in a crumpled heap, his clothes scorched, his eyes darker than a nightmare, staring up at a gray sky.

"Rhyl!" Calypso crouched beside Rhyl, feeling for his pulse. As his fingers touched Rhyl's skin, tendrils of *varing* burned into his fingers, but he didn't let go until he felt Rhyl's erratic heartbeat, like an injured bird. "Rhyl. Rhyl. Rhyl," Calypso chanted as the *varing* burned Calypso's skin black, forcing him to let go of Rhyl. His fingers ached, but as he watched, his skin healed and the pain receded.

Calypso rocked back and forth on his heels, unable to touch Rhyl, unable to do *anything*. Rhyl's knuckles were white as he gripped the vercuri dagger with his life, even in his dreamlike state. He was using it to pull the *varing* from the Forest, from the ground, pulling it into himself. But at what cost?

Rhyl's magic worked around him. Finally, when Calypso wasn't sure if he could stand the waiting a moment longer, Rhyl took a deep breath, then another, his eyes flashing blue and green, not black. Calypso reached for him, and this time, the *varing* was gone. His skin didn't burn. Rhyl's invisible fire of dark magic was extinguished.

Rhyl groaned, twisting. He looked inches from death.

"Rhyl …?" Calypso's fingers dug into the remnants of Rhyl's scorched shirt.

Rhyl didn't open his eyes, but his mouth quirked at the corner. "I'm fine."

"The Allmakers …"

"Gone," Rhyl rasped, then swallowed. "They died to show me …" Then, dis-obligingly, Rhyl fainted.

"Fuck," Calypso muttered. He lifted Rhyl gently, holding him against his chest. He was heavy, but Calypso was a *velidar* and asked the Forest magic to help him. Thankfully, even after everything, the magic answered.

The sentinel trees were no longer a tight barrier. It was as if they'd shrunk. Calypso didn't have to scramble (or drop Rhyl) to get out of the glade. The cracks had become more like scratches.

Lula as a white fox was waiting for him. Her amber eyes were dull, sad. Her nose twitched. Then she was merely a flash against the green, off to find Timur, no doubt, to inform him what had happened. At least Calypso would not have that unpleasant task.

Calypso carried Rhyl to where Honey waited and hoisted him up onto the saddle. He put in an hour's walk, enough distance between them and the glade. There was no way of knowing how the Allmakers' demise would affect Forest magic. The door of his house appeared when he called to it, and he nearly cried with relief.

CHAPTER 38

EVA

EVA SLEPT FITFULLY. By dawn, she was fully awake. Cotoch still sat with his back against the door. He looked like he hadn't slept. He only moved when servants brought food, accompanied by several huge guards. Eva was surprised Cotoch didn't lunge for the door.

The food was ample. They were even given several bottles of wine. At least they were well-fed prisoners. Eva didn't feel hungry, but she nibbled on the fresh bread.

"Allia would come gloat if she caught Pena," she told Cotoch.

"I know. If only I had a basin, I could search for Pena and know she was all right."

"You need a basin to find visions?"

"Yes. Do you not?"

"No. A *sanarii* can find visions in the elements. Air. Fire. Water. But a basin does make it easier." Before Cotoch could ask, Eva continued. "I don't use magic anymore. It is too dangerous."

Cotoch regarded her with pity or anger, Eva couldn't tell.

"Fuck it," Eva said and poured herself wine. Cotoch held out his cup. She filled it.

They drank and talked about their children. Cotoch talked about his headstrong daughter with a smile in his voice and an unyielding edge of worry. Eva assured him Pena's antics were nothing compared to the twins. Cotoch's daughter might have the ability to shift into the form of a wild creature, but Bren and Aralis *were* wild creatures. No one in Kitarra could tame them.

"Did you know that I loved you?" Cotoch said after a few more glasses of wine. Eva had had her fair share too. Was this Allia's plan? To let them drink themselves into a brainless stupor? If so, it was working. "Back then, I only knew how to hurt the things I loved," Cotoch went on.

What a terrible curse. What a terrible legacy.

"How did you change? How did you discover your wrongs?" Eva asked.

"My daughter. My wife—not Sandra—my second wife …"

She wondered if he would elaborate. She wasn't sure it was a tale she wanted to hear. But her mouth was heavy from the wine, so she didn't shush Cotoch when he continued.

Cotoch told Eva how he married one of the old king's daughters. Ana was already wed to another man, but all the other daughters of the king were barely more than children. Ana's husband was a brute, and it was not uncommon for a husband to give his wives away for strategic reasons. He complained she was a problem for him. Hadn't given him any children. Difficult. Prone to mustering the household into a flurry.

"Mustering?" Eva repeated with a laugh. Gods, the wine made her feel like a mushroom.

"It's a good description."

Cotoch wed Ana and secured his regency. But then Cotoch fell in love with her. Pena was born. Eva listened to how happy those times were for Cotoch, when Pena was little and everything she did was full of laughter. Even when they realized she could shift into a wolf, Ana met the challenge with love and patience. Cotoch took no other wives. He didn't want other wives.

Then a *vivus* came. Ana was out with Pena. It happened so fast. So fast.

Cotoch became silent. Even in her drunken state, Eva recognized his grief.

"Her death reminded me of every foul deed, every drop of blood that fell at my command and under my own knife. The *varing* took my beloved. And it is still less than I deserve." Cotoch's voice shuddered. Eva felt cold down to her toes.

Cotoch didn't look up. "Selene made the *vivus*. She used too much of the *varing* in her obsession with Vagar." Cotoch clenched his jaw.

"So, you let Vagar kill her."

"Yes. But it was my fault. I should have watched over Selene more carefully, put a stop to her endeavors."

Eva set her cup down and began pacing the length of the room. The wine made her steps an effort. She glanced at the window. It was night. When had that happened? She thought of Pena out there, alone. But there were far more dangerous things than the dark of night.

"We need to get out of here," Eva growled.

"If we could get word to Kitarra or Allati, they could send soldiers."

"Illiah can't come here."

"Eva, there is no scenario where we just walk out of this town," Cotoch grumbled.

"I have escaped this damned house once. And Stone escaped with Rhyl and Talo. Surely there is a way for us to get out of here."

Cotoch's sigh was long and grated.

"Or are you ready to give up?" Eva spat.

"Of course not. I just can't think straight. I would blame the wine, but I worry about Pena."

"Pena will be all right. She can hunt rabbits. She showed me."

This made Cotoch laugh. "Sometimes I half expect her to forget how to change back into a girl."

Eva gave him a weak smile. "Children are clever creatures. As worrying parents, sometimes we have a hard time remembering that."

CHAPTER 39

EVA

THE NEXT MORNING, guards took Cotoch away. Anxiety crept in with every hour Cotoch was gone. Eva's thoughts felt scattered. She tried to focus and devise a plan, but nothing stuck. By the time the sunlight waned, Cotoch was still gone. Eva worried that Cotoch was never coming back, that Allia had killed him. Without Cotoch to help her, Eva's chance of escape dwindled to nothing.

When the door finally opened with a rattle of locks, Eva's hope rose. But it was Caeris. At least he was alone, no guards, no evil queen.

"Where is Cotoch?" Eva was surprised it was the first question out of her mouth.

Caeris smiled, but it was cold. "We are asking him where to find his daughter. She has disappeared."

It was a relief to hear they had not found Pena. Eva knew Cotoch would die before telling them anything. Which only made her worry cinch like iron around her heart.

"I thought we could dine together." Caeris gestured for Eva to precede him.

Dining with Caeris was the last thing Eva wanted to do, but she would take any opportunity to leave the room.

It was just the two of them dining in a small chamber. The meal was lavish. Eva dismissed Caeris's offer of wine; her head still ached from the day before. Caeris was quiet, watching her eat in a way that made her uncomfortable.

"How did you meet Allia, Caeris?" she asked, trying to control the tension in her bones.

"A year ago, her boat crashed along the Jullayan coast as she fled Rodan. The Black Goddess showed her to me in a vision. I knew she would be my queen."

A long-forgotten nausea rose in Eva's gut at the piety in Caeris's voice. Black Goddess, indeed. So Crea had her claws into Caeris through Allia. What was Allia to Crea? A tool? A pawn? The false goddess had always craved violence and magic.

"Allia tells me you are lying about your relationship with Cotoch."

Eva schooled her face. She had always been a terrible liar. "What makes her think that?"

"Her gifts are strong. She sees visions."

"Then why would I be here with Cotoch?"

Caeris looked ruffled. Clearly, he did not know the truth.

"I am not lying, Caeris. I left Illiah in Kitarra to be with Cotoch." It was almost the truth.

"Why?"

"Illiah never forgave me for destroying the cendari tree."

"The source of his magic?"

Eva nodded, hoping this lie was not her worst idea yet.

"Here we thought the vercuri were the source of *candarii* magic." Caeris pulled Cotoch's—her—vercuri from the sheath at his belt. He ran his finger along the wooden edge. Eva could feel the *varing* pulse from the dagger. She could see it flicker behind Caeris's green eyes. "Tell me, Eva. Tell me everything."

Eva felt *candarii* magic gather around her mind, reaching for her will. Her mouth opened to speak, to give Caeris the truth he wanted. Her hands clenched into fists, weighed down by Caeris's will. She used all her strength to fight Caeris's *candarii* magic. Caeris's face resembled Illiah's so perfectly that it became one of her worst nightmares come to life: Illiah torturing her with the *varing*. But this was *not* Illiah. She pushed hard against the cage of Caeris's *candarii* magic and felt it give, then break.

Finally, Caeris slumped from fatigue, and with a flick of his wrist, the guards took Eva away. Eva's head hurt like he'd used an awl instead of magic. But he had not succeeded in breaking her mind.

Back in her room, she lay on the bed with her eyes closed. Her head ached with each heartbeat. The lantern dimmed as its wick burned low.

The door opened and guards shoved Cotoch into the room. He collapsed in a heap on the floor. His tunic was gone, his skin plastered with blood and dirt.

Eva grabbed the lantern, placing it beside him to inspect his wounds. The red light cast ugly shadows on Cotoch's face. Tracks made by tears stained his dirty cheeks. His eyes were wild. The lantern's flame dimmed, sputtered. Without thinking, Eva breathed magic into the flame, letting it blaze, giving her light to inspect the myriad of cuts along his arms and back. Her mind flashed back, and it was Illiah before her, locked in a cave, tortured by Imal, his skin bleeding from innumerable incisions and his eyes hopeless and dark.

She placed a finger on Cotoch's skin and used her *sanarii* magic to heal his wounds. There were many. She couldn't fix him completely, not after using so much strength to fight Caeris. She needed Cotoch alive if she was going to get out of this prison.

"This is fucked up, Eva," Cotoch whispered when she had done what she could. She tried to stand but nearly toppled as a wave of dizziness overcame her. She gave up and slumped beside Cotoch on the floor.

Cotoch was right. He was being tortured by another *candarii*, and Eva was healing his wounds with magic she had vowed not to use. Eva laughed, but even to her, it was the voice of a madwoman.

"What did Allia want?" she asked after a while. "Caeris said she was interrogating you about Pena."

Cotoch shook his head slowly. "Allia only wanted my pain."

Eva bit her lip. A flood of righteousness flowed through her veins.

Cotoch had earned his pain. And yet…her satisfaction had a sour rind, and she did not regret healing him. Somehow, it was a relief to know she could feel pity for a man who had once been so cruel.

"This is what I wanted, Cotoch. I wanted you to suffer."

"Sadly, I don't think you can take credit for this," he managed.

"That is the tragedy."

"But you healed me."

"I did."

"I thought you didn't use your magic."

"I don't. Stop talking."

He did.

CHAPTER 40

TSUGA

DRIP. DROP. *Drip, drip. Drop.*

It was an endless refrain.

Sometimes her cage was harsh and dark and desolate. Sometimes it was a blanket, keeping away the storm. Sometimes Tsuga placed her hand on the stone wall and felt the water pulse through her skin. Sometimes the darkness settled over her like wind. Oh, how she longed for the wind. She missed its weaving tapestry, tussling her feathers, bringing scents of the seasons. She yearned to hear leaves tinkling in a summer breeze almost more than she yearned for the sun.

Drip. Drop. Drip, drip. Drop.

Endless.

Then…something.

Tsuga pressed her hand to the inky wet walls of the crypts. She pushed. Odd. She could feel… she could feel the wind. For the first time since…for the first time in many lives of men, she felt the dark fall back. Away. As if …

She leaned into the long-lost sensation and *pushed,* and before her, around her, through her, was the river. The *simul rami.* Its ripples of magic, colors she had almost forgotten. She could taste it, feel it wrap around her, hear it singing with life, life, life. Her delighted laughter surprised her.

Finally, something had shifted—no, something had *broken.* Magic was hers to use as she wished once again.

Tsuga stepped into the river and emerged onto the windy plain the humans called the Tarm. The name she once called it was gone from her memory. That made her sad for a moment, but she couldn't remember why.

She half expected to turn and see her tree leafed with green and gold, its gray bark almost silver in the light of day. She half expected *he* would be waiting for her beneath its boughs, his arms outstretched, his face carved with joy. But she knew that was a fool's thought.

Her tree was dead forever.

But Mute was not. Not yet. And now that she was free, she would find him. She must. She would finish what she started. This time, she would not fail. But she would need an army. She would need magic.

"I'm coming, my love. Wait for me. Wait for me."

CHAPTER 41

RHYL

The fragmented conversation was like a memory that wasn't his, whispering in Rhyl's mind. His head felt like it had been torn into bits and pieces. Snatches of visions came and went. The glade of golden grass. A pool of stars. The Allmakers telling him to look, look, look. But the Allmakers were dead. Gone. That part was clear and oh so real.

Other parts were less so. His parents. A vision of his father, younger, on a boat, his skin crisscrossed with red half-healed scars. The Defender spoke in a halting voice to Aiyan. A promise. Death. Despair.

The vercuri. Nine vercuri. Trees. Flames.

Fuck, his head felt like it might burst. Or maybe it was being stitched back together.

The ceiling of Calypso's odd magical house spun above him. The wave of dizziness made him close his eyes. After a moment, his head settled and when he opened his eyes again, the ceiling had stopped spinning.

If Calypso's house exists, at least there is some magic left in the world, Rhyl thought absently. His muscles groaned like they had turned to stone. His entire body was heavy and sore like he had bruises on top of bruises. But he sat up anyway. The vercuri was still in his hand. Odd, that. He forced his fingers to loosen. They were stiff. How long had he been holding the thing? He noticed Calypso watching him.

"I can't touch that," Calypso said as an explanation, nodding to the wooden weapon. He ran a hand through his tangle of black hair making it stand on end. His blue eyes were wide, his cheekbones sharp as daggers. Rhyl's eyes lingered on them too long. Calypso leaned his elbows on his knees, but his leg was jiggling. Calypso realized he was fidgeting and stilled.

Rhyl was reluctant to put the vercuri down. It hummed with the *varing,* reminding him…Then he was back in the glade, begging the Allmakers.

"I don't understand. Show me again. Please."

"We can't. This is the end. This is all we have to give you."

Rhyl had blinked and the pool was dry and cracked. The stars, the dark glassy water, was gone. A hot wind tried to push him over. It smelled of ash and hot metal.

"No." Rhyl had hissed. The *varing* rose through the cracks in the dry earth like a thousand snakes. A primal instinct told him if the *varing* touched the edges of the glen, the dark magic would flood the *simul rami,* tainting it forever.

The *varing* had destroyed the Allmakers. The vercuri was a vessel that contained it. Was that how the vercuri worked?

Rhyl blinked.

He was again in Calypso's house. Calypso had moved a few steps closer; he looked like he was getting ready to catch Rhyl.

Rhyl took out a spare tunic and wrapped the vercuri in the fabric, as if a few layers of cloth could contain its poison.

"I feel like someone threw rocks at me," Rhyl told Calypso.

"Too much magic."

Rhyl groaned, lying back down on Calypso's bed. Calypso sat in a cushy chair.

"Food?" Calypso asked.

"No, thank you." Rhyl closed his eyes. Even the backs of his eyeballs ached. "In the pool...before the Allmakers ..." He couldn't bring himself to say *died*. "There was a man. A man made of *varing*."

"Yes. I have seen him before."

"You have?"

"I watched as he took over your father in Rodan."

"That was years ago." Rhyl pinched his eyes shut.

"But a part of him still lives inside Illiah."

"Yes. But why? Why Da?" Rhyl sat up to regard Calypso. The *velidar*'s blue eyes were almost black in the flickering candlelight. Candlelight that was both real and made of magic. Like Rhyl, made of magic and life.

"When I was ten, your mother traveled through the Great Forest. The *velidar* came to her and gave her extra magic to help her get to Kitarra. That was the first time I was pulled from my raven form."

"You spent the first *ten years* of your life as a raven?"

Something flashed in Calypso's eyes. Anger. Shame. Rhyl recalled how the other *velidar* thought of Calypso as less. As wrong. Other. *An abomination.*

"From that day on," Calypso continued, "the Allmakers have been guiding me, helping me find answers that will help you in your quest.

They tasked me with teaching you about Forest magic. They instructed me to go with you when you leave the Forest."

"If you come with me, you will be stuck as a raven," Rhyl stated.

"Yes."

"What was it like, the first time you shifted into a human?" Rhyl asked.

Calypso blew air between his teeth. "Strange." Then after a moment, "Wonderful. Like breaking free from a cage." His midnight eyes glanced off Rhyl's like a shooting star.

"Mila and Aiyan can shift between forms without Forest magic—why can't a *velidar*?"

"I'm not sure. But the *heera* are different."

"Mila is not *heera*. She thinks her magic is from the Forest Folk."

"I don't know, Rhyl. Magic does strange things when it mixes. Human and *velidar*. *Candarii* and *sanarii*." Calypso gestured to Rhyl.

"Do you think I could shift into a different form?" Rhyl ventured.

"Don't be ridiculous."

Rhyl had asked Aiyan the same question once. Aiyan had given him much the same answer but with more wisdom and less snark.

Calypso kept running his fingers through his hair, pulling at the black waves. "The Allmakers told me I can help you find the vercuri."

"How?"

"By giving you Forest magic. Here, let me show you." Calypso came and sat beside Rhyl and put his hand on Rhyl's chest. Rhyl marveled at the warmth of Calypso's fingers splayed against him. He had a sudden memory of his lips pressed against Calypso's, of touching his face, leaning his body against him. Fragments of a dream or a memory, Rhyl wasn't sure. Then he felt Calypso's magic pour into him, drop by drop. Warm. Intoxicating. Filling him, yet leaving him wanting more. So much more. He pulled away.

"Stop," Rhyl hissed.

Calypso's eyes narrowed, confused.

Rhyl couldn't express how it made him feel to have the Forest magic fed to him, but it felt strangely similar to taking the *varing* from someone's pain. Calypso's magic filled him in the same way and made him want *more*. And even willingly given, it felt…wrong.

Rhyl swallowed. "I don't want your magic. There are other ways to find the vercuri."

Calypso withdrew his hand and moved away, his face unreadable. "The Allmakers told me to stay with you."

How could the Allmakers ask that of Calypso? Rhyl's mind screamed with the injustice of it. But he didn't say anything. His head ached and his body felt wrung out like an old kitchen rag, but he could feel the Forest magic from Calypso pulsing through his veins like a promise. He silenced the voice in his mind that begged for more, that yearned for Calypso's fingers against his skin.

"Why you?" The question slipped past Rhyl's better judgment. He regretted it when Calypso stiffened.

"Probably because I lived among humans for so long. And…my parents were killed by wanderers."

"What's a wanderer?"

"A *velidar* corrupted by the *varing*. The *varing* twists our form and our mind, turning us into creatures lusting for violence and pain. Like a *vivus*, only stronger, like a *revenant* who was once a *velidar*."

"That's horrible," Rhyl whispered.

"Lulanan brought your mother to me. Eva took me out of the Forest and raised me."

"As a raven."

Calypso nodded, his face more solemn than Rhyl had yet seen it. "So, I know what is at stake."

Rhyl ached for the right words to say, to offer comfort. But his mind did not offer anything helpful. He thought about reaching and pulling Calypso into his arms, offering the solace of his body, his touch, but he didn't think that was what Calypso wanted.

"You need to rest," Calypso grumbled. Rhyl was surprised Calypso didn't shift into his raven form since it seemed to be his preferred method of avoiding conversations.

Rhyl wanted to give Calypso back his bed. But he still hurt. And Calypso was right, he *was* exhausted. He didn't know if he could even move. But the cracked, barren pool haunted him. Calypso's past haunted him. His mother had raised a Forest child, not just some foundling bird. And the wanderers…what a terrible fate.

"What will happen to the Forest now that the Allmakers are gone?" he asked.

"As long as the *simul rami* runs clear, the magic will sustain the *velidar.*" Calypso said. "Go to sleep, Rhyl. You need to *rest*."

Rhyl ignored him. "My mother destroyed the cendari tree in Kilev. She worries that it weakened the *simul rami*."

"If the *varing* continues to leak through the bounds of the *simul rami*, it won't matter how many cendari trees are left. Go to sleep. Now. I'm not talking to you anymore." Calypso emphasized his threat by turning his back on Rhyl.

"Usually when you don't want to talk to me, you turn into a raven."

"Oh, come now, I'm not that dramatic," Calypso said.

"Oh, Cally, yes you are," Rhyl said as he yawned. He couldn't see Calypso's face, but he somehow knew he was smiling.

Calypso's fancy blankets were soft, and Rhyl drifted to sleep with embroidered leaves against his face.

CHAPTER 42

CALYPSO

CALYPSO LAY FACING THE WALL, his back to Rhyl, listening for Rhyl's breathing to slow and slip into a rhythmic motion that meant the prince was asleep. Only when Rhyl was truly sleeping did Calypso turn to gaze at Rhyl, feeling like he might turn into vapor and disappear.

Calypso knew exhaustion was a hazard of the *sanarii*. A *sanarii's* connection to the *simul rami* was not a gentle one. Rhyl might sleep for an entire day and not wake.

Calypso did not feel tired.

Cally. Rhyl had called him Cally.

Too many thoughts and emotions skittered across his mind. He lingered on the feeling of holding Rhyl against his chest as he carried him out of the glade. He had been anxious to get Rhyl to safety, but his body had relished the moment like a thief, savoring the soft lines of Rhyl's shoulder and neck. Being close to Rhyl awakened a different creature inside him. His face burned with shame. He couldn't look at Rhyl without thinking of that kiss. Even with the ominous fate of the Allmakers fresh in his mind.

Calypso had known it would happen. The Allmakers had told him their magic could not withstand this new age of the prophecy. Magic was changing, and for the magic of the world to be in balance, they had to sacrifice their magic, their lives, to help Rhyl.

Calypso wondered what the Allmakers had shown Rhyl. Had they told Rhyl what they told Calypso? Did they tell their child of the prophecy just how difficult it would be to bring balance to the *simul rami* and *varing*? Would Rhyl wake and know the truth about Calypso's role in the prophecy?

Calypso.

Timur's voice rattled in Calypso's head, his grating energy more conspicuous than the sound of his voice. Calypso wished he could ignore it. But he couldn't. With great reluctance, he relinquished his blanket and his gaze on Rhyl and stepped outside to find Timur pacing, his green eyes wild, almost glowing. Rhyl's horse Honey watched, his ears twitching uneasily.

"The Allmakers are gone," Timur stated.

"I know. We were warned that their time was ending."

Timur shook his head. "It is happening much faster than we anticipated. There are more wanderers in the Forest."

A rush of fear slithered across Calypso's shoulders, making him twitch.

"The boy…the human," Timur said, "his *candarii* magic is the cause of this. The *varing* follows him. It is poisoning everything." Timur's eyes raked over Calypso as if he was already infected.

"When the Allmakers died, the *varing* leaked into the Forest. Rhyl contained it. He *saved* us," Calypso hissed. "The Allmakers brought him here. This is not his fault."

"His presence here is dangerous for us. The Allmakers could not predict the *varing* would poison us so fast. Rhyl got what he came here for, and now he must leave the Forest. Before dawn." Timur's growl deepened.

"Where is Lulanan? What does she say?"

"The Guardian rarely shows herself, you know that," Timur told him.

Not to you. But Calypso was not brave enough to say it out loud. Not when Timur's eyes flashed like the predator he was.

"Get the boy out of the Forest, Raven. Tonight. I want him gone before dawn." It was an order. "Or else." Timur's threats were not against

Rhyl. The *velidar* were not foolish enough to hurt the child of the prophecy. But Calypso had borne the brunt of Timur's wrath before, and fear for his own well-being and the memory of teeth and claw and beak on his feathers and flesh made him nod.

"I will get him out of the Forest," Calypso said.

Timur, clearly satisfied, disappeared into the dark. Calypso stared into the night forest, his mind numb.

Too soon. It was too soon. And…and now he was losing Rhyl before…before what?

Calypso patted Rhyl's horse on its soft nose before slipping back into his house. Rhyl was stretched out, still asleep, on Calypso's small bed. He didn't want to wake him. He didn't want to tell Rhyl his magic was poisoning the *velidar*. He didn't want to put that burden on his shoulders. But…wanderers. Fuck. Timur was right. It was too dangerous for Rhyl to stay in the Forest.

Calypso leaned over and nudged Rhyl gently. "Rhyl. Wake up."

Rhyl opened his eyes, his face all soft, he smiled–at him–and Calypso felt his cheeks burn. "What? You want your bed back?" Rhyl's smile grew, but he still looked half-asleep.

"There are wanderers in the Forest." Calypso sharpened his voice, hoping it would make Rhyl more alert. "We have to leave. Now."

Rhyl's face hardened. "How do I stop them?"

Calypso shook his head. "A wanderer is not like the other *vivus* or the *revenant*s. It will come after you because it senses your *varing*, your *candarii* magic. And now with the Allmakers gone, your *varing* will spread into the Forest. You endanger us all by being here."

"But …" Rhyl looked like he had a thousand questions. "Wait—*we?*"

"The Allmakers told me to go with you, remember?"

Rhyl didn't answer. He rubbed his chest absently—the place where earlier Calypso had pressed his hand giving Rhyl his magic. A wretched feeling spread through Calypso. Like hunger pangs, he reflected. Ridiculous. The Forest magic provided for the *velidar*. He hadn't felt true hunger in years. Not since he came to the Great Forest after Eva left.

Calypso felt Rhyl's hand on his wrist, his touch soft, then it tightened, holding him.

"I'm sorry, Calypso," Rhyl said. "But I can't let you come with me. It's too dangerous. It's too cruel."

"What?"

It was the only word Calypso could utter. *Sanarii* magic flooded through him. It amplified as Rhyl put his other hand against Calypso's neck, against his pulse. Calypso began to titter, tip, stumble. He was terribly tired, but there was nothing he could do to fight Rhyl's magic. Half-asleep, he felt Rhyl steer him to his bed, his hand pressed against his skin, still pushing his treacherous magic into him, forcing him into a stupor.

"I guess this is goodbye, Calypso," he heard Rhyl whisper.

When Calypso woke, he knew many hours had passed. He didn't have to look around to know Rhyl was long gone. Rhyl had left him behind.

CHAPTER 43

RHYL

BEHIND RHYL, the rock chasm was a silent scream, dark and jagged. Before him, the open air of the Midlands was like an abrupt awakening.

A dream. The Great Forest had felt like a dream.

A pressure built behind his eyes and his throat was tight. He looked back at the Forest again. Wanderers. Monsters. He shivered.

Tarran had scars from a monster of the Great Forest. It was a story not told often. But the evidence was undeniable. Years and years later, Tarran's scars were still visible. The *varing* turned people into crazed, monstrous versions of themselves. Rhyl thought of Corri. His stomach roiled. He leaned over and the contents of his meager breakfast reappeared.

Calypso was right. Rhyl was a danger. He brought the *varing* with him wherever he went. But he had contained the *varing* with the vercuri when the Allmakers died. Calypso had taught him how. If he hadn't, it might have been much, much worse.

"Be safe, Calypso," he muttered. Wrenching his gaze away from the Forest was like ripping a tree out by its roots.

As the days passed, the landscape on either side of the narrow path Rhyl followed transformed from open rolling hills studded with straggly trees to high scree slopes and thicker groupings of conifers. The change meant he was approaching Stonyhill, but the little winding path seemed endless, and each bend looked like the one before.

As he rode, Rhyl tried to piece together the strange visions the

Allmakers had given him, but his thoughts always turned to Calypso's little house. At first, Rhyl told himself he was merely missing a roof over his head and Calypso's food, but he knew that wasn't it. He could not picture the little house without Calypso and the amused tilt of his mouth, his raised brow. Those ridiculous cheekbones. And his lips. Calypso's lips made a mockery of his concentration.

The path wove through a rocky valley with steep slopes. He rounded a corner and brought Honey to a stop. Three travelers were ahead of him on the path, staring at him. The two men growled and drew their swords. The woman on the horse gazed at him with wide eyes that sent an alarm down Rhyl's spine.

"What's this?" the older man sneered. His face was dark with grime, and he was missing a few teeth. "A young pup all on his own?" The man licked his lips. "Where did you come from? And where did you get such a fine pair of boots?"

Rhyl cursed inwardly. This was why he needed to pay attention and scout the narrow bends and twists of the road with his *sanarii* magic. Rhyl thought about turning Honey around and running, but the haunted look in the woman's eyes made him stand fast.

"I am on my way to Stonyhill," Rhyl replied.

"Stonyhill, eh?"

Rhyl glanced up at the woman. Her eyes flashed with desperation.

"And where are you headed?" Rhyl countered.

"Nothin' to you, boy. But give me those boots, and that pack of yours—and your horse too—and we will let you be on your way, unharmed like."

Honey sidestepped, tossing his head as if suddenly understanding the peril of their situation. Rhyl rubbed the horse's neck to reassure himself as much as the beast.

Rhyl weighed his options. The two men were older but not old. Their muscles were corded, and they held their weapons with confidence, big swords that appeared of solid make and well cared for. But

Rhyl did not plan to draw his sword. He took a deep breath, preparing to summon his elements, when a sharp twang cut through the air. Rhyl ducked instinctively, if redundantly, as an arrow whizzed past his shoulder. The man's ugly sneer transformed into disbelief at the arrow sticking at an angle from his chest. A second arrow took the other man in the shoulder, then a third hit with a thud in his side. Both men dropped slowly, their lifeblood staining their quivering lips, their faces contorted in pain and despair as death came for them.

Rhyl could smell the *varing* from the pain and fear of the dying men. Instinctively, he pulled the *varing* around himself like a shield. Rhyl wondered why he didn't have an arrow in his chest.

"Rhyl!"

Five cloaked figures, including the archer, appeared. One rushed to the woman on the horse, speaking to her like a friend, a few went to the dead men, and one made his way to Rhyl.

"Tarek!" Rhyl leaped out of his saddle and ran to the big man. "Tarek—am I ever glad to see you." Rhyl's chest heaved with relief.

"What in the blazes are you *doing* here?"

"I—I'm on my way to Stonyhill."

Tarek looked the way Rhyl had come. "From *where*?"

"The Great Forest."

"The Great Forest," Tarek echoed, his brows arched.

"It's a long story. Thanks for not shooting me," he said to the archer, who was none other than Elish, Tarek's lover.

"I recognized you instantly, as impossible as it was to comprehend," Elish told him, his bow slung over his shoulder.

"I couldn't believe my eyes," Tarek said. "Still can't. You've grown."

Rhyl gave a shaky laugh.

"Upwards maybe, but he looks like he needs feeding up." Elish's words were curt but his eyes were soft and his hand on Rhyl's shoulder felt like home. "We all need a rest." Rhyl followed Elish's gaze to the young woman.

"Come, let's make camp," Tarek said.

"Here?" Rhyl asked, horrified to spend the night among the bloodstains.

"No. Over the rise." Tarek jerked his chin, but his voice was kind.

Rhyl helped the Iron Wolves dispose of the bodies. They placed stones over the dead men to discourage scavengers. They didn't want wolves—the four-legged kind—following their trail.

The young woman walked stiffly, but she smiled. Rhyl had questions for Tarek and Elish, but he helped them make camp in silence. They erected tents and set about lighting a fire. It had rained, and there was little dry wood, but Rhyl sent the fire blazing into the night sky regardless. The air was cool in the craggy hills.

"I forgot how convenient magic can be," Tarek mentioned, sitting down next to Rhyl, relishing the warmth of the fire.

"Ha! That roasted duck is making my mouth water. I may have magic, but I'm a terrible hunter."

"You don't look like you've been starving for too long."

"I was in the Great Forest," Rhyl reminded Tarek. "They took care of me well enough."

"The Forest Folk?"

Rhyl nodded. Tarek looked like he was trying to decide which question to ask first.

"Who is she?" Rhyl asked quietly, nodding to the rescued woman sitting with a blanket around her shoulders.

"Mara. She is from Stonyhill. She was out looking for mushrooms and herbs a few days ago and was caught off guard by the two men we killed. We've been tracking them since yesterday."

"Was she? Did they …?"

Tarek's eyes were soft and yet edged with steel. "What do you think?"

Rhyl swallowed, looking away from the young woman. In Kitarra, the punishment for rape was harsh. He could sense the *varing* in her body, twisting, corrupting her thoughts. If he wanted to, he could reach out and take it. The flow of the *varing* in his veins was the promise of a fire on a warm night. With effort, Rhyl squashed his longing, but it left behind a sour taste that might have been shame.

CHAPTER 44

CALYPSO

KNOWING RHYL had deliberately left him behind sucked the air from Calypso's lungs.

"I don't want your magic."

Calypso could not banish Rhyl's words from his mind. They circled, each pass cutting deeper, making his heart bleed out that much faster.

The Forest still vibrated with the *velidar*'s grief. The wanderers had not yet been found. Timur had instructed all the *velidar* to move to High Hill at the center of the Forest. Timur believed they would be safer there. Even with the Allmakers gone, the *simul rami* was still strong at the center of the Forest where the biggest trees held the purest magic in their roots.

Calypso did not seek safety with the other *velidar*. Instead, he perched at the top of one of the tallest trees along the Forest edge where he could see the Midlands stretch out beyond the Forest for miles and miles. He hopped from foot to foot on the branch. His wings itched with a restless heat, part anger, part failure. Rhyl was out there, somewhere in the Midlands, making his way back to Kitarra. Knowing Rhyl was as safe as he could be…was something.

Calypso knew he needed to turn away from his lofty perch and seek out safety with the other Forest Folk. But he couldn't force his gaze away from the horizon.

Calypso had waited so long…and for what? He had failed the Allmakers. The Allmakers obviously had not considered that Rhyl would rebuke his help, his magic. Calypso cursed the old spirits for their infuriating obliqueness. He might have even spit on their grave if they had one. No, he was no help to Rhyl. His friends were beyond his help.

They are not your friends. They left you a long time ago, a subtle voice whispered in his head. *Rhyl is no different. He left you behind. He does not want you.* Trying as hard as he could, Calypso had never managed to silence the voice.

The time after Eva left the Keep had been lonely. The Great Forest had called him home, but there was little comfort there. Only the trees and the magic and the Allmakers' creed had kept him from falling into despair. But he'd no true friends. His friends had left for a land far away and forgotten him.

But even if Eva and the others had forgotten about his existence, Calypso still cared about them. Eva and Illiah. Mila and Murryn and Tarran, who had always been so kind to him, even if to them he had just been a raven.

As a *velidar*, Calypso was tied to the Great Forest. The Forest magic nourished him, kept him from hunger and illness. Why, then, did he feel like his heartstrings were unraveling? Was this what failure felt like? No, it wasn't just failing the Allmakers that haunted him. The thought that he would never see Rhyl again…was death.

I can't stay here.

The feeling in his throat, in his aching gut, was suffocation. He was starving for something the Great Forest could not provide. He would rather spend the rest of his life a raven than live another day in the Forest, alone, ostracized, and a failure.

Maybe the Allmakers chose him because they knew he would follow Rhyl to the ends of the earth.

He spread his wings and let the wind take him away, away, away. He knew he was flying into a cage, doomed to stay trapped in his raven body. But as the trees dissipated to the grassland of the Midlands below him, he felt a new certainty. He was going to find Rhyl. It might destroy him, but he was entirely, exquisitely all right with that. He could not imagine a better end.

CHAPTER 45

RHYL

DESPITE THE REUNION, no stories were told around the fire. Rhyl was thankful the Wolves did not plague him with questions. He didn't think he could speak of his time in the Great Forest. His throat did a funny thing if he thought of speaking Calypso's name.

He lay down in front of the fire and fell asleep to the gentle murmur of the Iron Wolves and the shuffling of horses. He'd offered to take first watch, but as his body softened into sleep, he was thankful Tarek had told him to rest.

He was asleep. He knew he was dreaming, but it was also a memory.

Rhyl had just left Calypso with Honey and stepped beyond the roots and the huge trees to find himself in a field of tall yellow grass that grazed his knees and danced with a warm breeze carrying the scent of a dew-damp morning. The Allmakers' Glen. The trees he had just passed were a long way behind him—he had only taken one step. The sky above was startling blue, like Calypso's eyes.

Before him was a pool nestled in the grass. Perfectly round and perfectly still, its dark water was filled with stars as if it reflected the night sky.

"Child." A voice made Rhyl spin.

"Where am I?" Rhyl had asked.

"You are still in the Forest, but we have brought your mind here, to our space."

"Why can't I see you?"

The silence that followed his question felt sad.

"We are too weak. Too old. Our time is coming to an end."

"Why am I here?"

"We need to show you how to bring balance to the magic of this world."

Rhyl's heart hammered in his chest. This was it. This was his destiny.

"Look into the pool."

Rhyl looked.

It started with stars and blackness. So much light, and dark. Weightless, yet heavy.

A forest, verdant tangles. Lakes of fathomless blue and glittering reflections. Mountains tall, strong, like hands holding the world together.

Fire. Darkness. The mountains shook the forests and the lakes and rivers. Clouds moved with anger across the sky. Lightning. A storm to end storms.

When the dust settled, a voice spoke from the ashes. Asking for help. Begging. And it was answered.

The clouds parted. Rain poured down into the chasm caused by the impact. Hand grasped hand. Fingers brushed against wrist, as kind as the storm was callous.

Two spirits. One of the earth, one of the stars, and impossibly, there was nothing but love and tenderness between them.

"The lovers." Rhyl had breathed. He looked around the field. The light was fading. The grass stilled. No breeze lifted the dry stalks to dance. For a moment, he thought it was twilight, but there was something off about the quality of the light. Faded. Thin.

"You must look, Rhyl. There is not much time."

Rhyl obeyed and looked.

The man from the stars put his hand on the earth. Under his palm the varing wrapped and coiled like a snake. His eyes, once full of starlight, became dark. He stepped away from his love into the world of humans.

War. Ruin. The humans fought. Madness reigned. Creatures came from the Forest.

Monsters that had once been the velidar. *Blood ran down the rivers. The land turned rotten. Nothing grew. Disease took those who hid.*

The man watched in horror and delight. Horror because he knew what was happening was wrong, but the varing wrapped inside his veins whispered "More." He called out for his lover, and she came. How could she not?

"You must kill me. Look what I have done."

"How can I do that?"

"You know how. You know it must be done."

The spirit of earth wept; amber tears ran down her cheeks like sap. It took her a long time, a whole season to craft her weapon. And then she called her lover to her. He fought the varing, *and his eyes were bright once more.*

"Once you do this, you must destroy it." His eyes were wild.

The spirit nodded through her tears. She hesitated. How could she not? He beseeched her, softly, like the softest summer rain.

She plunged the spear into his gut. Then his shoulder. Then chest. He didn't bleed. Varing leaked from his wounds, draining the life and substance from him.

"Thank you, my love." Then he fell to the ground.

The spirit wept. When she rose, the body of her lover was gone, taken by the varing. She looked at the spear in her hands. She snapped it in half. Then again. And again until there were nine shards around her.

"She didn't destroy it. Not really," Rhyl said. The glen was dark. Empty.

"No. She did not." The whisper was faint. "Do you know what you need to do?"

Rhyl felt panic rise in his gut. "No! Show me."

"We have shown you."

"Show me again. Please."

But if they spoke, Rhyl could not hear them. How could they do this? How could they leave him like this?

The glen was dark, the pool of stars replaced by the *varing*. The dark river poured out of its bind, running free.

Rhyl took out his vercuri and drove it into the dry ground. The *varing* changed course and went toward the vercuri like water down a hill. Rhyl pulled the *varing* into the wooden blade. It burned his hands. A foul taste filled the back of his throat.

Fire.

Rhyl called fire and forced it to burn around him like a halo.

Fire in a forest? *Smart, Rhyl.* But he had no time to come up with a different plan. He knew if the *varing* leaked into the Forest, it was over. He had seen the army of *velidar* monsters. He imagined Calypso, part bird, part man, all monster. He could see a circle of dancing animals turning and contorting into nightmares. Wrong.

His fire guttered and went out. The *varing* was contained.

Rhyl's clothes were scorched. The ground was black. Tall trees circled him. The clearing, the field of grass was gone. The ground was hard and hot under his body. He felt like the sky was weighing him down. He couldn't move. The sun, the bright sky, was gone. The trees stood close, their branches leaning over him.

Rhyl was vaguely aware of someone shouting his name. He opened his mouth to reply, though nothing but a strangled noise escaped. It didn't matter. Calypso was there, crouched over him, eyes soft with concern. Calypso's arms came around him, holding him against his chest. Calypso called his name and Rhyl wished he could answer.

Rhyl woke. His body was coiled, his breathing tight. He struggled to surface from his memory of the Allmakers' Glen and remember where he was.

The Midlands. With the Iron Wolves. On his way to Stonyhill.

Tarek sat on the other side of the fire, on watch. The old man caught Rhyl's eye. Tarek raised one scarred brow in question. Rhyl nodded to indicate that he was all right.

He was all right. Calypso was safe now that Rhyl could not harm him or the Forest with the *varing*.

He turned the memory of the Allmakers around in his mind. The old spirits had perished to give him a riddle he did not understand. How many more would die before Rhyl understood what was needed of him?

He closed his eyes against the despair that settled over him. Soon, it would be dawn. And he would keep moving. What else could he do?

CHAPTER 46

CALYPSO

DAYS PASSED and Calypso did not catch up to Rhyl. Some days the sun was pleasant, but others, the wind pressed against his feathers, trying to worm into his warm skin. And his hunger was a sharp-toothed thing gnawing on his insides.

He questioned his sanity. Rhyl didn't want him. Rhyl would think he was a fool for leaving the Forest. What if Calypso was making the biggest mistake of his short life? Was he fulfilling his promise to the Allmakers or acting because of his selfish, lonely heart?

He was extremely disappointed with himself that he had not yet found Rhyl. He'd thought the road would be obvious, easy to spot from the air, but so far he couldn't find it. He was fairly certain Rhyl would head for Stonyhill. Rhyl spoke of the little establishment with warmth and familiarity, and for all Rhyl's magical abilities, he could not use magic to sustain himself. He would need stocks to get him home to Kitarra. Yes, if Calypso found Stonyhill, he would find Rhyl. *If…*

Rhyl mentioned that Stonyhill was north-east of the entrance to the Great Forest. Unfortunately, Rhyl's descriptions hadn't been instructions. But as a raven, Calypso could cover a lot of distance. He would head east and use his nose to pinpoint Stonyhill. Human settlements were smelly places.

A gust of wind caught his wings, lifting him, forcing his body to compensate by twisting. He cursed in his raven voice and pushed into the wind.

The rain Calypso had scented started to pelt his face. The thick clouds obscured the landscape, and he had no choice but to seek shelter in a dense pine tree. He perched, shivering, breathing in the cold mist, hopping from one foot to the other.

Maybe he should go back. The Great Forest would welcome him home. The magic would wrap around him and he would lie in his house, snug and warm and no longer hungry, surrounded by the things he had crafted from magic. But his things, his fine furniture and soft blankets, were just echoes of a life he would never live. He had always known that.

He put his head under his wing to hide from the wind and chanted in his mind: *Rhyl. Rhyl. Rhyl.*

The storm broke in the night. The wind died and took the dense fog with it. Stars appeared. Calypso drifted in and out of sleep until dawn came and he took wing using the rising sun as a bearing.

He worried the rain would dilute any scents. Then he caught the unmistakable trace of cows and goats and chickens—human habitation—and dipped his wings in victory and gave a cry. Another scent was on the wind, a trace of something…odd. He couldn't place it. And he didn't care. The valley below him could only be Stonyhill. It matched Rhyl's description with the small river tumbling through boulders and over logs and the buildings, low and comely, built close together like a clump of mushrooms.

He aimed for the roof of the largest dwelling. A waft caught his senses just before he landed. He changed course at the last moment, circling, beating his wings to keep aloft. The scent had been a trace on the wind, but now Calypso knew it. Blood and rot and death. He careened around, looking for the source.

Corpses. In the mud. Slumped beside the building. Arms and legs had been torn off, flesh askew, pale from the rain, but still, Calypso could see the rents along the skin. Something had torn at them with teeth. They had been ripped apart and left lying. Who would do such a thing? Or what? He flew over the fenced field. The livestock were also dead, but not… eaten as the people had been.

Nothing—no one—was left alive.

Rhyl.

Calypso flew from corner to corner of the little settlement, searching with his heart in his throat. But he didn't see any sign of Rhyl. No corpses with bright hair. No horse with a coat the color of oak leaves in fall.

Certain that none of the lifeless bodies were Rhyl, Calypso steeled himself to search inside the buildings. A door was left open. Calypso landed outside it, taking a few hop-steps toward the dark interior. His feathers rippled with fear. The stench grew stronger the closer he moved to the open door.

He couldn't do it. He backed away, taking wing to the nearest rooftop, seeking solace in height. Calypso refused to believe Rhyl was among the dead, but he would be coming.

Calypso settled down to wait among the ghosts.

CHAPTER 47

RHYL

WARM MEALS. Felis's welcoming house. By the Guardians, Rhyl was even looking forward to mucking out the barns and listening to Ren and Harly's bickering. He was eager to bask before the leaky fireplace in Felis's common room, though it left his clothing smelling like smoke. He'd missed Stonyhill. He'd missed being part of a family.

The valley lay below them. The sound of a raven came from the distance. Ever since leaving the Forest, every time Rhyl heard the rough call of a raven or the sound of wings beating against the wind, his heart contracted oddly, a knee-jerk reaction that was new to him. He would often see a pair of birds gliding in the air currents. Eagles. Sometimes ravens—regular, nonmagical ravens.

This raven's call grew louder, and just like the other times, Rhyl looked for it—he couldn't help himself. The raven was flying low toward them, its call growing louder and more anxious. Maybe it had young ones around. But that didn't make sense. It was well into summer. Its fledglings would be long grown and flown.

The raven came lower and lower and dove right toward Rhyl. Rhyl shrunk into the saddle, imagining its sharp beak in his eyeballs. Honey sidestepped in alarm.

"What's up with that fucking raven?" Elish cursed loudly.

Rhyl did not feel talons on his eyes, but he felt the bird's feet grip his arm. His first instinct was self-defense, but he stopped himself from swatting the bird away. The raven flapped its wings, trying to balance as its talons slipped on his leather greaves. It chirped a croak.

"Calypso?" Rhyl asked, disbelieving. "Cally?"

The raven bobbed its head.

Rhyl must be dreaming. (He had a few dreams featuring Calypso appearing as a raven before shifting into a naked man.) Rhyl blinked, his face burning. The raven was still there.

"Calypso? Your mother's raven?" Tarek wondered out loud, breaking through Rhyl's daze. Tarek would remember Eva's raven from when he worked as Eva's bodyguard.

"Calypso is one of the Forest Folk." Rhyl cleared his throat. "But *what* are you doing here?" Rhyl had gone to great lengths to keep Calypso from following him. He didn't casually use his magic to send someone into a state of sleep. He'd only done so for Calypso's safety.

Calypso glared at him with a dark eye. Dark, not blue. He would not answer. Could not answer. Because there wasn't enough magic outside the Great Forest to support a *velidar*. Rhyl bit back a few angry words. He should send Calypso back to the Forest. Tell him he was an idiot. But Calypso was shivering so hard it was a wonder he managed to stay perched on Rhyl's arm. Rhyl wrapped his cloak around Calypso until only his black beak peeked out.

"Right. You can't talk. You can't shift," Rhyl muttered. But just knowing Calypso was there with him, softened something inside him. Even if he was still angry. Calypso croaked. "Oh, hush. I can be both angry *and* happy to see you."

Tarek gave Rhyl an amused look, but didn't ask any questions. They moved toward Stonyhill.

"Wait." A wave of dark magic hit Rhyl like the sharpest winter wind. He could feel it like a dense fog in front of them. Calypso still trembled inside Rhyl's cloak. Maybe it wasn't just the cold bothering Calypso. "Something is wrong," Rhyl told the others.

"What is it, Rhyl?"

"Dark magic. I feel it everywhere." Rhyl wasn't about to tell Tarek and Elish how it called to him, whispering like a lover.

The Iron Wolves drew their swords as they rode forward, wary.

They noticed the dead livestock first. Tarek and Elish rushed into the village. Rhyl had a terrible premonition about what they would find.

The first body looked like it had been dead a few days. A man. Rhyl knew his name but refused to speak it, even in his mind.

There were more. Stonyhill was covered in death.

Felis's house was dark.

Rhyl couldn't go into the house. He stayed and held the horses' reins as the Wolves went into house after house, their faces melting from stern to desperate to grieving and hopeless.

"Felis is dead," Tarek said when he came out. "They are all dead." His voice shook.

A sob rose in Rhyl's throat. "What happened here?"

"We don't know."

"There is dark magic all over this place." Rhyl's voice wobbled like a boy's.

Tarek nodded. "Can you ask your raven?"

"He can't talk."

Tarek's mouth formed a thin line.

"I can try to find out what happened," Rhyl said. "But Cally, you need to give me some space." Calypso gave a garbled raven word and launched into the air.

Rhyl sat down with the wall of Felis's house supporting his back. He didn't have his basin or still water close by, so he called fire, feeding it with his magic. He looked into the flames and reached for the *simul rami*, but it was the *varing* that answered.

CHAPTER 48

RHYL

"RHYL!" Tarek's voice was far away. "Rhyl! Damn it, boy!"

It was the screech of a raven that made Rhyl open his eyes. He was lying on the mucky ground looking up at the sky. Calypso flew in circles above. Tarek loomed over him.

"Tarek."

"Are you all right? Your eyes are still not right."

"What do you mean?"

"Your eyes were black right through to the whites." Tarek was not one to lose his nerve, but Rhyl could see the big man's fear.

"It's the *varing*. I will be fine in a moment." Rhyl hoped it wasn't a lie.

"Sorcerer!" The shaky voice of the young woman made Rhyl sit up. She was pointing a finger at him. "You're a sorcerer. *You* did this!"

"He's just a boy, Mara. Leave him be." Tarek's voice left no room for argument. He gave Rhyl his hand and helped him to his feet. Rhyl glanced skyward. He couldn't see Calypso anywhere.

"Rhyl. What happened?" Tarek asked.

Rhyl opened his mouth to tell Tarek, but he retched, narrowly missing Tarek's boots. "It was wanderers," he said after wiping his mouth. "Forest Folk changed and twisted by the *varing*. Monsters," he clarified, realizing Tarek probably didn't know what that meant. "Evil creatures…do you remember what happened to Tarran many, many years ago, before my parents were married?"

Tarek gave the barest of nods, his eyes haunted. "Where are these wanderers now?"

"I don't know—I couldn't hold the vision long enough…I didn't see. But I think if they were still here, we would be dead. Or at least you would be dead…I would be …" Rhyl closed his eyes. What was he saying? Thoughts stirred in his mind that made no sense. The Allmakers' thoughts. He wanted to lie back down in the muck until his head cleared.

"Come." Tarek propped Rhyl up with a big arm. "We need to deal with the dead, and then we can sit down and…Fuck …" Tarek didn't say anything more. Not even Tarek had all the answers.

Tarek found a round of wood under the eaves, out of the rain for Rhyl to sit on. The others went about the task of finding and taking care of the dead. They would burn the bodies, it was decided. Rhyl told Tarek he would start the fire; he would use his magic to burn the bodies to ash.

Rhyl couldn't bear to watch as they brought Felis's body outside. He kept his eyes on the sky.

"Rhyl?" Tarek's soft voice roused him. Rhyl's body was tender all over. His stomach still reeled. "We are ready for you to light the fire. If you are up to it."

Rhyl nodded, not trusting his voice to speak. His throat burned with restrained tears, like he had swallowed his own fire.

Calypso sat on the roof. He cocked his head, a question in his eyes. Rhyl put out his arm and Calypso landed on his elbow and hopped up to his shoulder. The raven's weight and his soft feathers pressed against Rhyl's neck made it easier to breathe, easier to set his mind to the task asked of him.

The bodies had been laid with care on a pyre. Someone had gathered ferns and spread them like a shroud. The Iron Wolves and Mara, the last living resident of Stonyhill, stood a safe distance away, waiting for him.

Rhyl called fire, sending it to the wood and the bodies. Calypso shifted on Rhyl's shoulder but stayed perched while Rhyl worked his *sanarii* magic. It flared with unreal speed, burning brighter and hotter because it was fed with magic instead of tinder, hungrily consuming the dead. The heat became unbearable.

Rhyl turned and looked at the settlement, silent and empty. Tarek came up beside him.

"Elish and I have talked. We will go to Fishtown to find some good people willing to help Mara rebuild. Felis would want that."

Rhyl rubbed his wet cheek. "Mum will be sad to hear what happened."

"Aye."

"I need to get home," Rhyl said, feeling the urgency in his gut. He needed Kitarra's mountains at his back, the smell of the river in his nose and the sand under his toes reminding him of childhood summers. He needed his family, his home.

"You shouldn't go on your own."

"I won't be on my own. Cally will come with me. It seems I can't get rid of him—ouch!" Rhyl felt a sharp pain where Calypso pinched his ear with his sharp beak.

Tarek raised a brow. "The raven?"

Calypso gave an indignant croon in Rhyl's ear.

"If your mother knew you were alone–"

"I'm a grown man, Tarek." Rhyl didn't bother to keep the irritation from his voice. "And not only can I best any of your Wolves with a sword, but I can also make fire from nothing and call wind. I can protect myself." Tarek's mouth opened to protest. "I was distracted, before, with those men." He willed himself not to glance at Calypso. "It will not happen again."

Tarek looked disgruntled but didn't comment.

"Stonyhill needs you more than I do," Rhyl said in a softer voice.

"Let's find you some provisions, at least. Still, I have a feeling the next time we are in Kitarra, your mother is going to flay me."

Rhyl hesitated to follow Tarek into Felis's house. But hadn't he just assured Tarek he was a grown man and capable of taking care of himself? Rhyl squared his shoulders and accompanied the big man. Calypso, who as far as Rhyl knew, had made no such promises to manhood, returned to the roof.

Rhyl ignored the dark stains on the stone floor as he trailed Tarek to the larder. The monsters had come looking for violence and death, not stores of preserves. The larder was untouched.

With Tarek's help, he packed Honey's saddlebags full of smoked meats, dried fruit and nuts. Night was fast approaching. Tarek tried to convince Rhyl to stay until morning. Part of him yearned to stay, to bask in the comfort of Tarek's wisdom, to let himself be cosseted, if only for one night. But the pyre still burned. Rhyl could still feel the tingle of the *varing* at the edge of his senses, ,begging him to reach out. It wasn't an effort, exactly, to keep it at bay, but it wasn't comfortable either.

He let Tarek wrap his long arms around him and Elish kiss his cheek. He avoided Mara's dark gaze filled with disdain. She was not wrong to blame him for the death of her village, her comrades. Death followed the *varing*. And the *varing* followed Rhyl.

Rhyl rode into the twilight. Calypso flew overhead, his swift wing strokes quickly moving him out of sight, but Rhyl knew the raven wouldn't go far.

He rode until there was enough distance between him and Stonyhill that he could no longer feel the pull of the *varing*. It might have been midnight, Rhyl wasn't sure. He found a sheltered dell and dragged Honey's saddle to the ground. After he tethered Honey for the night, all he could do was pull his cloak around his shoulders and use the saddle for a pillow. Just as he slipped into sleep, feathers brushed against his face, and the warm weight of Calypso nestled between his ear and his shoulder. Rhyl sighed and surprisingly, he fell asleep with Calypso's cold beak against his cheek.

CHAPTER 49

CALYPSO

RHYL'S SHOULDER was Calypso's favorite perch, but he also loved the wind under his wings and in his eyes. Honey no longer flinched when Calypso took off or landed, which was nice for everyone.

As Calypso flew higher, Rhyl and Honey below quickly became a lumpy speck. Calypso always kept Rhyl and the road within his sights, though the dirt track through the Midlands could hardly be called a road. No wonder Calypso had trouble spotting it before.

The more distance they put between themselves and Stonyhill, the more the tight band in Calypso's chest loosened. Rhyl hadn't once mentioned sending Calypso back to the Great Forest.

As they moved through the Midlands, Rhyl searched with his *sanarii* magic for the wanderers. Calypso wondered if he would ever get used to watching Rhyl fall into a trance. When Rhyl tumbled through the *simul rami*, his body became statuesque. He didn't look alive, nor asleep. When Rhyl used his *sanarii* magic, the *simul rami* pulsed around him like a living thing, reaching invisible roots out to Calypso. It felt like sunshine, or maybe a flame. But like any flame, Calypso would burn if he got too close.

Rhyl reported that he didn't *see* anything threatening. If Calypso could have spoken, he would have told Rhyl to search using the *varing*. The dark magic called to its kin. But even if he could suggest it, he had a feeling Rhyl would disagree.

Rhyl left the road to make camp. Calypso soared down and perched on a skinny branch to watch, offering encouragement as Rhyl made a fire and began cooking a thin rabbit he'd shot with an arrow.

"I can't understand any of your noises, Cally, but why do I have the feeling you are mocking me?"

Calypso gave a raven version of a laugh, and Rhyl glared at him, though Calypso saw a smile twitch on his lips.

The sun set. Rhyl shared his dinner with Calypso. He might have comments about Rhyl's cooking, but he was hungry enough that the stringy meat went down just fine. Rhyl seemed to have more trouble and nibbled at his food, watching Calypso with an amused expression.

The night air grew cold. Cold for summer. Cold for Calypso. Outside the Forest, he constantly felt the chill penetrate his feathers. But Rhyl could create fire from nothing, forcing it to catch on the wettest wood. It could be worse.

"Ack! Your claws are sharp, Cally!" Rhyl complained as Calypso pressed against him. But Rhyl didn't shoo him away. Calypso couldn't deny that the best part of his day was when Rhyl settled for the night and allowed Calypso to hop and lie next to his neck. Rhyl had a lovely neck. Calypso was no sparrow or robin; he was rather large, but still, he felt like he fit next to Rhyl quite perfectly.

A violent burst of shivering woke Calypso in the dead of night. Rhyl's magic-fed fire had burned to cold ash. The night breeze clutched at Calypso's skin, torturing his limbs—arms and legs, fingers and toes. Toes. He flexed his human hands and legs, wondering what kind of new nightmare this was. It felt so real.

It *was* real.

He was human.

And naked.

Rhyl slept peacefully beside him, wrapped in his thick cloak. Calypso carefully extricated himself from Rhyl's side. A deep blush warmed his face. Waking up beside Rhyl, the length of his body against Rhyl's, stirred things that had no business stirring. His body—gods, his very human body was *not* taking this seriously even with his skin covered in goose-prickles and the perpetual shivering.

He couldn't help imagining Rhyl waking and wrapping Calypso's trembling body in his cloak, his arms tight around him. Foolish thoughts. Rhyl allowed Calypso the- raven to sleep close to him, but Calypso the man would not have the same luxury. It was possible Rhyl would wake and toss him out in the cold, angry and disgusted. Calypso was beginning to believe he had dreamed that stupid drunken kiss the night of the full moon.

But *how* had he shifted? He'd thought—he'd *been told*—it was impossible outside the Forest. Scenarios and snatched knowledge circulated in his mind, but landed nowhere because he was too fucking cold.

Honey shuffled uneasily close by. The horse huffed, his shining dark eyes focused on something in the surrounding trees. His ears flattened. He pulled at his tether in alarm.

Something was moving in the undergrowth. Or at least, Calypso thought he heard footsteps. Calypso strained his frustratingly dull human hearing. Then it moved again. It sounded like an animal, but not small like a squirrel or mouse. Bigger. A bear, perhaps? A deer?

Then he felt it. The *varing*. And it wasn't coming from Rhyl or his carefully wrapped vercuri. It was coming from the night, from that sound, from that *thing* out there in the forest.

Then he saw it. Them. The dark made it impossible to count how many; his human sight was rubbish. But there was more than one, and one wanderer was one too many. Terror froze his voice for a moment. He managed to scream Rhyl's name before his raven form enveloped him.

CHAPTER 50

RHYL

RHYL WOKE TO CALYPSO screaming his name. No, sleep must have made him delusional; all he could hear was the rough screech of a raven. Rhyl scanned the dark, his heart beating like a war drum. Something thicker than the shadows, denser than anything natural, shuffled in the undergrowth.

Rhyl called fire, and light blazed around him. He grabbed the vercuri from its wrappings in one hand, and in his other he drew his sword. He couldn't see Calypso—Rhyl hoped the raven had flown to safety.

His fire created strange shadows that danced along the branches of the trees, illuminating something more…solid. His fire revealed the form of a person—no, a creature. Rhyl's mind couldn't put its pieces together. All his logic told him was *wrong*. Sharp canine teeth beneath wide flaring nostrils set in a human face. Its jaw was elongated. Its chest bare. Its arms furred. But its eyes, slivers of black *varing*, made Rhyl's mouth dry. Its shape was disjointed, like the *varing* took everything dangerous and fearsome about a wild animal and placed it uncaring on a human body, disguising any recognizable features.

A wanderer.

Rhyl felt his world crumble. Was it Calypso, corrupted and transformed while Rhyl slept? No, a flash of his fire reflected off glossy feathers above him, circling between the trees. Calypso was airborne.

The *varing* slid off the wanderer in waves. Rhyl breathed them into his body, knowing it would take all his strength to defeat the creature—creatures. More stepped out from the trees into his firelight, each as hideous and wrong as the last. Calypso dove at one of the wanderers, his raven scream loud and angry.

"Calypso, get out of here!" Rhyl yelled at the raven. What was Cally thinking? Compared to the wanderers, Calypso was a spider under a boot.

Honey burst his tether and bolted into the forest. The wanderers ignored the horse and continued to creep toward Rhyl, their heads low, their eyes fixed on him. Hunting him. Rhyl's fire was holding the monsters back, but he didn't think it would last. Calypso had told Rhyl the *varing* gave the wanderers strength, making them even more dangerous. Rhyl fed his magic to his fire and the blaze grew like its own monster.

Rhyl poured the *varing* into his *sanarii* magic. He wasn't sure why or how—it was almost instinctive—and holding the vercuri made it easy. His flames turned from red to bright blue and spread up the vercuri's blade. Rhyl swung the vercuri, and the fire leaped from the wooden blade toward the creatures with the grace of a sharp whip. Good. Rhyl swung again, this time concentrating to control the arc of magic. The fire surged, catching on the creatures.

Their howls of pain were horrifying. Rhyl wanted to put his hands over his ears and close his eyes, but instead he intensified the fire, focused its heat until it was almost a molten rope flowing from the vercuri. Despite their ragged screams, the creatures kept coming. One lunged for Rhyl's face. Rhyl blocked it with his arm, thrusting his elbow into its neck. The impact dazed the creature for a split second that Rhyl used to slice across its belly with his vercuri. Black, sticky blood spilled onto the moss. A smell rose from the dead creature, thick with rot and excrement, like the wanderer had been decomposing from the inside for weeks. Rhyl coughed, nearly retching as another leaped, then another. Rhyl crouched, slashed, just able to keep ahead of their incredible speed.

He didn't count how many fell until there was only one wanderer left. It didn't lunge for him like the others. It stood still, watching him with those dead, glassy eyes. The wanderer's form had hints of hoof and antler, but any beauty or grace had been replaced by the wrongness of the shape and shadow.

"*You* are the abomination," Rhyl whispered. He took a step toward the wanderer. It didn't move or flinch. Rhyl could hardly look at it, but he knew he needed to end the *velidar*'s suffering. The *varing* dripped from its ruined life. "Give it to me," Rhyl heard himself command. The wanderer crouched and raised its head, baring its neck to him, offering him its life, its magic. A thrill fluttered down Rhyl's spine as he sliced the beast's neck with the flaming vercuri and felt the *varing* fill him.

The roaring of Rhyl's fire magic was the only sound in the night.

Rhyl moved away from the corpses, sucking in breath after breath of night air. He let his flames gutter. The bodies–wolf, deer, hawk–were charred to the bone, almost impossible to discern against the blackened earth. The gratifying intoxication as the *varing* surged through his veins melted away, leaving sorrow.

Rhyl breathed out a sob and sank to his knees, then onto his elbows, his nose hovering above the ground. He wasn't sure if it was despair or fatigue that pounded his lungs like a hammer. Calypso landed beside him, his long sharp beak a hairbreadth from Rhyl's eye.

"Fuck," Rhyl said, breathless. "Fuck. Fuck. Fuck." Then he retched onto the moss.

CHAPTER 51
RHYL

"WE SHOULD SKIRT MAHLAS, hedge the mountains, and keep close to the trees in case we need cover," Rhyl told Calypso. Calypso chirped thoughtfully, snapping his beak. His missive of agreement. Or so Rhyl assumed. He didn't speak raven. Their one-way conversations were aggravating. If only he could mind-speak to Calypso as he could with Talo. He'd tried. It didn't work. Which wasn't a huge surprise. Rhyl could speak to Kitarrans with his magic, but Rhyl could not speak to the wolves or vice versa. Calypso's *velidar* magic was similar to Aiyan and Mila's, so it made sense he wouldn't be able to speak to Calypso. But it was no less disappointing.

Before them stretched the wide-open valley that was the Tarm. The mountains to the north were bare; the snowy peaks had melted under the summer sun. The forest was a deep green where it met the golden of the grassy Tarm. Far to the west, he could see the smudge of mountains that marked Kitarra.

Home. Rhyl could nearly taste the briny smell of the river that hung around Kilev in the summer. He could almost hear Talo's welcoming laughter.

The entirety of the Tarm still lay between Rhyl and the safety of Kitarra. He could not allow himself to feel comfortable. Even with his *sanarii* magic to help him see the road ahead, the Tarm was a dangerous place. And he had no way of knowing if they were being stalked by more wanderers. Nights were uncomfortable. Rhyl hadn't slept properly in the days since the attack. He debated reaching out to Stone or Talo. He yearned to. And he would, he decided, but not until Mahlas was behind him.

Calypso croaked and took off, his wings beating the air as he circled up and up. Rhyl closed his eyes and followed Calypso with his *sanarii* magic. It was not quite the same as flying, and he had no idea if Calypso could sense his presence. Like Calypso, he searched the road ahead for people and saw nothing. The way was clear. Reluctantly, Rhyl's consciousness returned to his body. As he rode, he kept the black speck that was Calypso in his sights.

Calypso kept to the skies for the better part of the morning, then disappeared. The raven would reappear shortly. Rhyl berated himself for worrying. No need to feel like a cat under a rocking chair, as Stone would say. And Calypso had been in a sour mood. Maybe the raven needed space. Rhyl was pretty sure Calypso was tired of his cooking. Or perhaps he was just tired. Rhyl sensed Calypso was plagued by nightmares, but Rhyl couldn't talk to him about it.

Calypso reappeared and flew low over Rhyl's head with a loud cry. Rhyl sagged in relief. Calypso circled back, flapping his wings anxiously. Rhyl decided to skip berating the raven for disappearing.

"What is it?" he asked.

Calypso flew a tight circle with more cries that almost sounded like Rhyl's name. Rhyl sighed, steering Honey off the road to follow the raven. The tall grass came up to Honey's knees. Calypso led Rhyl to a thicket of scrubby trees, a good place to make camp, but it was midday. What was the raven thinking? Rhyl wanted to put more miles behind him before stopping for the night.

Calypso perched in the tree and made a horrendous amount of noise.

"I'm coming!"

Calypso clearly wanted him to walk into the thicket.

Rhyl dismounted and scrambled through the tangling brush. Calypso hopped to the ground. Rhyl paused. Beside Calypso crouched a wolf, almost invisible in the leafy undergrowth with its tawny fur marked with brown. Rhyl reached for his dagger, his heart shuddering with panic, thinking of Calypso's neck crushed by the wolf's strong jaws. But no, the wolf's ears were pressed against its head in fear. And it was small for a wolf, and skinny—young, he realized. Just a pup. Rhyl put out his hands, a stupid instinctive gesture better for a person than an animal. The wolf stood a bit taller, ready to dart. It glanced at Calypso with dark, clever eyes. Damn, the wolf's eyes were like Mila's and Aiyan's—too clever for an animal.

The young wolf disappeared and a child—a girl—crouched in its place, her dark eyes round, her mouth quivering. Her skin was caked with dirt. Her thin arms wrapped around her shoulders.

Rhyl took his cloak and wrapped it around the child, slowly, careful not to scare her.

"He said you could help me." The girl's voice was small but had an edge to it.

"Who?"

"Calypso."

This girl could talk to Calypso. Rhyl blinked away the envy that briefly robbed him of speech. Useless emotion. This was a child, alone in the Tarm. A *heera* child.

"Who are you?"

"My name is Pena."

"Where did you come from?"

Her lips shook. A few tears ran down her face. She wiped her nose on Rhyl's cloak. She looked so cold. Rhyl piled a few sticks and set them on fire with a flick of his wrist. The girl's eyes widened further.

"You're Prince Rhyl," she whispered, her eyes flicking to his bright hair. "I have heard of you—and your magic."

Rhyl smiled at her. "Are you hungry?"

Surprisingly, she shook her head. "I'm a good hunter."

Rhyl swallowed his nausea at the thought. "Here, sit by the fire. Warm up."

"Thank you. I like your magic."

"I like yours."

She smiled shyly, moving closer to the fire, almost tripping over his long cloak. "You are right. He is quite nice." This she said to Calypso. She grimaced at Calypso's silent reply. "I can't speak to you in my head in this form. It's too hard." She sounded exhausted.

"Pena, I want to help you get home," Rhyl told her.

She sighed, her eyes drooping. "Papa told me to go to Kitarra." She lay down, curled up in Rhyl's cloak.

"Your father sent you off alone?" Outrage sparked in Rhyl's chest. Though she didn't get far. Mahlas was less than a days ride away.

She shook her head vigorously, her dirty hair moving like a wild thing. "He couldn't come with me. The door was locked. He was trapped. Him and …" She looked up at Rhyl with an expression he couldn't read. "Eva." Her eyes widened. "Eva is your mum, isn't she? You look like her. Papa says I look like *my* mum."

Rhyl sat down heavily beside her. "Where is she?"

"My mum is dead."

Rhyl shook his head. It was like having a conversation with his brothers. "I am so sorry to hear that, Pena. But where is *Eva*?"

"In Mahlas. With Papa."

Rhyl bit his lip. Pena's story sounded ludicrous, an unlikely fabrication that only Aralis and Bren could come up with. Being twins compounded their deviousness. Rhyl's heart hurt. "Pena, please tell me what you know of my mother."

Rhyl listened with clenched teeth as Pena told him about Eva's arrival in Attingard with "Uncle Vagar." She told Rhyl that she—Pena, not Eva—was going to Kitarra to learn about magic. Her voice bubbled as she told Rhyl she was going to meet a wolf just like her. They were traveling to Kitarra when they stopped in Mahlas where a "bad woman" said she was going to kill her if she tried to escape. She locked Papa and Eva away.

"You were very brave to get away, Pena."

Pena smiled, then yawned.

"Rest now, Pena." Rhyl patted her shoulder. She smiled at him, now full of trust. Calypso gave Rhyl a meaningful look before he hopped to settle beside her. She stroked the raven from head to tail like he was a cat. Another shock of envy rippled through Rhyl at the ease of affection she showed Calypso. He shrugged off his annoyance. Pena smiled, then closed her eyes and appeared to be deeply asleep. Poor thing.

Rhyl made sure the fire would not go out before walking to Honey. It seemed they were making camp for the night. And he needed to retrieve his second cloak from his saddlebag. The summer night was cool.

Outside the thicket, he sat in the long grass, letting the wind whip around him. Every gust made the grass hiss, eclipsing all other sounds. With the wind came the sound of horse hooves beating the earth and a child's scream. Not real. A memory. The scream was Talo's. Rhyl didn't have the energy to chase away the childhood memory invoked by the wind and the grass and seeing that poor lost child.

He had been younger than the wolf-girl by some years when Cotoch kidnapped him and Talo, holding them in Mahlas until Stone and Irri rescued them. Rhyl could hardly remember those few days of running across the Tarm, but he remembered his arms aching as he clung to Irri's back. It was only many years later that his parents told him the only reason they had escaped Cotoch that day was because Rhyl had killed their attackers with magic. And then he had healed Talo from near death.

It was too much power for the young boy he had been. It was too much power for him *now*. How many men had he killed already? How many more would he kill in his life? What kind of legacy was that?

He set the thought aside for another day and closed his eyes and reached for his *sanarii* magic. The *simul rami* came around him, lifting him away, connecting him to the wind. *Eva. Mother. Mummy.* He begged the magic to take him to her.

The *simul rami* took him to the city of Mahlas, to a large house where the hallways were patrolled by guards wearing red and black, a sigil of black feathers on their shoulders. Then a room. A bed. There a woman paced, her face lined, dark shadows under her eyes. *Mummy.*

A door opened, and a man fell into the room at Eva's feet. The door slammed shut, and the lock clicked in place. The man could barely keep himself from collapsing onto the floor. Eva looped her arm in his and helped him get to the bed and spoke his name. Rhyl felt the *varing* pulse through him in answer to his anger.

The man had dark hair, looked about the same age as Rhyl's parents, maybe a bit older. He opened his eyes; they were brown like the wolf-girl's. Cotoch.

Pena was wrong. She looked very much like her father.

CHAPTER 52

CALYPSO

CALYPSO WATCHED RHYL leave the thicket with the subtlety of a storm cloud. Understandably, Rhyl was upset and confused about what Pena had told them about his mother. Rhyl would search for the truth in the *simul rami*.

Calypso was torn. Rhyl was vulnerable when he was gripped by *sanarii* magic. But Calypso knew there was no one for miles, and right now, the girl—Pena—needed his presence more than Rhyl. And if Calypso was being honest, Rhyl didn't really need him at all. It was impossible to ignore Rhyl's petulant looks. Having Calypso around frustrated the prince, he could tell.

Rhyl didn't return to the thicket until nearly dark. Calypso was just about to leave to go find him when Rhyl thrashed his way through the dense tangle of trees.

"Calypso." Rhyl's voice cracked. "My mother is being held captive in Mahlas."

Pena woke at Rhyl's harsh voice.

It's okay, Calypso told her. *He is just upset because he worries about his mother.* Calypso crooned to let Rhyl know he was listening.

"What is your papa's name, Pena?" Rhyl asked, his eyes sharp.

"King Cotoch."

Rhyl looked like he might scream and pull his hair out by the roots. But instead of raging, he kept calm, but stern, reminding Calypso of Illiah. Pena shrank into Rhyl's cloak. Calypso wondered if she was on the verge of shifting.

Calypso knew who Cotoch was and what he had done to Rhyl's family. The Allmakers had shown him Cotoch's evil deeds in the *simul rami*. Eva's hurt was not only Rhyl's to carry; Calypso cared for the *sanarii* princess too.

Rhyl fixed his blue-green eyes on Calypso, his face still reflecting his inner storm. "What was my mother doing with Cotoch? She looked *concerned* for him, Cally. It doesn't make sense. I searched for answers, but I still don't understand." He put his head in his hands. "I have to get her out of there."

"And my papa?" Pena asked.

Rhyl's face twitched, but Calypso doubted Pena could see Rhyl's disgust. "I can't promise anything, Pena."

Calypso cursed his inability to speak to Rhyl. How did Rhyl think he was going to get Eva and Cotoch out of Mahlas? Why was Cotoch captive? He'd thought Mahlas was Cotoch's city. It didn't make sense. He didn't know much about Mahlas or how far they were from it. He didn't know anything. He was just a raven. Or worse, a man stuck in a raven's body.

Not for the first time, his bird form chaffed. His feathers itched. He had shifted that night the wanderers came, but since then, nothing. Calypso was beginning to accept waking up next to Rhyl in his human form had been a concoction of his rebellious imagination. Maybe he was slowly descending into madness.

"Can you tell me about the people who locked you up?" Rhyl asked Pena, fishing around in his pack for some food. He gave Calypso a handful of nuts and dried meat. Pena ate a couple of nuts, but she still claimed she wasn't hungry.

"I don't know. Eva knew the man—the other king. But they still locked us up."

"What was his name? What did he look like?"

Pena scrunched up her face, stroking Calypso's back with her fingers. "He was tall. Dark hair. Old, like Papa, but not *old*. His name was…Caed?

Cael? I can't remember." She looked like she was going to cry. Calypso crooned, tickling her finger with his beak. Pena smiled.

"Caeris?" Rhyl asked.

"Maybe?"

Rhyl bit his lip. "How is that possible?" he thought out loud. Rhyl's eyes danced with malice and desperation. Calypso wanted to reach out and press Rhyl against his chest and tell him it was all right. But he couldn't because he was a fucking raven. And also because it was a gesture Rhyl might not appreciate.

"What is it, Cally? You have grumpy written all over your face."

Calypso let out a squawk that was all frustrated rage. Pena jumped, pulling the cloak around her.

"What does he say?" Rhyl asked Pena, alarmed.

"Nothing."

Calypso hopped into flight and dove past Rhyl into the high branches of the thicket where he was hidden by the night. He broke off small sticks with his beak and shredded them. His raven body had never felt so tight and uncomfortable. He didn't know how to shift. He'd tried. Every night, he'd tried. And failed.

CHAPTER 53

RHYL

RHYL'S MIND was on the verge of shattering like fine glass. He had to get his mother out of Mahlas. The thought of her captive, in danger, far from any help, locked in a room with Cotoch, made him both furious and terrified. There wasn't time to call for help. He would not wait idly for his father and Stone to come to the rescue. Not when he could get her out.

A plan churned in his mind, but his concentration strayed. Calypso didn't leave his roost high up in the thicket, and Rhyl couldn't think of a way to coax him down.

In the morning, Calypso continued to act peculiar. The frustrated look on the raven's face was obvious. Maybe Calypso regretted leaving the Great Forest. Rhyl *had* tried to stop him, but the stubborn bird had come, anyway. Maybe Rhyl should've sent him back after Stonyhill.

Rhyl shook the raven out of his thoughts. He needed to concentrate on the task at hand.

The best chance Rhyl had to rescue his mother was to infiltrate Mahlas at night, using the cover of darkness as his ally. He searched the *simul rami* and discovered what he could about his mother's situation and the city of Mahlas. Between fervent bouts of planning, he fed Pena and Calypso. Pena offered to hunt him a rabbit. He declined. He wasn't about to send a little girl out to hunt, but he didn't say it out loud.

At daybreak, Rhyl asked Calypso to stay with Pena. He told them that if he didn't meet them by nightfall the next day at the edge of the forest, they were to go to Kitarra without him.

He left the thicket on foot, leaving Honey with Pena and Calypso. If need be, Pena could set the horse loose and Pena could run as a wolf to Kitarra. Calypso would fly above and keep the girl safe. The two of them could make their way to Kitarra together.

He didn't look back.

As night fell, the wind died down and it was quiet. The tall walls of Mahlas were dark against the vast expanse of stars. The gatehouse was the only bright point in the night. The farms hedging the town looked asleep, lights extinguished. Or had everyone withdrawn inside the city?

The vercuri hummed at his belt. He flexed his fingers as the *varing* called to him. Oh, how his mother would disapprove of what he was about to do with magic. But he would burn down the whole damn city if necessary to get her out.

Rhyl's dark cloak made him invisible, enabling him to approach the gate unseen. He took a moment to observe the three guards huddled around a fire at the gate. It really was cold for summer. Every so often, the guards would peer into the night, probably out of duty or boredom. Rhyl reached with his magic. He could feel their pulses, their lifeblood.

Rhyl had learned the basics of how the human body worked from Aiyan. He knew what happened when a person was stabbed in the heart versus the arm. He knew about the organs and that a person had a finite amount of blood and that a body needed air to breathe and what happened when that airway was blocked. His father and Stone had continued the lesson by teaching him how to use the body's weakness to greatest effect with blades and muscle. But Rhyl also had magic.

Rhyl used *sanarii* magic to pull the air from the men's lungs. He watched them try to catch a breath, eyes bulging in fear. One by one, they dropped. Rhyl instantly released his hold and dashed forward. He didn't want to kill them, if he could avoid it. A choke hold was something taught in the Forge, but it didn't last long, magically induced or not. And if the guards saw him, he would have to kill them.

Rhyl leaped past the unconscious guards, thanked the Guardians he didn't have to waste time with the gate's locks—it was wide open—and made his way into the dark city.

More guards patrolled the gloomy streets. But Rhyl was not concerned. He'd trained with his father and Stone and Aiyan, all of them fucking legends. He made slow progress toward Cotoch's house, but he was not seen.

As Rhyl walked, moving from dark shadow to dark shadow, a growing sense came over him. Pulled him. The *varing*. He could not fathom the source, but he found himself following the pull, down a side alley, down another dark road. He crouched low at the entrance to another courtyard. In the dark, he could just make out darker shadows, moving, shuffling, a groan here or there. People.

A sense of terror swept over Rhyl. They just stood there, swaying slightly, as if asleep on their feet. Rhyl could not count how many; they were crowded into the courtyard, several hundred, perhaps. He knew they were *revenant*s. By the *varing* consuming them, by some dark instinct that he, as the child of the prophecy, possessed, he knew. His visions in the *simul rami* had not shown him this horror.

He crept up to a man of middle years. He got close enough to see the man's face, his clothes. Rhyl lit the smallest light in his palm, holding it up to illuminate the poor soul. The person did not flinch in the sudden light, did not move. The man licked his lips. Something about the simple, primal gesture made Rhyl's skin crawl. His eyes caught on the bright weave of the man's tunic, now filthy, covered in grime. It was distinctly a knit from the mountain men near Withe. Rhyl doused his light and backed slowly the way he'd come. A terrible premonition burned like acid in his heart. Kitarrans. The missing Kitarrans his parents worried about. *Revenant*s. But why were they here, herded like sheep, deep in some sort of unnatural trance, in Mahlas?

Rescuing his mother seemed even more important. What if she somehow became like those poor people? A husk, a shell of her former self?

Rhyl retraced his steps and made his way toward Cotoch's house. He calmed his breathing and focused on the task at hand. Find his mother. Get her the fuck out of this cursed city.

Even if Rhyl had not seen it in the *simul rami*, the main house was impossible to miss. He went around to a servants' entrance, which was also guarded, but only by one guard. Rhyl used his magic once more, but this guard he gagged and tied, wrists and ankles, and stuffed him in a dark corner.

Inside the house, the lanterns had been extinguished for the night. Rhyl fought to get his bearings. He didn't want to call fire to light his way. He needed to be a shadow in the night. Pena's insights about the layout of the house had been vague and had not included the servants' wing, but Rhyl found the main hall and managed to remain unseen by several patrol guards as he made his way upstairs. So many guards.

All the doors looked the same. Rhyl ran his hand through his hair, groaning inwardly. He needed to find her. He needed to get out of this house before an alarm was raised. Maybe he should have killed the gate-keepers outright. Maybe he should have set the city wall on fire. That would have been a good distraction. He had considered it.

The floorboards creaked under his step. Rhyl cursed silently and moved on slowly. Around a corner, a single lantern illuminated two guards standing outside a door. They looked half-asleep at their posts. Rhyl stepped and the board beneath his boot groaned. The guards turned and saw him.

"*Fuck*," Rhyl whispered to himself.

One guard charged while the other ran off in the opposite direction. Rhyl could hope it was out of cowardice, but more likely he was sounding the alarm. Rhyl unsheathed his sword. The guard already had his drawn. He was fast and huge, but he was no expert. Rhyl swerved easily and plunged his sword into the man's gut. He didn't have time to do anything else. It all happened so quickly. Magic. Rhyl should have used magic.

The door was locked. The key was…damn, who knew where. Rhyl

kicked the door handle. Hard. Pain radiated up his leg from the effort. But the wood splintered and the metal fell to the floor with a clang.

His mother was inside. Her face registered her shock.

"Rhyl!" Her voice was part rage, part love part *I can't believe you are this reckless.*

"Hello, Mummy Dear."

CHAPTER 54

EVA

"WHAT IS THAT NOISE?" Cotoch said, sitting up with a grunt.

Eva heard it too. Like waves pummeling the walls of the hallway, then their door. The hinges splintered as the door fell. The figure in the doorway was haloed by light and magic, his starlit hair framing his face like a living thing.

"Hello, Mummy Dear."

"Rhyl!" Eva exclaimed. Her son cocked his head, his sideways grin so like his father's. She wanted to rage at him. She wanted to inspect him for injuries. She wanted to hold him close to make sure he was intact. "What are you *doing* here?"

"Rescuing you, of course."

His presence opened a wound of terror in her heart, but also joy. So much joy. She took his face in her hand and kissed him on his brow, his cheek. "Foolish boy!"

"We need to get out of here," Rhyl hissed, transforming from her little boy into a warrior. He looked past her at Cotoch, his eyes icy.

"He comes with us," Eva said. "Can you do it, Cotoch?" His injuries were raw, and Eva was fairly certain he had several cracked ribs.

"Yes."

Rhyl looked Cotoch over with a glint, a sharp edge Eva had not seen before. She didn't like it. No more did she like the dead guard in the hall. Her son, her dear son, a murderer. No, a warrior. A protector. Like his father. But still, she wanted to wrap Rhyl in her cloak and shield him from his own power.

Cotoch took the dead man's sword. "This way," he gestured, his voice weak.

"The trail up the hill," Rhyl concluded.

"Yes." A ghost of a rueful smile crossed Cotoch's lips.

"No. We need to go to the crypts," Eva argued.

Both men stopped in their tracks.

"Eva, are you insane?" Cotoch spat.

"We will not get another chance to talk to Tsuga."

"Tsuga." Rhyl said the name like it meant something. "The old spirit."

"Yes," Eva answered anyway.

Rhyl chewed the inside of his mouth. "You think she knows where the other vercuri are?"

"I do. So does Cotoch."

"There are a few hidden doors. We might be able to get down there and then out without anyone knowing," Cotoch told them.

"As long as Allia and Caeris haven't found the doors."

"Right."

"So Pena was right about Caeris," Rhyl muttered.

Cotoch looked at him sharply. "Pena? Where is she?"

"Safe," Rhyl assured him.

"Quiet. We need to move silently," Eva reminded them.

Cotoch led them to the end of an old hall. The plaster on the walls was peeling around a large fraying tapestry. Cotoch pushed it aside and pressed against the wall. Nothing happened.

"Rhyl, Eva, push. I can't—" He was too weak.

Eva helped Rhyl push the wall, and slowly it gave way to form a small door. Beyond, was darkness. Footsteps reverberated down the hallway. Many footsteps. The house was waking up.

Eva wondered if they were trapping themselves. This was a terrible idea. Then it was too late to turn back. Rhyl pushed the door closed behind them. It was like being eaten by silence and dark.

"Anyone think to bring a lantern?" Cotoch quipped, his voice shaky.

Rhyl lit a fire in the palm of his hand, casting shadows around the rough-hewn passage.

"Ah."

"How do we call her?" Eva asked.

"With a vercuri," Cotoch replied, looking at Rhyl.

"But—" Eva let the argument die when Rhyl put his hand on the sheath at his belt. "You took Kitarra's vercuri?"

Rhyl gave her a look. Illiah's sardonic gaze peeked from Rhyl's eyes. "Stone gave it to me."

"Call her," Cotoch said, his voice strained.

Rhyl closed his eyes, and Eva guessed he was calling Tsuga with his *candarii* magic. It was not a call with the voice, but with the *varing*. Eva could feel it permeate the dark, coiling around her senses. She felt Cotoch's eyes on her, assessing. She bit her lip.

Rhyl opened his eyes and they were black, eclipsed with *varing*. Eva pressed her hand against her mouth to stop her gasp of horror.

"There is no one here," Rhyl announced. "The crypts are empty."

CHAPTER 55

COTOCH

"IMPOSSIBLE," Cotoch spat. The spirit woman couldn't die or she would have done so under his knife long ago. Neither could she escape. Cotoch peered into the dark, knowing how futile it was. He wouldn't see her. Only the vercuri could bring her to him.

"Are you sure?" Eva asked her son.

"No. Yes. I don't know." Rhyl rubbed his forehead. The boy was clearly exhausted. "Here, try it for yourself."

Rhyl handed him the vercuri. Cotoch did not think it was because the prince-ling trusted him. It was because Rhyl knew Cotoch was suffering and weak, and if it came to it, there would be no contest between them.

But the boy was right. Tsuga was not in the crypts. He gave Rhyl back the vercuri.

If Tsuga was gone…how? She had been trapped in this eternal dark for years and years. If the stories were to be believed, she had cursed herself. Cotoch had not seen the spirit woman since he left for Allati. Being king had changed him. Ana had changed him. He had long given up any desire to be in the crypts. They were a nightmare. A testament to his darker side and the urges of *candarii* magic. Urges he had fought since he fell in love with an Allati woman.

"Now what?"

"Follow me. There are many paths and doors in and out of these crypts."

Cotoch led them slowly through the dark.

"What's down here?" Rhyl asked, moving toward a corridor, away from Cotoch's guidance, taking his meager *sanarii* light with him.

"Much of the same," Cotoch muttered. He almost stumbled on the uneven ground. Allia had fucked him up. He was so tired. His legs didn't always follow his command. Eva had used her *sanarii* magic to heal the worst of Allia's torture, but still, Cotoch was weak as a babe and every step brought his pain to life. "Rhyl, stop!" Cotoch's shout bounced off the rocks.

Rhyl did, holding his hand in front of him. His fire flared and revealed the dark pit he had almost stepped into. It wasn't bottomless, but it would have been a nasty fall. Rhyl's light danced across things in the pit. Eva turned away, but Rhyl did not. He leaned forward, his light flaring. Cotoch knew what he would see.

"There are bones of *people* down there," Rhyl said, his voice an icy threat.

"Come, we need to move on. We are almost there," Cotoch said, his voice quiet. Their chance of escaping Mahlas was dwindling. Possibly gone. In the dark, it felt like time ceased to exist, but that was an illusion. Above them, Allia and Caeris would be searching, guards would be swarming. "This way will lead us close to the back wall and the track up the hill. Let's hope there aren't too many guards between us and the Tarm," he told them.

They came to the end of a passageway. Cotoch was thankful after all these years that he could still tell one from another. The door was old and small, but the latch turned. Cotoch pushed it open a hairbreadth and peered through the chink. Then he closed it.

"There are three guards in the hall."

"I can take three guards," Rhyl said. Confident bastard. Like his father.

"Sure." Cotoch had seen the aftermath of Rhyl's abilities. He admitted Rhyl's confidence was not hollow. Again Eva looked like she wanted to say something, but held her tongue. "Ready?" Cotoch asked.

"Ready."

They burst through the door. Rhyl made for the guards and took them down in three strikes. Incredibly fast. Cotoch felt a pinch of envy. He was good with a blade, but he had never been that good. Like water flowing over rock, with furious power and grace. Fucking child of the prophecy.

"This way." Cotoch led them down the hall. The lanterns were bright. The relief of being out of the crypts was a heady thing.

They halted where the hallway intersected.

"This way. Follow the hall, take the stairs at the end. The door is behind the painting with the boat and stars," Cotoch whispered.

"Hey! You there!" a guard shouted. More were coming around the corner.

Rhyl charged forward, his sword cutting a swath through the armed men. But more men came from behind. How much of Allia's army was descending on them? They were nearly trapped.

"Go. I will hold them off," Rhyl said.

"Foolish boy. *I* will hold them off," Cotoch growled.

Rhyl opened his mouth to argue. Cotoch was right to call him foolish. But Eva grabbed her son by the sleeve and pulled him along with her down the hall, leaving Cotoch to the guards.

Four guards. Cotoch held his sword aloft and squared his stance. It was a bluff; he was ready to crumble. He swung as they tackled him. They should have overpowered him, but he managed to take them down. Maybe he wasn't as weak as he thought. Or maybe he was merely lucky. Maybe his *heera* ancestors were watching over him. His breathing was labored but he was still standing, wasn't he? He hoped Rhyl and Eva had found the door. He hoped he had bought them enough time.

Allia's *daeum* Kitarran appeared in the hallway. For a moment, Cotoch's exhausted brain thought it was Stone, but then he remembered that Stone was in Kitarra. Stone had betrayed him not once, but twice. Then he realized that was a long time ago, and he was a changed man. Then he realized he was about to die.

The Kitarran, Liam, was Allia's henchman, her slave. Her *daeum*. For days, the young Kitarran had wrenched Cotoch's pain at Allia's command. Now, the Kitarran monster stalked Cotoch, a long, pointed dagger his weapon of choice. He was young, younger than Stone had been when Cotoch found him. But this Kitarran boy was big and strong, not the half-starved drowned desperate thing Stone had been. His eyes were colder than ice carried on the wind.

Cotoch swung to block the Kitarran's strike. He was too slow. The Kitarran's blade scraped down his and swung up to meet Cotoch's flesh. Warmth flooded his chest. A sharp pain made him hunch as the Kitarran drew back, his blade covered in Cotoch's red, red blood. Cotoch stumbled against the wall, leaning heavily on his shoulder, trying not to slide to the floor. He coughed out a mouthful of blood. His lungs wouldn't take in air. He was drowning in a sea of knives. His head hit the ground. At least his death would be quick. At least he would not die on Allia's table.

CHAPTER 56

ASHA

ASHA TUCKED HER KNIVES into the pouch at her belt. The mere presence of her throwing knives felt both treacherous and comforting. She'd bought the knives secretly at one of Kilev's summer markets. The merchant's stall had been filled with miscellaneous items, not just weapons. The seller had been a seedy man with greasy hair and bad teeth. Not the kind of person likely to spread gossip or ask questions about her purchase.

In Rodan, Asha had been forced to give up her knives when she left for Kitarra. Her master had insisted that no one in Kitarra could know she had been trained to kill. No one could know how deadly she was. Master instructed her to act shy, to be soft around the edges. But Asha's knives had been her one possession that meant something to her. She'd desperately missed practicing. She'd missed the concentration of the aim, the strain in her arm, and the metal against her palms, the satisfaction as her blade hit the target with deadly precision. With her blades, she was in control.

She wished she could show Talo.

The Queen's Keep was built against the mountain; the forest rambled right up to the palace walls. Over the weeks since Asha's arrival, she'd ferreted out paths and secret places. Her favorite was down an old path. The overgrown moss and ferns showed its disuse. At the end of the little path was a clearing beneath a cliff, overhung with arching trees and ferns. In the clearing was a forgotten statue—a stone sword with flowers carved to look like they were growing over the hilt. The stone was green with moss. An old stump close by provided the perfect target for Asha's knives.

Asha approached the clearing, already pulling her knives from her pouch, eager to sink their blades into the stump. This time she was confident she would cluster them all with two fingers' width. She didn't notice the other Kitarran until she was nearly on top of him. She hastily shoved her pouch closed. Her lack of observation was a failure. The Kitarran stood with his back to her, one hand resting on the statue. But he'd heard her and spun, his yellow eyes narrowed. Asha's eyes flicked to his hand, which curled around something she couldn't see.

"Prince Arrain," Asha garbled. "I'm sorry—I didn't mean to interrupt." And it was clear she *was* interrupting. The prince's face was taut, his mouth a firm line.

Then his expression softened. "It's all right, Asha. It's a good spot, is it not?"

"It is. I often come here."

"Oh?"

"I feel safe here." Asha didn't know why she said it, but it was the truth. Talo's father seemed the kind of man one spoke truthfully with.

"I've only come here a few times," he said quietly, letting his hand slip from the statue.

Asha felt she was missing something. "What is this place?" she asked.

"Do you not know?" His voice was kind. Asha shook her head. "This is Talo's mother's—Emri's—grave." His face looked anguished. His wife, Talo's mother, had died when Talo was born. Could he really grieve for a woman dead all these years? Was that love?

Asha moved to stand beside the prince and looked at the statue as if for the first time. She put her hand on the moss-covered stone. There was no name, no indicator of its purpose. "I wish I'd known that."

Prince Arrain smiled sadly. He was still holding something. He shifted it to his other hand. Asha smelled something; it came from that strange vial he held. It smelled like…It smelled like *Her.*

"What is it, Asha?"

Asha flattened her expression. She wanted to assure him it was nothing. "What are you holding?" she asked instead.

Arrain held up the vial like he just remembered he had been holding it.

"This is my secret." Then his eyes glanced at the stump pocketed with knife marks and back at Asha, but he didn't say anything. "It's culla powder. A potent herb rendered into a drug. It either enslaves or kills. Have you seen it before?"

"Why do you have it?"

He sighed. "Talo hasn't told you?"

"Nothing about this."

Arrain's mouth twitched into a less gentle smile. "I was once a slave to an evil man. Through this drug, he held me hostage. Or so I thought. But actually, I held my own chain. I still do." He held up the vial. The gray powder caught the light and looked almost molten. "If I don't take this, I will die. And after all these years, my body is starting to feel its strain."

His hand shook as he held the glass vial. He opened it and a strong waft assaulted Asha. It *was* familiar. Asha had to fight the panic the smell induced. She could almost feel her master's hands on her face, her master's magic in her mind, twisting her body and her will. The smell was a cage. She wanted to run, but something, Arrain's sorrow, perhaps, kept her feet firm.

Asha watched with mild horror as Arrain put a small pinch of the gray powder on his palm and then in his mouth.

"Do you come here to talk to Emri?" Asha asked a few minutes later.

"No."

Asha was sure it was a lie. But it did not make her respect him less. Lies were necessary sometimes. Lies were what kept one alive.

"Why do you come here, Asha?"

It was a test. But if she told Arrain the truth, she didn't know what would happen. Her master was a fickle, cruel person, and Asha might wake to find her master had done something irreparable. She might wake to find Talo's lifeblood on her fur, on her knives.

If she lied to Arrain, she would continue to betray Talo and his family.

But if she told Arrain the truth, he could lock her up, put her behind bars where she wouldn't be a danger. She turned to Arrain to open her mouth, to beg him to do just that, but she couldn't make the words form on her tongue. Her mind became sludge, blinking between consciousness and dreams. And the smell. Her master's magic wrapped around her will, her mind, taking the last of her freedom with her speech.

CHAPTER 57

AIYAN

AIYAN COULDN'T SLEEP.

The night was filled with sounds. His open window allowed his wolf hearing to pick up the soft noises of the Healer's Hall. The murmurs of nurses and healers, the groans of patients, and the occasional scream of a woman in labor. He trusted his healers. They were exceptional at what they did. No, his unease was from something else. Something unseen. Something only his wolf could sense.

With Queen Arrah's blessing, the healer's hall was built beside the public bath house, and Aiyan and Mila's house had been built behind that, right against the forest. Beyond the sounds of the Healer's Hall, Aiyan could hear crickets, owls, a few optimistic frogs.

He sat up. The blanket fell off his shoulders and he shivered. Even Kitarra's summers were cold compared to the heat of Rodan. Aiyan wondered if he would ever truly grow accustomed to it.

"What is it?" Mila asked, her voice muffled by the blanket as she rolled toward him, a bare leg looping over his. His heart still thrummed with excitement knowing Mila had chosen him. Over and over, she had embraced him with her love, her body, her mind. She shared his journey embracing his *heera* nature, and together they had started the Healer's Hall. Without her, he would never have found his way back to the gentle nature within his *heera* ancestry.

But he wasn't sure she could help him now.

"It's Asha," Aiyan told her.

Mila groaned. "Talo's little Kitarran?"

"She is not what she claims."

"I know." Mila surprised him by answering. "But she is hurt, traumatized. And if she won't let us in, how can we help her?"

Aiyan ran his thumb over his bottom lip. "I want to help her."

"You are the most patient man I know, Aiyan." Mila rubbed her hand down his back. "The most skilled hunter. You know what you need to do."

When Aiyan turned back to Mila, she was asleep, her mop of black hair curling onto his pillow. Aiyan smiled. She had always had more faith in him than he had in himself. It was why, after all their years together, he still did not deserve her.

He could find out the truth about Asha. It would be simple. All it would take is a subtle touch and more subtle magic. With skin to skin contact, Aiyan could use his *heera* magic to read a person's memories, find out anyone's most dangerous secrets. He did it very rarely. He despised prying into people's vulnerable thoughts and emotions. It was violating, and Aiyan wanted no part of that.

But was Asha a danger? He didn't know. He wished he had the ability to search for answers in visions like a *sanarii*. If Rhyl were home, Aiyan would ask the boy for help. A wave of misgiving hardened inside Aiyan. Rhyl was a capable young man, but they still all worried about him. He hoped Rhyl would come home soon.

CHAPTER 58

EVA

EVA WAS AFRAID she would lose the track. It was narrow, and the rocks were loose and they couldn't keep a light, it was too risky. Dawn was still a ways away, for which Eva was thankful. The bright lights of Mahlas below hid them in the shadows. They needed the cover of darkness to shield them until they reached the forest. But she kept glancing behind her, straining her eyes to make sure Rhyl was still close.

Eva tried to keep her mind on her footing. The ground was uneven and it was dark, dark, dark. After days and days of confinement, the wide expanse of sky called to her. With the wind in her face and the stars above, she felt a bit giddy. She wanted to swing her arms wide and call the energy of the night to her. But she kept her mind on the path, moving as fast as she could.

She thought of Cotoch, left behind, to what fate she didn't know. She did not mourn him, but she did silence the cruel voice in her mind saying he had finally earned redemption.

At the top of the hill, the dead cendari tree greeted them.

"This way," Rhyl said, tugging her sleeve for her to follow. Rhyl led her through the tall grass toward the looming shapes of the mountains. The forest was a dark swath before them. Dawn was coming. They reached the forest, and the trees wrapped around them like a shield against the brightening sky. Eva allowed herself to breathe. Rhyl, too, seemed to relax. He halted, bent over, his hands on his knees.

"Rhyl, are you all right?" Eva asked, rubbing his back.

"Cotoch is dead," he whispered. "I saw him fall."

Eva hissed through her teeth but stopped herself from berating Rhyl for wasting energy on *seeing*. "He died so we could escape," she stated.

"A hero's death. Will that make it easier for Pena?" Rhyl looked up at her, his eyes bright in the faint light.

"How did you find Pena?"

A ghost of a smile played on his lips. "It's a long story."

Eva wrapped her arm around Rhyl's shoulders and squeezed. He leaned into her. The comforting touch was lulling, but they both knew they needed to keep moving.

She saw Honey first. Her son's horse stood patiently tethered to a tree. Then she saw the wolf. A leggy thing the color of bark and fall leaves with brown eyes. It whined and bounced over to them. Rhyl glanced up at the trees. Pena shifted, her face ashen.

"Papa?" she asked. Pena read Rhyl's expression and her lip wobbled.

Rhyl bent down. "I'm sorry, Pena."

Pena burst into tears. She waved Eva away when Eva tried to tuck the girl into her arms. Pena shifted into a wolf and skulked under the trees.

"Will she run?" Eva asked Rhyl.

"I don't think so," Rhyl murmured. Pena just turned her back to them like the most rejected creature in existence. Eva's heart broke.

"Rhyl, we should go to the Vale. We can rest there and call reinforcements."

"You know how to get there?"

"I think so."

Rhyl nodded. He looked like he was about to fall. He leaned on Honey.

"Rhyl, sweetheart."

"We need to press on, Mum," Rhyl said. "You ride Honey."

"No, you need to ride more than I."

Rhyl glowered. Eva was about to argue—**she** and Rhyl had always excelled at arguments—when a raven swooped down, giving Eva a fright.

The raven landed on Honey's saddle, which Rhyl had yet to occupy. "Mum, do you remember Calypso?"

She gave her son a look. Rhyl had listened to enough of her stories to know she would never forget her raven, how she missed him even after so many years.

"Wait, are you saying this is Calypso?" Eva asked dumbly. The raven looked at her with knowing eyes. Eyes too clever and too shrewd for any common bird. Eyes that brought back memories. Joy suffused the old ache like a balm. How was this possible? She wanted to demand explanations, but Rhyl looked dead on his feet. And there was an army behind them and a man who had given his life for their escape.

Eva wanted to hold Calypso and tell him how much she had missed him. She wanted to hug Rhyl and never let go. She wanted to tell Pena it wouldn't hurt forever. But there was no time. They needed to move. They needed to be soldiers because there was a mad queen behind them. There was no room for hesitation. Not if they were to survive long enough to get to Kitarra.

CHAPTER 59

EVA

EVA HAD FAITH they would find the secret way into Tayeh's Vale. It was a testament to Rhyl's exhaustion that he didn't question her as she paused several times, hesitating about the direction. Eva doubted enough for both of them. It felt like a lifetime ago since she had been there with Stone, and Stone had been the one to lead her. She had been hurt, her body and mind.

But the Vale was a place of magic, after all. Tayeh's place. And she could feel it pulling her.

It wasn't until she saw the rock, the one that still looked remarkably like a bull even after a dozen years, that she breathed a sigh of relief. By the time they reached the Vale's entrance, the sky was bright and the sun danced in the morning mist that lay about the forest, mist that grew thicker as they approached.

"This way," she encouraged. The path descended quickly. Soon they were wading through ferns, making their way down to the bottom of the valley where the hot creek poured through the cave and met the mossy forest.

"It's exactly how I imagined it from Stone's stories," Rhyl exclaimed. Eva smiled.

The Vale was narrow, and at its bottom the creek poured from a maw in the side of the hill. Inside, the cave was tall and wide and bright. The floor was smooth rock and sand. A small section of the cave had been carved into a living space with a level stone floor, an ancient wooden table, old chests, and a place to sleep. It was remarkably free from signs of rodent habitation.

Rhyl let Honey's reins drop at the entrance to the cave where there was a bit of mossy grass.

The little room built into the cave was dusty from neglect with leaves piled in corners. Eva pointed Rhyl in the direction of the sleeping alcove. He didn't complain about her ordering him around. Rhyl pulled his sleeping furs with him but didn't utter a word. He closed his eyes and Eva was certain he was asleep instantly.

"Come, Pena, look at this." Eva coaxed the young wolf over to where the creek poured out of the rock. It had not changed in the years since Eva had been in the Vale. She blinked, thinking of how hurt and ill-minded she had been. Because of Cotoch. Because of Pena's father.

Pena sniffed the water, and her ears perked a bit.

"Come bathe with me? It will feel wonderful."

Pena looked thoughtful, then shook her head and slunk back to sit at the entrance.

Eva stripped off her clothes and sank into the hot pool. Gold glinted from the rock like stars. The element called to her magic. She'd spent years ignoring the *simul rami*'s pull. But she had used it to help Cotoch, her enemy, like a snared fox gnawing off its own leg to survive. They would not have escaped Mahlas without Cotoch's help. Being Allia's prisoner was a fate she refused to contemplate. But now in the Vale without imminent danger, she was afraid of her magic. She could wait for Rhyl to wake and let him call Talo or Stone.

I have become a coward, she thought.

No, she would call Stone. She owed her amourii that. He and Illiah would come with a host of soldiers. They would march to the ends of the earth to find her.

Illiah.

His absence was a constant ache. Since leaving Kitarra, she'd done her best to push him from her thoughts. And knowing she had left him willingly, without saying goodbye, hurt like a festering cut. She wondered if he was still angry with her. Of course he would be. But would he forgive her, at least a little, when she saw him again? Part of her wanted to melt into his strong embrace. Part of her recoiled from telling him what their son had done in Mahlas, to rescue *her*. Guilt settled over her. She shivered thinking of Rhyl's eyes, black with *varing*. If she had not gone to Allati, she would never have been in Mahlas, and Rhyl would not have felt the need to rescue her.

Somehow, not even one season had passed since she had seen him, and Rhyl looked so much older. He was…a warrior. A man. But he would always be her child, her little one that she had lost and found.

She wanted to ask Rhyl about his journey. Cotoch had told her Rhyl had left Kilev, heading southeast, but his *candarii* visions couldn't tell him more. Eva had her suspicions. And Calypso's presence almost confirmed them.

Calypso left Pena's side where the young wolf lay, a fuzzy brown blob, in the sun. Calypso hopped to the edge of the pool, a rock in his beak. Eva laughed softly. Calypso dropped the rock into the water. Eva fished it out with her toe and gave it back to him. He crooned. It was a game they had played years ago at the Keep. Eva shook the water off her hand so she could run a finger down his glossy feathers.

"Where did Rhyl find you?" Eva marveled. "And how did you know him after all these years, a man grown?"

The raven's expression looked defeated.

"I missed you, Cally. Every time I saw a raven fly by, I would think of you. Every. Time."

Calypso made a funny chirp-thrum noise in his throat. He hopped back across the stone floor to Pena.

It was time.

Eva closed her eyes and used the magic of the mineral spring to search for Stone. Like using a stiff muscle to swing a sword, it hurt. But it came easier than she expected. She had missed him.

Eva!

Stone.

Where the fuck are you?

She had expected Illiah to be furious with her, but she hadn't expected such raw anger from Stone.

In the Vale. With Rhyl and Cotoch's daughter and a raven.

I can't wait to hear this story, he clipped. *Are you all right?*

I'm fine.

Where were you?

I went with Vagar to Allati. Then Cotoch and I went to Mahlas. But in Mahlas we were taken prisoner by King Caeris of Jullayah.

I'm having a hard time understanding this …

Oh, it gets better. Allia, Imal's sister, is Caeris's queen, and she is intent on invading Kitarra.

Even better…I don't know where to start asking and my head already hurts. What do you need?

I need you to come to us in the Tarm before Allia finds us. Bring an army.

Fuck, Eva. Where is Cotoch in all this? He growled.

Rhyl says he is dead…long story.

I'm relieved you came to your senses and called me. I will assume you had your reasons to wait until now. But you are fortunate this hurts my head because I have many words for you, milady!

Come get us.

We will. Give us seven days and we will be there. Can you last that long?

Yes.

Eva did not waste magic saying goodbye. Stone's head would feel like the business end of an ax for the next few hours. Oddly, Talo did not have the same effect from Rhyl's magic. But Stone was…different.

Eva finished bathing and dressed, wishing she could have grabbed some extra clothes since hers were filthy from their escape. *Such a spoiled lady I have become.*

She made a fire—the hard way, with tinder and kindling and flint that she found in one of the dusty storage chests. She would make tea from the wild mint beside the creek.

As she worked, she tried not to think about the hurt in Stone's voice. She tried not to think about Stone relaying her message to Illiah, how he would wilt with relief to hear she was safe. But her guilt was a relentless warrior that gave her no reprieve.

CHAPTER 60

ILLIAH

ILLIAH SURVEYED the newest recruits. It was difficult to look past how young they were. He had to remind himself when he met Diea, now one of his best captains, she had been barely fourteen. These young men and women were all over sixteen. And they would train for four years before they would see any real hardship. In those four years, they would be tested. Some would fail. Not everyone was cut out for the life of a Peace Guard or Queen's Guard.

The recruits stood at asana, nervous as hell. Illiah was aware he had a reputation for being fair but stern. His soldiers respected him. But since Eva had gone missing, Illiah admitted he had an edge no one wanted to cross. He heard the mutters and hushed silences. Perhaps it was why the newest residents of the Forge looked ill.

Illiah took a deep breath, but it did not calm the monster inside him.

Movement caught Illiah's eye, and he turned to berate the intruder. It was Stone, his expression hard as marble, which indicated something of great importance.

"You are dismissed," Illiah announced to his recruits.

"Sir?"

"Now. Go."

The recruits hurried out of the training yard with a few confused backward glances.

Stone leaned in close so his voice would not travel. "I know where Eva is."

Illiah put his hand on Stone's shoulder to steady himself.

"She's in the Vale, Cotoch—"

"I knew it," Illiah hissed through his teeth. Gods, Illiah couldn't breathe. He would kill Cotoch. This time, the scum would die.

"It's not what you think—Illiah, Eva said Cotoch is dead."

"What?"

"Eva is unhurt. Rhyl is with her."

"Rhyl?"

"They are being pursued by Jullayans," Stone continued.

"Jullayans? Did I hear you correctly?"

"Apparently King Caeris is on his way to Kitarra. His queen—"

"Caeris is married?"

"For fuck's sake, stop interrupting me like a fool and I will tell you."

"Fine." Illiah folded his arms. He wanted to hit something.

"Eva thinks Caeris is a threat. She said Caeris's wife is Allia, Imal's sister. A *candarii* sorceress. I'm as confused as you."

"Shit."

"Yeah."

"So Caeris could be under this woman's control?"

Stone shrugged.

"Stone, how do we know Eva isn't …" Illiah felt like such a piece of shit. A betrayer of a husband. "She ran away. What if she is not of sound mind? What if Cotoch enthralled her and this is a trap?"

Stone glared at him. "She is all right. More so than you are right now."

Illiah pushed the monster down.

"Right now we need to get to Eva and Rhyl before Caeris does," Stone told him. "Eva told us to bring an army and meet them at the Tarm."

"Did she say how many men Caeris has?"

"You would go to war with your brother?"

"Is he my brother if his mind is poisoned by the *varing*?"

Stone looked grim. "We need Aiyan and Mila."

"Talo will want to come."

"We need him here."

"Agreed. But he is not going to like that."

Stone shrugged. "He knows his duty."

"Get Diea. I will find Aiyan and Mila."

Aiyan hesitated in Illiah's doorway. The wolf's eyes bored into him with displeasure.

"You got my message?"

"You and Stone are going to rescue Eva and Rhyl."

Illiah nodded.

"Mila and I will come."

"Thank you."

Aiyan still did not step into the room. He eyed the gold basin in front of Illiah with obvious unease.

"I will do this with you or without, Aiyan," Illiah said sharply.

Finally, the wolf came into Illiah's study and closed the door behind him. "I am aware."

"But thank you for coming." Illiah forced softness into his voice.

He'd already filled the gold basin. With Aiyan standing sentinel, Illiah looked into the water, letting the *varing* pulse around his ears, letting his inner eye focus on the dark river that was the *varing*.

Caeris. Brother. Twin. Candarii.

The *varing* showed him Caeris and a woman in Mahlas. Caeris looked annoyed, frustrated. Illiah hadn't seen his twin brother for years. He looked less weather-worn than Illiah—softer around the eyes and mouth. His hair had less gray, but maybe it was just the lack of a beard.

The woman was dark-haired. Dark-eyed. Beautiful. Sharp. Like a vicious weapon, her displeasure made her appear dangerous.

Allia.

The voice belonged to Mute, not Illiah.

She is a broken thing. Beware.

Illiah was in the habit of telling himself the voice of Mute was his imagination, but…it was getting harder to ignore. Illiah was terrified to answer in case it allowed Mute to overpower his will once again and force Aiyan to fulfill his promise.

Illiah focused on the vision. He could feel the *varing* twine around both Caeris and Allia. But with Allia, the ropes of *varing* moved freely, and with Caeris, the *varing* encased him like a cage. Caeris was her prisoner. A young Kitarran stood behind Allia. The *varing* pierced his arms and legs and held him like a puppet. His eyes were wild, his pain potent. Illiah could feel Allia take the *varing* from his pain, manipulating it.

Other presences he couldn't see or name hovered in the peripherals of Illiah's reach. Then the *varing* snaked through Illiah's control and like a wave in a flood, it poured down on him. He felt Mute rising…

…and woke, lying on the floor.

Aiyan's voice drummed through the room. The *heera* chant vibrated in Illiah's bones. He didn't want to get up. Aiyan's voice, his magic, was soothing, like a warm fire on a winter night. The *varing*, the vision, was gone.

Aiyan let his chant die. "Was it worth it?" he asked.

Illiah did not miss the sardonic tone.

"Caeris's queen *is* Allia. I thought she was dead."

Aiyan's amber eyes narrowed. "I thought so too. Queen. Fuck."

Illiah rubbed his head. It felt too full. "She has a Kitarran. A young man. He has the look of a *daeum*."

"Impossible."

Illiah pressed his fingers into his forehead. The backs of his eyes hurt.

"What do they want, I wonder?" Aiyan mused.

"Eva might know."

"When are you leaving?"

"Within the hour."

"Don't wait for us. Mila and I will catch up. But…Illiah,"–Aiyan pierced him with his amber eyes–"there was another one in the hall today."

Aiyan's words drenched Illiah like ice water. Aiyan continued, "A young man. He killed his uncle. We sedated him, and he is resting. But the *varing* rages like an infection, and my *heera* magic is not enough. He might not make it. I——" Aiyan swallowed.

"What is it, Aiyan?"

"I tested a theory. I talked to the young man's aunt. She was upset, I took her hand." Aiyan couldn't look Illiah in the face. Aiyan abhorred physical touch; with a few exceptions since his *heera* magic worked through skin-to-skin contact. Aiyan had told Illiah touching a person with *heera* magic was like finding a vision about that person. It let him know their hopes and dreams, their fears and shame. Aiyan hated it because he felt it too invasive. But he had used it. Aiyan must have felt desperate.

Aiyan continued, "The aunt…she knew how her husband mistreated the boy. She ignored it. The *varing* infected him long ago. And his sister, also abused, is among the missing."

Illiah's heart was in his throat. He didn't need to see the young man to know his pain, to know the feeling of the *varing* pulsing through his blood robbing him of his mind, his life. Trauma seemed to attract the *varing*, but Illiah had known that already. But could trauma also cause someone to become a violent, mindless *revenant*?

"You think she may have become a *revenant*?" Illiah asked.

"I think so. But I don't know where she went——Where any of them went. Until now. But what if Allia has them?"

Illiah thought of the ropes of *varing* in the periphery of the vision. *Candarii* sorcery grew from pain and despair. It made sense that the *varing* unchecked would do the same. Too much *varing*. Magic unbalanced. And if someone was able to gather and use it…Illiah had a feeling he understood why Allia was coming to Kitarra.

CHAPTER 61

CALYPSO

"ALLIA IS SEARCHING for us." Calypso overheard Rhyl tell Eva. Calypso rode on Eva's shoulder, so it wasn't hard to overhear their conversation. Eva rode Honey and Rhyl walked with Pena as a wolf at his side. Their small procession left the Vale two days earlier. Kitarra was still a long way ahead, even as a bird flies. "How far away are they?"

Calypso knew *they* were Stone and Illiah.

"Stone told me they just passed the standing stones. I told him we are on our way." Eva's voice sounded uneasy.

"Da will take a small group on horses to meet us. They will travel faster."

"I agree. Stone will be with him."

"If the Jullayans catch up to us, I can stop them." Rhyl sounded confident. Arrogant prince. Calypso wished he could tell Rhyl just how silly he sounded. Silly and brave.

"Perhaps. But I don't want you to," Eva argued.

"Would you rather we were at their mercy?"

"Of course not!"

That was how many of their conversations ended, with a disagreement. Maybe that was why Rhyl hadn't told Eva about the Great Forest. Or Stonyhill. Or that Calypso was actually a *velidar*. (Not that it mattered since he was stuck as a raven.)

Calypso took flight, ignoring Eva's protests as his wings brushed against her face. The wind took him up and up. The sun was warm on his black feathers. It would be a hot day. The Tarm looked like a sheet of gold beneath him.

As the sun began to descend into the mountains to the west, Calypso made lazy circles toward Eva and her shoulder when he saw something below. He dove for a closer look. There was Illiah, riding a black horse with a white blaze on its nose, and the big Kitarran—Stone—was running alongside him, keeping pace with the horse. Then Calypso noticed the two wolves prowling in the grass toward Eva and Rhyl and Pena.

He let out a cry of triumph no one would understand. The black wolf, Mila, looked up. He made a loud vibration in his throat that was more of a drumbeat than a song before he circled back to find Rhyl and the others.

He wanted to tell Pena their rescuers were close, but his cowardice overcame him. Eva still thought he was just a raven. Pena had promised she wouldn't tell Eva she could speak to him, and so far she had kept her word. But what child was good at keeping secrets?

It didn't matter. Rhyl saw Stone and Illiah and let out a cry. Illiah pushed his horse forward. Stone ran like the wind on his long Kitarran legs.

Calypso stayed aloft, watching as Illiah dismounted and ran to his wife, his son, embracing one, then the other, then both. Stone's smile was all teeth. Pena crouched, her tail between her legs, pleading with Calypso for help as the two big wolves came toward her. They shifted into their human forms. Pena's front paw came up, her weight shifted to her back legs as she prepared to bolt. Calypso dipped down and dove over her ears.

It's all right, Pena. They are good people. I promise. Don't be afraid.

I'm not afraid.

Calypso laughed inwardly at that. Pena was trying to be brave, poor thing. He wished he could shift to human and take her hand in his.

Aiyan looked up at Calypso, one brow raised quizzically. Calypso froze under his amber gaze.

Raven.

Wolf.

Then Aiyan smiled, but at him. Calypso landed on Rhyl's shoulder because Illiah had his arms across Eva's, making Eva's shoulder uninhabitable.

"You have an interesting companion there, Rhyl," Aiyan noted, his chin indicating Calypso.

Please don't tell Eva what I am, Calypso begged the wolf-man. Aiyan looked confused but nodded.

"This is Calypso," Rhyl said.

"Calypso?" Illiah exclaimed. "Are you sure? How is that possible?" He narrowed his eyes at Calypso suspiciously.

"Ravens are long-lived birds, and exceptionally clever, Illiah," Eva gently berated her husband.

"We need to get moving," Stone told them. "Bedtime stories are for when we are back in Kitarra." The big Kitarran's tone made Calypso uncomfortable. The small group moved as if they could all read one another's thoughts. Calypso felt like an outsider. A liar.

Within a minute, they were making haste toward Kitarra. Calypso stayed on Rhyl's shoulder, digging his talons into his cloak for purchase, gripped by an irrational fear that they would leave him behind.

CHAPTER 62

ILLIAH

ILLIAH KEPT EVA AND RHYL within his sights. Not that he was concerned for their safety; his gaze fell toward them like gravity. Eva was perfectly whole. Illiah's worst fears had not come to pass.

Eva was safe.

And Rhyl. Rhyl had hardened. Illiah watched his son, noticing the lines at the corners of his usually laughing mouth. But Rhyl's face softened when the raven sat on his shoulder. Rhyl had always loved animals.

The Kitarran army's camp was a stone's throw from where Illiah as a newly appointed First Defender had met with Cotoch years ago.

Cotoch was dead. A riot of emotions accompanied the fact. Relief. Regret that he had not died under Illiah's knife. Pity. Guilt. Pena was an innocent. She did not deserve the grief that hid in the back of her eyes. Illiah had seen too many children with the same look. Enough for ten lifetimes. Aiyan and Mila had not hesitated to take the girl under their care. She would do well with them and in time, he hoped her little heart would blossom.

The elaborate Kitarran camp was more comfortable than any camp had a right to be. A pavilion had been erected for them. The sleeping tents were connected by a large sitting area complete with couches and braziers. There were enough guards and scouts that no one would get within ten miles without their knowledge. Illiah let himself relax. Irri and his spiders had already gone to scout Mahlas to determine what he could about the Jullayans.

Nella, Illiah's uandian greeted him with an ecstatic display, which only intensified as the dog greeted Eva and Rhyl. Nella barked as Rhyl's raven flew into the tent, but with a word from Illiah, she quieted.

Two serving boys came in carrying buckets of heated water. Illiah would have to speak to the camp master about age restrictions; the two boys looked far too young. Then Illiah looked closer at the boys and swore under his breath before shouting, "Bren! Aralis! What in the Guardian's name are you doing here?"

Bren and Aralis grinned, their disguise dismantled. They ran to their mother and knocked her over, swallowing her in their embrace. Eva's shouts of laughter made Illiah bite his tongue against the reprimand he wanted to pelt into his unruly sons. Eva ruffled their hair, kissing their dirty foreheads. The grime was likely part of their disguise, but with the twins, Illiah couldn't be sure.

"Is there no command too strict for you two to break?" Illiah huffed. The boys ignored him. Heathens. Illiah tossed his hands in the air. "They take after you, you know," he told his wife. Eva raised a brow in contradiction.

"Da, how could you expect us to stay home and just wait?"

"Yeah, we missed Mum, too, you know!"

"And me? You missed me, too, right?" Rhyl asked as he hooked an arm over each of his brothers roughly, calling them pirates, kissing them on the cheeks one after the other. He introduced them to his raven. Illiah still could not believe Rhyl found Eva's pet raven in the Forest. It was… suspicious. But he didn't ask any questions. Not yet. His fatherly instinct told him to let Rhyl rest. His warrior instincts told him there was time. And something in Rhyl's expression made Illiah want to gather Rhyl into his arms and never let him go.

Food was brought. The haunted look left Rhyl's eyes as he ate like he hadn't seen food in months. Aiyan and Mila joined them with Pena who was a human girl once more and dressed in clean, practical clothes. Bren and Aralis also reappeared clean, their cheeks rosy.

Bren and Aralis sat by Pena, and for once, almost behaved themselves. Pena was quiet, her eyes round. But Illiah saw her smile, just a little, when Bren explained how they managed to pass as servants in order to come along. They boasted how the camp master had no idea who they were. There had been a moment, Aralis explained, when Bren hadn't known what a dugout was, which almost blew their cover.

Something warm settled inside Illiah. It felt like old days when Rhyl was still a boy, when he and Talo were almost as obnoxious as the twins. Almost. But Talo was in Kilev, and his absence was felt.

Rhyl was quiet, but he also didn't stop eating.

After the meal, Bren and Aralis offered to play a game with Pena. To Illiah's surprise, she agreed. Bren and Aralis could be overwhelming, but they were kind boys, under the noise and dirt and wildness.

With the children gone, Illiah turned to his wife. His darling wife.

Eva cleared her throat and took a sip of wine.

"So," Illiah invited.

"So," Eva echoed. She took a deep breath. "Vagar came to me in the forest behind the Queen's Keep. He gave me a vercuri and told me Cotoch wanted to help me—help us—help Rhyl."

"And you went with him. Alone."

"Can you imagine if you had talked to us first?" Stone cut in with a laugh. He wasn't even being sarcastic. That Stone had forgiven Eva already made something inside Illiah jealous. Why couldn't he forgive Eva as easily? Yes, he was overjoyed to see her. He loved her like a forever ache, but that ache sharpened knowing she had left him. But . . .

"We would never have let you go," Illiah admitted. Knowing it was true didn't make it all right. Shame hit him hard.

"You would never have trusted anything that came from Cotoch's mouth. If he had sent an embassy to Kilev, you would never have heard him out," Eva reminded them.

Illiah was silent because there was nothing to say.

"So I went with Vagar."

"Knowing it would torture us?" Illiah couldn't help himself.

Eva sighed. "Yes."

"At least Rhyl had the decency to tell Talo what he was planning. At least one person knew," Stone quipped. Maybe he hadn't entirely forgiven his amourii.

Eva looked guilty, but also defiant. What she had done was beyond reckless, but she was brave. Illiah couldn't help but feel pride alongside his anger, and his pride grew stronger the longer she sat close to him. He reached out and squeezed her hand. She laced her fingers with his, even though his hands were cold.

Eva looked at Aiyan. "Caeris's queen is Allia, Imal's sister."

"I know." Aiyan looked at Illiah. "Beric told me she was dead."

"Maybe he thought she was," Illiah offered. In all their years of dealing, Illiah had no reason to think Beric was a liar.

"Allia has a *daeum* Kitarran," Eva said. "A young man named Liam. Where he came from, I have no idea."

"Asha was hidden away. Perhaps there were others," Illiah said, feeling ill at the thought.

"I think we should send a formal invitation to Caeris, invite him to come here and talk with us," Stone suggested.

"You think that is wise?" Eva looked at Illiah.

"I think with our army behind us—"

"And me," Rhyl quipped.

Illiah growled. "And you."

"What do Caeris and Allia want?" Stone asked Eva.

"Magic. Caeris claimed it was for the Goddess, but Allia...I don't know what her motives are, and I would bet money that she has Caeris eating out of her hand like a trained hound." Eva glanced at Illiah, her eyes round with worry. "I don't want them anywhere near you," she added.

Illiah cupped her face, running his thumb along her lip. "Crea can't hurt me."

"She doesn't want to hurt *you*, she wants to hurt *everything*. She wants chaos. She wants *him*."

Mute.

"It will be all right, Eva," Aiyan said. "We are strong enough."

"Mum, I'm the child of the prophecy. What can go wrong when I'm around?"

Eva smacked Rhyl's shoulder, making his raven squawk in alarm.

"I'll arrange a message," Stone said.

"Well, Rhyl. Besides the raven, what else did you come home with?" Illiah asked, eyeing Calypso on Rhyl's shoulder.

"The Allmakers are gone."

Rhyl's words settled around the table like a cloud over the moon. Illiah didn't know much about the Allmakers, but he felt the ominous nature of the news.

"Gone?" Eva echoed.

"Dead."

"The Forest?"

"The Allmakers' magic disappeared, but there is still magic in the Great Forest. That was the reason the Allmakers went there in the first place." Rhyl's confidence, his humor, was slipping. "But now there are wanderers outside the forest."

"What is a wanderer?" Stone asked before Illiah could.

"A *velidar* who's been corrupted by the *varing*, caught between forms—animal and human. A beast. A monster. Like a *revenant*, but more wrong, more evil. Stronger. More predatory. Ruthless."

"Like the one that attacked Tarran all those years ago," Eva whispered.

The monster that attacked Tarran had come for Illiah and taken over his mind. He had almost killed Eva that day.

Eva squeezed his hand. She remembered that day too.

Rhyl took a deep breath. There was more. Illiah knew it would be bad.

"The wanderers attacked Stonyhill," Rhyl said.

"No …" Eva breathed.

"Tarek and Elish and the Wolves are all right, but everyone else… Felis…It was a massacre."

Eva started to cry. Illiah tucked her into him, cradling her.

Eva locked her wet, blue-green eyes on Illiah. Her fingers curled tighter around his. "They will come for you."

"They will come for the *varing*," corrected Rhyl. Gone was the little boy Illiah had carried and nurtured. Before him was a warrior, blooded and vetted. Illiah despised the necessity of it.

"Allia has Cotoch's vercuri," Eva announced.

"And the ability to create a *daeum* army," Aiyan added in his clear voice. "We think the missing people in Kitarra may have been turned into *revenant*s. And we fear they may have left Kitarra …"

"To seek a source of the *varing*," Illiah finished.

"There were *revenant*s in Mahlas," Rhyl told them. "I saw them. A horde, waiting, as if enthralled."

"How many?" Illiah asked.

"I don't know. Hundreds."

"Fuck," Stone whispered.

A heavy silence followed. Illiah didn't know what to say. It was beyond his experience and skill. They were wading through the dark.

"Cotoch told me he was the one who destroyed Imal's *daeum*," Eva mentioned.

"What?"

"And I believed him."

"I wonder how he did it," Aiyan said thoughtfully.

Illiah bit his tongue; he didn't want to talk about Cotoch. The bastard was dead.

Nella stood up and put her head on Illiah's lap. Eva reached over and rubbed the dog's soft ears.

"This can wait until tomorrow. We are all weary," Aiyan said, standing, Mila's hand in his.

"I'll go check the watch," Stone offered. And with that announcement, everyone went their separate ways. Rhyl was almost asleep on his feet. Eva went to fetch Bren and Aralis and make sure they found their beds.

Illiah was tempted to send Bren and Aralis off to sleep with the servants, seeing as they had been disguised as serving boys long enough to convince the camp master of their usefulness. But everyone in camp now knew they were princes. Illiah would not risk their safety. Born into privilege meant they could be prey for those who saw them as symbols of greed and power.

And in the large tent, there was room—and privacy. Smart thinking, that. Illiah intended to seclude himself with Eva for the remainder of the night in the privacy the First Defender was accorded.

"Those boys." Eva shook her head as she stepped through the privacy curtains into their corner of the tent. Then she stiffened and didn't meet Illiah's eye. "You are still furious with me."

Illiah ran his hand through his hair. He took a step over to her and pulled her to him. "I wasn't really angry—just terrified."

"I am sorry for that."

"Don't be. I love you. That means I will always be a bit terrified. Because I need you."

"I need you too."

Eva kissed him, her lips warm and familiar and perfect. Illiah fell into her kiss, his hands cupping her face, tangling in her hair. He sucked her lip, biting just a little, moving his lips down her neck, her chest, tracing the contours of her body. She groaned, arching against his lips. Her hands reached for him, taking him, her desire and urgency making him hot and hard. There would be times ahead for slow lovemaking, for long touches and silken words, but this was not the time. They both needed too much, ached for too long. Eva's body tightened with her ecstasy as Illiah released his need inside her body, and they clung together, breathing as one.

Illiah felt Eva smile against his chest, and every broken piece within him melted and fused, stronger than before.

CHAPTER 63

STONE

STONE TURNED the smooth glass vial in the palm of his hand. He'd promised when he returned from his perimeter check, he'd let himself take a pinch of the culla powder. But Rhyl stood outside his tent, looking up at the stars. The boy should be sleeping.

"What's bothering you?" Stone asked, even though his skin was tight with longing. He hadn't taken his dose of culla for three days.

"I don't know. I can't sleep."

"I wouldn't either if I had a raven sleeping on my head."

"He doesn't sleep on my head."

"Cats are more cuddly."

Rhyl smiled and shook his head. Was the boy blushing? Was Stone missing something?

He put his hand on Rhyl's shoulder. "It's good to have you home. I'm proud of you for getting Eva out of Mahlas."

"Cotoch died so we could escape."

"So the bastard died a hero's death…Who would have thought it?"

"We went into the crypts below his house looking for Tsuga, the spirit woman. There was a—a pit in the ground full of human bones. His victims, Stone." Rhyl's voice settled into a whisper.

Stone's tingling skin turned into an ache. He hadn't allowed himself to think about Cotoch's atrocities, not while he worked for the man and not after.

"Poor Pena. If she ever finds out …," Rhyl muttered.

"And the spirit? Tsuga?"

"Tsuga was gone."

"I thought she was trapped."

"Somehow she was freed…I don't know. Magic is shifting. What happened in the Forest with the Allmakers…I feel like we are on that point of balance, just before the tip, just before the plunge and the fall."

Stone agreed, but he didn't want to say it out loud. "Was it worth it? Going to the Great Forest?"

"It was …"

"But?"

"Fucking spirits, Stone. The Allmakers were not as clear as I had hoped. They left me with…a head full of chaos."

Stone chuckled darkly. "From what I know of spirits and Guardians and prophecies, that sounds about right."

"Things are going to get bad, Stone. I feel it."

"But it isn't, yet. Don't overthink it."

"Great advice," Rhyl quipped.

"My advice to you is to go to sleep. You're dead on your feet, boy."

"Yeah, yeah."

Stone watched Rhyl head back to his tent.

Being alone came with a pungent relief—relief heavily laced with shame. With Rhyl off to bed, Stone could feed his body culla and cleanse himself of this want, for a few more days. He poured the powder into his mouth. Instantly, his throat burned and constricted as his tongue registered the strange taste. He gasped for breath, his body pressed by an invisible fist. Something was wrong. Culla was consuming, but this was flaying him from the inside. His head felt seared open. He felt magic around him, chaotic magic. He heard weeping. Water rushed over his face leaving his lungs bursting and his mind numb.

CHAPTER 64

CALYPSO

SATISFIED THAT PENA WAS SAFE and as comfortable as a grieving girl could be, Calypso went to find his own place to sleep. He found Rhyl tucked into a soft bed inside the large palatial tent. He settled next to Rhyl's neck and sighed. Rhyl was already deeply asleep. Calypso listened to Rhyl's even breathing and felt himself slip into sleep.

A wave of magic slammed into his mind. It moved through his mind and bones, a torrent of pain, cascading, crumbling, leaving him scraped and raw.

Then silence.

Then his mind pieced it together. Someone close was dying.

Calypso poked his beak into the sensitive spot above Rhyl's ear.

"Calypso? What the fuck?"

Calypso flapped outside, making awful noises that would surely wake up everyone. Stone lay on the ground, unmoving, his fur a bright shadow in the night.

Wolves! Calypso called.

Rhyl stumbled out of his tent, barefoot, his cloak in his hand. Calypso called to him. Rhyl stood dumbly, but Calypso could see the moment he processed that the lump on the ground was Stone. Rhyl rushed to Stone's side. Others came behind him. Mila. Aiyan. Illiah. Eva shivered in her loose gown and wet hair, but her fingers fumbled on Stone's neck. Calypso landed at Stone's feet.

"He's alive," Rhyl told his mother.

"Barely."

Aiyan and Mila crouched down, their approach more practical and less reliant on magic. Aiyan tipped back Stone's head gently and Mila felt over his body for injury.

"Poison," Mila announced, her nose scrunched. "I can smell it."

"Can you make him retch it up?" Aiyan asked Rhyl.

As far as Calypso knew, Rhyl had never used his magic to manipulate a person's body that way. "I—I—"

"Never mind. It might be too late for that," Aiyan said. Aiyan looked at Calypso.

I don't know what happened, Calypso told the wolf.

"Here." Mila held up an empty vial.

"Someone laced his culla," Eva said, her voice quivering.

"He is slipping away," Rhyl said, his voice anguished. He pressed his hands against Stone's chest as if he could push his life into him. Calypso had never felt so hopeless. He stood behind Rhyl. If he still had any *velidar* magic, he would give it to Rhyl. "I can't hold him," Rhyl whispered. Eva closed her eyes, her hands over her son's. Together, they tried to keep Stone from shattering as they pushed the poison away. But it wasn't working. Tears streamed down Eva's face.

Raven, Aiyan's voice whispered gently in his mind.

Calypso looked up to see the wolf smile, just a little. The only light was from the torch a guard held. Calypso felt cold, but his hand was warm where it rested on Rhyl's shoulder. Not wing or beak, his *hand*. He looked at Aiyan again and realized that he was no longer a raven, he was a man, and there was magic in his hand, and that magic—his magic—was flowing into Rhyl and Stone. He could feel the *simul rami*. He could feel Stone, through Rhyl, take a breath, his heartbeat gathering strength. The poison was receding from Stone, moving through Rhyl into Calypso. A slow burn started in his throat, followed by a wave of nausea in his gut. The poison was in *him*.

Shift! The poison should affect a raven differently, Aiyan urged him.

I don't know how! But even as he said it, Calypso felt himself grow small as he settled back into his raven form. The effects of the poison vanished.

Stone opened his eyes.

"What the fuck just happened?" His demand came out in an icy whisper.

Eva laughed a sob and flung her arms around his neck. Rhyl rocked back on his heels, looking like he was about to faint. Aiyan reached out and put his hand on Rhyl's shoulder before he fell. Mila moved quickly and took Rhyl's other arm.

Calypso flapped to Mila's shoulder where he could keep Rhyl in his sight.

A little while later, Rhyl was asleep, back in his bed. Calypso huddled next to his neck. Eva came in and kissed her son's forehead, then Calypso on his feathered head.

Calypso's thoughts were a mad whir. Had they seen him shift? Had it really happened? Calypso had amplified Rhyl's magic, somehow. Through Rhyl, he took the poison from Stone into himself. The Allmakers had never mentioned anything like *that*. But then again, the Allmakers had told him he couldn't shift outside the Great Forest. Why had they lied? Calypso felt betrayed.

The Allmakers had been nothing more than ancient beings, their magic oblique and vague. Perhaps they had been part of the world so long they didn't understand it anymore. They didn't know his heart; they never had. They hadn't betrayed him. They just hadn't understood what was important for him to know.

Calypso sighed and pressed closer to Rhyl's neck, tucking his head under his wing. At least he was with Rhyl.

The coming days would not be easy. Calypso still had to find Rhyl's weakness and push him toward greatness, as the Allmakers would say. Calypso despised the necessity of it. He should never have agreed to the Allmakers' plea all those years ago. But somehow, it had never felt like he'd had a choice.

CHAPTER 65

AIYAN

STONE RECOVERED QUICKLY. The raven seemed to have no ill effects from absorbing the poison. Incredible. Aiyan was relieved, but they were all unsettled. Stone's addiction was not well known, and no one had access to Stone's culla except Aiyan, Mila, or Stone himself. No one would know to lace Stone's culla supply with poison. And only a spy could have gotten physically close to Stone's culla. Which meant there was someone in Kilev who could not be trusted. Rhyl said he would search in the *simul rami* as soon as he regained his strength from healing Stone.

Aiyan was uneasy.

And the raven. He had worked with Rhyl to pull the poison from Stone. Yet Aiyan had a feeling Rhyl didn't know Calypso had helped him. Aiyan planned to have a chat with the boy once he returned to Kilev, but first he had a message to deliver.

A wolf in the dark of night, stalking through tall grass, is impossible to see.

Aiyan entered the city of Mahlas like a ghost. His *heera* sight showed him the *varing* draped over the city like a spider's gauzy web. Aiyan never forgot a scent. He traced Allia to the large house described by Eva.

She was waiting for him on the steps. The young Kitarran stood behind her. Aiyan paused, shocked by the rotting core of the young man. He *was daeum*. It was true. Allia had created a *daeum* Kitarran.

Aiyan shifted to his human form.

"Aiyan." Allia let her eyes wander down Aiyan's body from his *heera* mark to his toes. Her king was not with her, though if he was her puppet, he wouldn't care that Allia's face was full of lust. At least the woman was still predictable.

"What are you doing here, Allia?"

She smiled. "You have made a new life in Praedan, why can't I?"

"You are queen of Jullayah, isn't that enough? Why come to Kitarra?"

She sighed. "Don't you understand? It's never enough, Aiyan." Something raw and real flickered in her eyes. A shadow of the frightened young woman she had been. The woman who had been morphed under her brother's thumb into the hollow monster before him. Aiyan felt a pang of pity and longing to help her. But that was foolishness. Not everyone could be saved. And he had tried to help her once. He had tried to love her. Now he owed her nothing.

"I thought you were dead," he said.

"Is that why you left with *her*?" she spat. "Because you thought I was dead? Did you ever love me, Aiyan?"

"No."

Her eyes narrowed. "You are cruel, Aiyan. You were always cruel. It was why you were so good at killing. Is that what you do for the Defender? Kill? Sneak through corridors? Did he send you here to kill me too? Or his own brother? Or his little nephew? My son?"

Aiyan sucked in a breath. "You have a child?"

"I bore Caeris an heir five months ago. The babe is in Jullayah." She preened. "But do you want to see my true children?" Her eyes gleamed. Something like terror gripped Aiyan.

"Show me."

"Come." She stood and moved with a skip in her step, like a little girl. She held out her hand to Aiyan, her mouth twisted in a smile. "Look."

Aiyan let her take his hand in hers, trying to ignore the way her fingers curled around his. Through the touch, his *heera* magic showed him a mass of people. No, not people, *revenants*. They were alive but not alive. The *varing* poured from their skin like blood from a wound. He didn't need to wonder where they came from; he felt the answer in his bones. The missing people from Kitarra. Rhyl had been right. Allia had called them with the *varing*.

Aiyan nearly dropped her hand when he saw the wanderers. The creatures were neither beast nor man but wrong and twisted, and the only thing left in their eyes was hate. This was her army, not the men from Jullayah, but these creatures infected with *varing*, simmering with malice and need for violence.

Aiyan shook his hand from hers. "What do you *want*, Allia?"

Her smile grew teeth. "I want *everything*. Once, I waited for you to rescue me, but you never did. Now I don't need anyone to save me. I hold the power, Aiyan." She sighed, sounding bored. "Go now. Go back to your whore and your new masters and tell them I am coming for their child of the prophecy. I am coming for their trees. For their magic. Tell them. Run, Aiyan. Run like the wind. We are coming."

The sharp sound of her laughter followed Aiyan back through the thick grass to Kitarra.

CHAPTER 66

STONE

"WHY DO YOU LOOK SO WORRIED? I'm impossible to kill." The raspy quality of Stone's voice made his quip fall flat. Eva glared at him, her arms folded. Illiah's mouth twitched. Stone closed his eyes so he didn't have to look at them. Despite his glib speech, he felt like he had fallen into the void of death and been spat back out.

"Rhyl saved you," Eva said softly, patting his shoulder. He reached up and took her hand and squeezed her fingers in his. "You were poisoned."

"Someone got into my culla," Stone concluded.

Illiah nodded. "Your addiction makes you an easy target. Your death would weaken Kitarra considerably."

"There is a spy in Kilev," Stone said.

"So it seems."

"We need to take precautions," Eva said.

"If only we could ask Rhyl to look," Illiah huffed. "But I know the culla clouds things."

"And our boy has enough on his plate," Eva said.

"Agreed," Stone said, trying to keep his eyes open.

Aiyan erupted into the tent, shifting in a blink. His eyes were wild, dangerous.

"What is it?"

"Allia. Her army is coming. Now," Aiyan announced. He took a step toward Illiah and gripped his arms. "Her army is made of *revenant*s and wanderers."

"Shit," Stone said as Illiah leaped into action, shouting the alarm. It was a testament to their training that the camp woke and moved into an efficient order.

"I'm taking the children out of here," Eva said. "You should come with me," she said to Stone.

"No. I can fight." He sat up and a wave of nausea made him pause. He took a deep breath and felt better, stronger. He walked with Eva out into the dawn. With every step, his lingering fatigue shed away.

Rhyl appeared from his tent, the raven on his shoulders. Stone opened his mouth to tell Rhyl to find safety, but Rhyl's expression stalled him. Eva looked from Rhyl to Stone. She bit her lip but didn't say goodbye, just gave Stone's shoulder a squeeze, an unspoken message. *Keep my son safe.* Then she went to find the children.

"I see them," Rhyl whispered, pulling his sword. "Cally, go, find somewhere safe."

"Go with Eva. She is leaving with the children," Stone told the raven, then realized he was talking to a bird. The bird seemed to understand and took off. What the fuck? "We should draw them away from the camp," Stone said, feeling a strange awareness niggling down his neck, like he was being watched.

Illiah appeared beside him; Aiyan flanked them both. Illiah whistled and they moved, their troops following like a silent deadly tide.

The dawn was coming. The sky was gray, a few stars lingered. The shadows refused to give way to the coming day. Even with Stone's Kitarran eyesight, it was difficult to make out unnatural movement against the grass swaying in the night breeze.

Rhyl didn't look away from the dark grass around the standing stones. In one hand he held his mother's sword; in the other was his vercuri. Stone nearly jumped when the vercuri burst into blue flame.

"Stone, stop staring and draw your latha," Rhyl hissed.

A sound rose from the grass. A snarl. A scream. A hiss. The sound rode Stone's vertebrae like a saw blade. They burst from the dark, a blur of dark shadow, a glint of eyes.

Rhyl's flame blazed and reflected off more creatures. Stone didn't bother counting. He felt the presence of his soldiers behind him.

Rhyl swung, hitting something solid. Then they came. A flood of bodies and force and malice. Stone had fought their ilk before. The *revenants*, like the *daeum*, were strong and fast, their wills made of magic.

Someone cried out, one of theirs. Rhyl reacted with a shout, a cry, his fire blazed, growing, moving, reaching, illuminating the night and exposing their enemy. Stone lunged and attacked, his latha finding flesh and bone. He severed arm from shoulder and aimed for heads and hearts and tried not to think about the blood soaking into his fur.

Fuck. He hoped Eva had gotten away with the children. Though some savage part of him wished she were there beside him. She could be ruthless.

Illiah was with them now, fighting beside Rhyl, moving with efficient strokes that had earned him his fame as a swordsman when he was the same age as Rhyl. Something in the back of Stone's mind nagged him as his arms burned from the strain. They kept coming, the rotten, magic-infected bastards.

"Da!" Rhyl's scream was rending. Stone glanced and saw Illiah, slouched over as if a great weight pushed him down and he was fighting to get free. "No." Rhyl spoke the word like a thunderclap. The sharp noise was a shock wave. Magic cut through the air, knocking the breath from Stone's lungs.

Silence greeted them. Stone waited for another wave of attackers, but none came. Rhyl was on his knees, crouched like a shield over Illiah, his vercuri extinguished. Child of the prophecy indeed.

Aiyan appeared beside Rhyl and Illiah. Aiyan was covered in blood not his own. The wolf met Stone's eyes and his expression told him they were unhurt. Stone moved through the standing stones, stepping over body after body. Diea checked their injured, shouting orders. Chaos slowly turned to order. And with the gray light of dawn, the blood-soaked battleground became a graveyard.

CHAPTER 67

ASHA

"I'M NOT WHO YOU THINK…My master sent me here to …"

Asha couldn't even say it to her mirror, to her own reflection.

She tried again. "She threatened to kill me. She threatened to kill Liam…I had no choice. She took over my mind with magic. I think she may have done something to Arrain."

Asha's reflection looked back at her. Her dark fur, her golden and white patches. Her amber eyes. *Do I have my mother's eyes?* Her parents would be ashamed if they were alive to see her.

Asha needed to tell Talo the truth. Now. Unless she was wrong… her thoughts were foggy at best. Perhaps it had been a dream. Perhaps Arrain was not in danger. When her master took over her mind, she didn't always remember what she had done under thrall. She might not have sneaked into Arrain's chamber and laced his culla with poison stolen from the Healer's Hall. It might have just been a dream. Why would her master want Arrain dead?

But the truth sounded like the ravings of a madwoman. *Am I mad?* She wished it were so.

She owed it to them to *try* to tell them the truth. Even if they locked her away and called her insane. Even if that meant she would be banished from Kitarra, sent away from Talo, earning his hate forever, it didn't matter. Her lies had kept her alive, but now they were tearing her apart. Her fingers shook. Her legs trembled, but she was resolved. She would do this. And face the consequences.

"Can you tell me where Prince Talo is?" she asked the guard in the hallway.

"I believe he is with the queen. Would you like me to escort you?" The guard was a woman named Terea. Talo liked her. She made Asha nervous.

"Yes, please. If you don't mind."

"Not at all," Terea said with a smile.

Asha couldn't keep her hands still. Terea glanced at her fidgeting as she announced Asha's arrival. Queen Arrah was in her atrium, sitting on her pillowed chair. Talo sat on a chair close by. The queen smiled a little at Asha, but Asha had a hard time taking her eyes from Talo's to offer the polite greetings expected of her.

"Talo, off with you. I can see the girl wants a word with you, and you alone." Queen Arrah smiled and waved her hand.

"Thank you, Mua," Talo said, leaning over to kiss his grandmother. He reached out a hand to Asha. She wanted to take it, to feel his long fingers encompass hers, but she didn't.

They walked along the edge of the atrium. The air was warm next to the glass. Asha loved the atrium. Its thick air reminded her of Rodan, of the days when she would find refuge in the solace of the heat of the day, the only time when her minders were too exhausted to boss her around.

"Your fur is such a striking color in the sun," Talo said.

Asha dipped her head, feeling her skin warm. "Thank you."

"Is something wrong, Asha?"

Asha took a breath in preparation for her dive into the frigid water that was the truth.

"Talo!" A shout came from behind them. It was a Peace Guard, Vayn, who was often following Talo around, his personal guard but also a friend. "Talo! They're home. Rhyl is home! Eva is with him!" Vayn grinned.

Talo was so excited, he wrapped his arms around Asha and kissed her forehead. "They're home!"

So Asha was pulled along behind Talo to share in his joy, feeling more like a traitor than before. But if something had happened to Arrain, then

Vayn would tell Talo straight away. He would not have greeted them with a smile. Asha gave her head a shake. She *was* imagining things.

And the prince of the prophecy was home.

CHAPTER 68
RHYL

FUCK. Rhyl wanted to sleep for a week. His arms still ached. His head still throbbed. But only three of their soldiers had died from Allia's attack. He had stopped the monsters. He had stopped the massacre. At dawn, they had counted nearly two dozen bodies. If Allia had sent more, Rhyl might not have been able to stop them. Already, what he'd done had nearly drained him. But still, there were three families who would be mourning. What he had done was not enough. Would it ever be enough?

He couldn't help but feel like there was grit around his heart. He had wanted this for so long. To be home in the palace, a soft bed to sleep on, good food to eat. Training with the Peace Guards. The hot pools. Teasing his little brothers. Talking with Talo.

But instead, as they rode through the city up to the palace, he found his answers short, his mood for conversation eclipsed.

He didn't know where Calypso went. Likely he'd flown off after Pena, Aiyan, and Mila to the Healer's Hall, which made sense. Calypso could talk to the shifters. Calypso would not be as lonely with someone to talk to. Rhyl was glad Calypso found companionship. Really, he was. But something lurked around the corners of his heart; it might have been envy.

The palace was blessedly unchanged. Rhyl had almost expected that home would no longer feel like home. That he would walk under the arch that led to the royal apartments and feel like a stranger. But he didn't. Talo met him there and wrapped him in a welcoming embrace.

"Eek. You need a bath," Talo said but hugged him hard, pressing his forehead against Rhyl's. "I missed you."

"And I you." Rhyl held his brother tightly and his spirits soared, for about a minute.

"Where are the parents?" Talo asked.

Rhyl's parents and Stone dove into council with the Defender's captains immediately upon arriving to discuss the threat that Caeris and Allia posed. Rhyl was thankful he was not required to participate. He did not want to think about that unsettling woman. He did not want to think about her monsters. He did not want to think about the smell of their charred flesh burned by his fire.

Had Talo been saying something?

"I asked if you were all right," Talo said.

"No. Not really."

Talo's face suddenly looked ten years older. "Come, I'll tuck you into bed." He wrapped an arm around Rhyl's shoulders and tried to steer him down the hall.

"I'm not an invalid. I'm having a bath before I go to bed."

"All right, then. I will see you after your nap."

With great relish, Rhyl shucked his dirty worn out clothes. He embraced the cool air of the courtyard before plunging into the hot water of the mineral pools. He did his best to ignore the black branches of the cendari tree because they reminded him of the dry, black pool where the Allmakers had shown him their secrets. Useless secrets. Rhyl resisted the urge to throw rocks at the stupid dead tree.

No one else came into the pools while Rhyl bathed. He wondered if everyone had been warned to give him space. He squinted through the steam, thinking he heard the beating of wings, but no raven appeared. It was just the wind rustling through the forest on the mountain. A sound that was as much home to Rhyl as his mother's voice.

CHAPTER 69

CALYPSO

KILEV WAS FULL OF PEOPLE. Calypso had *known* that but experiencing it firsthand was another thing entirely. People and colors and textures and noise—it was street after street, house after house. Wending through the city to the Queen's Keep, Kitarra's palace, felt like getting lost. He left Rhyl's shoulder and flew up and up until the city looked like a maze. But the palace was easy to identify, and beyond it was the forest and the mountain and tall Kitarra Peak. The peak leered, and Calypso knew he would be daunted to fly toward its spire.

Calypso? It was Aiyan. *We want to talk to you.*

You are *talking to me.*

Just come here, will you? Mila added.

Calypso hadn't known Aiyan long, but he'd known Mila before when he was a raven-child and she had been the headmistress of the Keep. He'd seen visions of the wolves in the *simul rami* over the years, but that was a poor comparison, he realized. Aiyan was both far scarier and far kinder in real life. His amber eyes were piercing and knowing, and yet full of deep understanding. They were also the two most beautiful people Calypso had ever seen. Aiyan's dark skin was like a sunset, and Mila was as pure as the first snowdrop at winter's end. He had admired them for their beauty, but after knowing them, even for a short time, they felt parental to him. He was glad they had taken Pena under their wing—err, paws.

Where am I going? he asked.

Aiyan told him where to find the Healer's Hall and how to get to

Mila and Aiyan's house. It wasn't far from the palace. A square, simple building tucked into the forest and mountain.

Calypso was relieved when he found the right house after two mishaps. Some people didn't like big black birds landing on their open windowsills.

Mila smiled as Calypso hopped in. Pena was there, looking tired but happier than he had seen her since hearing about her father's death. Aiyan sat, taking a sip of freshly brewed tea.

There was a homeyness to their house, a calm that soaked under Calypso's skin. He settled on the arm of the couch and croaked. Pena stroked his feathers.

"Aiyan thinks he can help you shift," Pena said, her smile growing.

Truly?

Aiyan nodded.

But—but how?

"Aiyan had to teach me how to shift." Mila looked at Aiyan with a secret smile. "I didn't know how at first either."

But I have always been told it is impossible! Calypso argued.

But Calypso *had* shifted. That night the wanderers came for Rhyl. He had woken as a human. He had tried to shift since then, but nothing worked. He had given it up as his imagination. Except he shifted when Stone was poisoned…Calypso didn't want to recreate either of those situations.

Aiyan cocked his head like a wolf on the hunt. "Maybe you were told a lie to keep you—the *velidar*—in the Forest."

Mila looked thoughtful. "I think my mother's mother was a *velidar*. Perhaps they tell lies to keep you young *velidar* from leaving the Forest to seek love elsewhere. And leaving shifter babies all over the realms."

That does sound plausible, Calypso admitted.

"And there's no harm in trying, Calypso," Mila chided him.

Calypso realized he was shuffling from one foot to the other. He stopped and readjusted his wings. Mila was wrong. Fear of failure made his stomach flip over and his spine turn to ice. What if it didn't work? The disappointment would crush him. Or what if it did work? Then what? That was almost as terrifying.

"Do you want to try?" Aiyan asked.

Right now?

"Sure." Aiyan took another sip of his tea.

Mila grinned.

"Can I stay to help?" Pena asked.

"If Calypso agrees."

Calypso chirped at her.

"There is less magic here. You must find a way to use what is part of you," Aiyan told him. "We all have a little magic, even if one isn't *sanarii* or *candarii* or *heera*."

Mila added, "Before in the Forest, your source was the Forest itself. The *simul rami* flows through us all. You must find *your* source and use it."

It made sense. Calypso reached for his magic as he would've if he were still in the Great Forest.

And found nothing.

I can't find it, Calypso whimpered.

Do you feel safe here? Mila asked.

I do.

Are you sure? It will be impossible to shift if you let your negative emotions control you.

I—I think I feel safe.

But you want this so badly, Mila said, as if reading his thoughts.

I spent the first ten years of my life as a raven. This form is me. But now it is not enough.

I understand, Mila said. *I denied my wolf for more years than that, out of fear. But once I accepted both my forms, I felt...free.*

You are afraid of your human form, just like Mila was afraid of her wolf, Aiyan concluded.

Calypso was about to argue, but Aiyan's words held a kernel of truth. *I—I…You are right. I am afraid.*

That we will reject you.

Calypso flapped his wings.

We will not reject you, Calypso. Nor will Eva and Illiah. Nor Rhyl. Aiyan's wolf eyes sharpened as he read Calypso's body language. *Love is a risk, Calypso. Do not throw it away out of fear.* Aiyan glanced at Mila. *And those you love will always hurt and disappoint you in some way. No one is perfect. But you must accept that you, too, are not perfect. You must accept yourself for everything you are. You are enough, Calypso. Now, search for your magic. It is waiting, we can see it. Reach for it.*

Aiyan began to hum, first low in his throat, then his chant grew into a wordless song. Calypso could feel his intent, his meaning, his truth. It was joy and sorrow and love, love, love.

Calypso caught the spark of magic inside him, closed his eyes, and hung on, knowing it was his thread to the *simul rami*. His source. As he clung, it grew brighter, stronger until he could wrap it around his core, his being, and take it. Then it was like the Forest magic, but weaker. He couldn't be nourished by it or manipulate it like the magic of the Great Forest, but he could use it to wrap his body and change his form. He felt himself shift. His feathers became skin and his face morphed from beak to nose. It was like tickling sunlight. He sneezed.

He was breathing hard when he opened his eyes. He felt stiff all over. The world had shifted. His sight had shifted. He tossed his head to get his black hair out of his eyes. Both Aiyan and Mila looked smug. Pena grinned, her hands clasped. Calypso felt cold and hated it instantly. Mila smiled and put a soft blanket around his shoulders.

"I did it." Calypso's voice shook.

"You did!" Pena squealed. Her little arms barely fit around him.

Calypso's mind and heart were so full of what this could mean. He was human. He was a man. He was no longer a raven. He could see Rhyl. He could speak to Rhyl. He could…he…would have to tell Eva. Calypso doubled over. His chest hurt. Mila rubbed his back.

"It's all right, Calypso. Breathe, just breathe."

"Don't shift back yet," Aiyan warned. "If you shift out of panic, out of instinct, it will be harder next time. You must hold on to this form longer, until you are calm."

Calypso closed his eyes. Mila continued to rub his back and Pena held his hand. It only took a few more breaths and then he felt less panicked.

"Thank you," he told them.

Mila cupped his jaw. "Oh, darling, we are happy to help you."

Pena stepped back to inspect him. "You are very handsome as a man, Calypso." The girl giggled.

"I'm cold," Calypso whined.

Aiyan put his warm hand on Calypso's shoulder. "Now that you are calmer, try shifting back and forth a few times."

Calypso did. Each time was a little easier. But by the fourth shift, he was suddenly too tired to shift back into a man. And too cold. As a raven, he had a layer of feathers to warm him.

Aiyan gave a low laugh. "Come, it is time to rest. Tomorrow is a new day."

"You are welcome to stay here, Calypso," Mila offered.

Thank you, but I should go find Rhyl.

He hopped over to Pena and rubbed his beak against her chin before flapping out the window. He flew toward the Queen's Keep, low into the courtyard, over the pools. The dead cendari tree stood out like a canker. Calypso hesitated, but then landed on a black branch. He felt sorry for the dead tree.

A Kitarran came out into the courtyard. She was alone. She slipped out of her robe and hissed as she touched the hot water. Calypso recognized her from Rhyl's description as the girl from Rodan. Asha. Rhyl had gone on at length about how Talo doted on her, bringing her gifts and trying to make her laugh. Calypso had told Rhyl it sounded romantic. That had been back in the Great Forest.

Asha looked sad. Extremely sad. Calypso hopped along the branch, drawn to her agony, not that he could help her. He wondered if Talo saw her sadness or if she only wore it when there was no one around who might see it.

Daylight was fading and Calypso realized he didn't know where Rhyl's room was. And that he might have missed dinner. Rhyl had mentioned that his room opened onto the courtyard. Calypso hop-flapped from window to window. One of the windows was open. Calypso peered inside. Rhyl was sprawled, tangled in the blankets, so deeply asleep he was as good as dead. Had Rhyl left the window open for him? Calypso felt a pang of wanting. But maybe Rhyl had just felt stuffy in a room disused for many weeks.

Food was left on the table. But it looked untouched. Calypso helped himself to some leftovers and hopped over to the bed and settled on the pillow beside Rhyl's face.

CHAPTER 70

CALYPSO

CALYPSO WOKE HUNGRY. Rhyl was still asleep. Calypso was tempted to wake him and show him how he could shift into a man. He let himself imagine shifting and kissing Rhyl awake. He squashed his thoughts and hopped off the pillow and flew to the table. He nibbled some cheese. The window was still open to the courtyard so Calypso went to see what he could find. He found Eva bathing. She was alone. It was barely after dawn. The sunlight was thin and hazy, slowly moving down Kitarra Peak.

He landed on the edge of the pool.

"Cally!" Eva's smile was just as Calypso remembered. As a raven-child, his favorite game involved stealing her soap and hiding things in her towel.

He assembled his courage and used those happy memories, and her smile, and shifted.

Her eyes widened in surprise. Calypso carried Aiyan's words of comfort in his head. But as her smile faded, his doubt grew into a living thing. He wondered if it was too late to change back into a raven and fly far away.

Then her smile grew into a grin, her eyes wet with happy tears. She covered her quivering mouth with her hands. She was crying, which made Calypso cry. He wiped his hand across his wet cheek and hopped into the hot water with her before he started shivering.

"Eva." He felt his cheeks spread in a grin.

Then her happy tears turned into tears of despair. "I *left* you. I left you alone! Oh, Cally, can you ever forgive me?" She cupped his face in her hands, inspecting him.

"I was all right," he told her. He'd survived the loneliness, the isolation. He had his duty to the Allmakers.

"How did I not know you were a *velidar*?" she exclaimed. "Oh, how I wish I had known! You are wonderful as a raven, too, you know. But…I always wanted you to talk to me."

"How selfish of you," Calypso teased.

"And I always thought you were a handsome devil." She pulled at a strand of his black hair. Then she ruffled his hair in the same way he'd seen her do with Bren and Aralis. Something clicked in his heart.

"I always thought so."

"Rhyl knows," Eva assumed.

"He knows I'm a *velidar*. Not sure about the handsome part. But until last night, I didn't know I could shift outside the Great Forest. I was stuck as a raven once again."

"Poor thing. Which is why you were never a boy." Her eyes were thoughtful. "You left the Forest with Rhyl, believing you would be stuck as a raven?"

"Yes." Calypso wished he could tell what she was thinking. "Aiyan and Mila helped me learn to shift."

"Ah." Eva's smile grew again.

A servant arrived and glanced curiously at Calypso. "My lady? Princess Cassandra is asking for Rhyl. Most desperately."

Eva groaned. "She wastes no time. Thank you, Lia. Tell Cassandra she may join us for breakfast in an hour. And, Lia dear, can you fetch an extra towel for Calypso?"

The servant, Lia, nodded and came back in a moment with a thick piece of linen.

"And, Lia, please make it known that Calypso is …" She looked at Calypso with a small frown. "He is family," she concluded. The servant nodded and bowed to Calypso before leaving. "Likely the news of our return has spread like wildfire through Kilev."

"I imagine your leaving caused quite a stir."

"Right."

"Uhm…I don't have any clothes," Calypso said absently, but he was thinking about the young woman desperate to see Rhyl. "And I'm hungry."

"Come. Both of those problems are blessedly easy to fix." Eva hopped out of the water with a splash, wrapping her wet body in her towel. Calypso did the same, trying to imitate the way she wove it around her body so it didn't fall to the ground. He followed her inside her chambers. Her rooms were larger and grander than Rhyl's, and obviously shared with her husband and Rhyl's younger brothers.

"Wait here," Eva told him as she went into her bedchamber.

Calypso wrapped the towel tighter around his cold body, inspecting the room where Rhyl had grown up. The room was elegant, but it also managed to feel snug, comfortable, like a home. Like Mila and Aiyan's house.

"Uh, who are you, and what are you doing here?"

"And why are you naked?"

Bren, followed by Aralis, walked out of their room, their hair mussed, their clothes wrinkled.

"I'm not naked. I have a towel."

"Boys, this is Calypso." Eva reappeared with Illiah trailing her. She must have told him because he looked unsurprised as he walked over to thump Calypso on the shoulder.

"Welcome to Kitarra, Calypso," the First Defender said.

"Rhyl's *raven*?" Aralis said, his mouth twitching into a smile. "You're a shifter!"

"Amazing," whispered Bren.

"That's why you aren't wearing any clothes," Aralis noted.

"Yes." Calypso's cheeks burned, even though he knew nudity was nothing in Kitarra.

"Come, let's go to the stock room and find something for you to wear," Eva said, leading Calypso out into the hallway. "Princess Cassandra is joining us for breakfast," Eva called behind her to her family.

Illiah groaned as loudly as the twins. Eva ignored them.

The hallways were still quiet and empty as the palace began to wake. What would he say if Rhyl emerged sleepy-eyed from his room to see Calypso traipsing around the palace in a towel?

"Over here." Eva led him down some stairs and into another hallway. It looked like they were in the servants' wing. There were fewer statues, and the lanterns decorating the archways were less elaborate. But it was still beautiful.

The stock room was full of crates and chests. The smell of lavender and cedar made him sneeze.

"Here, try these. Later we can go out to Kilev. There are endless shops." Eva opened a chest and started pulling out tunics and soft breeches. Calypso ran his finger along the fabrics and delicate seams. He pulled out a tunic in a shade of emerald-green with blue stitching. "Can I have this one?"

"Ooh. That is lovely. Here is the undershirt. Then that goes over top. And you need small clothes." More rummaging. Eva tossed some garments at him. She started laughing when he began dressing, slowly, carefully, like he'd never done it before. Because he hadn't.

She tossed him a few pairs of boots to try. The first pair was too big. The second fit, but they were a bit stiff, like cages for his feet.

Eva beamed. "You look marvelous."

"Thank you."

"Now, breakfast."

"Yes, please."

Eva looped her arm in his.

Calypso marveled at the feeling of the clothes against his skin as he walked with Eva back upstairs. He had never worn clothes not made from magic. He felt…human.

Back in Eva's chambers (Rhyl was not there), Calypso went for the tall, polished mirror to look at himself.

The way his black hair flayed around his face reminded him of feathers, but he couldn't find a way to tame it. But the way the blue of his eyes matched the blue thread of his tunic was satisfying.

Eva came to stand beside him. "You look like a prince from a tale. The girls are going to swoon over you." She sounded exasperated which made Calypso wonder if Rhyl usually had girls swooning over him.

"Calypso," Stone said as he entered. "Aiyan told me."

Calypso felt like he should bow or…he didn't know. He tried something, bending at the waist, and the big Kitarran laughed and put his hand on Calypso's shoulder and squeezed it. "Where's breakfast?"

"Cassandra is joining us," Illiah told Stone with a tone that made Eva glare at him.

"Talo and Asha too," Stone replied. No one mentioned Rhyl.

"Excellent," Eva said. "I was sorry I couldn't get to know Cassandra… before." She glanced carefully at Illiah.

A soft knock on the door. Stone opened it and ushered Talo and Asha in. Eva introduced Calypso.

"The *velidar*?" Talo said, bowing to Calypso. "Rhyl told me about you."

"He did?"

Talo grinned. "A little. Rhyl and I can talk, mind to mind. It was difficult with him so far away. And then for the last few months…never mind. Where's breakfast? I'm starving."

"Ah, here is Cassandra."

The young woman looked shy as she entered, surrounded by— well, everyone. She had a round face and round…other parts. "Good morning," she said, curtsying. Perfectly. Like a damn princess.

Then a handful of servants came carrying trays and dishes and pitchers of steaming drinks and bowls of summer fruit. Calypso smelled sausages and freshly baked buns and his mouth watered. Still no Rhyl.

Eva greeted the servants, thanking them. She knew their names and asked after their families. Bren and Aralis teased the older serving woman and she pinched their cheeks.

Calypso was told where to sit. Beside Eva. Rhyl was still absent. They were eating without him, it seemed. Princess Cassandra looked relieved when Talo gestured for her to sit beside him and Asha. Calypso envied the beautiful glossy blue fabric patterned with flowers of Cassandra's bodice and the gold bracelets around her delicate wrists.

"I'm sure Rhyl will be here soon," Eva said. Calypso opened his mouth to say something but realized Eva was talking to Cassandra, not him.

"Should I fetch him?" Cassandra offered.

Calypso almost choked on his sausage (which would have been a shame as it was very good). Calypso wanted to object, but there was no need. Rhyl walked in, freshly dressed, looking more princely than Calypso had yet seen him.

Rhyl halted on the threshold. He opened his mouth but nothing came out.

"Rhyl, how good of you to finally join us," Calypso said, smiling to hide the wave of nerves that made him want to shift.

CHAPTER 71
RHYL

BREAKFAST *time, sleepy boy!* Talo's voice was loud inside Rhyl's head.

Breakfast? How was it morning already?

Thanks, Rhyl replied hoping Talo could hear his sarcasm through his mind-speak.

Rhyl hadn't slept so deeply for a long time. He rolled onto his back, instinctively expecting to feel Calypso sleeping by his neck. He'd left his window open intentionally, and he could have sworn he'd felt him there while he slept, but he was alone.

He dragged himself upright. Then dragged himself to the basin and splashed cold water on his face. He needed to shave but didn't want to make the effort. He rummaged through his wardrobe for clean clothes. The soft fabric felt strange on his skin without a layer of travel grime.

He could almost imagine the last few months had been a dream. The horror of the wanderers, Stonyhill, Allia's attack—just a nightmare. The Forest, a strange fantasy. And Calypso…Something tightened in Rhyl's chest thinking of the raven-man as a figment he had concocted. He shook his head.

Where was Calypso, anyway? Probably with the wolves and Pena. The tight thing in Rhyl's chest grew sharp.

Rhyl walked into the courtyard garden, looking up at Kitarra Peak. The stony mountain looked like a jagged tooth outlined in the low morning light. He had missed the old hunk of rock.

But soon enough, he would have to leave again. He needed to find

the other vercuri, and he had an inkling as to how to do it. The Allmakers'
last words and parting visions had been coalescing in his mind, and he
was beginning to piece them together. Cendari trees. Rivers of magic.
Summons. Intent. He almost had it.

The smell of hot breakfast wafted into the garden, making Rhyl's
mouth water. He was never good at thinking on an empty stomach.

He entered his parents' chamber through the courtyard door. They
sat at the table, eating. They had not waited—nor should they have. Rhyl's
parents had always accused him of dawdling. Talo had not warned Rhyl
that Princess Cassandra was breakfasting with them. Rhyl felt a pang of
remorse that he hadn't given the young lady a single thought since he had
left. His mother did have high hopes for an alliance through marriage
with Rodan.

Cassandra was not the only guest; a young man sat beside Rhyl's
mother. His clothes were a vibrant shade of emerald, despite his demure
posture. His face was framed with black hair and his blue eyes found Rhyl.

Rhyl drew a breath. An invisible emotion landed on Rhyl's chest.

"Calypso," he said.

Calypso in his human form.

Impossible.

Rhyl was surely dreaming. An impossible dream that made his face
heat and his body uncomfortably…tight.

Calypso's mouth twitched into an almost smile. "Rhyl, how good of
you to finally join us."

CHAPTER 72

CALYPSO

THE TALK AROUND the table fell silent. Calypso felt Rhyl's gaze move from the tips of Calypso's hair down to his human toes tucked under the table. (Not that Rhyl could see his toes.) Rhyl didn't make a move to sit or say anything. Calypso could feel everyone watching. Surprising Rhyl like this, in front of his whole family, had been a terrible idea.

"Raven got your tongue?" Calypso quipped, but it came out shakier than he intended.

Rhyl almost smiled, but he still looked like a fish struck on the head. "Calypso," he finally said.

"Rhyl. Sit!" Eva said. "As you can see, we didn't wait for you."

"Good morning. Lady Asha, Princess Cassandra," Rhyl stammered with a sudden fit of politeness.

He took the empty seat between Calypso and Cassandra. Calypso caught Stone's gaze across the table. The Kitarran prince winked at him. Calypso's cheeks flushed and he took a sip of tea as an excuse to hide his face but the tea was too hot. He singed his tongue.

"Rhyl, I'm so pleased you are home," Cassandra said, pouring Rhyl tea. "You have been very missed. I can't wait to hear about your adventures."

Calypso swallowed another sausage. Eating helped him resist the urge to nudge Rhyl with his leg under the table or throw things at Cassandra.

"Tell me, Calypso, where are you from? I haven't seen you around court before," Cassandra asked over Rhyl.

Bren started to say something, but his father gave him a look.

"Calypso is my…my—" Rhyl began.

"Friend. I'm his friend," Calypso finished.

"Calypso was my foster son in Jullayah," Eva explained. "Don't look at me like that, Illiah. It's true."

The talk around the table was light. Cassandra and Talo and Asha told them of the goings-on of court. Petty things, but Calypso was perfectly content to sit and listen.

Cassandra paused in her description of some up-coming occasion featuring dancing and alliances—whatever that meant—to lean forward and smile at Rhyl and Calypso. "Rhyl, we should all go, Talo and Asha, you and me, and Calypso can escort that lovely young thing, Lady Raina! It would be fun."

"I'm sorry, Cassandra, but I'm not interested in 'escorting' *women*," Calypso told her.

The silence that followed Calypso's statement was deafening. *In for a pinch, in for a pound,* Calypso reflected. And Calypso wasn't going to lie, even if it was merely by omission. He felt Eva's eyes on him. He met her gaze, and she smiled her approval. But he couldn't look at Rhyl. Not to save his life.

"Oh. I guess…there might be some—boys, men," Cassandra said, flustered. She applied herself to her breakfast. Asha leaned over to talk to her, but Calypso didn't hear what they said because Rhyl leaned toward him.

"How is this possible? That you shifted?" he asked, his lips close enough that his breath tickled Calypso's ear.

"Aiyan and Mila."

"You look…colorful."

"Your mum found me clothes."

"You look…like you fit."

"What does that mean?"

"You are a wild creature, and you look like you belong here."

Calypso bit his lip. "Are you saying I *don't* belong here?"

"No!"

Calypso looked at his plate.

"When I saw you, I thought I was still dreaming. A good dream," Rhyl added in a whisper.

"Rhyl, after breakfast, we are headed to council," Illiah said.

Calypso silently cursed the Defender for interrupting.

"We need you there, Rhyl. And you, Talo," Illiah went on. "And you, Calypso."

Cassandra wasn't invited to any councils, Calypso thought smugly. He felt the desire to preen. He ate another sausage.

CHAPTER 73

CALYPSO

CALYPSO SPENT MOST of the council thinking *How did I get here?*

Rhyl discussed his time in the Great Forest. They talked about Allia, her history in Rodan. Her army of *revenants*. The attack. Rhyl's magic. The vercuri. Rhyl's magic, again. The wanderers. Calypso could still smell death and rotting flesh at the edge of his mind. He could see the bodies in Stonyhill. He'd nearly jerked when Rhyl's hand settled on his. The warmth of his skin, the way his thumb moved along his wrist, shook the memory away.

The discussion turned to the *daeum*.

Calypso had seen the horror of the *daeum* in visions. He imagined an army of *daeum* not made from men, but from wanderers. Rhyl wouldn't be able to defeat them all.

"What does Allia want?" Rhyl asked.

"Allia suffered at the hands of her brother. She is corrupted." Aiyan leaned onto his elbows. "She wants power. Magic."

"But if she is looking for magic, why come to Kitarra? Why not the Great Forest?" Rhyl asked.

"The cendari trees," Calypso answered. They all looked at him. "The trees are the true source of the *simul rami*. And the true source of the Guardians."

"Then why did the Allmakers settle in the Great Forest?" Eva mused.

"Because their magic was too strong to stand alongside the trees," Calypso explained. "Like too much hot sun beating down, drying out the land, making it uninhabitable. That is why they made the Kitarrans, to guard the trees."

"Did you learn what you must do?" Eva asked her son.

"I think so," Rhyl replied.

"What is it?"

Rhyl didn't answer.

"Rhyl, we want to help you," Stone said softly, sensing Rhyl's hesitation.

"I don't think you can help me. You never could. This is something I have to do alone. Don't look at me like that." Rhyl glowered accusingly around the table.

Calypso knotted his hands together out of anger. Rhyl was acting like a martyr. Like he had no choices. Like a sacrificial beast laid out to some forgotten god. But then, maybe he was.

"Is that what the Allmakers told you?" Stone asked.

"The Allmakers showed me…things. History. People. I don't know. It's difficult…to explain …"

"Caeris and Allia have Cotoch's vercuri," Eva said.

Rhyl and Talo blanched, but the others look unsurprised.

"We need to find a way to get them back," Eva continued. "There is no doubt that we need the vercuri. Rhyl and I can sense them, as *sanarii*, but still …"

"It feels like an impossible task," Mila finished.

"Can we steal the vercuri from the Jullayans?" Talo asked.

"Too risky," came Illiah's instant reaction.

"How many do they have?" Talo asked.

"Cotoch said he had two."

"That means two vercuri are still unaccounted for," Rhyl said quietly.

"Yes."

"Can you ask the Guardians?" Calypso suggested.

"We have. They can only search within their realm," Eva said.

"And Tayeh is gone," Calypso stated. "Rhyl, if you use a cendari tree as an amplifier, you might be able to find the last two."

Rhyl looked at his mother. Eva's expression pinched. Calypso understood why Rhyl had not tried. Eva's fear from her own experience had kept Rhyl from using the cendari trees. Calypso could understand her fear. But she was wrong. Rhyl would not destroy the cendari trees with his magic as she had. That was why he was a child of the prophecy. He could use magic in a way others couldn't.

"But we need Cotoch's vercuri, and that is beyond our reach," Talo stated.

Illiah had been mostly silent during the council. He looked thoughtful. Like he was planning something. He stood up.

"Thank you for coming. We will adjourn for now. Stone? You will report to the queen?"

Stone nodded.

"Talo, I need you to gather the captains. We need to prepare in case Allia sends her army over the border."

"Yes, Defender."

"Calypso, you are to orient yourself with the Queen's Keep and Kilev. Don't fly too far. We may need you to answer some questions about magic." It was the command of the First Defender. But Illiah followed his order with a half smile.

"Yes, Defender." Calypso tried not to sound smug. The Defender's recognition made Calypso feel like family. Like he belonged.

After the council, Eva showed Calypso to a chamber that was to be his. It was small but grand. Calypso wanted to tell Eva that he would be happy to sleep on Rhyl's bed with him…but then he realized there were reasons why he shouldn't say that.

So he accepted the room graciously.

Rhyl laughed when he found Calypso under a swath of fabric.

"Aren't you supposed to rest?" Calypso told him.

In answer, Rhyl flopped onto Calypso's bed. "I am resting, see?" He closed his eyes. "Will you come with me to the cendari tree?"

"How far of a journey is it? I'm already accustomed to fine fabrics and soft beds. I don't know about sleeping in trees," Calypso teased, resisting the urge to flop down beside the prince. He could still feel Rhyl's thumb along the back of his hand. He wasn't sure what it meant.

"Not far. A day or two in the mountains."

"You really haven't tried using a cendari as an amplifier?"

"I have, actually. In Withe, a few years ago."

"Without Eva knowing."

"She has her reasons to be afraid."

"I know."

Rhyl plucked destructively at the threads of Calypso's blanket. Calypso wanted to swat his hand. "I could feel it. The *varing*, waiting just beyond the tree's roots. I was scared I would do what she did and kill it."

"You won't. You have enough control."

Rhyl huffed. "Why did you leave the Forest to come after me, Cally?"

"You know why. The Allmakers told me to stay with you."

"But you were almost a raven—forever."

Calypso shrugged. "There are worse fates."

Rhyl looked like he was almost going to say something. Calypso could see his mind working in the backs of his blue-green eyes.

"There is a feast planned for tonight," Rhyl told him, eyeing Cally's new tunics. "Everyone will be there. The queen wants to meet you."

"What should I wear?"

"The blue one." Rhyl nodded to the tunic draped across the chair.

"Don't be ridiculous, blue is boring. I'll wear the gold one."

Rhyl laughed. "Where did you even get these?"

"Mila brought them."

Rhyl shook his head, smiling. "A grand chamber. Fine clothes. I think you have been adopted by the royal family."

Calypso blushed. Rhyl yawned, making a noise like a cow.

"Go have a nap," Calypso told him.

Rhyl stood and nodded. He was in the doorway when he looked back at Calypso with a wistful smile.

"I don't know if I can sleep without a warm raven on my neck." Then he left.

CHAPTER 74

CALYPSO

YUP, Calypso was in trouble.

Rhyl's smile was sunlight that tingled along his skin. Rhyl's blue-green laughing eyes made Calypso feel drunk. Rhyl's tunic was green with gold trim and matched Calypso's, but Calypso wouldn't let himself believe Rhyl had done it intentionally. Nor would Calypso let himself think that Rhyl turned his smile on him more than any other.

Calypso's feet still felt oddly tight in his new boots, but it wasn't uncomfortable. He rather liked the way the boots pressed tightly against his calves.

"Stop preening and hurry up!" Rhyl demanded, still smiling.

"I'm not preening," Calypso muttered. Rhyl's eyes lingered on Calypso's legs. He picked up his pace, hoping Rhyl did not see his flushed face.

Rhyl led him through an ornate door into a grand hall with a tall, domed ceiling, inlaid with designs that reminded Calypso of trees and branches. Maybe roots. The arches were gilded with what looked like gold and jade. In the center was a long table carved to reflect the design in the ceiling. Calypso wanted to trace his fingers along the smooth edge, but Rhyl was introducing him to Queen Arrah, who smiled and patted Calypso's cheek with the affection of a doting grandmother.

Rhyl snagged Calypso's attention again, this time by pulling on his sleeve, gesturing for Calypso to sit beside him. Calypso noticed the others had already taken their seats. The queen sat at the head, the rest of the family sprinkled like an array between nobles.

The feast was served. The overlapping sounds of several conversations rumbled against the domed ceiling. Calypso ate, enjoying the food immensely, as did Rhyl. At one point they caught each other's eye, each with a mouthful, and Rhyl started to laugh and almost choked. It was hardly princely. The meal *was* a far cry from skinny rabbit. Calypso wasn't sure if he had ever been happier. It was hard not to imagine what it would feel like to run his fingers through Rhyl's starlit hair or kiss his laughing mouth.

He swallowed the thought with a sip of wine.

Rhyl pushed his leg up against Calypso's, touching from the knee to ankle. Rhyl's long fingers curled around his under the table. The gesture felt less like affection and more like a tether, as if Rhyl was afraid he might disappear. Calypso caught Rhyl's eye. Rhyl's mouth twitched. A question. Calypso squeezed Rhyl's hand in his, and Rhyl grinned. Calypso's heart soared.

After the feast had been eaten and dessert devoured, there seemed to be an unspoken agreement and the younger dinner guests disembarked. Talo led the exodus with a look to Rhyl and Asha at his elbow. Cassandra grinned and looped her arm in Asha's.

"There will be no dancing tonight," Rhyl whispered in Calypso's ear as an explanation. Calypso nodded. Kilev was wreathed in grief. Calypso saw it in the frail hands of the queen, in the tight lip of the Defender.

Talo and Rhyl led the small group to the large formal garden outside the grand hall. The air was scented from flowers and warm with the late summer breeze. Lanterns glowed and the half-moon sat suspended above the river below. They sat on the soft grass between the rose hedges, and Talo produced a bottle of wine. Talo and Rhyl sparred with stories about their childhood. Rhyl's goal was to find an embarrassing story about Talo to share with Asha. Which only encouraged Talo to do the same. Rhyl, it seemed, was hard to embarrass. Talo's retribution was failing.

Calypso was distracted by Cassandra and her outrageously lovely laugh. She also had a wit to match. And in her accented voice, everything sounded beautiful. He couldn't help but remember that everyone wanted Cassandra and Rhyl to wed. An alliance between Rodan and Kitarra by blood made sense, even to Calypso who knew nothing about politics. And Cassandra was lovely. Why *wouldn't* Rhyl want her for a wife?

"Remember last year when you and Corri stole Da's latha and put grease on the handle?" Talo said.

Rhyl grinned. "It was to get him back for eating my birthday polii." But Rhyl's grin faded. Calypso remembered Corri was Rhyl's friend who had died…He'd seen a vision of that night. The blood. Corri had been a culla addict, an easy victim for the *varing*. The influence of the *varing* and the culla forced Corri to slit his wrists.

"You have to try polii, Calypso, you'll love it!" Rhyl said, distracting Calypso.

"Tell me about polii, I keep hearing about it!" Cassandra said. Calypso was not the only one grateful for the change of subject. Rhyl went into great detail about the delicacy that was served once a year (twice a year if Rhyl begged the palace cook to make polii for his birthday).

"And with autumn approaching, the Darkest Night is not far away," Rhyl said. "You are staying until spring, Cassie, are you not? You will get to try polii yet."

Since when had Rhyl started calling her Cassie? Cassandra glowed under Rhyl's attention.

"I am. Unless there is a reason I get to stay longer." She looked at Rhyl, completely unabashed. Rhyl blushed. Calypso wanted to pull her hairpins out.

"How long are *you* staying, Calypso?" Cassandra asked, as if it was a competition. As if Calypso was the competition. *Was* he the competition?

Calypso leaned back on his elbows and looked up at the stars. "I don't know," he replied honestly.

"As long as you want, Calypso. You are family," Talo told him. Calypso smiled. Talo's offer was heartfelt.

Asha yawned. Talo asked if she was ready to retire. She nodded, taking his hand, leaning her head on his shoulder. The young Kitarran seemed fragile, Calypso observed. But maybe that was just compared to Cassandra's vivacious nature. The two women, one Kitarran and one human, were stark contrasts. But there was something about Asha… something Calypso couldn't put his finger on. She seemed to care about Talo. But sometimes she looked like she was a wild thing caught in a snare.

Cassandra also watched the two lovers leave. Calypso wanted to rip the smug smile from her perfectly shaped lips. She turned to Rhyl and Calypso.

"I think I'm ready for bed as well. Would you walk me to my room, Calypso?" Cassandra asked.

"Me?" Calypso started. Why would she ask *him*? Was this an expected courtesy? Why hadn't she asked Rhyl? He looked at Rhyl, silently begging for help.

"Cassandra, I'm sure a guard will see you to your chamber," Rhyl said. "I have something I need to discuss with Calypso. Alone."

Cassandra took the dismissal for what it was. She gave one of her perfect curtsies and left.

The garden felt huge and empty with just Calypso and Rhyl and the stars and the breeze and the long river winding below. The lanterns burned low.

"What did you want to discuss with me?" Calypso asked.

Rhyl laughed. "You didn't *want* to walk her to her room, did you?"

"Nooo," Calypso assured him.

"Good. I'm sure she just wanted to pelt you with questions about me. Her favorite pastime."

"I didn't know you two were close."

"We're not. I hardly know her. But she wants to marry me."

Calypso's bile rose. "I got that impression." Calypso noticed how close Rhyl sat to him, almost touching. "Tell me about Corri," Calypso said. Stupid. Why did that come out?

"Why?"

Calypso shook his head, wishing he still held a wine glass. It would give his hands an excuse. And his mouth, for that matter. "Never mind. I don't know why I said that."

"Are you jealous of a dead man?" Rhyl asked.

Calypso made a noise with his teeth. "Why would I be jealous?"

Rhyl shrugged, smiling like a cat.

"Because you…and him …?" Calypso couldn't say it.

"It wasn't like you think."

"I don't know *what* I think." Calypso flicked the air with his fingers. Movement calmed him.

"I killed Corri." Rhyl wasn't smiling now. "The *varing* killed him, but only because I was there." There was an alien tone in Rhyl's voice, something dark and lost, and it made Calypso wish he had learned to wield a sword to chase it away.

"Rhyl, you can't blame yourself for the *varing*. You are not its source. You are not *it*."

"I know."

"And you have more control over the *varing* than you realize."

"What makes you think that?"

"You kept the wanderers away. That night, you used both *candarii* and *sanarii* magic to save us. You couldn't have done that before you came to the Forest." Rhyl remained silent, so Calypso continued, "I can feel the *varing*. I know it is part of you, but unless you are holding the vercuri, it doesn't affect me. You could kiss me and it wouldn't bother me. Me—a *velidar*!"

"You want me to kiss you?"

Calypso cursed his choice of words. He was also a terrible liar, so he didn't bother saying anything.

Rhyl leaned forward. His soft, full lips pressed against Calypso's. Calypso froze, even when every sense he had was thick and hot.

Rhyl drew back. "I'm sorry…Have you never kissed a man before?"

Calypso wanted to smack him. And kiss him. He shook his head in disbelief.

"What?" Rhyl asked.

"You! Don't you remember kissing me? The night of the revel? In the Forest? You were drunk, and pissed for some reason, but you kissed me. Then passed out from your overindulgence."

"No. I did not!" Rhyl looked genuinely horrified. Then thoughtful. "I thought that was a dream. You didn't say anything. Why didn't you say anything?"

"What was I going to say?"

"Cally."

Fuck, when Rhyl spoke his name like that, Calypso saw stars. He slipped his hand along Rhyl's cheek, his thumb tracing the stubble on Rhyl's jaw. He pulled Rhyl toward him ever so slightly, assuring Rhyl this was okay, this was good, this was necessary—Calypso was desperate to feel the warm press of Rhyl against him.

Rhyl leaned. Into him. Against him. Calypso's clumsy hesitation dissolved, and he ran his hand under Rhyl's shirt, against his smooth muscles. What started as soft and sweet turned into a clash of skin against skin, a war of need and want and touch.

"Don't rip my shirt," Calypso said with sudden concern. "The embroidery!"

Rhyl collapsed in a fit of laughter but managed to say something that Calypso interpreted as "Take it off."

"Here?"

"No!" Then he stopped laughing. "Will you come to my room?"

"As long as you don't expect me to shift back to a raven just to keep your neck warm."

"No, that was not what I had in mind." Gods, Rhyl's eyes were electric.

Calypso swallowed.

"Follow me, you ungrateful raven-man."

"Haven't I already proven I would follow you anywhere?" He meant it to sound witty, but it came out in an emotional whisper that made Rhyl push him against the wall, hands under his shirt, his mouth hot on his neck, his hard body pushing, grinding, begging. Rhyl grabbed Calypso's hands with a groan.

"Not here," he whispered against Calypso's ear.

Calypso nodded, grinning like an idiot against Rhyl's lips. They pried themselves apart.

The walk to Rhyl's room felt like miles.

With Rhyl's door closed behind them, they flung themselves onto the bed, laughing. Rhyl made a show of helping Calypso take off his tunic, undoing each elaborate button with exaggerated care.

"Just rip the thing already," Calypso begged, his voice thick.

Rhyl laughed and did no such thing. Instead he used deliberate slowness until Calypso lay naked beside Rhyl. Rhyl's fingers brushed Calypso's skin, lingering, teasing, a promise that made Calypso's blood surge. Rhyl followed each gentle touch with his lips, using his mouth to bring Calypso to the brink, then tipped him into the void where he was completely undone.

Rhyl kissed him deeply. "You all right?" Rhyl asked, his eyes soft.

Calypso didn't answer, just smiled, and pushed his nose against Rhyl's neck. He wrapped his arms around Rhyl, pulling him in close, marveling at the shape of Rhyl under his fingers, his mouth. He wanted to memorize every curve, every edge of Rhyl's body. He yearned to pull every last sigh from Rhyl's lips until the prince was dismantled and limp. But when Rhyl muttered, his fist clenched against the bedsheets, what sounded like "Fuck me," Calypso was the one who was almost undone. Again.

After, they lay like leaves fallen in a storm of their own making. Rhyl flicked Calypso's nose, and Calypso smiled without opening his eyes.

"Stay with me tonight? Not as a raven?" Rhyl asked.

"Yes. I will."

CHAPTER 75

ASHA

ASHA DIDN'T KNOW RHYL WELL, but watching him was fascinating. It was a reminder how comfortable Rhyl and Talo were with each other. Their mutual trust was mesmerizing. They teased each other relentlessly, but loved each other deeply. She'd had a little of that, long ago, with Liam. When they were children. Over the years, she'd pushed the longing for friendship away where it couldn't torment her.

Asha noticed the looks passed between Rhyl and his friend, Calypso, at breakfast and then at the feast in the grand hall to celebrate Rhyl and Eva's return. And with Calypso's admission that he preferred men, Asha read the meaning behind those looks easily. Cassandra seemed oblivious. Asha hoped she wouldn't have to explain it to her. Cassandra's father's lover was a man, after all. Surely Cassandra was clever enough to realize …

"I like Calypso," Talo mused, proving that Talo was also aware of his brother's inclinations. As they walked down the quiet hall, Talo curled his hand around Asha's. Asha stifled another yawn, though it was her nerves, not fatigue that made her feel off.

"You like teasing Rhyl more," Asha deduced.

Talo laughed. "Yeah. Bringing up Corri in front of Calypso was a bit mean, I guess."

"Rhyl and Corri were lovers?"

"I don't know the details."

"Why didn't you tell Cassandra? All this time, you knew Rhyl was attracted to men."

"And women. Cassie had a chance."

"Maybe leaving the three of them alone was a bad idea."

"Nah. It will force them to sort it out."

Asha bit her lip. She needed to tell Talo. She needed…"Talo?"

"Yes, Asha?"

"It's a beautiful night. Let's go look at the moon." By the old ones, she needed courage. She needed open air. She needed …

"You aren't too tired?"

She shrugged.

"Ah, I know just the place."

Talo led Asha through the dark courtyard up into the forest behind the palace. There was a twisting trail, and they followed it up and up.

"Are you all right on these roots and rocks?" Talo asked. Asha wanted to bound ahead of him, to prove that the wild was no match for her. But she didn't. She did tug playfully on his tail.

"Lead on, My Prince."

Talo laughed softly.

They emerged from the forest onto a mossy bluff. The twinkling city lights tried to compete with the stars but failed. The moon shone brighter than them all, reflecting off the river. A cool breeze ruffled Asha's fur.

They sat, side by side. Asha let Talo put his arm around her shoulders and didn't move when his hand slid down her side to her waist. Maybe she should have had less wine with dinner. Maybe her common sense would outweigh the delicious warmth of Talo next to her. She knew it was selfish, letting Talo touch her, enjoying his affection.

She turned to tell him everything. Talo's face was close to hers, and even against the night, his light blue eyes devoured her. She didn't move away when he leaned in and pressed his lips to hers. Her body arched against his. Warmth flooded her and stars burst through her body, warming her from the inside out. His hands pulled her toward him, with gentle urgency.

Asha drew back, just a little. "Talo?"

"Yes, my love?"

She opened her mouth to release her truth. She'd been a coward, but she could not take the weaker path, not any longer. But the words died in her throat. The smell of magic was thick in the air around her. The magic pushed her down, into that cage inside her mind. She fought. But she collapsed into that place, a prisoner. Her mind screamed Talo's name, knowing he was in danger, knowing her mind, her body, were no longer her own.

Asha fought. Her mind was wrapped and bound. As she sank, the foggy oblivion offered her snippets of memories, taunting her. Or perhaps strengthening her. She couldn't tell.

There were only two Kitarrans at the villa in the country. Asha and Liam were told they were the lucky ones, the little Kitarran children taken from the city of Kara to the country, where there were trees and dry fields and in the distance forested hills. How lucky they were not to be in Kara where slaves were thrown into pits and left to die in the streets.

There was fresh water, a spring pure and plentiful, at the center of the villa. Though often clouds of brown smoke would leave the horizon hazy and make the air smell strange. One of Asha's earliest memories was of thinking clean water was an odd thing to boast about. Was water not plentiful? But as she grew older, she understood that was foolish. Rodan was a dry, hot land, and the well in the center of the villa gave the trees their green leaves and ripened the fruit.

Asha was told the city of Kara was a dusty, dirty mess. Though Liam overheard the servants whisper that the new emperor was fair, and Kara and Rodan thrived. But it didn't matter because Liam and Asha were never allowed to leave the villa and its gardens. Still, Asha dreamed of visiting the city of Kara, seeing the wide ocean where, across its depths, was Kitarra, her homeland.

Of Kitarra, she was told very little. No one spoke of it, not really.

She was told it was a wild, cold place. But Asha was good at eavesdropping. Liam told her it was because she was Kitarran, and Kitarrans had better senses than humans.

Liam was the same age as Asha. Neither had any memory of their parents nor where they came from. But they didn't ask questions. Questions led to punishments. Gruel for meals and scrubbing floors. Asha very much liked her cool fruit and spiced meat.

Liam and Asha were tutored together. Their lessons included the languages of Rodan and Kitarra, and they could speak and write in both. They were taught combat with a sword and with fists. They were taught to ride a horse, which was tricky when they outgrew the little pony in the stables. Both Asha and Liam were faster and stronger than any human. As they grew older and taller and stronger, Asha could sense the servants' fear as they watched them spar. Part of her relished their apprehension.

Once a season, a different tutor would come. This woman, a human—Asha had never seen another Kitarran other than Liam—they were told to call Master. This woman had long, black hair that brushed the small of her back. Her face was stern, her features too hard to be called beautiful. She was friendly, and Asha grew to trust her, even if Liam was wary.

When Asha was twelve, their master came to live at the villa with them and took on all of their training herself. Liam and Asha were no longer tutored together. Liam would tutor with Master in the morning and Asha in the afternoon. Almost as soon as this new routine began, Asha noticed a change in Liam. He was…less. His green eyes grew dull and lost their curiosity, their laughter. His fur looked flat. He didn't tease her or tell her stories as he had since they were little. Asha tried to ask him what was wrong, but he would just offer her a facade of his old smile and tell her not to worry.

Then one day, Master turned to Asha.

"I have a mission for you, Asha," she said.

"A mission?"

"Yes. Why else do you think you have been fed and trained and taught all these years? I have a job you must do for me."

A hint of unease niggled at Asha's mind. But still, the idea of something new excited her.

"What is it, Master Allia?"

"Well, it will take many years to prepare, but I want you to travel to Kitarra."

Asha's heart soared at the thought. Kitarra. The land across the sea. She would leave the villa. Her mind jumped between all the things she might see and do. Then her excitement stumbled. "Is Liam coming too?"

"No, not Liam."

"Oh. I can't leave without Liam."

Master raised a single brow, her expression like a blade. Asha shrank before her displeasure. But didn't Master understand? Without Liam, Asha wouldn't have courage to leave the villa.

Master snapped her fingers and a guard came in with Liam. Liam didn't look at her at all. His shoulders slumped. His tail hung limp.

"You and Liam are both excellent warriors, Asha," Master said, twirling a strand of hair in her fingers. "You have been excellent students, and I am exceedingly pleased. But there is one lesson I need you to learn." Her mouth twisted, and something flashed in her eyes that sent a shock of fear down Asha's spine. "Liam, hurt Asha."

Asha hissed in shock. What a ridiculous thing to say. Liam would *never* hurt her. Liam was her friend, her heart. But Liam stepped toward her, his eyes empty. Cruel. Not his at all. What had Master done to him? What had happened?

Liam raised his dagger. Asha blocked with her arm just as he struck. The blade cut through her silk sleeve into her flesh. Asha bit her lip against the pain. But her muscles had been trained, and instinctively she struck his neck with her fist, knocking him back. Liam came at her again, and she used a proper deflection this time, knocking the dagger out of his hands. It skittered across the floor.

"Liam! Stop!" Asha begged, a sob catching in her throat. Liam didn't seem to hear her. He stalked her, his eyes black, his breathing heady, like he was breathing in her pain and fear instead of air and life.

"Liam, stop," Master commanded. Liam stood still. Master huffed in disappointment and clicked her tongue at Asha. "Asha. If you do not go to Kitarra, Liam will die. I will tell him to cut his own throat. This is the lesson: You must *always* do as I say."

"You…are a monster," Asha whispered.

"No, darling, I am going to be a queen."

EVA

HOME.

When Eva's bedchamber was lit by a single candle at the end of a long day, that was when it felt the most like home. Like the walls and tapestries closed around her, and she was safe. Sometimes she felt the remorseful pang of the Keep left behind with its lofty towers, and the Great Forest at her back. But Kitarra, the Queen's Keep, was the place where she raised her children and found her family in Stone and Talo and Arrah. It was the heart of her life, and she would never call another place home.

The feast had felt so *right*. Like old times. Full of smiles and laughter. Arrah looked like years had fallen from her face. The children had been happy. But Rhyl …

"I can't believe Rhyl," Eva muttered to Illiah as she shed her clothes preparing for bed. "He seemed so odd toward Calypso!" Illiah lay on the bed. She couldn't see him, but she could feel his eyes on every piece of her exposed skin. It made her smile. Then he started laughing, so she turned and demanded an explanation.

"Darling, could you not see it?" Illiah asked, pulling her on top of him and running his hands along her.

"See what?"

"You, my dear, are incredibly perceptive, intuitive, clever, but you have a blind spot when it comes to Rhyl."

"What are you talking about?" She leaned into him. His hands were deliciously warm as they moved across her body.

"Rhyl was not odd, he was just…besotted, maybe? There is more between those two boys than you know."

"What are you saying?" Eva squirmed into a position to see his face better. She loved his face, his nose, his cheeks, the shape of his lips. She kissed them lightly.

Illiah grinned. "Well…the Rodan princess is going to be very disappointed."

"Are you saying that Rhyl is attracted to men? That he and Calypso…?" Illiah raised his brow.

"*How* did I not know this?"

Illiah shrugged. "I have no idea. Rhyl and Calypso were holding hands under the table. Hey, where are you going? I thought—"

Eva slipped from his arms—no small feat—and threw a thick robe over her nakedness and marched down the hall to Stone's door. She didn't knock.

Stone was sitting in asana, cross-legged, breathing like a statue. He opened one eye and raised one brow.

"Stone, Illiah tells me that Rhyl prefers men." It came out in a huff.

A sharp tooth peeked out as Stone's lips stretched into a grin. "So you finally figured it out."

"No! *I* didn't! Illiah told me."

"Ah, so your pride is hurting."

Eva bit her lip. Maybe her pride was a little bruised. Rhyl was her *son*. How could she not know this? How could she have not seen it? Why didn't Rhyl tell her? She thought of all her comments about women and wives. She'd even, obliquely enough, told Rhyl about the importance of pleasuring a woman. She felt like an idiot for making assumptions.

"Does it matter?" Stone asked her.

"If Rhyl falls in love with a man? Of course not!"

"So, this is just about your ignorance on the matter."

"Why didn't you *tell* me?"

"Eva. The boy didn't want me to—it wasn't my business."

"Rhyl asked you to keep this from me?"

"Not in so many words, no. He is not ashamed. He is not hiding it. He was holding hands with Calypso under the table——"

Eva threw up her hands.

Stone continued, "It's not something that should have to be mentioned. It just is."

"If I had known, I wouldn't have put all those girls in his path."

"There weren't that many girls. Be kinder to yourself."

"Your sarcasm is not needed."

"Oh, I think it is." Stone, the bastard, was enjoying her wounded pride. "And besides, if it makes you feel better, Rhyl likes women too."

"Men *and* women?"

"Does *that* bother you?"

"No. It doesn't. Not at all…I just wish he'd told me."

"Well, don't hold your breath. Sons don't tell their mothers *everything*."

Eva flopped down on Stone's bed. "And *Illiah* knew. How many times have I harassed him about his lack of intuition when it comes to our children? But this time, *I* had it all wrong." Eva wanted to wipe the smirk off Stone's mouth. "Calypso is a fine boy, but …"

"Go easy on the raven-child. I think there is more hurt behind his fine blue eyes than he lets on."

"Part of that is my fault."

"Eva, don't take that on too."

Eva covered her face with her hands. "I just want Rhyl to be happy. And Calypso."

When Stone didn't reply, Eva removed her hands and looked at him.

"There is more to Rhyl's story about his time in the Great Forest," Stone said. "He is withholding information. I think he is trying not to hurt you."

"He could never."

"What I mean is, he doesn't want to cause you undue pain. He knows how much you have been through. And what this prophecy has cost you."

"At least Calypso is a better option than Corri." Eva felt terrible for speaking ill of the dead, but she knew, of all people, Stone would not judge her.

"A *velidar* who believed he was a raven for Guardian knows how many years."

"*My* raven."

Stone smiled. "Only your son would fall in love with a raven."

CHAPTER 77

RHYL

RHYL WOKE, aware that he was not alone. He grinned, reaching out to Calypso sleeping beside him. He was ecstatic he didn't wake up beside a black bird, or worse, woken to find that Calypso had abandoned him during the night.

"I'm still here." Calypso obviously had similar thoughts. He smiled, shyly. Rhyl stretched out, letting every inch of available skin—a considerable amount—touch Calypso and then wrapped him in his arms. Calypso pressed his face into Rhyl's neck.

"I've never been so aware of my body," Calypso murmured.

"What does that even mean?"

"You know what it means."

"Do I?"

"I'll show you."

Sometime later, Calypso asked if it was time for breakfast. Rhyl made a comment about insatiable carrion birds, and Calypso smacked his shoulder.

"I am going to bathe first. Coming?" Rhyl said.

"I guess."

"It's all right, Calypso. This isn't the Forest. No one will care about us."

Calypso looked doubtful. Rhyl sighed. He could understand Calypso's hesitation. He wanted to slay all the fucking *velidar* who let Calypso think he was an abomination.

"What will your parents say?" Calypso asked.

"The Defender won't care. Mummy won't care, but she will be surprised. I think. I never told her."

"That you like men?"

"Right."

"Why not?"

"I don't know. It never came up."

Calypso shrugged as if that made sense.

Rhyl tossed him a towel and wrapped himself in another one, leading Calypso out to the courtyard and the pools. He wove his fingers through Calypso's. The simple touch thrilled him in a way he'd never imagined. He bit his lip. Calypso's fingers were capable of making him lose his composure.

Calypso tensed beside him. Rhyl's parents and Stone were also bathing. Rhyl fought a strange instinct to hide Calypso from them. But he had just finished assuring Calypso that he was a grown man entitled to seek companionship where he chose. He squeezed Calypso's hand.

His mother called to them, her voice full of laughter. Calypso seemed to recover his bravery. He shrugged, dropped his towel, and hopped into the hot water to greet Eva, exclaiming in a loud, insinuating voice that he'd had the best sleep in his life. Rhyl was the one left at the edge of the pool, blushing hard.

Calypso splashed him. "Get in here. I want breakfast."

Illiah and Stone looked at Eva and burst into laughter. Rhyl shared a confused look with Calypso.

"What's so funny?" Rhyl asked the parents after he had fully submersed himself.

"Your mother and I had a bet. She lost," Stone explained.

"You had no witnesses! The bet is void," Eva exclaimed, pouncing on Stone like she was trying to drown him. Stone flipped her into the water. She emerged like a drowned cat. "Illiah, avenge me!" Eva demanded through her laughter as Stone bested her.

Illiah did no such thing. He closed his eyes and leaned his head against the pool edge. "Calypso, remember at the Keep when you used to try to steal my towel while I bathed?"

Calypso grinned sheepishly. "A little."

"You were such a rascal."

"Was I?"

"It's too bad we didn't know you could shift to human. You would have been a useful scout," Illiah mentioned.

"Da!" Rhyl said. "He was just a child."

"How old are you, Calypso?"

"I found him when I was thirteen, so that would make you twenty-four?" Eva stated with a question.

"Around there."

Rhyl was about to mention that Calypso had spent the first decade of his life as a raven, but Aiyan lopped into the courtyard, his fur flecked with what looked like blood. They all took notice. Rhyl gripped the pool edge. Calypso put his hand on Rhyl's shoulder.

Aiyan shifted. The blood was suddenly stark and horrible against his bare skin.

Illiah and Stone were both out of the water in an instant. But Aiyan looked at Rhyl.

"A *vivus*. In the Healer's Hall."

Rhyl recognized the moment his happiness, his hope, drained away.

"It killed five people. Mila and I destroyed it."

"There's more," Illiah assessed.

"Three of the five killed rose as *revenant*s."

"I didn't know that was possible."

"I didn't either," Aiyan said. "Rhyl, the *vivus* took Corri's shape." Aiyan's voice was full of pity.

Rhyl was thankful he hadn't eaten breakfast. He felt like he might throw up.

"Rhyl?" Calypso took his hand, grounding him.

Rhyl dropped his hand and grabbed his towel, launching out of the pool.

"Rhyl!" Calypso called.

But Rhyl ignored him. He was a fool—such a fool. Everything he touched became cursed. *He* was cursed. The prophecy had cursed him before he had taken his first breath. What was he doing, taking Calypso as his lover? Letting himself think he could *have* a lover. Live a normal life. No, he had been selfish. How could he do this to Calypso?

"Rhyl!" they called.

"No." Rhyl addressed them all. His face was wet from the pool, maybe it would hide his tears. He looked at Calypso, hoping he saw the truth in his eyes. "This is my fault."

He could see them all bristle and open their mouths to argue, but he turned his back on them, closing his ears to their words. They didn't know. They hadn't been there with the Allmakers.

Back in his chamber, Rhyl dressed, strapping his sword to his hip. He needed to go to the cendari tree in the north. He would use its magic to find the missing vercuri. He'd sort through the Allmakers' memories in his head. He would figure this out. He would be the child of the prophecy.

"Rhyl?" Calypso came in quietly.

"I have a job to do."

"The prophecy."

Rhyl nodded. It hurt to look at Calypso. It hurt to think of the night before. Of Calypso, his skin, his mouth. How it felt to be with him. Like every happy memory. Every clear sunrise. Every bright moon. How could everything shift so quickly? Rhyl's sun had been eclipsed by midnight in an instant. "I have to do this, Calypso. Alone. I was a fool to…to think you and me…to think this was a good idea."

"What are you saying?" Calypso's voice held an edge that made his voice unrecognizable. Rhyl's fault.

If he looked at Calypso, it would destroy him.

"Forget last night, Calypso. Go back to the Forest. You can't help me. You should never have followed me."

"I—"

"You can't help me!" Rhyl said, letting the *varing* creep under his skin, sending it deliberately toward Calypso. He turned and saw the moment Calypso sensed the dark magic, fear lacing his bright blue eyes. "Leave." Rhyl intentionally pushed the *varing* into his voice, watching as Calypso's expression turned from sorrow to fear to anger.

"Fine," Calypso said so quietly Rhyl almost didn't hear. Then between one breath and the next, Calypso shifted into a raven. Rhyl hadn't realized his window was open until Calypso flew through it. Gone as quickly as a breeze and just as quiet.

Gone.

What had Rhyl just done?

The invisible weight of what he'd said to Calypso pulled him down, crushing him. His knees hit the stone floor and Rhyl blessed the pain that moved through him from the impact. Pain of the body was welcome over the pain in his heart that made it a struggle to keep air in his lungs. He stood, holding the table for support as he shoved his feet into his boots. His chance of catching up to Calypso was slim. A raven could cover ground much faster than a man forced to wend through hallway after hallway after stairway. But it didn't matter. He needed to try. He needed…fuck, he'd used the *varing* on Calypso, a *velidar*. What kind of monster was he?

Aiyan. Aiyan and Mila could call Calypso back. Then Rhyl could explain himself. Rhyl needed to apologize and try to make this right.

Calypso wouldn't really fly back to the Forest, would he? If he did, Rhyl would follow him. The prophecy might destroy Rhyl, it might kill him. What if he died without telling Calypso how much he loved him? His heart ached with regret. Calypso…he needed Calypso.

He stumbled past the guards into the courtyard, but there was no raven in sight. No Aiyan. His parents were gone. They were probably in the council room discussing Aiyan's news and Rhyl's abrupt departure. He went back into the palace.

Rhyl came around a corner and startled Asha. "Asha! Do you know where Aiyan is? He was just here."

Asha smiled. "Yes, I can take you to him."

"Thank you!"

Asha picked up her skirt and led Rhyl down the hall. Rhyl wrote an apology in his mind as he went so he would know exactly what to instruct Aiyan to tell Cally. When he looked up, Asha had led him to one of the guest rooms. "Where is Aiyan? No one uses these rooms." Rhyl spun toward her, confusion and desperation making him slow. A warning rippled through Rhyl's mind. Asha's smile had been off.

"Aiyan can't help you," Asha said.

Her eyes…her mouth twisted in a way that seemed out of place. Her expression was like a mask, a terrible farce of the Asha Rhyl knew.

He caught a glimpse of a small blade as she lunged toward him. When Rhyl was a child, Aiyan would tell him stories about the vipers of Rodan. The small, deadly, lightning-fast serpents the color of sand. The perfect predator. Asha moved like light, like water, like the deadly serpents of Rhyl's childhood fascination.

Rhyl dodged her blade. As a *candarii*, he was faster than any Kitarran. Even Stone. He knocked her down, pinning her to the ground. There was a strange scent to her fur. Not the Kitarran grain-like smell all Kitarrans had; this was the smell of magic. But not his magic or Forest magic or *heera* magic. His mind almost snagged it, but Asha threw him off in a burst of energy, knocking him onto the stone floor, her blade skidding against Rhyl's ribs. A fiery pain lanced through him.

That was when he noticed what was off about her. Her eyes were the wrong color. They were black instead of green. Rhyl reached for her leg and gripped hard, trying to find the source of her strange magic.

Asha plunged the knife into his side and he screamed. Pain washed over him in waves and he did not let go. He pushed his magic into Asha, in her mind. Her mind, her will, was brimmed with powerful and violent magic. But underneath was another force, another person. Asha, just Asha, and she was fighting to free herself from the magic. He felt her extract the knife from his side, only to plunge it into his shoulder. The fiery pain came in waves. Still, he did not let go.

Rhyl began to unravel the magic that held Asha captive in her own body, but the pain made it difficult. His shirt felt wet and warm with blood.

Asha loomed over him. Quiet Asha. Mysterious Asha. But she was fading. Everything was blurred, and Rhyl just wanted to sleep away the pain.

But he couldn't silence the question. If the real Asha was trapped inside her mind, then who was this trying to kill Rhyl?

CHAPTER 78

ASHA

ASHA, trapped in her mind, saw a pinprick of light, like a hand reaching for her in the dark cage of her memories, offering her a way out. She pushed through the thick black that was her master's magic, reaching, stretching. The light grew. Asha could see, for an instant. She was walking down the hall, but just as quickly, she was pushed down into the prison once again.

Asha screamed.

Then magic slipped from her mind and everything was clear. She stumbled against the onslaught of memories. She'd tricked Rhyl into following her, then attacked him. She'd aimed for his heart, but he'd fought her. Her dagger had pierced his side instead of his heart, then again in his shoulder—gods, he lay at her feet, his eyes glazing over. But now, her mind was her own.

His hand released her ankle. She had not noticed he was holding on to her. Blood trickled down his torso from the wound. Asha dropped the dagger. It bounced onto the tile floor, splattering blood onto her fur.

"Rhyl!" She crouched beside him. His eyes were fading, not just with pain, but with the *varing*. Black tendrils chased away the blue of his eyes. "Rhyl, stay with me. Stay with me, please."

She ran to the hall and screamed for help.

"Asha?" someone answered.

Cassandra.

"Cassie, get help! Rhyl is hurt!"

Cassandra hurried over to her.

"No, go get help!" But Cassandra wasn't listening. She closed the door behind her. Asha heard the lock slip home.

"Cassie?"

Oh, gods. Cassandra's eyes were…not right. Like Liam's had been. How was this possible? How could her master enthrall Cassandra?

Cassandra pulled a dagger from her belt. It was the brightest thing in the room.

"No, Cassie, no!"

Cassandra lunged at Rhyl's throat. Asha leaped, knocking Cassandra's knife to the side. Asha easily disarmed Cassandra and immobilized her. Cassandra fought like a wildcat, like there was nothing that could stop her. But Asha was a Kitarran, and she had been trained to be ruthless. Cassandra's body, though controlled by a sorceress, was still a soft, pliable thing. Asha dug her claws into Cassandra's skin; it was the only way to hold her. She slammed Cassie's head down onto the table, and Cassandra went limp.

Rhyl, unconscious, was still bleeding into the rug from the wound Asha had caused.

"Asha?" Someone banged on the door. Asha's fingers slipped on the lock, leaving red streaks behind, but she managed it.

Aiyan brushed past her. Asha sobbed in relief to see him. Several Queen's Guards came behind him. Asha's sobs blurred her sight. Aiyan crouched over Rhyl, his hands checking Rhyl's body. A guard took Asha's arm.

Aiyan turned to the guards, his amber eyes like a piercing flame. "Take them and place them under guard," he ordered. His eyes were those of an assassin.

Asha swallowed her sobs, her throat burning, and forced the words out. "Talo is in danger! Please, *she* is everywhere. *She* can infect anyone! Please, keep Talo safe."

"Who?"

"Allia."

As the guards led her away, Asha thought, perhaps, she had seen recognition on Aiyan's face.

CHAPTER 79

ILLIAH

"RHYL'S BEEN ATTACKED. He is badly wounded."

Illiah was the First Defender of Kitarra. He was a leader. He was a fucking hero. But Mila's breathless words almost forced him to weep and wet himself for fear.

Rhyl.

Illiah had all sorts of nightmares, but the worst ones involved his sons.

"What happened?" Rhyl had been upset by Aiyan's news. They all were. But Calypso had gone with Rhyl, and who better to calm him than his lover? It was obvious Calypso cared deeply for Rhyl. What could have happened?

Mila shook her head. "Aiyan told me Rhyl was hurt, and to find you, then he rushed off." She paused. "He is with Rhyl. Come."

"Where's Eva?"

"She is on her way."

Mila led Illiah down the hall. Down a flight of stairs, still in the palace, down another hall. Guards stood at attention outside one of the guest rooms. Stone was there too, just behind him, his large presence a mere shadow in Illiah's mind.

Illiah pushed past, Mila on his heels.

Rhyl lay crumpled on the ground. Aiyan was moving over him, chanting softly. Illiah felt Stone's hand on his elbow, steadying him. Aiyan had already removed Rhyl's tunic and had a cloth pressed to his side, saturated with blood. Blood was smeared on Aiyan's skin, on the floor. Rhyl's blood. His son's blood.

"Where's Eva?" Illiah hissed.

"I'm here." She brushed past him and joined Aiyan beside Rhyl, putting one hand on his brow and one on his stomach, just below the wound. "He lives, barely."

"He's a strong boy," Aiyan whispered.

The room went silent as Eva did her work, using her *sanarii* magic. No one stirred. Illiah dared not breathe, lest somehow his breath would push away the life from his son.

"I can't do it. I can't keep him. I can't pull him back." Eva shook. "There is too much *varing* inside him."

Illiah didn't think. He reached down and put his hand on her shoulder and pushed. It was not gentle. It was a blow in the dark and Eva lurched, gasping for air, then realized what he was doing. Illiah had no idea if the *varing* would help, if the dark could strengthen the light.

"It's working," Eva whispered, her voice strained.

Now that Illiah had welcomed it, the *varing* rose to greet him, eager, powerful. His eyes shifted. Shadows crawled along the walls, their hands reaching out, reaching for him and Eva and Rhyl. Mostly for Rhyl. The man was there too. Illiah's mirror. His dark reflection. Mute.

Mute was close. So close. He reached out a hand to touch Illiah's face like a brother lost. But Illiah felt another touch first. A hand clasped his shoulder, then another. Illiah heard a wolf's snarl. He opened his eyes. Aiyan was holding him by the shoulder. Eva was slumped on top of Rhyl, and Stone was there beside her, lifting her, cradling her. Illiah shoved Aiyan away, meeting his yellow wolf eyes. What he saw on Aiyan's face was a promise made long ago.

"Not yet," he whispered to Aiyan. And then Aiyan nodded, his jaw relaxed.

Illiah touched Rhyl's throat and felt a pulse just as Rhyl's eyes fluttered open.

"Is she all right?" Illiah asked Stone. Stone nodded, smoothing Eva's hair from her face, his lips a thin line. "Rhyl? Can you hear me?"

Rhyl gave a very faint nod. "Everything hurts."

Illiah's relief came as a sob as he cradled his son. Rhyl started shivering. Aiyan had a blanket and Illiah helped him wrap it around Rhyl. Rhyl tried to sit up but could only get onto one elbow, so Illiah held him. Eva was awake but weak as a newborn. Stone gathered her onto his lap. Illiah turned his old jealousy into gratitude, thankful Stone was there to help Eva when Illiah could not.

"Where is Cally?" Rhyl whispered, his voice rough as gravel. "I need to find Calypso."

"You almost died, Rhyl."

"We will find him," Aiyan assured him.

"I said something awful to him. He left…my fault."

"Shh. We will find him," Stone crooned.

"I don't think I can walk," Rhyl said.

"The guards are bringing a stretcher," Stone said. He stood with Eva in his arms.

"I need to know what happened here," Illiah stated. With Rhyl away from the edge of death, the First Defender inside Illiah had returned. Illiah had never seen Aiyan look so old and tired.

"It was Asha," Aiyan said.

"Asha?" Illiah choked.

"She…she and Cassandra are responsible. They are under guard."

"Where?"

"Their chambers."

Then Talo rushed into the room. "Rhyl! What happened?"

Illiah glanced at Stone. There was no way to shelter Talo from the truth. Illiah felt sick. Telling Talo the woman he loved was an enemy would be as painful as the wound she had inflicted on Rhyl. But there was no magic to cure a heart broken from betrayal.

CHAPTER 80

ASHA

ONE GUARD SAT IN HER ROOM, watching Asha pace. How many kept watch outside? It didn't matter. Asha wasn't going to escape. And besides, she had nowhere to go. Cassandra had been taken somewhere else.

Please let Rhyl live, Asha begged. The dagger had not reached his heart. But Asha knew enough about wounds to know it had been grievous.

A guard opened the door. "Come."

Ten guards flanked her as she was led down the hall, too many for her to best even if she wished to dash for freedom. Freedom. Ha. There was no freedom for her in a world with Allia in it.

Asha rubbed her eyes with the back of her hand repeatedly. She told herself to stop crying. She owed it to them to explain, and she refused to do it sobbing and sniveling like a child.

The guards led her to the council room.

Aiyan, Illiah, Stone, and Mila. There were four of them—no, five. Talo was in the shadows, leaning against the wall. She caught his expression as she passed. Had her face looked like that when Liam had tried to kill her? Her tears kept coming. Cassandra sat in a wooden chair, her face red from crying. Asha was put in a chair next to her.

"You owe us an explanation," Stone said to Asha.

"You owe *me* an explanation," came Talo's voice, rough from tears of his own.

Aiyan stood before them, his eyes veiled. What did he see that others could not?

Asha looked at her hands.

"I'm not who you think I am," she told them. "My master is a woman named Allia. She sent me to Kitarra to gain your trust. She planned this all." Gods, what if they didn't believe her? Now that she spoke it, it sounded ludicrous.

Mila's curse startled Asha. She looked up at them. Aiyan's eyes were no longer veiled. Fear, sadness, and regret betrayed the seriousness of her truth. They knew Allia.

"She ordered you to kill Rhyl?" Aiyan asked. Stone and Illiah were silent. Talo paced as if trying to contain himself. Asha noted the latha at his belt.

Asha shook her head. "No. She can take over my mind, my body. She can turn my will into her own. But I broke free, somehow—Rhyl...I know this all sounds crazy." She closed her eyes, trying to gather her thoughts into words. Asha remembered how she'd come back to herself when Rhyl touched her. Asha shook her head to clear her thoughts. Maybe *She* had merely let her go. "I called for help. Cassie came, but Allia enthralled Cassandra and attacked Rhyl a second time."

Cassandra was as pale as the moon. "I didn't do anything. Asha is lying."

"I'm not. I beg you, I'm not lying. Allia...can make others do things they would not normally do. She can change them somehow. Like they are under her spell," Asha tried to explain. She dared to meet Talo's eyes.

"Is that what she did to you?" Talo asked. His tone was a laceration.

"Yes. Sometimes."

"But she didn't always need to, did she?" Aiyan said. "She had other ways to get you to do what she wanted."

Asha nodded, swallowing a sob.

"Why, Asha?" Talo spoke. Aiyan shushed him.

"I didn't want to. It wasn't me—I had no choice." Asha hated how her tears threatened to rob her of speech. How they made her look fragile and pathetic, but she couldn't stop crying. "She took Liam."

"Who is Liam?"

"A Kitarran, an orphan, like me. My friend. We were raised and trained together in Rodan."

"What happened to Liam?" Aiyan asked, looking at Illiah knowingly.

"She changed him. She told him to kill me and he almost did. He was my dearest friend, and he would have killed me without hesitation."

"Liam is the *daeum* Kitarran Allia has in Mahlas that Eva spoke of," Aiyan said softly. Asha didn't understand the strange word. *Day-um?*

"If Allia found a way to make a *daeum* Kitarran, why not change Asha too?" Illiah said.

Aiyan was watching Asha as if she were a puzzle. "She couldn't. Not quite. May I touch you?" Aiyan asked Asha.

Asha nodded. Anything to help them believe her.

The room held its breath as Aiyan placed his hands, one on either side of Asha's face, cupping her ears. His skin was cool against her fur. She thought it would feel the same as when Allia had pushed her magic into Asha's mind, but it didn't. It was almost soothing. Asha found that she could close her eyes and breathe deeper. The room seemed to disappear. Then she smelled magic, but it was an earthy smell, like moss in the sun. Peace. Like the forest at dawn. Like sunrise. Cool rain on hot sand.

When he released his hands, it felt like a light had gone out. She blinked.

"It's hard to sense, but there is something there, like *candarii* magic, but strange. I have no idea how Allia managed it."

Asha dared to hope that they actually believed her.

"Can you get rid of it?" Illiah asked.

"I don't know."

"Please." The plea escaped her before she could stop it.

"I can try. Later. I need to see to Rhyl. He was stable, but he is still grievously injured."

Asha put her hand over her mouth. "I'm so sorry. I am." She was crying again. She swallowed her tears and looked at Talo. His face was a thousand shades of anger. She wanted to beg Talo for forgiveness, tell him she loved him, but no, that would be selfish. Cruel.

Stone nodded. "Put the girls in their chambers, and keep them guarded."

In solitude, Asha wept and wept.

CHAPTER 81

AIYAN

AIYAN STOOD OUTSIDE Asha's door. Exhaustion saturated every fiber of his body. He yearned to shift into his wolf form and curl around Mila and sleep the feeling away.

At least Rhyl was healing. His parents' magic had saved his life. But Rhyl should never have been in danger. Aiyan had felt something off about Asha from the first. How had he not seen it?

Aiyan knocked gently on Asha's door. "It's Aiyan. May I come in?"

The guard gave him a strange look. Just because Asha was a prisoner didn't mean she didn't deserve respect, but Aiyan was not in the mood to school the guard. He did glare at him, just a little, which never failed. The guard swallowed and stepped back involuntarily.

"Come in," Asha's faint voice answered.

The guard opened the door with a clank of keys and let Aiyan inside.

Asha sat on her window seat, knees pressed against her chest. The fur on her face was wet with tears. She looked young and lost and scared.

"I'm hoping you will speak with me about Allia," he said in Rodan.

"Of course."

He moved slowly and sat across from her. She watched him with tired eyes.

"How old were you when you first met Allia?"

"I was quite young—I don't know my exact birthdate. Maybe four?"

"What did she do to you?"

"At first, not much. She had tutors for us, for Liam and me. We learned languages and numbers. We were taught to read and write in both Rodan and Praedan. We were taught how to fight with knives and bows and swords and our hands."

"Were you treated kindly?"

"No. Not really. At the time, I thought it was kindness. We had good food to eat and plenty of water, and clean clothes. But now I see how Pena is treated, and Bren and Aralis. Liam and I were expected to learn quickly, and when we didn't, we were punished. Mostly by being separated and isolated." Asha drew in a sharp breath, her eyes full of memories. "Then when I was about twelve, Master–I mean, Allia— came to live at the villa. She would spend time alone with Liam. When he came back from those times, he was quiet and sad."

"When did she first take over your mind?"

Asha looked at her hands. "I was about thirteen, I think. She did the same thing that you did. She would put her hands on my face and little by little I would feel her take over. I fought her once. Only once. She killed a servant, in front of me, out of anger. I was terrified she would kill me or Liam."

"Was it the same with Liam?"

"No. She *changed* him. When her magic leaves my mind, I come back to myself. Liam is always…lost."

So Allia had had years to warp and train Asha's mind into her weapon. Aiyan knew Imal, Allia's brother, had never had Allia's patience. Perhaps that was why the old emperor failed to take the minds of the Kitarrans. Or maybe there was something about Liam's mind that was different.

"May I?" Aiyan held out his hands.

Asha nodded. Aiyan could see her effort not to flinch when he touched her face. With a gentle touch, the same he would use on a patient riddled with pain, he used his *heera* magic and reached into her mind, her memories. Her fear was strongest, mingled and amplified by her helplessness. But woven among the fear was a faintly glowing thread of light that was her love for the other Kitarran, the one whom Allia had taken, Liam. Good. Aiyan could work with that.

Gently, Aiyan began to rip the pieces left by Allia, bit by bit, freeing Asha's glowing thread from Allia's tightly woven chains.

Asha tensed against his fingers. The glowing thread disappeared, swallowed by a familiar magic. Aiyan was consumed by Allia. The smell of her skin and her dark hair. Aiyan's memories overwhelmed him. Allia was there, wearing Asha's skin, in control of her Kitarran body. She lashed out at him, using Asha's claws to dig into Aiyan's face. Aiyan felt blood drip down his skin and moved to block her, but she was fast.

"Aiyan! How dare you take what is mine!" Allia hissed through Asha's voice.

"Allia," Aiyan spat. "You can't have her." He began to sing. Allia had *heera* magic, but she had not been raised by a wise woman. She did not know there was power in words and voice and vibration. Aiyan pushed his magic through his chant; he reached for Asha and held on to her, pushing out Allia, his touch no longer gentle or kind. It was forceful and *heera* strong. He should have known Allia would not let him take the righteous path. She would force him to fight and claw and growl. But if that's what it took to cleanse Asha of Allia's evil grasp, he would fight until every last strand of the woman was eradicated.

Asha woke.

"You're bleeding! What happened?" She put her hands on her head as if it ached.

"She came. We fought. I won," Aiyan told her, breathing hard.

Asha gaped.

"I don't think Allia will be able to take over you again." Aiyan would not have told her if he had doubted it. That would have been too cruel.

Asha's lip quivered. She clearly did not trust her hope. "What about Liam?"

Aiyan shook his head. "Liam is different. I don't know if he can be saved."

She nodded.

"You are free, Asha."

She turned her glistening eyes on him. Her mouth curved in a small, sad smile. "Thank you, Aiyan."

"It is my honor. No one should be forced to live inside a cage."

CHAPTER 82

ILLIAH

"AIYAN."

"Illiah, come in."

Illiah respected Aiyan greatly. They were friends. But the ease Illiah felt with Stone or Turk had never come with Aiyan. Aiyan was not a brother, he was a howl in the night, a glimpse of shadow in the late afternoon. He was a story told to errant children.

Long ago, as they sailed to Kitarra from Rodan together, Illiah had forced Aiyan to make him a promise. An oath between only the two of them. Not even Eva or Mila knew. The oath was why Aiyan had always kept Illiah at a distance, and Illiah had never begrudged Aiyan for it.

"Pena, would you please go help Fia? I need to speak with the First Defender."

Pena nodded and picked up her books before walking past Illiah and his guards.

"Pena is a brave thing," Illiah mused as he took a seat.

"Are Rhyl and Eva still sleeping?"

Sleeping was too gentle a term for what magic did to a *sanarii*, but Illiah nodded. He regarded the wolf, the shadows of grief under the man's eyes. "What happened when you spoke to Asha?"

Aiyan had been an assassin, but he had chosen a different profession since coming to Kitarra. The assassin turned healer. He tended the sick and dying with a kindness and strength Illiah marveled at. After years of taking lives, he now saved them. Illiah had never asked Aiyan to step into his former role, but he was relieved Aiyan volunteered to interrogate Asha because he had been close to asking. Illiah did not want to turn that task over to anyone else. The matter was too nuanced, even if she had nearly killed Rhyl.

Aiyan clasped his hands and rested his chin on his thumbs. He took a breath. A warrior before the assault. "Asha is free from Allia's enslavement. I used my *heera* song to break the bond."

Illiah was glad to hear it. He knew what it felt like to be controlled by another. Poor Asha. But whatever the wolf had done to win Asha's freedom, it left a mark. Illiah had never seen the wolf look so haggard. "How did Allia bind her to begin with?"

"In Rodan, Allia was exceptionally good at enthralling. She could take Imal's *daeum* from his control without him knowing. If anyone could make a *daeum* Kitarran, it would be her."

Imal had been a powerful sorcerer. His army of soulless monsters, the *daeum*, had nearly destroyed Jullayah, then Kitarra. Only a greater monster had stopped him.

"But you never saw her enthrall a Kitarran?" Illiah asked, pushing his monster from his thoughts.

"No. Imal tried again and again to create Kitarran *daeum*, and failed. I don't know how Allia managed it." Aiyan was lost to the shadows briefly. "But Asha is not a *daeum*. What Allia did to her is different. A *daeum* has a unique dicidium—you know I can see the wrongness of it easily with my *heera* sight. But Asha's aura looks the same as any Kitarran. I saw no reason to suspect her."

"And the Rodan princess?"

"The same."

"We need to know how easy it is for Allia to enthrall someone. Does she have to meet them? Know them? Or is anyone susceptible?"

"I don't think she could enthrall just anyone. Some are harder to control than others. *Sanarii* are easier for *candarii* to control, for instance." Aiyan grimaced as he said it. "And Cassandra is from

Rodan. Perhaps she and Allia crossed paths. I haven't asked her yet."

"Asha is not *daeum*, but Allia does have a *daeum* Kitarran. Eva saw him in Mahlas."

"Asha said his name is Liam."

"Maybe there was something amiss about the boy?" Illiah offered. "In Rodan, the *varing* could only consume me *after* Imal had broken me."

"Perhaps. Eva said it was Cotoch who killed the *daeum* that day in Kara," Aiyan mentioned, his voice soft.

"She told me that as well. But why would he?"

"Long ago, in Rodan, Cotoch was disgusted by Imal and his *daeum*." Aiyan shrugged.

"Cotoch who coerced a realm with magic to put him on the throne," spat Illiah.

"The Allati have not suffered from his leadership…quite the opposite." Aiyan's mouth twisted. "But we are getting off topic. Cotoch is dead. He is no help to us." Aiyan regarded Illiah. "I never told you this, Illiah. But you are an amplifier. Magic moves through you like an open road. That was why Imal wanted you."

"What does that mean?"

"It means that Rhyl could use you."

"Use me how?"

"To strengthen his magic. Like Imal did."

"Why didn't you tell me this?"

Aiyan rubbed the back of his neck, stretching. "Because I'm a coward, and the last thing I want to do is fulfill my promise."

Aiyan's words trickled like winter rain into Illiah's heart.

CHAPTER 83

RHYL

THE LIGHT CAME INTO FOCUS as Rhyl opened his eyes. He was on his parents' bed; his mother lay beside him. She looked asleep. Dark circles haloed her eyes, making her faint wrinkles stark. Rhyl had never seen her look so old and worn. He reached out and put his palm on her brow, recalling how Aiyan had told him to rest, but he needed to make sure his mother was all right. Eva had saved him with her *sanarii* magic, and now he used his magic to give her strength. Not that he had much to give. He felt weak as a lamb born in a winter field.

"Rhyl," she murmured. Then she groaned. "How do you feel?"

"Terrible."

"Me too. What happened?"

"I still don't know. I can't really piece it together." He remembered Asha, then grimaced. The sickening feeling of the knife in his side was imprinted on his nerves.

Stone sat in the shadows, his eyes on Eva. Rhyl recognized the bond they shared. Amourii. "Stone, what do you know?"

Stone cleared his throat. "Asha told us she has been under the control of Allia, a *candarii*. She threatened her into spying on us."

"And Cassandra?"

"Asha claims Allia used her magic to enthrall her."

"If Allia can do that, no one is safe."

"Not necessarily," Eva said. "Allia didn't enthrall *us*. Surely if she could, she would not have needed to send Asha here to gain our trust. And there must be a reason she could control Cassandra."

"Aiyan wonders if it is because Allia is also *heera*," Stone muttered. "Rhyl, Illiah has ordered you to be under Mila's or Aiyan's guard at all times."

"Has anyone seen Calypso?" Rhyl asked, ignoring Stone's statement.

Stone shook his head. "Last we saw he was following you."

The pit in Rhyl's stomach gaped. He pressed the palms of his hands against his eyes and groaned.

"If he loves you, he will come back," his mother assured him.

"That is not how it is supposed to be. I should go to him," Rhyl growled. "But I can't even stand up. And I have no idea where he is."

Stone patted Rhyl's knee sympathetically. "I'll find some food. Food helps."

Stone left. Eva sighed. "This is where, as your mother, I should tell you to be strong, that this will pass. But this fucking hurts."

Rhyl grimaced. Everything behind his eyes throbbed. He closed his eyes, trying to connect to the *simul rami*. He needed to find Calypso, even just to know he was all right. Nothing happened. There was nothing to connect to in his parents' chambers. He needed the wind, or fire, or the gold basin. His muscles felt pummeled as he forced his body to move.

"Where are you going?"

"I need to find Calypso." To his surprise, his mother didn't argue or tell him to rest or berate him until he listened to her reasoning.

Mila was sitting outside the door as a wolf. Her black fur gleamed in the torchlight, an extension of the night. Night. Rhyl lurched. He hadn't noticed the dark windows in his mother's room. He'd lost a whole day. He would never find Calypso in the dark. Even if the *simul rami* could show him Calypso, how could he know where he was if it was the middle of the fucking night? He wanted to punch something.

"Do you know where Calypso is?" he asked Mila.

Mila shook her head.

"Can you contact him?" Rhyl's throat was tight with hope.

Mila's wolf face looked sad. She cocked her head, then shook her head once more and touched her wet nose to Rhyl's hand, her tail wagging softly. Rhyl drew a shuddering breath.

Calypso could take care of himself. But what if he didn't come back? What if he was already on his way to the Great Forest, far beyond Rhyl's reach?

Fuck the prophecy. Rhyl needed to find the man he loved.

CHAPTER 84

ASHA

WHEN ASHA HAD FIRST ARRIVED at the Queen's Keep, the elegant chamber given to her had felt imposing with its high ceilings and lavish rugs. Now as she paced its length, the walls, the ceiling, pressed down on her, squeezing the life from her, breath by anxious breath. She wanted to run, to fly. By severing her connection to Allia, Aiyan had given her a gift beyond measure. And she knew exactly what she was going to do with it.

She was going to kill Allia.

At Allia's command, Asha had been trained to be cunning and deadly, to be a weapon, a blade in the dark. Asha had the tools she needed to avenge Rhyl and Liam and Talo…She couldn't regain Talo's affection or trust, she knew that, but Allia would die by Asha's blade, and that would have to be enough.

Asha's room was guarded by several Queen's Guards. Even if she could fight her way out, she refused to inflict more violence on Queen Arrah's people. She would save her violence for Allia.

From what she'd overheard, Allia was in the city of Mahlas. Asha was thankful for the time she'd spent studying the maps in the palace library. She knew Mahlas was well outside of Kitarra's borders. The physical distance did not worry her. But where she would find Allia, she would find Liam. And Liam, as Allia's slave, would kill Asha if he could. Asha was not sure if she was prepared to kill her oldest friend.

But the truth settled over her, along with an old ache. Liam was not that boy anymore. Liam, the boy who had held her hand and taught her to carve a stone, was gone. Allia murdered him the day she ordered Liam to fight Asha.

Asha's anger was more useful than tears. She let it wash over her, infusing her grief with its strength.

She studied her chamber with the eye of a prisoner looking to escape. The only window was constructed of tall panes of glass that did not open. The window faced the royal courtyard patrolled by guards.

Asha cataloged her strengths. She was a good fighter, but since she was not willing to harm any Kitarran, she would have to rely on her speed and agility. Most of the Queen's Guard were human; she could easily outrun them. But they might shoot her in the back. Also some of the Queen's Guard carried throwing knives. She would have to take the risk and trust the dark of night to cover her.

She would do it tonight.

A guard brought Asha dinner. Soup and a piece of bread and a chunk of cheese. She ate it only because she knew her body would need all the strength it could get, but her nerves made eating a chore. The window was black with night when another guard collected her empty dishes.

Asha waited until midnight when the shift was almost over and the guards on duty would be tired and slow from their hours of tedious watching. At least she hoped. She held no illusions—the Queen's Guard were the best warriors in Kitarra.

She had a small bag with a few bits of food she'd hidden away. She slipped in a few coins. That was it. Stone had confiscated her throwing knives, and oh, how she missed them. She changed out of her dress into pants and a close-fitting tunic and her leather vest. The leather would not stop an arrow or dagger, but it might protect her from the broken edges of the glass. She couldn't risk a cloak catching on the glass or anything else. She needed to move like the wind.

Asha sat at her window and listened. During the day, the courtyard was alive with voices, guards, servants, the royal family, but now in the dead of night, there was only the faint movement of guards. She thanked her acute Kitarran hearing. A human would be hopeless.

When she was sure (as sure as she could be) no guards were directly below her window, she picked up the washing basin, the heaviest object she could find in her room small enough to throw.

She aimed.

Threw.

For a terrifying moment, she thought the basin would bounce back and crash onto the floor. But the glass shattered. She didn't wait for the pieces to settle before diving through the small opening carved by the basin. She tucked and rolled onto the ground outside. A shard grazed her arm.

From the corner of her eye, she caught a glimpse of the guards. But she was already running, ignoring the burn of her arm and the pinch in her foot. She must have stepped on a shard.

The guards, weighed down by weapons and stumbling in surprise, were not fast enough. Asha had already leaped and landed on the top of the wall—a challenging feat for a Kitarran, impossible for a human. She ran along the wall, making her way beyond the palace, waiting for the knife in the back of her leg. She closed her ears to the shouts of outrage from the guards. Soon the palace would be alive, and Asha needed to vanish.

The bite of steel didn't come. She leaped from the wall to the roof, using her momentum to combat the steep angle. Running above the hallways and ornate courtyards was like entering another world. Part of her yearned to pause, to look down on the subtle lights of Kilev, to watch the moon play off the Ilba River and Kitarra Peak behind her. But that was a pastime for a court lady. Asha was a traitor. She had no place in Kitarra.

With a quick assessment, she surged over the gap between the roof to the next section of the wall separating the palace from the rest of Kilev. She teetered there, catching her balance. The wall came to an abrupt end where it met the massive wall of the Forge. The only way forward was a long drop into the forest. There was a tree, its branches reaching toward her like a promise, but it was the farthest jump yet. She bit her lip. Time was slipping away. She could hear the alarm rising from the palace behind. Ahead, the wall around the Forge was lined with guard towers, and Asha knew those towers were always occupied.

The wall around the Forge was also dotted with windows. Above and below each window was a stone sill. The sills were narrow, but the windows were close enough that she could leap from window to window. If she fell, it would be a nasty drop. Pointy rocks jutted toward her like teeth. If she could get down two levels, she could make the last drop into the forest without breaking her ankles.

She leaped to the first window ledge, digging her fingers into the tiny crevices of stone. Her fingers ached as she clung to the narrow ledge. Her outstretched tail kept her balanced. As she jumped to the last window, her legs wobbled. Beyond, the forest was dark and welcoming. She took the last leap. The landing was harder than she'd anticipated. A sharp pain lanced up her foot—she needed to check for glass—but she didn't think it was twisted or broken.

She allowed herself a moment to breathe. She yearned to head into the forest, but she thought of the wolves. They would track her more easily in the trees where her scent would be discernible among beetle and squirrel. Better to stick to the city roads, camouflage her scent with the people and other Kitarrans. But she needed to be out of Kilev by morning. She was too distinctive. She cursed her patchwork fur.

A hand clenched onto her arm. She had not heard anyone approach. The Kitarran's fingers cinched around her biceps, and she bit her lip to stop from crying out in pain. She could see his face and crumpled to the ground under the force of Talo's glare.

Talo was alone. If she knocked out his knees, she might break free from his grasp, but she couldn't bring herself to hurt him.

"Are you going back to *her*?" Talo growled. Anger danced in his eyes like a living thing.

"I am going to kill her," Asha vowed, but it came out weak and fearful. Like Asha as a child standing before Allia, feeling like dirt under her fingernail. *No. I am not that girl anymore.*

Talo let his grip slacken, and Asha raised her chin and stood. Talo's hand was still on her arm. "You want vengeance?"

"Yes," Asha told him.

Talo took a breath. "I believe you."

"You—you do?"

Talo nodded. He let go of her arm.

"Are you letting me go?" Asha dared to ask.

"No. I'm coming with you."

CHAPTER 85

STONE

IT WAS THE MIDDLE OF THE FUCKING NIGHT, and Stone was not a young man anymore. Gods, he was tired. Mila was at his side as they poured into the First Defender's room. The hallway behind them was filled with guards.

"Asha is gone," Stone announced.

Eva appeared at Illiah's side, a fine robe covering her nakedness.

"And we lost Rhyl," Mila said.

"What do you mean, you lost Rhyl?" Illiah demanded. "I told you and Aiyan to keep an eye on him."

Mila bristled. "I am not your soldier, Illiah. Rhyl came to me asking about Calypso, then went back to his chambers. Then Bren and Aralis—"

"Bren and Aralis are the reason you lost Rhyl?" Stone said with a huff. He had not been told that.

"They caused a distraction so Rhyl could leave his room without anyone noticing."

"What kind of distraction—never mind, I don't want to know." Eva pressed her forehead against Illiah's shoulder.

"Those boys," Illiah growled.

"Don't blame them," Mila said. "Well, I guess you can blame them a bit. But they think Rhyl hung the moon, so they would do anything for him."

"You're not wrong."

"Where is Talo?" Illiah asked.

"I don't know," Stone answered.

"He is gone too," Mila said.

"What. The. Fuck."

"Children," Eva said in the same tone. Stone shared a look of frustration with her.

"What do we do?" Illiah asked, looking a thousand years old.

"What can we do?" Stone countered.

"Rhyl is more powerful than any of us. We have to trust he knows what he is doing," Eva said.

"They are clever children," Illiah mused.

"They are no longer children," Mila berated them. "It is time to let them lead."

CHAPTER 86

CALYPSO

RAVENS COULD NOT CRY. Their eyes lacked the capacity for tears. But Calypso felt his grief in every feather, right down to his scaly toes, and it blinded him all the same.

He didn't know which direction he flew, but the smell of the river faded, and before him loomed mountains peaked with jagged rocks and patches of old snow. He flew lower, skimming the forest. He flew and flew and flew until his wings ached, forcing him to land on a rock in a small clearing.

He shifted back to a human, letting his body purge its grief, letting the tears stream down his face until he lay weak and half-frozen in the grass. His head felt clearer, but he shivered. The discomfort from the cold was secondary, almost calming.

He couldn't do what the Allmakers wanted of him. He couldn't go back. He couldn't face Rhyl.

"My, my, what have we here?"

The voice startled Calypso. He shifted back into a raven, ready to take flight.

"Don't fly away, little raven. I need your help."

Calypso studied the person before him. Tall. Old. A voice like a man, but not a man judging by the long dress, and the bright bracelets and bells looped around her arms. Her—his?—eyes were lined with charcoal, creased in the corners from age. She wore an ornate shawl woven with every color imaginable over her head, hiding her hair. She held out a long, thick cloak.

Calypso shifted back into a man and took the cloak, wrapping it around his bare shoulders.

"Calypso. That is your name, is it not?" The voice was so deep and masculine, so at odds with the person before him, Calypso wondered if he had somehow hit his head.

"How did you know?"

"I'm a seer. My name is Magda. But you can call me Mags." She smiled, revealing more wrinkles. It was a trustworthy kind of smile. "Come. Tea and food always help."

The woman Mags led him into the forest to a wagon that must also be her house. It had a roof and a door. A thick-legged horse grazed on dry grass nearby. It didn't even look up when they traipsed past. A stew pot bubbled over a small fire. The aroma made Calypso's mouth water.

"Is it a coincidence that you were so close, or did you see me coming?" Calypso quipped, but if he was being honest, he wasn't sure where the joke was.

Mags lifted a gray eyebrow. A whole garden of wrinkles emerged on her face. "Have some stew. I have news for you."

The stew was quite good.

"So, raven-boy, you and I both know more about the prophecy than anyone. Me, because I am a seer, and you, because you are the Allmakers' lackey."

"I…guess?"

"Have you unraveled it?"

Calypso shook his head.

"You lie." But she laughed, a deep sound, and the lump in her throat bobbed. "I have seen you. And him.

"*Those who were strong are now weak.* The Kitarrans, obviously. The *varing* has weakened them.

"*With healing hands, the babes will speak.* This could be Aiyan and his healing potions and *heera* ways. Or it could be Rhyl. But how exhausting would that be, if Rhyl had to heal everyone?" She huffed before she continued. "*Light turns to dark and colors shift.* The *varing* poisoning the *simul rami,* of course.

"*Two rivers join when two lovers rift.* Hmm. Tsuga and Mute. Or not? Sometimes I wonder if the prophecy refers to Eva and Illiah. Or you and Rhyl?" Her eyes glinted. "*Watch for the child of two thrones*—Rhyl, indisputably.

"*Born with magic in his bones,*

"*A child lit by the stars.* Rhyl is a very pretty, boy, wouldn't you agree?

"*Watch for him, for he shall be ours.* Oh, the Kitarrans watched for him, all right. Now for the other part."

But Calypso said it before she could, "*After he has proved love's true form*

"*The child will call the storm.*

"*A king, a prince, a fox, a crow, four a circle make.*

"*To send the dark one to the stars for true love's sake.*

"*Snap the tether, set me free*

"*Restore the river of magic to its rightful tree.*"

"Ah. So you *do* know this part," the seer said.

Calypso wanted to disappear into his stew bowl.

"I know what the Allmakers told you to do," Mags said.

Calypso closed his eyes. His chest tightened. He had always hoped that what the Allmakers had told him would not come to pass. He had hoped…but he should have known, after last night. After lying with Rhyl in his arms, he should have known. "*After he has proved love's true form…Only you can help him understand what his magic is and what it can do.*" The words of the Allmakers, spoken years ago, had never left him.

"*How can you ask this of me?*" Calypso had screamed. "*You are making me into a monster.*"

A heavy silence had filled the Forest. "*Calypso, this is the only way.*"

"Do you love him?" Mags asked now, pulling Calypso from the memory.

"I do." Oh, the words ached.

"Do you believe he loves you? Would you lay your life at his feet and trust that he would not squander it?"

"I do. I would." Calypso's stomach turned. Maybe she had poisoned the stew. He almost wished for it.

"The Allmakers told you to find Rhyl's weakness."

Calypso nodded miserably.

"Then you know what must be done."

Calypso retched up his stew. When he was finished, he wiped his mouth on the back of his hand. "I must become a monster."

Heavy gray clouds hovered over the Tarm. The air felt tight as Calypso flew over the endless grass. He could sense them. Her. The *varing*.

His wings felt like rubber and his heart raced with fear. It was all he could do to stay aloft, to stay on his course.

He would do this. For Rhyl.

But it wasn't just Rhyl. It was for Eva. For Illiah. Mila. Murryn. All the people he loved. He was doing this for them. Because without the prophecy, the *varing* would spread like a disease through all the realms. Death and chaos would follow. Calypso was not a warrior. He could not wield a sword or lead an army. He could not use magic to call fire and destruction. But he could do this. He could be the spark that caused the cleansing fire.

Calypso landed on the grass. He shifted and called her name.

She appeared slowly, as the mountains appear when the clouds dissolve after a storm. Her skin was dark green, some parts smooth, some like tree bark. Feathers crested her head and ran down her spine. Moss and lichen grew like armor over her chest and legs. Her eyes were gold, as old as the rocks and the rivers, but they ran with magic.

Behind her was an army made of shadows and ghosts, of monsters and nightmares.

Calypso held his fear tight so he would not run. He hoped it would not hurt, but he thought he could bear the pain of it, knowing it had purpose.

"Raven-boy." Her voice was cold and clear as a winter creek. With a flick of her wrist, a twist of her hand, Calypso felt his body knot and tighten. Dark magic surged in his veins and his limbs tore and contorted. He screamed and his mind was red, red, red.

CHAPTER 87

ASHA

THE WIDE SKY. The dry air. Dust in her lungs. The Tarm reminded Asha of the hills around the villa in Rodan where she had grown up. But the fierce heat was lacking. She did not miss it.

Their journey from Kitarra had consisted of exhausting days and short nights. The first night, Asha apologized to Talo, for everything. He told her in a curt voice that it didn't matter. Every night since, they had stopped, eaten, and taken turns sleeping while the other kept watch. There had been no time for sentiments, though whatever Talo had felt for her seemed to have dissolved when Rhyl almost died.

She glanced at Talo now. He studied the city of Mahlas from their vantage point. The tall grass gave them cover, though Talo's tawny fur gave him an added advantage.

"All right, I sneak in, kill Allia in her bed, and sneak out," Asha repeated. It was the short version of their plan.

"Brilliant," Talo muttered, his sarcasm reminding Asha he was full of reservation.

"I'm very good at sneaking."

"Hmm. Good thing I am too."

"You are *not* coming." They'd argued over it for days. Asha was a nobody; Talo was a prince. If Asha died, no one would care. If Talo died…she couldn't even finish the sentence. "It's too risky."

"I'm coming, Asha."

Asha growled at him. He smiled at her with teeth. She should have sent him away before they left Kitarra's border. He was irritatingly stubborn. But she still found herself fighting a strong urge to kiss him. She turned her attention back to the town.

They waited for the sun to dip below the horizon and for the night to bring them cover. Talo lay, twitching. He did not have Asha's discipline. He had not been forced to master his every movement and thought as Asha had. Talo would always be a prince. Asha had always been a weapon.

A cover of clouds came with the night, shielding the stars and moon, making the lanterns of the city glow with a hazy light.

"I was hoping for rain to help cover my—our—sounds," Asha whispered.

"It might rain yet."

"We can't wait any longer." She made to move but didn't. "Talo, stay here. Please. You are the prince of Kitarra. You are too valuable. And I can't live with myself if something happens to you because of me."

"You mean that." It wasn't quite a question.

"I do," she answered anyway. In the dark, the blue of his eyes was washed out to gray, but she could see his expression clearly. It would be so easy to lean forward and brush her lips against his. He did have lovely lips. And she might be going to her death. If she died without kissing Talo—

"Too bad. Let's go." Talo's hushed whisper startled her. He moved slowly in a crouch down the steep slope. Asha had no choice but to follow.

At the bottom of the hill, the tall building acted like a wall. They scaled the side of it to the roof with only minor difficulty. Talo was light on his feet, just as he promised. But Asha knew Talo had exceptional skills, even for a prince. Or perhaps because he was a prince. Asha had seen him on their voyage, dancing around the ship's sails. She had seen him in practice, working with his latha like it was an extension of him. He was born to it. His mother had been First Defender. His father was…a man out of legend.

They moved across the roof to the main part of the large house, their footsteps soft as falling leaves. They swung down into a darkened window left partially open—a small blessing—landing in near silence. They didn't know the layout, so they were forced to move slowly, checking each room. Fortunately, it was easy to see where the servants' quarters were divided from the main building. Allia liked her finery, and Asha knew she would be in the grandest part of the house.

"Let's hurry," she said. Talo's Kitarran hearing would pick up even the faintest whisper.

The next room they searched was large and richly furnished. A gold basin sat upon a dais, filled with water. Asha had seen a similar basin in Allia's room in Rodan.

"This must be her room," Asha said, searching from corner to corner. "Where is she?" she growled.

"What is this?" Talo pointed to a basket filled with a dried herb. He rubbed the crumbling leaves between his fingers, inhaling. He made an awful face. "I thought it was ragwood, but it's something else."

"Ragwood is what culla is made from?"

Talo nodded.

Asha looked closer at the herb, smelling it. The waft hit her nose. "This is a plant from Rodan. Reaver's grass, it's called. Allia forced me to eat it once, and it made me so sick." Asha remembered the two days she spent in agonizing pain. The scent brought the memory to life. But Asha hadn't seen it since. Allia never mentioned it after that day.

"Did she feed it to your friend too?" Talo said.

"Yes. I think so."

"Before he…changed? What if she is using it like culla?"

Asha nodded. Could there be a connection between the herb and Liam's fate? Did it matter?

"Allia also uses culla. I remember smelling it on her."

"How do you know what culla smells like?"

"Your father."

"Someone's coming," Talo stammered. Asha heard the footsteps too. They were loud, made by more than one person.

Asha grabbed Talo and went for the window, planning to escape to the roof, but the door opened, and light from handheld torches flooded the room. Talo and Asha drew their knives and pressed into the deepest shadows beside a tall wardrobe. They had not been seen.

Carefully, Asha peered around the edge of the furniture. Allia entered the room followed by Liam, his tall form obvious. Two other guards trailed them with torches. Asha's heart heaved seeing her old friend. There was nothing childish about him now. Nothing that reminded her of the boy she had loved.

Between the guards sagged a prisoner. The guards shoved the poor captive onto a chair while a serving woman went around the room and lit lanterns. Asha swore the woman saw them, but her gaze hardly wavered from her task, and she said nothing.

Allia didn't speak. The only sound was the grunting breath of the prisoner. His skin was rent with cuts and bruises; half his face was swollen.

Asha felt Talo's lips close to her ear. "That's Irri, the Defender's spy. He saved my life." Even with his voice barely audible, Asha could hear Talo's anguish.

Asha did not know that her hatred for Allia had not yet reached a tipping point, but it flared within her, rising. Talo put his hand on her shoulder, sensing her desire to pounce.

Allia took the basket of dried herbs and selected a few stems. She crushed them in a mortar, mixing them with a gray powder from a bottle that Asha knew was culla, giving Talo's suspicion life.

Irri watched her from his good eye, which widened. "What are you doing?" he garbled through bruised lips.

Allia smiled. "You'll see. Bring the other one."

Two more guards came into the chamber, dragging another prisoner. The second prisoner's livery matched those of the men who held him. Their comrade.

"No," Irri spat, straining at the ropes that bound him, even though it was agony. "You are a monster," he said to Allia. "He is innocent."

"Irri?" the other prisoner mumbled, his face as injured as Irri's. "Irri. I'm sorry. This is my fault …"

Allia, finished with her mortar, picked up a long wooden dagger. Asha felt Talo tense beside her.

"If my potion is going to work, I need you broken. You are Illiah's spy—don't deny it. And even with my herbs and magic, your mind is much harder for me to penetrate than a foolish Rodan princess. But you gave me the perfect tool with your lover here." Allia grinned. "Nothing better to break a man than watching a loved one suffer. Trust me. I've tried many methods." Allia didn't pause. She took the wooden sword and dragged it down the guard's face. Irri raged. The poor serving girl turned away, hiding in the corner of the room. Even the guards looked sickened. This was one of their own. Liam's eyes looked brighter, eager.

"We have to stop this," Talo whispered.

"There are too many," Asha whispered back. But oh, how she wanted to leap and sink her knives into Allia's neck. If she had been alone, she would have tried it, and likely died. But she couldn't, not if it meant Talo would share that same awful fate.

"She does not mean to kill Irri but make him her slave," Talo said.

"Wait." Liam's voice made Asha jolt. It also made Allia pause, though she looked slightly annoyed. "There is someone here…hiding."

Asha and Talo shrunk back. Talo pulled out his latha.

Without warning, Talo kissed Asha—a burning trail across her lips. The kiss left her too startled to do anything as Talo leaped from their corner, his hands raised in surrender, dropping his latha.

What was he *doing*?

"I was waiting in the shadows to kill Allia. I surrender," Talo said, stepping forward, away, drawing their attention from Asha's hiding place.

Allia narrowed her eyes at Talo. With a jerk of her chin, Liam pounced and pinned Talo's hands behind his back. Asha shrunk against the wall, terrified Liam would see her.

"Why would a prince—you are Prince Talo, are you not?—play

assassin?" Asha heard Allia ask. Asha dared not risk a glance. Talo had sacrificed himself; she could not make it in vain.

"You know why."

"Rhyl. Of course."

"And Asha. I loved her, but she was nothing but your pawn." The malice and disgust in Talo's voice made Asha die a small death. She heard the truth in his words.

"You poor prince," Allia mocked. Then she cocked her head. "Kitarrans are such fine playthings. Liam, take the prince somewhere secure while I think about what to do with him."

"What about these two?" Liam said.

"Take them away. It's getting late. Put them together so they can have some time before we start again. It should help the…process."

Gods, Asha could hardly contain her fury. But if she struck Allia now, Liam would kill Talo instantly. Fuck. What was Talo *thinking*?

The door closed and silence reigned. She listened as the footsteps retreated. She'd lost her chance to kill Allia, and now Allia had Talo.

"Psst."

A small voice made Asha nearly bite her tongue.

"I can get you out of here." It was the serving woman. "Come."

The serving woman surprised Asha again by pushing against the wall, revealing a fine crack that became a small door.

"Go down this tunnel. Keep to your left. You will find others down there. Say the word *starless* and they will know you are an ally." She said it very quickly, shoving a candle into Asha's hand and pushing Asha into the hole. Asha didn't even have time to thank her before the door closed, leaving her bewildered in the absolute dark.

CHAPTER 88

RHYL

HEAVY MIST HUNG in clumps against the mountainside, but the arching branches of the immense tree pierced the fog like a crown atop the hill. Of all the cendari trees, Hilltop was the most remote, the most difficult to reach. Rhyl guessed that was the reason the Kitarrans had never built a settlement around it as they had with the others.

The lonely mountain valley was only accessible on horseback or by foot. No wagon could weave up the hill alongside the boulder-lined creek. The trail was mostly overgrown; only small stacks of rocks laid out by forgotten pilgrims marked the way. Rhyl wondered if his mother had added her own little rock towers to the path when she and Stone had made the pilgrimage years ago. Rhyl had been ten years old, and his mother and Stone had been gone for weeks, visiting the cendari trees around Kitarra. It was the only time he remembered her leaving him behind.

Honey was a sure-footed horse and had no trouble carrying Rhyl up the narrow, winding trail. They emerged from the dense forest into the clearing at the top of the hill. Rhyl's breath caught. The cendari tree was *giant*. Its canopy spread like a city above him. The wind picked up, and the thick leaves tinkled like bells. He imagined a life among its branches, sleeping nestled in the giant wells between its limbs. He shook his head dispelling, the fanciful thoughts.

Rhyl's heart hammered as the percussive call of a raven echoed through the mist. He waited, breath held. But he knew it was not Calypso, even if his heart hoped. This raven sounded wild, its voice heavier.

A hook pulled at Rhyl's chest. He yearned to run back down the mountain and search for Calypso. Before he left, he'd tried to find a vision in his basin, but the *simul rami* showed him nothing. Maybe it was because Calypso was a *velidar*, or maybe the *simul rami* didn't want to part with its secrets. And if Calypso didn't want to be found, Rhyl had no hope.

He'd stumbled out into the courtyard and stared up at the sky. The massive dead cendari tree stared back at him. He could almost understand the desperation that had propelled his mother years ago and caused the death of the tree.

He'd needed a way to amplify his magic. With the cendari tree in Kilev dead by his mother's magic, he needed another cendari tree. He could have gone to Withe, but he couldn't face Tarran and Murryn and Susor. He wanted to do this alone—needed to do this alone. So he'd made the journey to Hilltop. He'd left Kilev days ago. And each day that passed had been excruciating.

Now, Rhyl rubbed the heel of his hand against his wet cheek and drew a shaky breath. *Help me,* came his silent plea, reaching out to the tree, to magic, to hope.

Rhyl dismounted. Honey, always happy to forage for grass, bent to the task even though it started to rain and huge drops hit the leaves and the ground in a clatter. The rain could not reach the base of the tree. Rhyl navigated through the roots to touch the silver-gray bark. It was cold and smooth, like a river stone. Then he felt the *simul rami* tingle against his fingers. It surged up his arm into his body, filling him with magic.

Hope flared within him. This could work. It had too.

He sat at the base of the tree, his back between the roots.

He closed his eyes.

He reached down into the river of magic.

Where are you?

A tangle of darkness greeted him. The *varing*, waiting, asking, begging, offering.

Calypso ...?

Nothing.

Grief felt like drowning. Like fire. Anger tore at Rhyl's chest, and he clawed with rage at the magic of the *varing* and the *simul rami*, screaming into the eternity that was the river of magic, demanding it show him Calypso. Rhyl called and searched and felt the magic rip apart and shatter under his grief.

He woke lying on the damp ground.

His throat ached. His head swam as he sat up, leaning against the tree's bark. He closed his eyes briefly in a silent apology to the tree. He could hear the rain cascading off the cendari leaves like a thousand tiny rivers. He opened his eyes and waited for his vision to clear.

A spear lay at his feet.

It was slender and longer than he was tall and white as cendari bark. Its long tip flared, then tapered like a point of a needle. He half expected the spear to disappear, a figment of his imagination. But when Rhyl reached out, his fingers curled around the shaft. It was solid, as real as life.

The Stormspear. Somehow, in his outrage and longing, he had pulled it from the *simul rami*.

Magic spread through the spear, burning up his arm like a flame. He cried out in shock and pain. A vision followed the pain and seared into his mind. The vision was not new to him. He had seen it in wisps and scattered pieces, but suddenly, with the spear in his hand and the cendari tree at his back, it unfolded clear and precise.

A grassy hill, and upon it, the tall cendari tree was in bloom. Tsuga, the spirit woman, stood with the Stormspear in her hand. Cendari petals fell from the blossoms and the leaves were shriveling.

The spirit's eyes were gold and held the sorrows of a hundred generations.

He came. Mute. Behind him, monsters and revenants. Death. Evil. Pain.

He stood before her like a sacrifice, arms out, placid. She whimpered as she drove the spear into his heart. Flesh tore from flesh. Blood seeped and cascaded. His face changed from peaceful acceptance to anger. He reached out his hand as if to strike her, but it was too late. His strength was done.

Petals fell over his body like a shroud. The monsters fled. A wave of magic pulsed and Tsuga screamed in grief and held her lover's body. Then she faded and vanished and all that remained of their union was his body beneath the cendari tree where it would rot and turn to dirt.

In the space of three breaths, the tree's branches turned black.

Rhyl blinked. The pain and the vision rescinded.

But Rhyl knew the man, Mute, who had died beneath the cendari tree was not dead at all. He was encased inside the *varing*, inside Rhyl's father's body.

Rhyl swallowed the bile rising from his gut. As the child of the prophecy, he needed to finish what the spirit woman had started—to kill the man in the *varing*. Illiah and Mute were one. He could kill Mute while he wore Illiah's skin. But Rhyl was not a hero. He could not kill his father. He couldn't.

If the Defender was there, he would command Rhyl to use the spear and kill him. Illiah was ready to die to rid the world of Mute's evil. A fucking hero, his father was.

The air sizzled with energy. The rain stopped. The air, the mist, circled Rhyl and the spear. The leaves of the tree shook as a violent wind pummeled them, and Rhyl understood why it was called the Stormspear. He glanced up at the cendari tree and his breath caught. The cendari leaves were curling, the tips of its branches turning black. The tree was dying.

"No, no, no, no!" Rhyl shouted, holding the spear, willing the magic to stop.

"It's all right, Rhyl," a voice spoke beside him. He spun to see Attin, the Guardian of Allati, his long hair tousled in the storm, his bright white wings fanned wide. "Sacrifices have to be made. We can win, but not everyone can live to see it."

Rhyl swallowed his tears. For some reason, Attin's words made him think of Calypso. Which didn't make sense, but everything made him think of Calypso.

"Any other words of advice?" Rhyl quipped, not bothering to keep the bitterness from his voice.

Attin gave him a tired smile and disappeared.

Fucking Guardians.

CHAPTER 89

ASHA

ON THE OTHER SIDE of the hidden door, the dark was so absolute that without the candle, not even Asha's Kitarran vision would help her. The candle wavered, and Asha felt a wave of panic at the thought of being enclosed in the dark. With what little light the candle gave, she could see steps leading down into the abyss. It was not a way out, it was a way down. Leading where, she had no idea.

Talo was right. Allia would not kill him. She was too clever for that. He was a prince. But that didn't mean she wouldn't hurt and torture him… Allia was cruel and relished the pain of others. But Talo was strong. Brave.

Asha vowed to make Allia's death slow.

Asha couldn't go back for Talo. She was in no position to fight Liam. No, she needed to find another way. The reality almost destroyed her.

A brighter light appeared from the depths. She spun, her hand over her eyes against the piercing light. Strong hands grabbed her, and a cold blade pressed against her throat.

"Starless," she garbled out.

The knife at her throat relaxed but didn't relinquish its touch. "What have we here?"

It was two women. One held a torch, the other the knife against Asha's throat. "A Kitarran?"

"Who are you?"

"A serving woman helped me. She sent me down here," Asha told them.

"Why are you hiding from the Bitch Queen?" the taller of the two women asked, her eyes full of suspicion.

"It's a long story. But I came here to kill her." Asha was gambling that they were indeed Allia's enemies. Or at least victims. Was there a difference?

The two women looked at each other. "Better take her to the boss." The woman finally lowered her knife.

Asha weighed her options. She could knock them down, steal their torch, and escape back into the house. But then what?

"If you are an enemy of Allia, then you have nothing to fear from us," they told her, as if reading her thoughts. Asha knew her chances with them were better than in the house above. Perhaps there was another way out of this dark lair.

They took her to a cave-like room lit with more torches. There was no furniture. Only a few crates and blankets. It smelled like sweat and old blood.

"What did you find, Willa?" a man—the boss, Asha assumed—asked. His dark eyes widened, then narrowed when he saw her.

"She came in through the door by your chamber. She knew the password. She claims to be hiding from Allia. Claims she came to kill her like some kind of assassin."

The man raised an eyebrow at her. A silent question. But there was something in his expression that made Asha uneasy. An edge. A rage. He was sitting in the stale dark, but Asha could feel his power.

"I came to Mahlas to kill Allia," Asha repeated. "But…it didn't go as planned."

"Unfortunate. Tell me," he commanded gently.

"First tell me who you are," Asha said. "Why are you here—what is this place?"

He resettled his weight carefully. His eyes pinched. He was injured, Asha realized. He lifted a canteen and handed it to her.

She hadn't realized she was so thirsty until the water touched her lips.

She took a few big gulps and stopped herself from draining it. "Thank you."

The man nodded. "My name is Cotoch. Allia left me for dead, but these women found me, helped me down here, and have kept me alive. Allia has purged Mahlas of guards loyal to me. Those guards were husbands. Lovers. Brothers. They did not take it well." He jerked his chin toward the women.

The women watched Asha with shrewd eyes filled with anger and grief. Asha felt a surprising kinship with them.

"Allia hardly notices us, thinking serving women beneath her, lacking the ability to thwart her," one woman said with a sneer.

Asha turned back to Cotoch. "I've heard of you. I was told you were dead."

He smiled mirthlessly. "I almost was."

Asha tried to remember everything she knew about Cotoch. Eva had spoken of him like an ally, but it was a story she knew little about. Ill blood ran between Cotoch and Illiah, a past full of hate. But she had no options. He was the only help she would get. And his daughter was in Kitarra.

"My name is Asha. I came here with Talo to kill Allia." She held up a hand when Cotoch opened his mouth. "Let me explain. I was raised in Rodan. Allia was my master. She...she was cruel to me and my...friend, Liam. She played games with our minds and manipulated us into doing— becoming—what she wanted. She turned Liam into her slave. She used her magic to control my body, locking me in my mind. She sent me to Kitarra as her spy. She took over my mind and forced me to attack Rhyl."

She told him about Talo surrendering to keep her safe.

"Your Liam is the one who did this to me." Cotoch pulled his shirt aside to expose layers of bandages and bruised skin.

"Liam is in complete thrall to Allia. A *daeum*, I have heard it called," Asha said.

"Yes. He is."

Asha told herself not to cry, but tears felt close.

"And you? If she took over your mind, how did you get free?" Cotoch asked.

"Aiyan helped me. But I was not like Liam. Not a—a *daeum*."

"Allia is a monster."

Asha eyed him. Cotoch was a monster too if Illiah could be believed.

"It's a good thing you didn't kill Allia," Cotoch told her.

Asha choked on her dismay.

"Without a master to control them, a *daeum* will turn feral, ruled by their lust for blood and pain. They cannot be stopped." Cotoch's voice faded away so Asha almost didn't hear his last word. "And a *daeum* Kitarran is not the only monster in Allia's arsenal. Did you see the army she has gathered?" Cotoch did not wait for her to answer. "She has monsters, the likes of which are only seen in nightmares. Wanderers. Creatures half human, half animal. Men and women whose minds she controls, who fight with the strength and speed of someone with no care for pain. Not wholly alive, but not dead."

"Allia must be stopped. She has Talo." Asha could not keep the growl from her voice. She yearned for Allia's neck beneath her claws. "It's my fault. Talo wouldn't listen when I told him I would go in alone. He wanted to help me."

Cotoch whistled through his teeth. "Princes are known for their arrogant honorable idiocy," he remarked. Then he winced. "But I am sure he had his reasons—"

Cotoch's words fell into a void. The torches blinked abruptly into darkness, as if the air had been sucked out. Asha inhaled sharply. The darkness felt alive. A strange fear made Asha's fur stand on end and her tail twitch, but she could not pinpoint the source. It was like waking from a forgotten nightmare. One of the women was sobbing.

"What—?" Cotoch began but couldn't finish. Another wave of magic snatched Asha's breath from her chest. She felt it pound between her ears.

The torches flared back to life, reflected in Cotoch's wary eyes. She reached out to the wall to steady herself. Cotoch looked as shocked as she felt.

"What *was* that?" she asked him.

"You felt it too?" Cotoch's weak voice was barely more than a whisper.

"I did. It felt like magic."

"It was…something happened. The *varing* pulsed and shuddered like thunder after a lightning strike. I felt …" His voice drifted. His eyes glazed over. Asha looked to his women, who waited quietly. They looked nervous, but the one had stopped crying.

With a small shake of his head, Cotoch focused his intense dark eyes on her. "The *varing* has shown me…Rhyl has reformed the Stormspear. I think he is coming here."

"Here? Why?"

"Because this is where are all the monsters gather."

Hope flared within her. Perhaps the child of the prophecy could stop Allia.

CHAPTER 90

EVA

"ILLIAH?" Eva approached Illiah where he stood leaning on the window ledge overlooking Kilev.

"He did it. Rhyl has the Stormspear. The vercuri are gone."

"Yes. I felt it too." Eva knew Rhyl had created the Stormspear. Where, how, she had no idea. But at that moment, when she felt the magic pulse, then shift, she had also felt Rhyl's path slip from her fingers. What happened to her son was no longer in her control, if it had ever been.

Illiah turned to her. She didn't like the hopeless look in his eyes. She wove her arms around his frame, marveling for the thousandth time how perfectly he fit against her and she against him. She slid her hand under his shirt, against his smooth skin. His finger curled around the base of her hair, pulling her against him so he could kiss her.

It wasn't until much later, when Illiah rose and dressed, leaving Eva naked, her body humming with lingering sensations Illiah had left her with, that she realized their lovemaking had felt like goodbye.

CHAPTER 91

ILLIAH

LEAVING EVA was a small death. Illiah drank in the curve of her thigh and the apex of her hip. Her tangle of starlit hair, the small wrinkles at the edge of her eyes. Illiah loved to make her smile and watch her wrinkles deepen, each fine line a mark of the years they had spent together, loving each other, raising their children.

An old ache in his chest grew to a sharp point. He turned away.

He was just strong enough to not look back.

The night was stale. The halls were cool and silent. Summer was waning. Illiah had to pause and press his forehead against the marble wall, gathering every ounce of his strength to fight the *varing*, to force it—*him*—down. He had waited too long. The moment magic pulsed as the spear was reformed, he'd felt Mute's slow strangulation of his will. Eva was his weakness—he had wanted just one more night with her. And now...

For days, he had felt Mute growing stronger, stretching inside him, tearing at his soul. The cage he had built to contain Mute was cracking, about to shatter. He had hoped...for what, he didn't know. But Illiah was out of time, out of strength. If Mute broke free...Illiah could not let that happen.

Mute subsided, forced down by Illiah's will. For now. Illiah quickened his pace and continued toward the Healer's Hall.

Aiyan was awake. Illiah wondered if the wolf knew he was coming or if Aiyan was always restless. Mila was nowhere to be seen, for which Illiah was thankful. He needed Aiyan alone.

He met the wolf's yellow eyes. Aiyan inclined his head in acknowledgment.

Illiah held his dagger out to Aiyan. "I can't hold him any longer, Aiyan."

Aiyan took the dagger. Carefully. Watching Illiah's every move with the wariness of a wounded predator facing an adversary.

"Please." Illiah knelt in front of Aiyan. He lifted his chin, exposing his neck. Aiyan would make the killing blow quick, almost painless.

Oh, how Eva would hate him for taking this path. She would not understand that it was the only way. He had never told her about the bargain he'd made with Aiyan years before. Illiah regretted that her memories of him would be tainted by her hatred, her anger, of what he was about to do. But what choice did he have? He could not let Mute take over once again. Mute would destroy Kitarra and everything and everyone Illiah loved.

"Now, Aiyan. I can feel him rising," Illiah begged. "They are calling him—me. I don't think I can refuse their call. My mind is burning."

A shaft of light lit along its edge as Aiyan raised the blade. Then Aiyan put his hand on Illiah's face, his fingers touching his forehead. Aiyan's *heera* magic was in his head, in his body. The *varing* rose against it. Mute crashed against it, fighting, writhing to break free.

"Do it!" Illiah said, grabbing Aiyan's wrist.

He'd tried to do this himself—he had held the blade to his wrist, ready to make the cut. Illiah had blacked out and when he came to, the knife was gone and his head was clear. Each time Mute had stopped his hand and put the knife away. Illiah needed Aiyan to finish what Mute would not allow him to do himself.

Aiyan sheathed his dagger. He released his *heera* magic, dropping his fingers from Illiah's face.

"What are you doing? You promised." Illiah's voice was a strangled growl.

"Illiah, we were wrong." Aiyan's voice was soft and full of wonder. And sadness. "This is not the answer."

Betrayal rose in Illiah like a wave in a storm. His mind pulsed with rage, with magic. His anger came with the *varing* and with it a wave of power that was Mute.

We are waiting.

They called to him. Illiah put his hands over his ears. His lungs ached as a sob escaped. The voices were pulling him into darkness. Pulling him away. Down. Drowning him in an ocean of *varing*. He tried to fight it, had been fighting it for a long time, but he had grown weak. And they were so persistent.

Come to ussss.

"I am coming," Mute whispered back.

CHAPTER 92

RHYL

THE CENDARI TREE died before Rhyl's eyes.

His fault. His fault.

The storm following Rhyl raged above him straight out of an old tale. Dense, churning clouds. Lightning flashed in their depths. A storm caused by magic. With the spear in hand, Rhyl used his *sanarii* magic to calm the storm, but he could not dissipate it. At least the rain had stopped.

His mind was numb. It was difficult to piece one thought to the next because they all tangled around the pit in his stomach. To fulfill the prophecy, he would have to take his father's life. Round and round, his thoughts took him to blood and sacrifice, and Rhyl wanted to scream and weep because he was just a boy in love and he wanted to live. And if he killed his father…Rhyl knew part of him would die.

He couldn't find Calypso in the *simul rami* or the *varing*. Maybe it was better that way. Better to never see him again.

Rhyl readjusted his grip on the Stormspear. Now, as the energy settled within the spear and the initial shock of magic subsided, it felt warm. Alive. Rhyl cursed it.

Thankfully, Honey had not shied from the strange magic. Rhyl leaned against the horse's smooth shoulder briefly, then pulled himself into the saddle.

As he rode out of the forest, the trail became a road once more. A plume of smoke rose from a small camp. Kitarra was full of friendly folk. They were probably trappers, come from the high country now that autumn was creeping down the mountains.

Rhyl approached the camp. The wagon was brightly painted with flowers and ferns and woodland creatures. A man and woman sat around a hearty fire. Rhyl smelled spices and fresh cooking. He greeted them, dismounting.

The pair were older. Their hair grayed. They smiled at him.

"Welcome, Prince Rhyl." The old man gestured for him to join them. Rhyl was used to being recognized because of his unusual hair, but he had his hood up, so how did they know him? He was wary, but he held the Stormspear. There was nothing to fear from two old travelers. And some food might help settle his roiling stomach.

"Thank you," Rhyl said, letting Honey's reins drop to the ground. Honey was too well trained to wander, and the horse looked thankful for the chance to graze. Rhyl plunged the spear into the soft earth where it stood like a sentinel. The thing was a bit awkward. And since it was no ordinary weapon, he doubted the dirt would dull its edge.

"Here." The woman handed him a bowl of stew. Rhyl stared at the woman longer than was polite. Her voice was very deep and the angles of her face were masculine.

The man was older, his face lined with wrinkles, but his shoulders were squared and he held himself like a warrior, though he stretched his leg out before him like his knee ached.

"So, you found the Stormspear," the man said.

Rhyl's mouthful of stew burned down his throat as he nearly choked on it. "Who are you, exactly?"

The man's face stretched into a grin. "My name is Eelan. And this is my partner, Mags."

Rhyl looked from one to the other. "Mags the seer. And Eelan …" The name sounded familiar.

"I knew your father when he was younger than you are now," Eelan said with a tired smile. "I set him on his path."

Rhyl wasn't sure anyone could take credit for that sort of claim. But then he remembered. "You gave my father his vercuri."

"I did."

"And you gave Stone—Arrain—the prophecy," Rhyl said to Mags. She inclined her head.

Rhyl put down his stew. "Why?"

"For Kitarra. For everyone. For good. For love. For life."

Rhyl couldn't speak for the astonishment that moved through his body like a current. His gaze dropped to the ground, to a black feather covered with dew in the grass. He picked it up, twisting it between his fingers. The feather was Calypso's, he was sure of it. It was a simple matter to shift his mind, reach for the magic of the spear and see a vision.

Calypso lying on the grass, in tears. Mags handing Calypso a cloak to cover his nakedness. Calypso sitting at her fire eating hot stew. They spoke. After, Calypso flew off. East.

A terror so complete poured over Rhyl with a wave of physical pain. He was pulled down, his limbs twisting, bending, wrenching but not breaking. Not Rhyl's pain. *Calypso's.*

Rhyl dropped the feather. His sight returned to normal.

"Where is Calypso?" Rhyl asked, his voice like steel.

"He is doing what the Allmakers asked of him." Mags's deep voice was tired and sad.

"After he has proved love's true form

"The child will call the storm.

"A king, a prince, a fox, a crow, four a circle make.

"To send the dark one to the stars for true love's sake.

"Snap the tether, set me free,

"Restore the river of magic to its rightful tree."

A cry escaped Rhyl's lips. Because he knew—he *knew*—what the *simul rami* had shown him, and what it meant. But it couldn't be true. Why Calypso? The Allmakers were gone–they couldn't tell him. And there was no *time.*

Rhyl stood, stew forgotten. He pulled the spear from the earth and tucked it under his arm. Eelan and Mags called out to him, but Rhyl was already riding through the forest.

His duty was to find Mute—his father—and to restore the balance of magic and stop the *varing* from spreading violence. But all he could think about was Calypso. East. Calypso had flown east.

The spear showed him the Tarm. The grass. The wind. Then he saw the writhing army that was more nightmare than real. There was Tsuga, the spirit woman. She sat beneath the dead tree, waiting. There was Allia as she walked through the horde. A Kitarran, his eyes dead, strode behind her. Allia's face was smug. She looked at Tsuga's creatures as if they were the most beautiful things.

Rhyl could hardly look at the wanderers. They were disgusting epitomes of wrong and evil. But one caught his attention. Pale skin. Dark hair. Black feathers. Face contorted with a raven's blue eye and a human nose and sharp teeth that were neither. Calypso had turned into a wanderer.

Rhyl screamed out his anger and pain, and the Stormspear shuddered in response. The *varing* ran down the lengths of his arms to his fingertips, burning, searing, waiting for his command.

CHAPTER 93

EVA

THE SIMUL RAMI RAN bright and clear. It carried Eva across wind, forest, and mountains until she was there, in Mahlas.

Tsuga sat beneath the dead cendari tree. In the light of day, there was no mistaking her spirit form made of things from the forest, bark and moss, feather and root. Her lips were red like a mushroom. Her hands twitched restlessly, her golden gaze darted back and forth.

Tsuga sensed her. Her eyes locked on Eva's. And narrowed.

"You took him from me," Tsuga seethed.

"What do you mean?"

"You took him from me," Tsuga repeated. Tears appeared on Tsuga's cheeks like morning dew.

Eva thought of Illiah. And the man in the *varing*, Mute.

Tsuga was right.

"He is mine. You cannot have him," Eva said into the wind.

Tsuga shook her head. "I will have him. He will come to me. He has no choice. They are calling to him." She stretched out her stick-thin hands and around they came to her. From the grass, they rose. From the air, they formed from magic and shadow and flesh; *revenant*s, people consumed by the *varing; vivus*, evil intentions made real; and the wanderers, the *velidar* corrupted and warped, their bodies both animal and human. An army of monsters fueled by dark magic.

"No. You cannot have him!" Eva shouted. But fear already formed along her resolve. This was an army. They were calling to Illiah, to Mute.

Eva's *sanarii* magic could feel their pull, their sway. Would Illiah be strong enough to fight that call? What of Rhyl and the Stormspear? How could he stop this evil with all the magic in the world?

Eva tore herself from the vision and forced herself to wake. Her body felt the strain in every joint and muscle. The *simul rami* danced on the edge of her mind, but so did the *varing*.

She threw a robe around her shoulders and ran out into the hall, calling for a guard.

"Where is Illiah? Find him!" she ordered, satisfied as the guard leaped to do her bidding.

Eva went to Stone's room only to find it dark and cold and empty. Stone was gone. So was his latha and his sword. Eva looked for his trove of culla. Gone.

Stone! Eva reached with her *sanarii* magic. She could feel it sear along the *simul rami* and into Stone's mind.

Eva. I'm sorry.

Where are you?

I have something I need to do.

Not you too. Please, no. Don't leave me.

A pause.

Illiah is gone? Stone asked.

Eva's mind raged and wept. *Yes. I think he is going to the Tarm. Tsuga has an army of monsters. She is luring him there.*

Tsuga? The spirit? What does she want?

She wants Illiah—Mute was her lover. Where are you?

There is something I have to do. I can't help you. I'm sorry, Eva.

Eva shed her magic and severed her connection to Stone. She picked up the first thing she could lay her hands on and threw it across the room. She screamed her frustration. Her nails bit into her palms. She tasted blood. She went back to her room and picked up her sword.

CHAPTER 94

STONE

BEFORE STONE, the Tarm stretched like an ocean of grass. Behind him was Kitarra and every promise he had hoped to keep. And for years he had. He had been a good father. A good prince. A good amourii. He had loved and lived, just as Emri would have wanted.

He pressed onward, the wind drying the teardrops on his fur. He was almost at the border. He had made good time in the last two days since the seer had come to him in a dream.

After thirteen years of searching for the seer, she had come to *him*. "I think you may need this now," Mags had said.

The words that followed were the missing part of the prophecy. They burned into Stone's mind, and he knew why Mags had kept it from him until now.

When Stone had leaped from the cliffs all those years ago, giving his life to the river below, he'd heard a voice. *"Not yet."*

And now he knew why he hadn't died that day when he jumped from the cliff. Part of him had known for a long time. It was why his dreams were full of the dead and why his mind wandered.

His role in the prophecy was not yet finished. Three nights ago, in a dream, Mags showed him the last part of the prophecy. Now knowing turned into action, and he left Kitarra behind. Maybe Eva would forgive him for abandoning her again. Unlikely. It was easy to stay angry at the dead.

But this was right. It was how it was meant to be. All these years, he had done his best to be Eva's amourii. To be the prince reborn. To be a father to the son he had abandoned. To be better. But it had never been enough to make up for his mistakes. This was all he had left. His sacrifice. Death.

He had packed light, taking his latha, his sword. A cloak to keep off the rain. A few doses of culla. Because even now, the thought of withdrawal made his blood run cold. No, he would die a warrior's death, not the death of a coward, an addict. That was one piece of honor he could retain.

His only hope was that someday Eva would understand.

CHAPTER 95

ILLIAH/MUTE

MUTE RAN, propelled by a force that was familiar but filled him with dread. The Stormspear. He would never forget the undeniable pull of the weapon. He could hear the calls of the wanderers, creatures created by the same magic that crafted the Stormspear. Their voices had filled his ears for all the years he had been trapped in the *varing*. Now he was embodied once more, but the voices still called to him. He remained trapped, just by another chain. The Stormspear had been reborn.

His legs burned from running and his eyes blurred from the rain. Illiah's body, his flesh, was fortified by the *varing*, but still, his feet were rubbed raw. The pain lanced through his mind but did not slow Mute. The *varing* controlled him as surely as the rain falls on the mountain hills and is pulled eventually out to sea. There was no denying the Stormspear. But this flesh body was faltering. His legs buckled and he fell into the mud.

Illiah woke. His mouth was full of grit. He moved carefully, lifting his face from the muck. His clothes were coated with mud and debris. He rolled onto his back and saw the sky. The movement made his legs ache, but it was nothing compared to the fiery pain in his feet. He didn't dare take off his boots.

He sat up carefully, trying not to move his feet abruptly. He took in his surroundings. By the tall grass and gaping sky, he appeared to be somewhere in the Tarm. He couldn't see a road or any sign of habitation. Had he run all the way from Kitarra? How many days had he lost inside Mute's mind? He closed his eyes against the pain.

Mute was still there. The man who was a mirror version of himself made of *varing*. Mute stood waiting, huddled. Weak. Hiding.

She is calling me, Mute whimpered.

"And we must go," Illiah replied. Tsuga had almost destroyed Mute once but failed. Perhaps she could succeed this time.

She will kill you.

"If it means ridding the world of you, I will let Tsuga kill me. I am ready to die."

Mute cowered in Illiah's mind. *Not her. It's not Tsuga who calls us.*

Then Mute screamed. Illiah felt a pain unlike any he had yet felt. It was as if his skin was splitting down his spine.

"No." But Illiah's will was frail. Mute slipped over his mind like a black cloak.

No one is ever ready to die.

Then Illiah felt empty and drained. He collapsed back into the wet grass.

CHAPTER 96
RHYL

WHEN RHYL WAS A CHILD, he and Talo were kidnapped by Cotoch. Rhyl didn't remember very much about that time and their escape with Stone and Irri from Mahlas, but he did remember the panic, the feeling of being followed, the need to move faster and faster. He remembered clinging to Irri's back, knowing that if they weren't fast enough, they would not make it home.

Now, Rhyl was not running away, he was running toward, but the manic energy that drove him felt the same. The feeling of being too slow, of time playing tricks, the claws of desperation raking through his chest. He pushed Honey faster and faster, praying to the Guardians the horse's strength would hold. But for what? He could not save Calypso.

He would only find monsters in Mahlas.

Rhyl shifted the spear in his hands. It was not heavy, exactly, but sometimes his fingers tingled and itched as the magic hummed and spoke to him. It was waiting. He could feel it. Like the pause before the exhale, the magic wanted to move. And so he moved.

Calypso, where are you… Rhyl whispered to the spear.

The spear led him to Mahlas.

The dead tree stood on the hill above the city. Rhyl let Honey stop. The horse snorted and tossed his head. Rhyl dismounted, not taking his eyes from the thing in the grass beneath the dead tree.

Rhyl took a step back, reeling, and nearly dropped the spear.

A dark thing stood there, watching him. Not a thing. A creature. No, not a creature. It was Calypso, but not Calypso. It was a monster. A thing twisted by magic and caught between life and tragedy.

Rhyl wept to see him.

He took a step forward. The thing that had been Calypso snarled. The sound crawled up Rhyl's spine and sliced open his heart.

"Cally," Rhyl whispered. Begged. His voice only agitated the monster. Its movements were wrong, too quick, too jerky.

As he rode from Kitarra, Rhyl's mind had turned over the terrible truth: he didn't know how to help Calypso. He'd ridden toward his doom with nothing, armed only with his need to help the man he loved. But now, with Calypso in front of him, clarity finally came. The Allmakers had shown him what to do. Calypso had shown him what to do. It was like the sapling in the Forest.

Rhyl readjusted the spear in his hand. Its magic flowed through him. He anchored himself to it and used magic to pull Calypso to him. At first, it just made Calypso scream and screech, a horrendous sound. But Rhyl kept pulling. And pulling. He wiped his tears on the back of his sleeve. He had to do this. He could not fail. *He could not fail.*

Calypso leaped, landing on Rhyl's back. Claws rent into the meat of his shoulder before he knocked Calypso down, immobilizing him with knee and arm. Rhyl was stronger than the wanderer because the spear was infusing him with magic. His shoulder burned, but he ignored it because *this was Calypso.* Calypso who held his heart and his body and his life.

Rhyl put his hand on Calypso's awful face. The *varing* flowed through Calypso like breath. The *varing* seared through Rhyl's fingers, his to control. His to command. And so was Calypso. So he ordered the *varing* to come to him, to fill him instead. Hope was his only tether.

Calypso thrashed, almost breaking free from Rhyl's magic-infused will. Sweat dripped down Rhyl's forehead, but he knew if he let go, it would mean failure. His veins burned as they filled with *varing.* His arms ached. And still he pulled the dark magic from Calypso. Calypso's face morphed and shifted, growing uglier and more wrong. Rhyl groaned, then screamed with the effort of holding Calypso in place. At last, Calypso went limp, the remaining residue of *varing* drained from his body.

Their labored breathing came as one, and slowly Calypso's features rearranged and became the face Rhyl knew.

Finger by finger, muscle by muscle, Rhyl relaxed his grip, unsure if he could believe he had freed Calypso from the *varing*.

"You're crushing me," Calypso whispered in a strained voice.

There were red marks like burns on Calypso's skin where Rhyl had pressed against him.

"Can you move?" Rhyl asked, hearing something approach. He looked up to see other wanderers creeping toward them. Rhyl's chest hurt. His arms hurt. His head hurt. He reached for the spear, holding it firm. Rhyl wanted to inspect Calypso, to make sure every bit of him had returned well and truly, but he kept his eyes on the other wanderers.

"Yes, but it hurts," Calypso said with a grunt.

"We need to get out of here." Rhyl's voice shook.

Calypso swallowed and nodded. Rhyl lifted him by the elbow, still holding the Stormspear firmly. Rhyl had been taught that a *candarii* grows stronger with the *varing*, but all Rhyl felt was exhaustion. Whatever magic he had used to pull the *varing* from Calypso, it had taxed him. It was all he could do to support Calypso and hold the spear. He could not fight the wanderers. All he could do was try to run.

Calypso hissed. "Don't touch me. It hurts."

"Can you shift?"

"No."

Calypso began to shiver, his skin covered in beads of cold sweat. Rhyl pulled off his cloak and put it around Calypso's bare shoulders while keeping the lurking wanderers in his peripherals. The wanderers maintained their distance.

Calypso began babbling. Something about Allmakers. About wanderers. And Rhyl. And the Stormspear.

"Shhh," Rhyl told him, keeping Calypso moving by holding him around his waist, the cloak a barrier between them.

"Ah, if it isn't Prince Rhyl, the child of the prophecy." A woman's voice carried across the wind.

Rhyl turned awkwardly. He didn't want to let Calypso fall. A woman walked through the wanderers toward him. Allia. She looked strong in the twisting way a small, lean animal is strong. She had long black hair that glistened like obsidian, reminding Rhyl of Aiyan. Her face was beautiful, but it turned Rhyl's stomach. Around her, the wanderers ranged like a nightmarish honor guard.

"Give me the spear, child."

Rhyl gripped the spear tighter. Calypso sagged against his shoulder, slipping. Rhyl's heart pattered unevenly in his chest. He raised the spear. Blood trickled down his arm from the claw wounds. The spear felt as heavy as a cendari tree, his magic thick as mud.

The woman came closer, trailed by her disgusting pets. Rhyl took a few steps but almost fell. Calypso's eyes fluttered, and Rhyl worried he would lose consciousness.

The woman stopped a few steps away from them. She held out her hand expectantly. "Give me the spear."

Rhyl aimed the spear point at the woman, but his arm trembled and the spear wavered. It was so fucking heavy. "If I give it to you, you will kill me."

The woman saw his weakness and smiled. "Of course."

The breeze caressed his face. The air above them raged with the power of the spear. The clouds boiled. Thunder echoed along the valley plain. Calypso slid closer to the ground. Rhyl could not hold both Calypso and the spear. And he could not leave Calypso behind.

He threw the spear at the woman's chest, but his throw was weak, off-kilter. The woman followed it with her eyes. The wanderers growled and roared. Rhyl pulled his last thread of strength and called to his *sanarii* magic. He called air and earth and pushed them in front of him, making a barrier of dust and wind. He pushed and pulled. The earth around the woman's feet thrust and rumbled. Rhyl's mind fogged over, but he did not let go of Calypso. He hoisted Calypso in his arms and ran, leaving behind a storm of dirt and rocks and wind that even a nightmare creature could not escape.

CHAPTER 97

RHYL

RHYL LEFT THE STORM BEHIND. Honey was faltering. It was all Rhyl could do to hold Calypso in front of him so he didn't fall as they rode hard through the forest. Allia's army was not pursuing. She had what she wanted. Maybe the spear would be enough to hedge Allia's blood lust.

Fuck. He'd lost the spear. He would be lying if he said he had had no choice. He had chosen Calypso.

Rhyl dismounted and led Honey down the tricky trail to the Vale. Calypso sat silent and hunched on Honey's back. Rhyl had to concentrate, putting one foot in front of the other. He was so tired. The Vale pulled him like a moth to a flame. He could almost see its magic. He prayed to the Guardians it would keep them safe.

Calypso looked like he had swallowed a pint of poison. His skin was gray and gleamed with sweat. Rhyl pulled him off Honey's back and helped him into the cave, forcing Calypso to get into the hot pool to warm up.

"Don't fall asleep and drown on me, all right?" Rhyl told Calypso. Calypso gave him a washed-out smile and closed his eyes, leaning his head on the rocky edge of the pool.

"I won't." His voice was nearly nonexistent.

Rhyl peeled Honey's tack from his tired body, letting the saddle drop to the ground. He should rub the poor horse down, but he just didn't have the strength. He wanted to make a fire, some tea.

His feet were like lead, slowing his movements. He kept a close eye on Calypso to make sure his head was above water. There was a stockpile of dry wood, so he made a fire. It took longer than usual for his *sanarii* magic to answer his call, but it did, and he sat back and watched the wood catch. He rummaged through his pack for something to feed Calypso.

"You came for me," Calypso said, hobbling over to the fire, wrapped in a blanket.

"The things I said…I should not have said them," Rhyl offered, knowing how inferior the statement was.

Calypso plopped down beside Rhyl. "It hurt."

"I'm so sorry, Cally. So very sorry."

"You aren't the only reason I left the Forest."

"I know. I'm a spoiled prince. I don't think these things through."

"You were trying to protect me." Calypso pushed his shoulder against Rhyl's.

"As soon as you flew away, I knew I'd made the worst possible mistake by saying those things."

Calypso smiled, a little. He leaned forward and kissed Rhyl, parting his lips with his tongue. Rhyl wanted to live in that kiss, to curl up inside it and never leave. But Calypso broke away from him with a curse.

"Kissing you feels like being burned."

Rhyl realized Calypso was not joking. "It must be the magic. I had to tear the *varing* out of you. No wonder you feel singed."

Calypso leaned into Rhyl, protected by the fabric between them. Rhyl gave a small gasp as he inadvertently pressed against the lacerations on Rhyl's shoulder. Without a word, Calypso carefully peeled back Rhyl's torn shirt to expose the injury.

"I did this."

Rhyl shook his head. "No. Dark magic did this."

With great care, Calypso took a cloth, wetted it in the hot spring, and gently washed Rhyl's wounds. They weren't deep, but they were nasty, and Rhyl had to grit his teeth from crying out.

"You need a poultice. There is self-heal just outside the cave."

"Does this mean you forgive me?" Rhyl asked.

"No."

"But …?"

Calypso sighed with his whole body. "Rhyl, I have to tell you something."

"What?"

"You aren't going to like it."

"Oh?"

"Yeah …"

"Tell me already."

"Years ago, the Allmakers called me to the Forest. They told me I had to find your weakness and push you to your breaking point. That was the reason they wanted me to come with you. Only then would you be ready to defeat Mute. Well, actually, their message was more convoluted, but …"

Rhyl stared at Calypso. That was what Eelan and Mags had meant. "Why?"

"You are their weapon, Rhyl. And the best way to strengthen a blade is by tempering it."

"That was a *test?*"

Calypso swallowed, his eyes haunted. "Yeah. I realized I was your greatest weakness. And I realized that if you could save me from being a wanderer, then you would be strong enough to fulfill the prophecy."

"Fuck." Rhyl pressed his hand against his aching head. "If the Allmakers weren't gone, I would hunt them down and destroy them."

Calypso laughed softly at that, which warmed Rhyl right to his toes. Then he frowned.

"I lost the Stormspear," Rhyl told him.

"Oh. I was hoping I'd imagined that in my delirium."

Rhyl shook his head. "The woman—Allia—took it. I don't think that was part of the Allmakers' plan."

"No. I don't think so," Calypso said softly. "Can she use it?"

"She is *candarii*. *Candarii* can use vercuri—the Stormspear."

"Right." Calypso adjusted, settling against Rhyl's shoulder. "What does the Stormspear do?"

"I don't know…exactly. I didn't bother experimenting."

"It's all right, Rhyl."

With Calypso warm beside him, it was hard not to be lulled into the lie.

CHAPTER 98

MUTE

MUTE OPENED HIS EYES. "Where am I?" he asked. The body that held him was strange. It was not Illiah. Impossible.

He tried to reach out with the *varing* but came up against a wall, a shackle. The Stormspear. Ah, the Stormspear could force him into a body not aligned with his spirit. Though the flesh would not hold him long.

He turned to see a woman holding the spear. The magic of the spear—Tsuga's magic— settled over him like a thousand chains, draining him. But this was not Tsuga. This woman was a stranger. And human.

Memories whispered to him. There had been a time when he had walked upon the ground in a body that was his, not forced upon him as it was now. In those years he had seeded the realms with his children, children who could touch magic. At the time, he had not realized his impact on the nature of this world. But now he knew.

"Who are you?" he demanded, though it was an effort.

"I am a queen, and you are my king," she answered with a smile as cold as hoarfrost.

"You should not wield the spear. It is not for you." Mute could feel the woman's magic. Her magic was not just chained to him; its tendrils reached an army of monsters all birthed by the *varing*. An army that should have been his to control, but with the Stormspear reborn, his power, his will, was gone.

The woman's face pinched, and the *varing* flashed like lightning across her irises. Mute felt the chain of magic linking him to the spear cinch and with it, pain.

"You are mine, your magic is mine, and now, I will rule," she proclaimed.

"Then you have made a mistake. This magic is not mine, nor is it yours. It flows and moves through the world, but if you force its path, it will only wreak havoc," he told her.

Another woman appeared beside the queen. This woman was a spirit. She had wings of coal black that stretched behind her. Something twisted like a knife in Mute's gut. He knew her. His daughter, his first child of this world. Then he remembered. Before she had become a spirit, Crea used the *varing* and created an army to destroy the innocent, to claim the land for herself. But the Allmakers had tricked her, turned her into a spirit woman along with the others. Guardians, they were called.

"It worked," Crea said. "Now, use the spear on me. Restore my mortal form."

Allia turned to the woman. Mute saw the moment when the Guardian with the black feathers who had once been his daughter knew her fate. Allia had no intention of giving Crea what she wanted.

"I gave you everything!" Crea screamed. "You are the queen of Jullayah because of *me*."

"You are a fool. And you can't hurt me because you are *nothing*."

Mute tried to call out and warn her, but his cry fell too late. Crea was a cruel creature, but she was his daughter. The spear point drove through Crea's heart, surprising her. She was a spirit, but the spear was a thing of magic and sacrifice, and it tore through her like fire through wax. Crea screamed again and disappeared.

Allia laughed as she turned back to Mute and ran a finger down his skin. The *varing* flared around them, and the voices of the wanderers wailed, piercing the inside of Mute's skull, making his eyes tear. The *varing* lashed out, and Mute was propelled into the river of darkness, away from the mortal body Allia tried to capture him in. But it was not freedom. It was just another prison.

CHAPTER 99

CALYPSO

CALYPSO FELT RHYL WATCHING HIM, but it was hard to look the prince in the eye and say the things that were on his mind. The memory of being a wanderer was too strong, too awful, the *varing* snaking around his being, his soul, warping him into something terrible. He had wanted to kill Rhyl. He enjoyed ripping his flesh and basked in his pain.

And Rhyl carried the *varing* inside him. A weapon, waiting, ready.

But Rhyl had come for him. And with his magic, Rhyl had made him whole, and Calypso dared to hope, to wonder if Rhyl loved him. But he couldn't bring himself to ask. No, asking felt like begging.

Rhyl was quiet too. He had lost the Stormspear, and Calypso could tell he felt ashamed, like a failure. Perhaps he regretted saving Calypso.

From the corner of his eye, Calypso saw Rhyl's whole demeanor change. Rhyl looked like he was in the throes of a bad headache, but his eyes were glazed like he was in a vision.

"What's wrong?" Calypso asked.

"Talo," came Rhyl's distracted reply.

Calypso waited, twisting his fingers together, the human equivalent of flapping one's wings.

Rhyl slumped as his connection to Talo dissolved. Calypso caught him, holding Rhyl against his chest. The *varing* was gone. Calypso could touch Rhyl without becoming seared meat.

"What is it?"

"Talo is in Mahlas, captured by Allia. He has been for some time, but only had the strength to tell me now."

Calypso inhaled through his teeth.

"Talo and Asha went to assassinate Allia, but got caught. Da is there, too, and Cotoch. All captive."

"What? How?"

"I don't know." Rhyl sounded hopeless. "I need to go to Mahlas. I have to help Talo," Rhyl mumbled against Calypso's skin. "I have to get the spear back."

"How did you find the Stormspear?" Calypso asked.

"I went to the cendari tree at Hilltop."

"And it just…appeared?"

Rhyl shrugged. "I was looking for you, desperately. Then the spear appeared. It took so much magic. The cendari tree died. It was awful."

Calypso held Rhyl tighter. "Fuck."

"Yeah."

"The cendari tree's magic was pulled into the spear," Calypso mused. Then, "You were looking for me?"

Rhyl groaned against Calypso. "I couldn't think of anything but you." He looked up at Calypso, his blue-green eyes bright. "And now Allia has the spear."

"But can she use it? You are the child of the prophecy, Rhyl. I think that means something. I think you are the only one who can use the spear. Besides its maker. *Candarii* use the vercuri, why not the spear?"

"We can only hope. Cally, I need to get to Mahlas."

"You can't do anything weak as a kitten."

Rhyl huffed a laugh that was anything but amused. "I have to go to Mahlas. Now. I have to do this."

"I am coming with you."

Calypso could sense Rhyl wanted to order him to stay in the Vale where he was safe. But instead, Rhyl kissed him long and slow, and Calypso let him. The last time Rhyl had kissed him, his lips had wandered to his neck, his shoulders, lower and lower until…Fuck, Calypso wanted to lose himself in Rhyl, in every curve and hard edge and shared breath.

But he drew back and pressed his forehead against Rhyl's and whispered, "I don't know if you heard me the first time, but I'm coming with you to Mahlas."

"I heard you."

CHAPTER 100

ASHA

ASHA HAD GROWN UP IN A CAGE. A cage that looked like a grand house with a yard and trees and a small garden fed from a well. A tall wall had enclosed the villa, and Asha had been forbidden to go beyond.

And now, closed in by dark and tunnel and earth, she was in another cage. She told herself the dark was temporary. But the earth pressed against her and she longed for the sunlight and air. She longed for Allia's death. True freedom lay with the woman's lifeblood pooling at her feet.

Days had gone by. Days Asha spent pacing in the dark, doing her best to keep her mind and body fit. Between waiting for Cotoch's women to return with fresh food or fresh information, she went through plans with Cotoch. It spoke of their dire conditions that they had yet to come up with a plan Cotoch felt confident would be successful. He knew the house, so Asha had to bend to his wisdom on the matter. But it stung. Every day that passed with Allia alive, prowling above her, shredded another piece of Asha's sanity.

"My lord, look who we found."

Asha raised her head to see several of Cotoch's serving women appear dragging a man. The poor sod, gagged and bound, was covered in dirt and blood. He struggled weakly against the ropes. Between the dim light and his filthy condition, it was hard to make out his features.

"It's Caeris, the Jullayan king," they told Cotoch. "We found him just outside the wall."

Asha's heart leaped. Maybe they could use him as leverage. She doubted Allia felt affection for her husband. The woman was incapable of love, but surely the king was an important figure in Allia's plans.

"Clean his face," Cotoch ordered, handing a woman a rag.

With his face somewhat cleaner, but still gagged, the prisoner glared at Cotoch, his green eyes desperate.

"Damn it, he looks just like Illiah," Cotoch muttered.

Asha tilted her head, inspecting Illiah's twin brother who was king of Jullayah. She wanted to think the king was another one of Allia's victims, enthralled, but she wasn't sure. He did look like Illiah, but Illiah was a good man. Asha had nothing but contempt for this fool who had let Allia take his crown.

"Should we hear what he has to say?" Cotoch asked.

"Are you crazy? He will scream murder and the whole house will hear," Asha said.

"No, they won't. Screams don't make it past the rock."

The surety in Cotoch's tone sent a chill down her spine. She pulled the rag from Caeris's mouth.

"I *am* Illiah," the captive said, his eyes wild.

Asha looked at Cotoch.

"Impossible," Cotoch spat.

"Illiah is in Kitarra," Asha confirmed.

"Prove it. If you are Illiah, what did I say to you the first time we met?" Cotoch demanded.

"You told me you raped my wife and that I was nothing more than a gutter-boy doing the bidding of Kitarra's queen."

Silence.

Asha cleared her throat. From Cotoch's expression, it was the correct answer.

Asha felt ill.

"What are you doing here?" Asha asked Illiah, helping him so he could sit with more comfort.

"It's a long story…" Illiah leaned his head against the stone wall, closing his eyes. He looked half dead. "What do you know of Imal's death, Cotoch?"

"Some."

"In Rodan, Imal tortured me, drawing the *varing* from my slow demise." Illiah paused to draw a few hard breaths. "But I am sure you know this, as you were the one who sent me there." Illiah opened his eyes to glare at Cotoch, then closed them again as he continued. "Through my pain, Imal released a man trapped in the *varing*. He took over my body, my mind, and he was powerful enough to kill Imal." Illiah's voice faded. Asha realized she was biting her claws. She thought she'd mastered that habit years ago.

"Mute—the man in the *varing*—is back," Illiah continued. "He took over my mind days ago, and brought me here, to the Tarm. But now… something happened. He—Mute—is gone."

"Dead?" Cotoch asked.

"No. No, not dead. Gone," he repeated.

Asha looked at Cotoch.

"Caeris," they said at the same time.

Illiah shook his head. "Impossible. Caeris is my twin, but magic does not affect him as it does me."

"My spies." Cotoch inclined his head to the women. "They reported that Caeris has been acting strange the last few days."

"We found you in the field, and we weren't even that surprised," Willa stated.

"Allia is not like other sorcerers," Asha reminded Illiah, untying his hands. Cotoch did not protest. Illiah grimaced when Asha untied his feet.

"You think Allia can control Mute?" Illiah asked.

"She has the Stormspear."

Cotoch's women had brought them the news. Cotoch had told Asha the tale of the spear. A tale from his mother's people in Rodan. A tale of two spirits who fell in love, but that love destroyed the balance of magic. The spear was created through sacrifice to bring balance.

"What? How? Where is Rhyl?" Illiah stood up, slowly. Something was wrong with his feet.

"We don't know," Asha told him, her voice wavering despite herself. "But Cotoch's spies don't think Rhyl has been captured by Allia."

"The house servants are spying for me above," Cotoch explained. "They reported that Allia has the spear but couldn't tell me how she came by it. Nothing about Rhyl."

"But Allia has Talo," Asha told Illiah, willing herself not to cry.

"Talo? How?"

"He followed me here. I came to kill Allia. But …" Asha told Illiah about how she and Talo watched Allia bring in Irri and another man, a Jullayan, how he knew Irri, how Allia might be using culla and something else to enthrall people. Illiah looked distressed, and Asha wished she had better news to offer him. "Talo surrendered to keep my presence a secret, to keep me safe, but also to distract Allia from hurting Irri. One of the women brought me here to the tunnels and Cotoch. But that was days ago."

"These tunnels are familiar," Illiah stated. Asha had the feeling he was hiding some deeper terror. The tunnels were rife with nightmare fodder. He hung his head. "Do you know what happened to Irri and his lover?" he asked without looking up.

One of the women, Lari, stepped forward and spoke up. "The guards say he is dead. He did not survive whatever Allia tried to do to him."

A sound escaped Illiah. Asha's heart wrenched to hear it. She'd heard of Irri's death a few days earlier.

"Eva said you died helping them escape," Illiah said, turning to Cotoch.

"I almost did. The women found me bleeding out in a hallway, and I told them to take me to the crypts. Tell me, how is Pena?"

"She is safe in Kitarra. She grieves. She thinks you are dead."

Asha didn't think it was the most useful thing to say. As a distraction, she turned back to more pressing issues. "If Allia used the Stormspear and Mute is now under her control, the only way forward is to regain the Stormspear."

"And if Rhyl is dead?" Cotoch said, glancing at Illiah like he might turn rabid.

"Then all hope is lost," Illiah said, his voice breathless.

"Talo can contact Rhyl. He will know," Asha said. "We need Rhyl, so we need Talo."

"Can you contact Rhyl?" Illiah asked her.

Asha opened her mouth in shock. "I don't know the first thing about how to do that. I ..."

Could she?

"Allia was in her mind once. I don't think Asha should risk sharing her mind with anyone," Cotoch mentioned. Asha felt thankful, because the idea of exposing her mind to another person, even Rhyl, was terrifying.

"Then we get Talo," Asha stated.

"It's too risky to get the boy. We've been over this," Cotoch said in a tired voice. "Your emotions get the best of you. According to Willa and Audry, Allia has not hurt Talo, and likely won't. He's an important hostage."

Illiah was watching Asha with a strange expression. "You are not what we thought at all, are you?"

"Allia turned me into a weapon, and I intend to turn that weapon against her."

A ghost of a smile touched Illiah's lips before he turned to Cotoch. "We could use the *varing* to find a vision and find Rhyl."

Asha didn't quite understand what Illiah meant by that. But it didn't matter. Cotoch's face was haggard.

"No. Not here in this dark place." The life was leeched from Cotoch's voice as he spoke.

Asha was tempted to kick Cotoch in his broken ribs. "We have been sitting down here in the dark for days. Enough is enough. You old men are as useful as a cracked kettle. I am going to get Talo on my own."

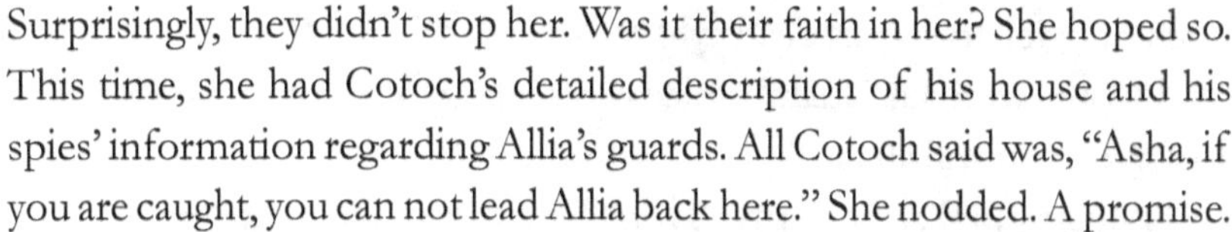

Surprisingly, they didn't stop her. Was it their faith in her? She hoped so. This time, she had Cotoch's detailed description of his house and his spies' information regarding Allia's guards. All Cotoch said was, "Asha, if you are caught, you can not lead Allia back here." She nodded. A promise.

Asha maneuvered through the halls of Cotoch's house in the dead of night when the hallway lanterns had burned out and the dawn had not yet come. The hour for stealth. It was quickly becoming her favorite time of day. Although she missed the sun.

Like a ghost, she approached the room where they were holding Talo, and in two precise movements, the two guards were down. She blessed the daggers Cotoch's women had found for her. Small, sleek weapons that fit in her hands like gloves. She snagged the key from a guard, twisted it in the lock, and slipped into Talo's room.

Talo was instantly alert.

"Asha?" he whispered.

"Talo."

"What are you doing here?"

"Rescuing you." She couldn't keep a smile from her lips. Talo limped over to her. He was injured. *Focus.* She could not let her rage overcome her urgency. "Lean on me. We need to get out of here." Asha bit her lip against the wave of relief that enveloped her as Talo gathered her close. His hands were around her arms, gentle, comforting, like a promise.

"I thought—I thought you were captured—they said they were torturing you." Talo released her just enough to cup her face in his hands, inspecting her.

"They lied—come, there is no time," Asha told him. But unease settled inside her as she led Talo down the dark stairs to the lower level of the house. They turned the corner to head down the dead-end hall to the secret door.

Five guards waited bearing torches. Five guards with Liam standing in front, weapons drawn. His Kitarran height towering above the others made the hall feel tight. She met Liam's gaze. Her heart gave a familiar lurch of grief to see his dead eyes.

"Come with me." Liam's voice was a fallacy of the boy she knew. "If you fight, you will all die."

Talo gripped Asha's arm. "Don't," he whispered in her ear.

"Listen to your boy, Asha. You never did have any sense," Liam sneered.

Even knowing a monster lurked under Liam's skin, the remark still hurt, still punctured the wound left behind that day Asha realized her friend had been taken from her.

But beyond her anger was a crueler thing. Behind the guards, the secret door to the crypts was open. Cotoch and Illiah were being taken out at knife-point. Despair crept over her. The crypts…gods, had Allia known all this time?

CHAPTER 101

ASHA

ASHA FELT TALO'S ARM come around her as Liam's men herded them into the hall. Cotoch was breathing in shallow, pained breaths and Illiah limped so badly, it couldn't quite be called walking. Talo's ears went back, and he hissed to see the condition of his foster father.

A low fire burned in the tall fireplace. Allia sat at the table and poured herself wine, sipping delicately. She held a tall spear, its shaft of silver wood ending in a fierce point. It didn't have the look of a lethal weapon. It looked other. Magical. It could only be the Stormspear.

Caeris sat at the same table. He looked just like his brother. Identical. But he didn't drink or eat. He sat still, watching his queen with dark, empty eyes. Asha could not see any rope or shackle, but he sat like a man bound. How long had Allia had her king enthralled?

Talo and Asha seemed forgotten, but the guards did not leave. Asha inspected the room for any object that might help them escape, but nothing offered even a glimmer of opportunity.

Illiah's eyes locked on the Stormspear. "Where is my son?" he demanded.

"The child of the prophecy?" Allia sang, twisting the spear in her hands. "I killed him."

Illiah made a noise in his throat like despair and collapsed onto his knees. Asha looked at Talo—could use magic to talk to his brother who was not a brother. Talo bit his lip and inclined his head slightly, but Asha read him well. Allia was lying.

Allia stood and stretched like a cat. She walked over to Illiah, collapsed on his knees, his face streaked with tears. She lifted his chin with the tip of the spear. Illiah stared at her, transfixed. Allia hovered the spear above his heart.

"Call the man in the *varing*." Allia's voice rippled with malice.

Illiah barked a laugh that was more of a sob. "I thought you already did. He is not here," Illiah said through gritted teeth.

Allia cocked her head. "Call him. I used the spear to bind him in Caeris's body, but he escaped. Caeris is not strong enough to hold him. But you…you are different. Somehow."

"No. I will not call him."

Allia narrowed her eyes. "No matter. Imal said that he had to break you to gather your magic, I can do the same."

"I'm not afraid of death," Illiah told her.

Allia smiled. And repositioned the spear, pointing it at Talo. "Not your death, perhaps."

The blood drained from Asha's face. Talo straightened his back. Asha twisted, lunging at Allia, almost knocking the spear from Allia's grasp.

"Liam, bind her hands. Hold her!" Allia commanded.

Liam's strong arms wrapped around Asha, immobilizing her. Liam had always been bigger and stronger than she was.

"Liam, please," Asha begged. "Liam, it's me, Asha."

"Gag her," Allia snapped.

A rag was shoved into Asha's mouth. Tears dripped down her face, but still she pushed at Liam and tried to spit the cloth out of her mouth.

Allia raised the spear, aiming for Talo's heart. "You, too, will be mine. My own prince."

And then Asha realized that Allia did not mean to kill Talo, she meant to turn him into her *daeum*, like Liam.

"It took years to make Liam my *daeum*, but with this"—she looked lovingly at the spear—"it will be a simple thing."

Asha screamed and screamed through her gag. The storm raged

outside; rain thrashed against the building. Asha wondered if it was screaming for Talo's life too.

Allia held out the spear, her dark eyes wild and hungry.

Asha drew a sharp breath. Something in the corner of the room, in the deepest shadow, moved, flitting green, then was gone. Then the storm quieted. The rain disappeared. Some silences speak of calm, of peace, but this silence was full of violence and death and grief. The pause, the quiet before the crash.

"You must kill him," a voice spoke into the room. A woman's voice like a brisk winter wind. The shadowy figure appeared briefly at Allia's elbow. Asha blinked. It was a spirit woman, her hair twigs and withered moss, her skin green but flaking. She looked like a dying forest. She was becoming more real, more solid. Her long finger pointed at Illiah.

"Quiet." Allia's voice rose in pitch. For an instant, Asha thought she sounded like a terrified child. She turned back to Talo.

"No, Allia, don't do this," Illiah whispered. "I will call him."

"Then do it," Allia ordered.

"No," hissed the spirit woman made of wood and feathers.

Asha stilled. Magic was building in the room. She could smell it, but to her it was invisible. She could only feel its presence, a cold kiss against her skin, a weight across her shoulders, a dread within her mind. Her worst memories came to the front. She fought to stay in the here and now, to be present, even if it meant watching Allia turn Talo, the man she loved, into a husk, a shell encasing violence.

A brilliant flash burst into being, followed by a sound so low, Asha felt it in her bones as it moved through the room. Asha blinked away the spots in her eyes. The low sound became a roar, a rush, then the glass panes in the windows shattered, and heat and flame burst into the room. She fell to her knees. They all did. The walls were coated in red flame that licked toward the arched ceiling. Everything was on fire.

CHAPTER 102

ASHA

A WAVE OF HEAT AND FIRE AND MAGIC swept through the room. Asha didn't feel the ground rise to meet her ,but she opened her eyes and found herself lying on the floor. They all were. The fire disappeared, swallowed by the night, leaving them in darkness. Asha took deep breaths of cool air, astonished there was no smoke. Through the broken windows, the faint light of the coming dawn peered into the silent gloom.

A figure stood in the door swathed in pale light. A woman. Two white wings spread from her shoulders, arching, swirling as if carved from mist. Asha blinked and saw it was not so. There were no wings. Just a woman wearing dirty clothes, her cloak ripped, her face covered in soot. Her bright hair tousled. But her blue-green eyes were sharp and lethal. Asha knew her.

Eva stepped into the room, over the fallen guards.

Allia lay crumpled on the ground not far away, and Cotoch beyond her. Illiah, to Asha's right, groaned. Eva moved to his side. Asha managed to pull the gag out of her mouth and twisted to see Talo, then Liam, both unconscious.

"Talo."

He didn't answer. Asha crawled over to him. Her head ached. A sharp pain blossomed on her shoulder. Talo's chest rose and fell. He was breathing. She nudged him hard. He opened his eyes.

"Asha?" He moved his body to inspect the room. "What happened?"

Asha jerked her chin to Eva, who left Illiah's side to come to them.

Eva's eyes were less menacing and more tired. She cut Talo's binds and handed him a dagger. He reached across to Asha and slit the blade through the ropes tight around her wrists. The pain in her shoulder flared. She couldn't move her arm.

"Is Allia dead?" Asha asked.

Eva crouched beside Allia. "No, I don't think so." She began to tie Allia's hands and feet, even though Allia was unconscious.

"Where is the Stormspear?" Asha wondered out loud.

Illiah was waking slowly.

"Illiah?" Talo spoke his name.

Illiah crawled over to Talo and grabbed Talo by the shirt. Somehow the aggressive gesture was affectionate.

"Rhyl's not dead," Talo told him.

Illiah smiled faintly. Blood trickled from the corner of his mouth. Then he turned and saw his wife. "Eva."

Eva almost smiled. She cocked her head. "Mahlas is on fire. Which may or may not be my fault." She looked at Cotoch unapologetically.

Cotoch came to a slow stand. The fall must have been agony on his ribs. "Tie him up," he growled, looking at Liam.

Talo nodded, reaching for the rope. Before he could reach Liam, Liam came alive, and leaped, drawing a dagger from his boot. The savage dark in Liam's eyes was a terrified wild thing suddenly released from its cage, with nothing but its instincts to lash out. He bared his teeth, his claws ready to eviscerate the nearest thing; Talo.

Asha moved and plunged her dagger into the spot between Liam's collarbone and his neck. The thin knife moved through the layers of Liam's muscles and found his heart. Blood poured from the wound as Liam's heart beat its last. He went limp and fell with Asha on top of him before his dagger could find its mark on Talo's neck.

Asha sobbed, rolling Liam's dead body from her. She extracted her dagger with a hollow wet sound. Talo caught her and held her close. But Asha pulled away, wiping her face with the back of her hand.

Before anyone could stop her, she drew the dagger, still red with Liam's blood, across Allia's pristine neck.

The gush of blood came over Asha's hand, soaking into her fur. No one spoke as Allia woke and gurgled her lifeblood onto the floor, her eyes wide and disbelieving. No one spoke as Asha stood and wiped her dagger clean.

The room was brightening. Dawn was close. Talo stepped toward Asha and pulled her into his arms. She clung to him so she would not shatter into a thousand tiny pieces.

"What is that sound?" Illiah asked. Asha heard it too. The clash of fighting. The rage of battle. Or a massacre.

"That is the sound of Allia's *daeum* ravaging Mahlas." Cotoch's voice was quiet and weak.

"Eva told me it was you who stopped them in Rodan all those years ago," Illiah spoke to Cotoch. "Stop them. You have done it before."

"It nearly killed me then," Cotoch whispered, holding his ribs.

Illiah narrowed his eyes at Cotoch. Asha could see the old hatred boil.

"There are innocents out there, Cotoch. *Your* people. Save them," Eva growled.

Cotoch straightened. His lip quivered. "If I succeed, tell Pena…tell Pena that I was not just a monster."

"I will tell her," Eva said, her eyes fierce.

Cotoch nodded. He drew a breath and closed his eyes. Asha held Talo tighter. Magic wrapped around them, invisible as air and as potent as a thunderstorm. The shadows felt tight and expectant.

Then it was gone. Cotoch fell to the ground. A moment passed before Illiah reached down and felt Cotoch's pulse.

"He's dead."

"Did he do it?" Talo asked.

"It's quiet," Illiah said, taking a step and tripping. Eva caught him. Talo let go of Asha and propped Illiah up.

"Where is the Stormspear?" Talo asked.

"Where is Caeris?" Asha asked.

"No ..." They all turned to Illiah. His eyes were black. His whole face took on the look of something other. It was Illiah, but it was not Illiah. It was a mirror. A dark pool of stars. Every instinct in Asha screamed a warning.

"Mute," Eva whispered.

"Eva," Mute replied.

CHAPTER 103

RHYL

BEYOND THE LINE OF TREES, there was nothing. A heavy mist blanketed the Tarm. The cool fog kissed Rhyl's face.

"What is this?" he murmured. The air was dense. Wrong. The Tarm was an open, windy place. The layers of stillness around him made him nervous. He couldn't see more than a length before him.

Calypso clucked and landed on his shoulder.

A crash of lightning and echoing thunder rippled over the plain, penetrating the dense fog. It was unlike any thunder Rhyl had heard. Unnatural. Honey screamed and reared. Rhyl managed to hang on, but his heart was in his throat as Calypso was tossed in the sudden gust of wind, his wings sideways, but he righted himself with a squawk of alarm.

Calypso landed in the grass and shifted, his face more stern than Rhyl had yet seen him. "What kind of storm is this?"

The storm echoed inside Rhyl's bones. Its restless energy was his. Its angry heart was his.

Then the clouds settled. The storm seemed to pause, waiting. What was Allia doing?

Rhyl reached with his mind to find Talo. It was difficult wading through the *varing* that buzzed wild and furious. He brushed Talo's mind, but the *varing* clouded everything.

He couldn't imagine what they would find in Mahlas, but he knew it would be bad.

"Talo's alive, but I can't talk to him. The *varing* has poisoned everything. We have to keep going."

Mahlas was close, Rhyl could *feel* it.

Calypso nodded and shifted back into a bird and took off, his wing-beats loud against the strange hush as he flew into the fog.

Rhyl bit back a plea for Calypso to come back. He had to trust that Calypso would return. He loved Rhyl, didn't he? He hadn't said as much. Fuck, why hadn't Rhyl said those words. *I love you.* Why hadn't he? Everything. Calypso was *everything* to Rhyl.

Rhyl tried to pull the *varing* to him, but there was too much. He could never contain it without the spear.

The dead cendari tree loomed ahead of him, revealed through the mist, branch by blackened branch. He could just see the rooftops below the hill, poking through the fog. The air smelled like smoke. Ash fell on his sleeve.

Another crack of lightning made Honey rear, and this time Rhyl lost his hold and slipped from Honey's back. He managed to land on his feet. Honey jumped, then stilled. The horse stood shivering, fighting every one of his equine instincts not to bolt.

Rhyl's hair stood on end. He heard a deep, guttural snarl from close by. He pulled his sword, tracking the direction of the threat. A wanderer rose from the long grass by the tree. Rhyl's mind could not take in its grotesque appearance, screaming threat and danger and wrong. He heard Honey bolt, but Rhyl didn't dare take his eyes off the creature before him. The wanderer leaped, its speed startling, even though Rhyl had expected it. He swung his sword to meet it, his blade glancing off its leathery flesh, neither animal nor human but both. A scream erupted, but it came back for him, its teeth bared.

The creature was on top of him, pushing him down. Its teeth sunk into his forearm, shaking his arm, his body. He screamed as pain and panic burned through him. The wanderer released its bite only to bite into Rhyl's shoulder. Then the wanderer dropped its hold, and Rhyl felt it slip away. Through bleary eyes, Rhyl watched the creature spin toward another attacker, its snarls deafening.

"Da," Rhyl gasped, sitting up, clutching his mangled arm against his chest. "Da!"

His father fought the wanderer, blade against teeth and claws. Illiah was fighting, but Rhyl could see he was weak, injured, perhaps. Even the Defender was no match for the wanderer fueled by the *varing*, and Rhyl remembered the wanderers were capable of enthralling a *candarii*.

"Da!" Rhyl's voice tore as he watched the wanderer swipe his father across the face. A gush of blood spewed into the grass as Illiah dropped. Rhyl struggled to his feet, lunging, pulling the *varing* around him for strength. The pain in his arm and shoulder flared, but he grabbed his sword and plunged it through the beast up to the hilt. As the wanderer died, warm blood fell over Rhyl's arm, black and sticky.

Rhyl fell to his knees. His lungs burned and his stomach roiled from the pain. He crawled over to where his father lay in a swath of bloodied grass. The distance felt like miles. Rhyl paused. A figure hovered over his father. A figure of twigs and moss and feathers. Her eyes were sad. The spirit woman. She traced Illiah's face with an insubstantial finger. She was almost transparent, not flesh and blood at all. Rhyl blinked. Maybe he was imagining her.

"You must finish this. Kill him," the woman whispered. Her eyes were wells of sorrow that Rhyl felt in his core. "It is the only way to end the prophecy. It is the only way to stop Mute."

Rhyl reached his father and pulled Illiah into his lap, clutching him close. Illiah's face was a mess of blood. Illiah reached his hand up, his horrid face moving, as if he wanted to speak, but no one could speak after such an injury. Rhyl put his hand over his father's face and reached for the *simul rami*. Rhyl pinched his eyes shut and concentrated on pulling his *sanarii* magic and using it to heal his father. He pulled and pulled, but inside Illiah was a writhing, dark mass of *varing*. Rhyl's *sanarii* magic could not fix him. He tried using the *varing* like he did to heal Calypso. But he'd had the spear then.

Rhyl grimaced, pulling at his hair, a noise of frustration ripped from his throat.

"You must kill him," the woman, Tsuga, whispered. She was close to Rhyl, her hand stroking his hair, but her touch was nothing, nonexistent. Like a ghost. "It is the only way."

Rhyl looked beyond, as if help was coming, but there was no one. Only the dense mist. Where was Calypso? A rumble of thunder was the only sign of life. He looked back at his father's face. Illiah blinked, hardly holding on to consciousness. A choking gurgle rose from his mangled lips.

He needed to end this. End his father's life. He chose love when he rescued Calypso and lost the spear. What right did he have to choose love again?

A glint in the grass caught Rhyl's eye. He realized he was looking at the Stormspear. Somehow, his father must have gotten it away from Allia.

Rhyl took off his cloak and put it under Illiah's head. He retrieved the spear. As his uninjured hand came around the wood, he felt its magic, alive, vibrant, flooding his body with warmth, strength. Power. A power meant for him alone. Rhyl shivered.

Images came to him. Visions. Memories from the Allmakers. The man made of *varing*. The woman with twigs and moss, plunging the Stormspear into the dark man's heart. Mute and Tsuga.

He looked at the dead wanderer that could so easily have been Calypso. An innocent, taken by the overflow of dark magic caused by the man in the *varing*. Mute. Rhyl had been born to hold both *sanarii* and *candarii* magic. The *simul rami* and the *varing*. He was the balance. This was what he had been born to do. This was the only choice left to him. He could not save his father. But he could end this. He could fulfill the prophecy.

Illiah lay with his eyes closed, his breathing irregular and shallow. Rhyl whimpered. Tsuga whispered in his ear, "It is the only way." Her voice was soft with pity.

Rhyl plunged the spear straight as an arrow into his father's chest, through bone and tissue, right into his heart. His death was fast and sure. Rhyl pulled out the spear and tossed it into the grass.

Rhyl slid to the ground.

Blood pooled beneath his father's body. Magic flared and sparked, rising from Rhyl like a flame. He screamed.

It felt all wrong. This was not balance. This was chaos.

He looked to the spirit woman. Her face was distorted with mirth. A sick feeling spread through Rhyl as she picked up the spear where Rhyl had discarded it. Her smile was curved like a blade as her red tongue licked the blood from the spear point. Her flesh was no longer hazy, no longer faded, but real and solid.

CHAPTER 104

MUTE

"SHE IS COMING FOR ME," Mute breathed. The city was burning. Eva had done this. For him. For Illiah.

But it wasn't enough. Mute could feel the *varing*, the magic. He could hear their voices, one by one, crying out in release, in agony. Her. Tsuga. His once beloved. The spirit would trap him in this world, in this magic. He fought the call, but he felt his strength waning. The spear called to him. And yet …

Eva was watching him, her white gold hair flecked with ash. Her blue-green eyes were round and wet with her shock. Her grief. Her shame. No, that wasn't fair. It was not her fault.

"Eva …" Mute's voice was thick, it didn't quite sound like Illiah's. He reached out his hand and cupped her cheek. Her skin was smudged with dirt. Her eyes were the hope of spring. Mute loved her because Illiah loved her. "She is calling me—us."

Eva didn't speak, but she gave him the smallest hint of a nod.

"Will he die?"

"I don't know," he answered.

Eva reached her arm around his neck, pressing her lips against his. Mute smelled her mossy, earthy smell. Her *sanarii* magic. So tender. So fresh. Then she let him go and turned away, hiding her tears from him. As if that would make it easier.

But Mute knew that goodbye was never simple.

STONE

TIME was a funny thing. Years had passed since Stone lost what was dearest to him. Years had passed since he, as Arrain, had chosen the merciless depths of the river. But sometimes, that pain still haunted him. It would come back, for an instant or a heartbeat, and clutch his chest, and he would see Emri's lifeless body before him. He would remember the last spark before it left her eyes. She hadn't said a word when she died. She had just…died.

The years had changed him, changed his memories. But still, he missed her with every fiber of his body.

The ache for her was like the ache for culla. Constant. Persistent. Shameful.

He dreamed of her sometimes. In his dream, he ran his finger down her back, tracing patterns in her black fur. Her laugh. Gods, he had almost forgotten the sound of her laugh.

It was inevitable that his thoughts turned to her now, looking down across the Tarm. Death was here, in this place. He could feel it. He could see the shadows hovering in the wind, settling among the dry summer grass.

Stone could feel the moment magic settled around him like a shield.

And then he saw them. A man with white wings. A fox trotting in the grass. A woman with black hair and black wings who looked recently spit out by death. The Guardians.

The woman, Crea, looked like she wanted to strangle the others. The fox shifted with the grace Stone knew was only achievable by the *velidar*. Her red hair fanned her freckled face like a sun halo.

They looked at him.

"So it has come to this," the man, Attin, said.

The fox woman walked up to Stone and put her small hand over his heart. "It is time."

Stone nodded.

"How long have you known, Arrain?" Crea asked with a sneer.

"Not long."

The silence around them was absolute. There was no wind to tousle the grass into a sign. There were no birds with their coarse voices. They were on a plain where magic kept time. Where magic was the door and lock and key.

They all turned to look behind them. Stone followed the gaze of the Guardians. His heart hitched in his chest. A Kitarran woman stood in the distance. Stone couldn't see her face clearly. But her fur was black as night.

"She waits for you," Lulanan whispered.

Stone's chest felt molten. His emotions rose like a thunderstorm, but somehow, the tears wouldn't come.

"Come," Lulanan said to the others. They stood around Stone and put their hands on him. His shoulders. His chest. His face.

A king, a prince, a fox, a crow, four a circle make. But Tayeh was dead. They needed a fourth Guardian. A prince.

"Why me?" Stone whispered.

"Because you know death," Lulanan said.

It felt like that day when he leaped from the cliff, the water breaking against his body, the intense cold that followed, and Emri's eyes held him as he sunk into the depths.

Crea had tears cascading down her face. Lulanan stood tall. Attin looked content. Ready.

A king, a prince, a fox, a crow, four a circle make.

Then they *pushed*.

Stone never thought magic could be so beautiful.

CHAPTER 105

RHYL

THE WORLD was gray and black. Above Rhyl, the wind whipped the clouds into a maelstrom. It should have been deafening, but Rhyl was shrouded in silence. Tsuga was at its center, her arms stretched out, one holding the spear, her face alight with a look of pure joy. Her joy was another's pain. Like a cat with a mouse.

The sky darkened like the gathering of night, but it was an unnatural darkness. Dusk was hours away.

Then the spirit woman laughed, spinning like a little girl, chanting, "My love, my love, my love."

Then the wanderers came, their eyes bright points in the swirling clouds. Their bodies seemed to absorb the darkness, making them more like living nightmares. A dream awakened.

Rhyl heard a raven call. He watched, frozen in panic, as Calypso dove toward Tsuga, the center of the storm. Like a dance, he shifted to a human, hand outreached to grab the Stormspear from Tsuga's grasp. A wave of wind and magic buffeted him. He twisted, turning back into a raven. He saw Rhyl and flew over to him and shifted.

"I can't get through it," Calypso said, clutching his arm like it hurt. "The magic is too strong."

Rhyl nodded, unable to speak. His throat was still constricted from watching Calypso fly at the mad spirit woman.

Calypso could not penetrate the magic. But he was a *velidar*. Rhyl was a *sanarii*. He was *candarii*. He drew a deep breath and focused. He pulled from the *simul rami*. He pulled the *varing*. He fed the magic into his veins and felt it coat his skin in an armor of magic.

He stepped into Tsuga's maelstrom, expecting to feel the wind slice at his clothes and the spear's magic deplete his strength. But that didn't happen. The magic bent toward him, so he pulled and took and gathered it.

"What are you doing?" the spirit woman growled. She cradled the spear against her chest. She looked to the wanderers yelping and growling around her. Rhyl pushed, reforming the magic around him and Calypso and Tsuga like a wall. The wanderers lunged, but they couldn't penetrate the magic sphere around them. Tsuga's eyes narrowed. "What *are* you?"

Rhyl didn't answer. Couldn't answer. He was using every ounce of his focus to call the magic, the spear. Tsuga cried out, and her hand around the spear became ethereal, ghostlike. Whatever power had given her the ability to hold the corporeal object was leaving her. As Rhyl's hand touched the spear, her magic dropped like a boulder. The wind, the storm itself, the magic, became Rhyl's. The wanderers. The *revenants*. They gathered around him like moths mesmerized by the fire.

With the *varing* and the spear, he could touch each of them and feel the writhing anger and hatred that was a sickness within them. There was no will, no thoughts, just hate and pain and anger. He could *control* them. And he could feel him. The man in the *varing*.

"Mute, come to me," Rhyl commanded.

A man walked out of the mist, his eyes blacker than night. Rhyl almost lost control from the shock. It was his father. Impossible. He'd watched him die. The body lay close by, its chest gaping and bloody.

"Da…I thought—I killed you."

"I'm Mute. And the man you killed was not Illiah, it was his brother."

Tsuga shrieked and lunged at Mute.

"You tricked me!" she wailed.

Mute reached out with Rhyl's father's hands and touched the spirit woman. Under his touch, she became less wraithlike once more. Mute cupped her face in his hands and pierced her with a look so full of love and longing. Then Mute's eyes shifted into hard anger, his face turned, and he clasped the woman against him, imprisoning her in his embrace. It was not kind and not loving. He looked at Rhyl with a monster's gaze.

"She is the reason for all my suffering," Mute declared. "She claimed to love me, but instead of setting me free, she trapped me in the *varing*. And doing so caused the *varing* to spill into the *simul rami*. I do not belong here, in this world. I never did. I fell here from another place, another time.

"I needed *you*, Rhyl. *I* made the prophecy and planted it in the mind of the Allmakers, the Guardians, the seer. I needed someone who could wield the light and the dark. Someone who could set me free and end this chaos." His words came quicker and quicker, and Rhyl struggled to understand his mutterings. It sounded like the raving of a madman.

Rhyl did not move.

Mute took a breath. "Rhyl, please." His voice softened. "Please."

Mute's black gaze reminded Rhyl of Calypso when he had been a wanderer. Something clicked inside Rhyl's mind.

The man was a wanderer. He was not two creatures forced into one body; he was two men forced into one mind, one of flesh and blood, and one of…something other. But the man was not the *varing*. The *varing* was only the poison.

"Rhyl, wait." Stone was at Rhyl's elbow.

"Where did you bloody come from?" Rhyl hissed, feeling tears at the edge of his resolve.

"I want…to be…free," Mute continued to beg in Rhyl's father's voice. "I want to go home."

Tsuga wailed, struggling against Mute. "The prophecy! You can only stop the spread of the *varing* by killing *him*." Tsuga was frantic, pulling at the binds of magic and muscle Mute held her with.

"Only you can free me, Rhyl," Mute told him, ignoring Tsuga. "Only you.

"Those who were strong are now weak,

"With healing hands, the babes will speak,

"Light turns to dark and colors shift,

"Two rivers join when two lovers rift,

"Watch for the child of two thrones,

"Born with magic in his bones,

"A child lit by the stars,

"Watch for him, for he shall be ours."

Rhyl would not kill Mute. He thought he had killed his father once; he would not do it again. There was another way. He knew that now.

"Mute asked you to make the spear to set him free, he trusted you. But instead, you made the spear as a tool to imprison him here, with you," Rhyl said to Tsuga. Her expression told him it was the truth. If he killed Illiah, Mute would be trapped in the *varing* once more, and the *varing* would continue to poison everything. That was what Tsuga wanted.

"I love him. I cannot live in a world without him." She looked at Mute.

"You must. I am not meant for this world." Mute's voice was full of softness, affection. Love. But also raw and brutal anger born from betrayal.

"My love …" She wept.

"What is love without sacrifice?" Mute asked her.

Tsuga did not answer. Watching them made Rhyl think love and hate were not dissimilar. Light and dark. What was one without the other? Rhyl swallowed hard. He vowed that if Calypso would have him, and they survived this mess, he would never cage Calypso out of fear or anger. He would choose the light.

"Tsuga," Mute called out to her with a lover's tenderness. Tsuga turned to him, reaching up to touch his face with her strange twig hand.

A simple gesture that spoke of longing and desire and a love so deep, Rhyl almost fell to the ground with recognition. Mute kissed her, and rain streaked down her bark skin and held her like a chain.

"Now." Mute's voice was soft. Rhyl realized Mute was talking to him. Rhyl gripped the spear, and for the second time drove it through another's flesh. It slid through Tsuga's strange skin with sickening ease. She slumped against Mute's chest, her body crumbling, wilting, her face full of sorrow and betrayal. Mute held her until she was ash, and that too slipped through his fingers, blown into the wind.

The wanderers fell. Their life force must have been tied to Tsuga all this time.

"It is almost done," Mute said into the quiet.

Then the spear began to disassemble. First in chunks, then flakes, then black dust. As the spear unraveled, so did Mute. First, black tendrils fell from Illiah's body. Then the tendrils turned silver and gray and became more solid. With each thread he untangled, it became easier and faster, and soon the sticky black threads of *varing* slipped from Mute like oil. It was like seeing magic become real as the *simul rami* seeped from Illiah's skin to become something *more*.

Stone's voice rose around them. *"After he has proved love's true form,* *"With spear in hand, the child will breach the storm."*

But destroying the spear wasn't enough. Rhyl reached and put his hand on Mute's face, his father's face, and reached into the very heart of magic, to the roots of the cendari trees, and used their light, their strength, to pull Mute from the *varing*, from the *simul rami*, from the very fabric of their world. Rhyl knew the cendari trees would not survive it. The only way forward was to destroy the magical link. Only then would the *varing* stop infecting the world through the rift Tsuga and Mute had created.

Rhyl opened his eyes. He started shivering. On the ground lay his father, his mother crouched beside him. Where had Eva come from? Rhyl could not tell if his father was dead or just unconscious. But a form—a person—stood in the tall grass. It wasn't the shape of a man, though it was something—something Rhyl's mind could not put a name to. Like a half-remembered dream.

"Mute," Rhyl whispered.

The wind died. Mute hovered, an impossible being made from the black of a lake at night, the space between the stars. His eyes glowed like coals in a fire, white hot, tinged with blue, then red.

"Please." Mute's voice was quiet, weak, waiting. But this time, he wasn't speaking to Rhyl.

"A king, a prince, a fox and a crow, four a circle make.

"To send the dark one to stars for true love's sake." Stone spoke, his hand on Rhyl's shoulder.

Around them, the Guardians stood in a loose circle. Attin, with his pure white wings. Lulanan with her hair like fire and skin like snow. And Crea, her face haggard, the black feathers of her wings dulled and fraying, her skin marred with lesions. Three Guardians. Three, not four.

Tayeh. Tayeh was gone. There was no one to take the last place.

Then Rhyl understood. A prince. Stone. How apt. Stone, who had defied death itself, not once, but several times.

The white fox nodded. "Stone?"

Stone joined the circle and linked hands with the Guardians.

Stone spoke the final verse, his yellow eyes focused on Mute. *"Snap the tether, set him free,*

"Restore the river of magic to its rightful tree."

The magic of the Guardians was a faint buzzing in Rhyl's ears. A wash of heat and softness that started as a slight breeze, a waft, but the magic built and built until a wave of energy robbed Rhyl of his breath, crushing him. He couldn't call for help.

When he raised his head, Mute, the other Guardians—were gone.

CHAPTER 107

ARRAIN

BEFORE ARRAIN was an infinite lake of stars. And a man. His skin was almost liquid black and reflected those stars like the clearest mirror.

"Thank you, Arrain," he said, his voice as soft and piercing as frost.

"What—what happened? Why am I *here?*"

"This is a place between your world, my world, and the others. A crossroads, if you like. I am free. Your world is free. The *simul rami* and the *varing* coexist once more. It's my fault. I was too curious, I leaned too close to your world and fell from mine. My essence, my magic was incompatible with yours. But I fell in love. My judgment was clouded." Mute smiled ruefully. "But I did not bring you here to tell you my story. I brought you here to thank you. And because she asked me to."

"Emri." Stone breathed her name, and there she was. She stood before him, her black fur rippling with light and fire, her eyes, Talo's eyes, bright and sure. He took her hand and she was real. Or he was not. He couldn't tell. He didn't care. In this place beyond the stars, this world beyond the living, they were together.

"Arrain," Emri whispered.

Arrain didn't know how long he stood with her in his arms. The stars had faded into the bright of day. They stood in a field of grass with the wind whipping around them and the grass swaying at their feet and the clouds cascading across the sky with the haste of lovers reunited.

"You have to go back," she told him.

"I know. But let me stay a little longer."

Emri laughed and held him close. He pressed his lips against her fur, her neck, her face, her black lips. There were things Arrain wanted to say. Like how it was unfair he was the one going back, how it was him who would watch their son live his life. But he knew in his heart that Emri shared every moment, every thought with him always and forever, even if she were no more than a whisper, a fragment of fractured sunlight in a dim room.

"They need you," Emri said, her voice less soft and more commanding.

"But I need *you*."

"And I am here. Always." Emri stepped away from Arrain, leaving a void. "Go. Go now."

Stone opened his eyes.

CHAPTER 108

RHYL

THE GUARDIANS were gone. Rhyl blinked. The sky was clear, blue as sapphires. Illiah and Eva lay beside Rhyl unmoving, but Rhyl could see his father's chest rise and fall. He crawled over to where Stone lay, still as death. He pressed his finger to the hollow of Stone's neck. He had to close his eyes and concentrate to find his pulse.

"Emri?" Stone's voice was so faint, Rhyl almost didn't hear him.

"No, it's Rhyl." Rhyl's voice was shaky and wet.

"Emri was just here, right here beside me." Stone closed his eyes again.

Rhyl felt something drop onto his shoulder. He looked to see a hand, a hand with fine long fingers that belonged to Calypso. His heart flew, but his body trembled. All he could do was collapse against Calypso, who then folded himself around Rhyl.

"It's all right now." Calypso pressed Rhyl to his chest tighter and tighter until Rhyl had to make a small noise to let Calypso know he needed to breathe.

"Da …" Rhyl untangled himself just enough to see his father stir.

"He is waking up." Eva was beside Illiah, tears of relief streaming down her face.

"The others. Mahlas." But Rhyl could hardly lift his arm. His legs felt like lead. Calypso was strong and Rhyl wanted to melt into him.

He reached out for Talo, for his magic, but there was…nothing. There was no link to his Kitarran brother. There was no *simul rami*. No *varing*. Nothing. The void crept inside Rhyl's chest with an ache, so he concentrated on the warmth of Calypso's skin. He smelled like a summer wind.

"Talo!" Calypso cried.

Talo walked toward him, exhausted and limping, propped against Asha. He saw Rhyl and grinned. Rhyl leaned against Calypso's chest and wept in relief.

A shadow passed over them as his father dropped a cloak around Calypso's bare shoulders. Illiah crouched and squeezed Rhyl's shoulder, but he said nothing. His green eyes were hollow and clear. His lips curved in a tired smile.

"I thought I killed you." Rhyl felt it needed to be said.

Illiah sighed. "I'm sorry, Rhyl." As if it were his fault. Rhyl hadn't the strength to argue. Illiah leaned down and rested his forehead against Rhyl's, his eyes closed. Calypso wrapped them both in his arms.

"Where did Mum go?" Rhyl asked. But he saw her. She was encased within Stone's long arms. They stood still, in their own world as Stone whispered in her ear, tears streaming down his face, tears that Eva wiped away with her sleeve.

Talo and Asha dropped beside Rhyl so Talo could wrap a fuzzy arm around Rhyl's neck. Eva untangled from Stone to kiss them all. For a time, no words were spoken, but Rhyl didn't need words. He didn't need anything but the knowledge that they were there with him.

"Stone, you are a Guardian," Calypso said eventually.

"I'm the same as ever."

"Exactly," Rhyl muttered.

Stone fixed them all with a fond gaze. "Let's go home."

CHAPTER 109

EVA

IT WAS DONE. Eva had wondered if the day would come. She had wondered what would be taken from her if the prophecy was fulfilled. Now, only time would tell how the new balance of magic would affect them.

But she doubted she would ever forget how the *simul rami* urged her across the Tarm, bringing her to Mahlas. Or how her *sanarii* fire felt flooding from her fingers in blazing arches of fire, carving her path into Mahlas, into Cotoch's house. She had felt unstoppable. And terrified. But it had worked.

Eva watched her husband lean heavily on a walking cane someone had procured for him. She could not heal his blister-torn feet, could not take away his pain. Her *sanarii* magic was gone. She had feared magic for so long after using it and killing Tayeh. But when it came to her survival and the survival of her loved ones, she had not hesitated to use it. At least now the choice was taken from her. Magic was gone.

And Illiah would recover, sooner if he would stay off his poor feet. But Illiah rarely took her advice. Illiah's stubborn nature could irritate her, but she knew she could be the same way.

Not many Jullayans survived the ravages of Allia's *daeum*, and those who had were traumatized, shocked, and in desperate need of a leader. With Caeris dead, Illiah was their rightful king. They told the Jullayans that a wanderer killed Caeris, which was partially the truth. Caeris would have died from his wounds. The fact that Rhyl had driven the final blow would stay a secret.

Irri was dead. Tortured by Allia, along with many of Mahlas's men.

His Jullayan lover, Teris, was still alive. Eva remembered him from the Keep years ago, a young recruit at the time. Irri and Teris had been lovers then, but in Jullayah, it had not been an easy romance. And Irri had left for Kitarra and never went back. Poor Teris, to be reunited briefly only to be ripped apart painfully. Eva would offer him a place in Kitarra, among Irri's people.

The *revenant*s were dead. When the magic released its hold, the *varing* had wasted them away to nothing, and there was no life for them to cling to. Their bodies would be burned; already a pyre was being prepared. It was too long a march to bring their bodies back to their loved ones in Kitarra. Eva would feel that loss for the rest of her life. She dreaded bringing that grief home to Kitarra, but it was necessary.

Eva watched Asha fuss over Talo's torn ear as she replaced the bloody bandage. Talo didn't seem under too much duress. Eva looked away when she saw Talo sneak a kiss.

Eva sighed. Love and loss. Kitarra would have its new young queen. Asha had proven herself. And it was clear she loved Talo with all her heart. Arrah would have no choice but to bestow her blessings upon them. And that, despite all the grief, made Eva smile.

A weight landed on Eva's shoulder. She berated Calypso who chirped smugly. Her *sanarii* magic was gone, but there must be some threads left because Calypso could still shift between raven and man. Rhyl must be sleeping or Calypso would never have left his side. Good. Her boy needed to sleep for a week, then eat a whole cow, and then sleep for another week.

Cotoch was dead. The people of Mahlas were cleaning up their ravaged city and building a pyre for their dead lord. He would not be burned with the rest. He would be given the funeral of a king. In a few days, once Aiyan and Mila arrived with Pena, they would light the pyre and send the lord to his final resting place as ashes on the wind.

Eva admitted Cotoch's death had been heroic. At the end of his life, he had accomplished something. Did it make up for his evil deeds? For the deaths he had caused? At least his legacy of cruelty would end with him.

Pena was a good child, with a good heart. Aiyan and Mila would mentor her with love and patience. Pena would never know the monster her father had once been and only remember the hero he had become in death.

Eva walked to the gate of the city and found Stone standing in the tall grass looking up at the clear blue sky. Autumn was coming. Cool nights and golden days. She linked her arm with his, and Calypso took off and flew up in lazy circles.

"I thought I was going to die for good, Eva," Stone said.

Eva leaned her head on his shoulder.

"She is waiting for me." Something in his voice made Eva shiver. The tone scratched against the old grief in her heart, the fear he would run away.

"Not yet, Stone."

Stone covered Eva's hand with his own. "I know. I will watch Talo and Asha wed and maybe I will be lucky enough to have a grandchild. Maybe two. Now that magic has balanced and the Kitarrans are no longer poisoned before birth."

Eva smiled, drying happy tears in his fur.

"And we will console Rhyl as he is tethered to the ground while his lover flies circles over his head." Stone laughed, watching Calypso twist and dive, more graceful than any dancer.

"And we will watch Pena grow and run."

"And we will watch the twins try and chase her."

"And we will live for them."

"And maybe die for them."

"All things have their cost."

"Eva?"

"Yes?"

"I am glad you saved me."

"Me too, Stone. Me too."

The grass shifted and moved and the breeze smelled like summer was saying farewell.

"But after then, perhaps, it will be time," Stone said softly.

"Perhaps." Eva held her tears and told herself not to weep over things yet to come.

RHYL

"WHERE *are* you taking me?" Rhyl asked Calypso for the thirtieth time. Calypso just grinned and pulled Rhyl's hand, leading him up the hill, deeper into the forest. "Did you at least bring food?"

"No, that was your job."

"Well, I forgot."

Calypso rolled his eyes. He paused in their hike, scowled, and brushed a piece of lichen from his crisp white linen sleeve embroidered with tiny leaves and insects. The exquisite shirt was a gift from Mila. Rhyl had observed that Calypso wore it more than any other item of clothing. Rhyl watched him, amused at his lover, a Forest creature—a raven half the time—who was wild and yet had more clothes than the four princes of Kitarra. Combined.

"It's not much farther," Calypso assured him.

Rhyl huffed and dropped Calypso's hand because the path, which wasn't really a path, became too narrow for them to walk side by side. Calypso scrambled up a rocky hill, if one could scramble while keeping one's clothes pristine.

At the top was a bluff covered in moss so green, it rivaled the fresh leaves of spring dancing in the sunlight. Rhyl looked down at Kilev, the Queen's Keep, the river, the lands beyond—the mountains, the glittering band that was the sea. The breeze tousled his hair, reminding him it was getting long. He breathed in the smell of fir needles and warm moss.

Music lifted from the city below. Kilev was still celebrating the birth of their new heir, a baby girl born to Talo and Asha just three days earlier. Healthy and squalling, fur as black as night, eyes the color of buttercups—a strange color for a newborn, everyone agreed. She didn't have a name yet, though Calypso was already calling her Linny. Rhyl had a feeling it would stick no matter what Talo and Asha named her.

The city and the Queen's Keep were entirely overrun for the occasion. Even more than when Talo and Asha wed. And each day, more well-wishers arrived from Withe and Pinnea and all the towns in between. Cassandra loved the influx of people. She still claimed to be looking for a husband, but Rhyl was fairly certain it was just an excuse to sample any interested young men. Rhyl could not imagine her leaving to go back to Rodan. She was too good a friend.

Rhyl had zero qualms about running off into the woods with Calypso to escape the busy palace, though Rhyl had foolishly assumed it involved a naked Calypso, a blanket, and nothing but the trees to bear witness to their endeavors. And to be fair, prior forest hikes had given him plenty of valid reasons to make such an assumption. No, *this time,* Calypso told him it was something else that required hiking and scrambling through the forest. And Calypso assured him with a look that made Rhyl exquisitely distracted, the weather was warm and fine and there was no reason not to add lovemaking to the day's activities.

"Come, over here," Calypso said, pulling Rhyl away from the bluff and back into the cool shadows of the forest. He stopped in a small mossy glade that looked like countless mossy glades they had already passed. "Here!" Calypso announced with a ring to his voice.

"And what exactly is so special about this place?"

Calypso grumbled. "This." He crouched down and gestured to a small plant.

Rhyl burst out laughing. "Calypso, this *plant* is why we are here?"

"You are such an *arse*. Look at it. Touch it," Calypso told him.

Rhyl, seeing Calypso's slightly crestfallen look, crouched and touched the small leaf. Something warm and tingly passed through his fingers. Magic. "Cally …" Rhyl breathed, in awe. "Is this …?"

"Yes. Yes, it is." Calypso grinned. "A cendari seedling."

Rhyl touched the tiny leaf with one finger, inspecting the thin stem of the tiny cendari tree.

"And look–" Calypso gestured to the glade. Rhyl noticed more seedlings. He looked farther into the forest. More. Little cendari seedlings dotted the moss like mushrooms.

It wasn't that Rhyl missed his magic. He knew the *simul rami* was still there, hidden, buried deep within the veins of all living things, and further still, the *varing*. Because light and dark were both existential. All he needed from magic was Calypso.

But knowing the cendari trees were not extinct, that life continued, that little Linny would see the cendari trees grow, was a gift Rhyl had not known would fill his heart with pure and absolute joy.

"Do you think we could bring one to the palace? Plant it in the courtyard?"

Calypso shrugged. "I think so, though I wouldn't dare try it without consulting Stone and Aiyan. It would be the perfect gift for Linny," Calypso mused. Calypso was already besotted with that little baby.

"Cally? Would you ever want children?"

Calypso's eyes cut to his. "What?"

"We could have a child. Maybe there is even a *velidar* child in need of a family."

"You are serious."

"I am."

Calypso closed the small distance between them and kissed him. "Maybe someday. But not yet." His eyes sparkled as he took Rhyl's hand and brought his palm to his lips. "It would be an adventure. But every day is an adventure with you, child of the prophecy."

Rhyl pounced, pulling Calypso with him to the ground. Calypso squawked and laughed, warning him to watch out for the cendari seedlings. Rhyl let Calypso roll him until his back and Calypso straddled him. Calypso's shirt was covered in little bits of moss and dirt, but he didn't seem to care as he leaned down and pressed his lips against Rhyl's.

"I love you," Rhyl told him, breaking the kiss with a smile.

"You tell me that every day."

"And you smell like moss," Rhyl murmured.

"Who cares? Just keep kissing me."

And he did.

PEOPLE

(BY REALM)

GREAT FOREST

Lulanan or Lula		Guardian of the Great Forest
Calypso		*Velidar*
Timur		*Velidar* leader, mountain cat
Midna		*Velidar*

KITARRA

Tayeh	tey-uh	Deceased Guardian of Kitarra
Eva or Evangeline		Princess of Jullayah
Illiah	il-ee-uh	First Defender of Kitarra, Prince of Jullayah
Mute		Spirit of the *varing*
Stone		Prince of Kitarra, Eva's amourii
Rhyl	ril	Eva and Illiah's son
Talo	tal-oh	Prince of Kitarra,
Aralis		Eva and Illiah's son
Bren		Eva and Illiah's son
Arrah	ahr-uh	Queen of Kitarra

Arrain	ahr-reyn	Arrah's son, later known as Stone
Asha		Kitarran raised in Rodan
Aiyan		Master of the Healer's Hall
Mila		Head Mistress of the Healer's Hall
Aisha	ey-shah	Captain
Tilley		Aisha's wife
Murryn		Mila's sister
Tarran		Aiyan's brother
Susor		Lord of Withe
Emri	em-ree	Deceased First Defender of Kitarra, wife of Prince Arrain
Irri		Kitarran spy
Turk		Keeper of the Long Isles
Scytt		Former First Defender
Corri		Scytt's son
Astera		Captain
Diea	dee-uh	Captain

ALLATI

Cotoch	King of Allati, Lord of Mahlas
Pena	Cotoch's daughter
Attin	Guardian of Allati
Pruit	Nobleman
Vagar	Lord of WindeKeep, Eva's half brother

JULLAYAH

Crea	kree-uh	Guardian of Jullayah
Caeris	ker-is	King of Jullayah
Allia		Queen of Jullayah
Teris		Soldier
Kaile	key-lee	War Commander, Lord of the Keep

THE TARM

Geral		Guard
Tsuga	soo-gah	Earth spirit

THE MIDLANDS

Felis	Master of Stonyhill
Tarek	Leader of the Iron Wolves
Elish	Leader of the Iron Wolves

RODAN

Cassandra	Princess, Beric's daughter
Imal	Deceased Emperor of Rodan, *heera*
Beric	Emperor
Allia	Princess, *heera*, Imal's sister
The Muro	Earth goddess of the *heera*

PLACES

JULLAYAH   joo-ley-uh
Caer Andri   kair an-dree   Capital of Jullayah
The Keep
Dwelllor's Knoll

KITARRA
Kilev   kee-lev   Capital of Kitarra
Withe   wahyth   Mountain city
Markeh   mahrk-ey   Border town
Drenev
Faevallen
Pinnae   Large city on the Long Isles
Hilltop   Cendari tree

ALLATI
Attingard   Capital of Allati
Windekeep   Vagar's estate
Wanderling Mountains   Stronghold of the Shadow Guard

GREAT FOREST | Home of the Allmakers and the *velidar*

Hill Top | Gather place for velidar

The Glen | Magical place of the Allmakers

RODAN | roh-dan | Land across the sea

Kara | Capital of Rodan

Praedan | prey-dan | Rodan name for the realms

THE TARM | tahrm | The valley plain between Kitarra and the Midlands

Mahlas | maw-lahs

The Vale, Tayeh's Vale | Secluded hidden valley

THE MIDLANDS | Land between Kitarra and the Tarm

Fishtown

StonyHill

WORDS OF INTEREST

Velidar	vel-uh-dahr	Old word for the Forest Folk
Forest Folk		People who live in the Great Forest
Sanarii	san-ahr-ahy	Mages who use the *simul rami*
Candarii	kan-dahr-ahy	Sorcerers that use the *varing*
Simul rami	sim-yuhl ram-ahy	Life magic
Varing	vair-ing	Dark magic
Daeum	dey -uhm	Enslaved warriors controlled by the *varing*
Heera	heer-uh	People of the forest in Rodan
Vivus	vi-vuhs	Manifestation of the *varing*
Revenant		A *vivus* inside a person
dicidium	dih-sij-yoo-uhm	An aura
Rauna		An old spirit

Allmakers		The old spirits who live in the Great Forest
Vercuri	vur-kyoor-ee	Magical artifacts
Rodaeri		Title of Rodan slave master, a Rodan aristocrat
Ro		Rodaeri prefix
Cendari tree		Special Kitarran tree that is a conduit for the *simul rami*
Stormspear		The spear the vercuri were carved from
Culla		Powdered herb used as a drug
Culla girl		Prostitute drugged into slavery using culla powder
Shadow Guard		Sorcerer hunters of Allati
Latha		Kitarran weapon
Iudarii trail	yoo-dahr-ee	Trial of a Kitarran warrior
Muhala or mua	moo-hah-luh moo-ah	Kitarran word for mother
Polii		Kitarran delicacy
The Dark Night		Kitarran winter solstice festival
Uandian		Kitarran guardian dogs
Kinadra		Kitarran word for wife, or life partner.
Amourii	am-ohr-ahy	Kitarran honor body guard, one who owes his master a life debt.

Sicara	A curved sword
Hisana	Kitarran word for rest, associated with combat training.
Ragwood	Herb that is refined into culla powder
Lamar	Rodan fibre animal
Golla	Rodan slave-pulled transporation device
Valisha	A herb
Gurdy Root	Herb for birthing
Bacara	A herb
Bojar	A herb
Reaver's grass	Plant from Rodan

ACKNOWLEDGEMENTS

As I finish this book, I finish a trilogy and say farewell to a cast of characters that I love and will miss. With this goodbye, I also close another decade in my life. A decade marked by grief and loss, but also finding my passions and the ability to reevaluate what is important to me and where I want my life to go.

For me, writing the Sanarii Chronicles has been acknowledging parts of myself and learning how to trust my inner writer and artist. In a world where creative people often fall through the cracks and are under appreciated, it can be hard to remember how valuable we are.

Thank you, Sonya, always. Although our adventures in the forest are few and far between and might not quite be considered adventures any more, I am so thankful for your friendship and enthusiasm for my world.

Thank you to my editor, Jenn Somersby, for your hard work, which has helped me grow as a writer.

To Quinton, Robbie, and Ben—you are my sun, my stars, my moon. All mistakes are mine.

ABOUT THE AUTHOR

Andrea Gibb lives on Sumas Mountain, in British Columbia, with her family. She is an artist and book designer. And when not writing, enjoys long, misty hikes in the forest with her dog.

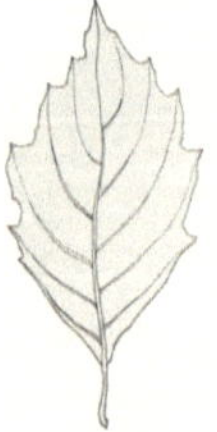

www.andreagibb.com

@andrea_gibb_author